DAUGHTERS

DAUGHTERS

KIRSTY CAPES

THE OVERLOOK PRESS, NEW YORK

This edition first published in hardcover in 2025 by
The Overlook Press, an imprint of ABRAMS

Abrams books are available at special discounts when purchased in
quantity for premiums and promotions as well as fundraising or
educational use. Special editions can also be created to specification.
For details, contact specialsales@abramsbooks.com or the address above.

First published in Great Britain in 2024 by Orion Fiction,
an imprint of The Orion Publishing Group Ltd.

Library of Congress Control Number: 2024948415

Printed and bound in the United States

1 3 5 7 9 10 8 6 4 2

ISBN: 978-1-4197-8107-0
eISBN: 979-8-88707-654-6

ABRAMS The Art of Books
195 Broadway, New York, NY 10007
abramsbooks.com

Kirsty Capes works in marketing and lives in Slough with her golden retriever, Doug. She holds a PhD from Brunel University London; her thesis investigates representations of the care experience in contemporary British fiction. Her first novel, *Careless*, was longlisted for the Women's Prize 2022. *Daughters*, published in the UK as *Girls*, is her third novel.

For all the girls I love

when i walked into the sea
i didn't think about what i would do
when the water hit my waist and kept going
my bare toes pushing under the wet sand for grip
it wasn't my choice to be here
which implies that choice belongs to someone else
but it doesn't

                              —*Emma Jeremy, "wet sand"*

Throw my ashes in the Canyon and my paintings in
the sea.

                    —*Ingrid Olssen, internationally celebrated
                       portrait artist. Spoken to her daughters,
                              on her deathbed (allegedly).*

SOMETIMES I DREAMED OF THE RICHMOND HOUSE.

I left it when I was a teenager, so I remembered enough for it to stick.

The house was our mother, and our mother was the house.

She made her mark on each window, ceiling, and wall.

With every year that passed, I returned to memories of the house and re-evaluated them through the lens of newly accumulated experience.

The way you feel about your childhood then is very different to the way you feel now.

Like a complex piece of music, the memories seemed to ebb away at times, soft and malleable, and rise to a horrendous crescendo at others.

I didn't think the desert would heal us. But by the time we crossed the state line, in our failing van, from Arizona into Nevada, I convinced myself that it would.

I thought that in inhaling the dry, hot, unspoiled air, we would be cleansed and purged.

New, whole, perfect versions of ourselves.

I didn't realize how deep the wounds went. I underestimated what it would take to cauterize them.

If the Richmond house had made me rotten on the inside, God only knows what it did to my sister.

EXTRACT FROM THE INTRODUCTION TO INGRID
OLSSEN: VISIONARY BY RICHARD TAPER
(FORTHCOMING FROM ORANGE RABBIT PRESS)

[. . .] Olssen had been a forty-a-day smoker from the age of sixteen. The development of a large-cell carcinoma on her left lung at
fifty did not come as a particular shock to anyone who knew of
the diagnosis. Olssen refused any treatment that involved radia-
tion or chemotherapy, according to her younger sister Karoline
Olssen—who, as she detailed the medical minutiae of the illness
that had led to her sister's death, chain-smoked five Chesterfield
Blues in the space of our forty-five-minute interview, with the
assistance of a jade-stone cigarette holder.

Ingrid Olssen believed and spoke only in absolutes, and one of
those certainties was that any chemotherapy that she allowed into
her body would ruin her brain and numb her fingers so that she
could never pick up a paintbrush again. Within a year of her diagnosis, the tumor had grown to three times its original size and
protruded from the front of Olssen's chest, stretching out the skin
around it, thin and shiny. Olssen's final (complete) self-portrait was
finished about three months before she died. In it, the artist is
standing in what most critics agree is a shallow cardboard box,
naked, her figure grotesquely misshapen. The canvas is five feet
and four inches long, the length of the artist's body, and the rendering is life-sized.* The tumor seems to be an alien straining
against her ribcage, desperate to burst through. The style of this
final self-portrait is frenzied, the application of the oils—darker
indigo hues for the flesh, more impressionistic than any of Olssen's earlier oil work, and lacking in the characteristic details
around the subject's eyes and mouth—is a frantic and imprecise
stylistic impasto. Olssen's face, indeed, seems to be melting away
from her skull. Karoline Olssen tells me that in the final year, her

---

* *Self-portrait #42*, oil on canvas, 2018.

sister began to hallucinate blackened and rotting winged demons the size of small children penetrating the house in Richmond and burrowing into the walls, where Karoline, alongside Ingrid's daughters, delivered hospice care in those last months of Olssen's life.

Her death was horrifying and heartbreaking for all close to Ingrid Olssen. Karoline cannot recall it without first dabbing at kohl-ringed eyes with a square of pale silk. After two years of grief, at the time of writing, the pain is still clearly very raw for Olssen's closest family members.

A moving yet controversial obituary was published in the *Observer*, written by Ingrid's younger daughter, twenty-two-year-old Nora Robb, who had recently completed a postgraduate degree at UCLA in Los Angeles, United States, majoring in Art History. She wrote:

At times I hated my mother. I hated her for how much she loved her work. More than she would ever love myself or my elder sister, Matilda. Growing up, the two of us were acutely aware of what little we could do to make her happy. Ingrid always told us that she was the observer, rather than the observed, although it was so often in her life that she courted a controlled cultural gaze. Olssen knew that her absolution lay in the reimagining of the world and the people around her. That the only way that she could understand the imbalance of the universe was to take what she saw and felt, and render it upon the canvas. She found ways to make people feel new and unfamiliar. With this mission, she was able to survive the wilderness. She once told me and my sister that when she died, we ought to throw everything she ever created into the sea. Ingrid Olssen never produced her art—never put brush to canvas or charcoal to paper—for anyone except herself. In that, her genius—and her destruction—lay.

Ingrid Olssen was cremated at Highgate Cemetery, twelve days after her death on January 19th, 2018. She was fifty-four years old at the time of her death. Her casket was made of cherrywood and inside was placed the April 1979 edition of *British Vogue*, the edition that had been on shelves the month she'd arrived in London from Hønefoss, Norway, as an estranged teenager. Also in her coffin were a bottle of Chanel No. 5 perfume, a pair of quilted leather gloves gifted to her by Carolina Herrera and a single red rose placed by her ex-husband Edward Robb. She left behind a catalogue of over four hundred works of oil on canvas, several hundred silkscreen and linocut prints, and other work ranging from the size of a postcard to the length and height of the western portico at St Paul's Cathedral. Her most celebrated work, *Girls* (charcoal and oil on reinforced canvas, 1999), remains on permanent loan to the National Portrait Gallery in London. Further works are displayed at the Museum of Modern Art in Los Angeles and the Tate Modern. Three paintings—including the scandalous *Edward and me on a bed of lies* (egg tempera on card, 1986)—are part of the permanent collection at the National Gallery in Oslo. All other components of Ingrid Olssen's portfolio— her oils, her prints, her sketchbooks (of which there are rumored to be over a thousand), her studies and the small number of works done in tempera—remain in her estate, inherited in equal parts by Olssen's two daughters and moved into storage at the time of her death.

It is unlikely that the world will ever see another Ingrid Olssen exhibition. Her estate is closely guarded by her family, who in general respect her wishes to keep it away from public eyes. What remains is a life marked by obsession, heartbreak, disaster and the snuffing out of a bright and blazing star in the landscape of modern European art. There is the question of Olssen's impoverished early life in a small Norwegian industrial community north of Oslo, alongside her younger sister, Karoline, and her widowed father, Lars, a pig farmer who died in the midst of bankruptcy in 2006. There is her migration to Britain in her adolescent years; her early education under the tutelage of one of the greatest European silkscreen artists of the twentieth century, Maurice Hoffmann.

Her frenzied entrance onto the London art scene of the 1980s and her indoctrination into the culture of tabloid celebrity; her whirl-wind affair and marriage to the Californian actor, Edward Robb. Her textured sabbatical as a mother to Matilda and Nora Robb, born 1986 and 1995 respectively. Her rise to prominence, and eventually international acclaim in the late nineties before her deteriorating physical and mental health led her to an early retire-ment, though the last ten years of her life (it has emerged) were her most prolific, and undoubtedly produced her most celebrated work.

This biography—written with the permission of Olssen's imme-diate family and personal lawyer—will document Ingrid's life, her work, her rise and her fall. With so little visual material publicly available, the Olssen and Robb families have kindly given me access to the private archives to share never-before-seen works and rare studies, captured here on pages 48-57 and 105-122.

Ingrid Olssen was untamable, flighty and feckless. Her life was marred by depression and addiction, as well as romance and celeb-rity, in equal measure. It is my hope that through her work, inter-views with her closest friends and family members, and a critical examination of her patchwork history as a young ingénue of her contemporaries, a tabloid sensation, a teenage prodigy thrown from poverty into the center of the cultural zeitgeist within the space of a few years, that we might somehow get a little closer to her; to understand some small portion of her genius.

CHAPTER 1

I DON'T REMEMBER SEEING NORA AT THE FUNERAL.

I didn't notice her arrive. I forgot to say goodbye, and, when I remembered, she seemed to have already gone.

She had tried to kill herself for the second time early in the spring, the year before our mother, Ingrid, died. Her roommate had found her in the damp bathroom of their UCLA dorm, dead leaves on the windowsill, swinging idly from the curtain rail like a sock caught on a nail by a thread. She'd been wide awake, holding each narrow elbow with the opposite hand, watching the house finches clean their feathers on the neighbor's roof through the frosted window.

She'd seemed to be waiting for something to happen.

Her second suicide attempt had been Nora's fifth brush with death. The fifth time she would extend a hand beyond the veil and feel the breeze through her fingers. Whatever it was that was lurking on the other side would take her by the wrist but never with a firm enough grip to pull her through. It wouldn't be the last time Nora shook hands with the grim reaper. There would be more.

At the funeral itself, everyone seemed to be waiting for something to happen.

Nora had written the obituary, so Aunt Karoline suggested that I deliver the eulogy.

I did—and as I read, I looked out to the congregation. The people my mother had collected throughout her life, who had loved her enough to come and watch her be put to rest. In the front row was Aunt Karoline in velvet black, a satin shrug the color of seaweed wrapped around her narrow shoulders. Her hair almost pink, so threaded through with white was the auburn. On Karoline's left-hand side was Maurice Hoffmann's widow, Angelica. On her right was Jules, an ageing, greasy-haired Los Angeles type who had at one time been a session drummer for Jefferson Airplane. He liked to tell people that he had survived the same strain of heroin that killed Janis Joplin. Further down were two Poet Laureates and one daytime television presenter. My dad, Edward, perched sheepishly on the end of the front row with his new wife, Marnie, who was the same age as me. He wore a pink polka-dot silk pocket square, which had become slightly crumpled over the course of the day and now hung limply across his lapel, as though it had lost interest.

Even now as I picture it, I can't think of where Nora sat. Who was next to her, what she was wearing, what kind of expression was arranged across her face.

The father of my daughter, Gus, waited in the back row, a respectful distance. He wore his nicest lawyering suit, which made him look a little bit like the kind of man who speaks on the phone at an obnoxious volume when on public transport. In reality, Gus was the kind of person who tended to ask people questions about themselves and listened to their answers. Nevertheless, it wasn't appropriate for him to be near the front, though he knew Ingrid as well as I did, or Nora did, and several boat-loads more than fucking Marnie did. He had been just as much a part of my mother's life as I or Nora had, despite us breaking up a year after Beanie was born, and a year before either of us were allowed to vote.

Our daughter, Beanie, sat back there too, though there was no reason for her to. She had done her make-up the way Ingrid always had—eyeliner so thick and black it made her eyes flare out across high cheekbones like the wings of a crow. I'll keep Dad company, she said. I shrugged and she squeezed my arm to show that it didn't matter to her. At fifteen, she seemed to have a thousand years of patience in her bones. She became more like Gus every day.

I looked around for Nora but I couldn't see her, out there in a sea of mourning.

After the eulogy, Aunt Karoline read a poem that she had written herself but that seemed to be overly derivative of Seamus Heaney. I could see the Poet Laureates eyeballing one another, unimpressed. Then, Sadie Nelson, bassist for punk sensation Acid Rain, who'd famously run away with Mum to Naples for a short time in the early 2010s to smoke opium in a squat, got up and played "Take On Me" on an electric guitar while Ingrid's coffin was slowly conveyed on a sort of airport baggage-check-type mechanism, and disappeared behind a thick red curtain. Nora had chosen the cherrywood for the casket and pansies for the flowers. They were burned, too.

In the remembrance garden, I found Beanie and Gus by the gates to the car park. We stood there together as various people from Ingrid's circle came up to us to offer condolences, shake hands, congratulate me on the great-ness of my mother and the footprint she had left, on the coincidence of my being born to her. Aunt Karoline dragged me into an angular hug.

You've done such a wonderful job, Matilda, she said. She would have been so proud of you.

Thanks, I mumbled into her powdery neck. The smell of the concrete was hard and cold. Thick, dark smoke rose from the chimney of the crematorium.

The eulogy was just beautiful, Mattie, someone I didn't recognize said from behind Aunt Karoline.

It was, wasn't it, Karoline agreed. Her lipstick was bleeding into the pursed smoker's wrinkles around her mouth. Really, so marvelous. So moving.

Sadie Nelson seemed to be having some sort of argument with a soap star next to the hearse. Aunt Karoline dashed away a tear with a handkerchief.

In the car on the way to the wake, which was to be held in the downstairs room of a pub off Richmond Common, Beanie said, Mum?

Yes?

I wasn't looking at her, my hands claws around the steering wheel, rigid. I hadn't seen Nora at the funeral. I had a horrible suspicion that she would ditch the wake; that she would leave me to deal with these horrendous people by myself. It was such a Nora thing to do. I was pre-emptively and uncharitably angry at her for it.

Nora, who only ever thinks of herself. Nora, who is always in some sort of permanent state of crisis. Nora, who can't even get her shit together for Mum's funeral.

Where did you get the eulogy from?

What do you mean?

The speech you read out today. You didn't write it, did you?

I glanced at her in the rear-view mirror. Her black eyes filled up the mirror, a streak of dark feathers across her face.

I got it off Grandma's Wikipedia page, I admitted.

Beanie grinned at me through the glass.

I thought it was a bit strange when you started listing her Controversies. Me and Dad liked it, anyway.

Gus—in the passenger seat—smiled with the corners of his mouth turned down rather than up. He didn't need to say anything. He had been a first-hand witness to the controlled self-demolition of Ingrid Olssen and her legacy since we were teenagers. And now he was here to witness the final blows as it all came crumbling down.

Nora wasn't at the wake, as I suspected.

Now that I think of it, I wonder if she had been at the funeral at all.

EXTRACTS [VARIOUS] FROM INTERVIEW TRANSCRIPTS, QUOTED IN INGRID OLSSEN: VISIONARY BY RICHARD TAPER (FORTHCOMING FROM ORANGE RABBIT PRESS)

Marnie Robb, actress and wife of Edward Robb:
I heard that Ingrid Olssen was born in the pigs' trough on a farm in buttfuck nowhere Norway.

Chad McCloy, journalist and host of television chatshow *McCloy Who's Talking:*
I heard she was the illegitimate child of a Scandinavian prince who got exiled after she tried to make a claim for the crown, or whatever. Which Scandinavian prince? I don't know. Whatever. Was she Swedish?

Angelica Hoffmann, wife of the late Maurice Hoffmann and Director of the Hoffmann Trust:
Maurice didn't know a jot about her when she turned up on the doorstep of his printing shop in Golders Green in the spring of 1979. I don't think he ever asked. That's the kind of man Maurice Hoffmann was. He took you at face value, he believed the things you told him and he trusted strangers. Here she was, this slip of a girl, barely sixteen, clearly malnourished, barely a word of English or a penny to her, and Maurice gave her a job. He didn't ask about how she got to London from wherever it was she came from, which someone told me was a dairy farm in the Swiss Alps. He just trusted her.

Edward Robb, actor and ex-husband:
She never told me a thing about how she grew up.

Karoline Olssen, sister and manager:
We were born on our family farm just outside of Hønefoss, Ring-erike, about sixty kilometers north-west of Oslo. Ingrid was born

in sixty-three and I in sixty-six or sixty-seven. Don't you dare print my age, Richard. Our father, Lars Olssen, was a pig farmer in a small village that sat halfway up a mountain. Our mother died when I was about four, I think. Something to do with her lungs. I don't remember much about her. Ingrid remembered a little more. We grew up there, on our farm, Olssengården. Our family had lived there for hundreds of years before our generation came along, slaughtering the pigs and farming the land. It wasn't glamorous, I tell you. At fourteen, Ingrid decided to forego the farmer's life and got herself a job at a papermill in the town. Our father didn't like that one bit. But Ingrid was a stubborn type of girl. That's what everyone liked about her. She never compromised on anything.

Edward Robb:
All I know is that she turned up in north London at Maurice Hoffmann's printing shop when she was sixteen and homeless, and within a handful of years she was the most celebrated young new artist of the decade. That was before I knew her, though. By the time she found her way into my life she was a stunner—drop-dead-at-her-feet kind of gorgeous—she looked like she'd never seen a hard day's work in her life. Cheekbones you could cut glass on. Skin so soft it was like it was made out of clouds. I'm a Texas boy, and I liked that about her. She reminded me of the girls back home. That was before things went sour, of course.

Karoline Olssen:
I think she felt that she was going to suffocate in Hønefoss. There are these enormous burial mounds there. From the early Iron Age, or so. They seemed to be everywhere. Surrounding us on all sides, though in reality it wasn't like that at all. It just felt like that, you see? Quite the tourist attraction. At all times, growing up, Ingrid and I were thinking about how we were surrounded

by dead bodies. Dead bodies in every direction, as far as you could see. We were living in a graveyard. I think that's why she ran away.

Nora Robb, daughter and performance artist:
No, I didn't go to her funeral.

CHAPTER 2

N<small>ORA IS STILL IN</small> L<small>ONDON, ISN'T SHE</small>? R<small>ICHARD ASKED</small>
<small>ME, FLINGING THE QUESTION OVER HIS SHOULDER.</small>

He was my mother's posthumous biographer and he was standing naked in
my kitchen. It was four-thirty on a Sunday afternoon in the spring. A little
over two years after my mother's funeral.

What? I asked, even though I had heard him fine.

Nora. She's in London, right? She started her PhD?

I hadn't seen Nora—in person, at least—in the intervening time.

Don't do that, I told him as I searched the fridge. Nothing edible: half a
block of yellowing feta and wilted spinach in the drawer. Even the marga-
rine had something suspicious growing on it. I itched to get some food in
before Beanie got back from her dad's place tonight. I dumped the marga-
rine in the trash and turned back to Richard.

He had the look of someone caught in the act.

Don't do what? he asked sheepishly. He handed me a mug of steaming
black coffee. I took it and pulled my dressing gown tighter around me. There
was a hole in the cuff, which I poked my thumb through, feeling the soft
flannel against the pad.

Work, I responded simply.

He grinned, a naughty schoolboy, mischievous.

Sorry, he said, still smiling.

If you want to get hold of Nora, you can contact her yourself. You have her phone number. You have her email address. There's no need for me to get involved.

I could hear the edge to my voice as I was speaking and regretted the sharpness before the words were even out of my mouth. Richard, the most forgiving, most apologetic man I had ever dated, pulled me into a hug, extracting the mug from my hands and setting it down on the kitchen counter.

I will do that, he said quietly. I didn't mean to upset you.

You didn't upset me, I lied. It's just weird when you bring up work stuff when we're together. As a couple.

I had been seeing Richard for six months, since the first time he interviewed me. Quite suddenly and without my say-so, it had become serious. I liked Richard. A lot. He was generous and thoughtful and considerate. He was also writing a book about my mother. Aunt Karoline had done all the work, commissioning him based on two flattering profiles he had written on Ingrid Olssen for culture magazines. He had narrated a short film about her work for the BBC that had won a BAFTA. He had interviewed her a few times himself when she was still alive. Aunt Karoline insisted that Mum had been quite fond of him, and enjoyed his writing on her. He was the perfect candidate to write the biography. I found it vaguely strange for him to be so interested in my mother, but I supposed that was the point of critics. And it was refreshing not to have to ask my boyfriend not to Google my name or the names of anyone in my immediate family. Richard had been pre-indoctrinated into the chaos when I'd met him: he'd already been an admirer of my mother and her work, and as her biographer there'd been no need for me to awkwardly laugh off old press clippings about Mum's behavior in the eighties and nineties. Richard had already seen all those clippings. He had a binder, in fact. It was unusual but helpful. After he'd agreed to write the book, Aunt Karoline had found the publisher and secured the advance, of course taking a fee for herself, in typical Aunt Karoline fashion. She'd then set about convincing me, Nora, my dad Edward, and an eclectic cast of characters from Ingrid's life, to participate. In the end I'd agreed to give an interview to get her to stop calling me at work.

Perhaps, too, through his book, Richard would do something none of us had managed: he would pull on the threads of my mother's life, unravel them and arrange them back together into some cohesive whole. I had read some of his journalism in anticipation of the interview; he was good—even I, someone who'd left school at sixteen with five GCSEs and whose day-job was helping kids process their feelings by drawing pictures, could see that—if a little melodramatic. Perhaps he would get to some truth of Ingrid that no one else ever could in her lifetime.

Richard had arrived at the two-bed Acton apartment I shared with my teenager, Beanie, the following week, his face ruddy-red and freckled, his glasses sliding down a shiny nose, his jeans faded and crumpled. He'd looked unassuming, but the way he'd watched me, and the questions he'd asked, were sharp as a laser point.

Referring to *Girls*, he'd asked early on in the conversation, Is it you and your sister?

I shrugged, unimpressed. Yes, it's us. Everyone knows that.

The composition is interesting, he said, almost to himself, fiddling with the notebook that sat tidily on his lap, the page unspoiled. He had the voice recorder on; the notebook seemed to be more of a prop, something to do with his hands while we talked. When recording, his clipped Surrey accent became more pronounced, as British actors did when they played parts in American movies. For someone who was a veteran in his field, despite only being in his mid-thirties, only a couple of years older than me, he seemed to be unsettled. He was ill at ease in my living room, perched precariously on the edge of the sofa, averting his gaze from the photo collage on the wall that Beanie and I had spent one evening putting together with a tub of cheesecake-flavored Häagen-Dazs and the *Twilight* movies back-to-back, pasting pink glitter and heart sequins around the frames of our favorite memories: trips to London Zoo, the aquarium, the day she'd found out she had won a scholarship for drama school and we'd celebrated by getting our hair dyed matching shades of blue. My blue had long faded and been flooded over with a chestnut brown as close as possible to my natural color. Beanie had kept the blue, and then moved on to violet, then pink, and now she was orange. She'd insisted that we have Ingrid and Nora in the collage too. I had no photographs of them, so Beanie had printed out Nora's headshot from the art faculty pages of the Goldsmiths University website where she was undertaking her PhD; Mum's photo was an old tabloid snap of her falling out of a nightclub in the eighties, writhing, spindly arms wrapped around my dad's neck as he struggled to hold her steady, permed hair all frizz, bouncing across her shoulder blades, a sparkling green minidress hiked up around her waist exposing turquoise underwear and the hipbones of a person who didn't eat. The pupils of her grey-blue eyes black moons in the flashbulb of the camera. Just a slither of white powder peeking out from her nostril—it could be missed if you weren't looking for it. I'd asked Beanie whether she was sure this was the picture she wanted on the wall to remember Grandma by.

She would love it, though, wouldn't she? Beanie had asked by way of reply. She would get a kick out of it.

Mum had always hated the serious artist portraits, and her own self-portraits, that had invariably accompanied any articles about her work. She'd called them—the pictures, the publications, the editors and journalists—vampires.

She *would* love it, you're right, I agreed with Beanie. She looked beautiful and effervescent and carefree. It seemed that even in that moment of bareness, of vulnerability, there was something the photographer had captured in her eye, a kind of knowing. That such a candid moment had possibly been orchestrated. There was never a moment with Mum, even when she was off her trolley on champagne and pills and powder, that she didn't know exactly what she was doing. It was a photo of her from before she'd had children.

I'd heard Beanie on a video call to Nora one evening not long after, updating her on what was going on in our lives. Nora and I had always had a tricky relationship. Ever since I'd left the Richmond house at sixteen to have Beanie, we'd periodically collided like two dying planets: always in moments of crisis. The times that Nora had almost died or in the final days of our mother's life. Nora didn't really have her shit together, and she never said it but I knew she resented that I'd left when she couldn't, all those years ago. When I was being honest with myself, I resented it too. Nevertheless, Beanie and Nora got on like a house on fire. Perhaps because there wasn't much of an age difference between them: I'd had Beanie when I was sixteen and Nora was seven.

Now that Beanie was past the age I had been when I'd given birth to her, and Nora was in her mid-twenties, they had the most in common compared to any other moment in Beanie's life. I'd suddenly felt like the odd one out, encroaching on them. Nora didn't like to leave the house all that much, except for her work at the university, and she didn't like to have visitors either. Consequently, their relationship had existed almost exclusively online. Beanie had shown Nora, via FaceTime, the pictures we had chosen of her and Ingrid to go on the wall.

See, we used your university headshot, Beanie had said excitedly. Look how posh and serious you are. A proper artist.

Take it down, Nora said crisply on the other end of the line while I hovered in the kitchen, eavesdropping.

What! Why?

It's horrible. I hate that picture.

I think you look lovely in it.

I look like a fraud in it. I'm not joking, Old Bean. Take it off the wall. I'll tell your mum to do it, if you don't.

You won't tell Mum, Beanie said, scoffing. You don't talk to Mum.

Just do it, Beans, Jesus.

Fine, Beanie said sullenly. I'll take it down. It's not like you'll ever see it, anyway. You never visit us.

Beanie didn't take it down. I chose not to ask her why.

As I'd sat opposite Richard, I'd looked up at the collage. In the corner was a postcard reproduction of *Girls* that Beanie had amusedly picked up from the gift shop at the National Portrait Gallery while on a school trip.

What do you find interesting about the composition? I'd asked him, humoring him. I reminded myself that I had agreed to just the one interview. One hour, that was it. Once it was done, Aunt Karoline would be off my back, I could get on with my life without pretending to be moved by the increasingly banal takes of yet another wanky art critic, no matter how well he could compose a metaphor.

We'd sat for *Girls* in Mum's studio, under the sash windows in the

Richmond house, for twelve days over the course of a month when Nora was four and I was thirteen. Mum had chosen lukewarm marbled blues and oranges. She'd liked the way the sun had hit our faces. She'd ripped out all of the light fixtures in the house one winter, like weeds pulled out at the root, and from then on we'd lived by candlelight or sun. Nora had been too young to sit for so long, really, but she had already learned that to be in the presence of our mother with a brush in her hand was to be still and quiet.

She'd painted the two of us in first. I'd had no interest in the technique and the choices and the influence of her work at that time. I had never really grown to enjoy it at any time, in fact. I was interested in Robbie Williams, not dying a virgin, and no one at my new school finding out who my mother was and sticking printouts of her pastel nudes to my locker. Nora had always been the one fascinated by the colors. She'd placed her little hands on the palettes that Ingrid had left lying around the house—balanced on window-sills and tucked under easels, and once or twice in the fridge among furring cheddar, open bottles of flat Moët, half-full cans of beans and overripe man-goes whose skin had become wrinkled as the juices inside turned—and swiped the oils across her face. Never mind the chemicals, the acetone on brushes and palettes to clean the old pigments away. She'd run her hands across the hard, cold walls. She'd marveled at our mother's work. Had stared at that portrait of us, enraptured by the blues and the swipes of orange and golden-yellow tones. The way Ingrid had made us both somehow ugly and beautiful at the same time.

Well, Richard said, I always was intrigued by how she made you so monstrous.

It was true. In *Girls*, she gave us a look of savagery, in the set of our jaws and the curve of our eyebrows, as though there was something tempestuous and unknown and frightening within us, trying to get out.

And how she bent her own body away from the both of you, Richard continued.

She'd painted herself into the middle of us, after she had finished paint-ing us. The composition was that of reaching. Nora not quite resting her head on Ingrid's right shoulder and me with a hand clawed upon her arm. Most people interpreted the pose as deeply maternal, almost that of the

Madonna. But I couldn't tell whether the touches she'd had us give her were ones of comfort or entrapment.

She'd leaned it against the wall—it was too big to hang—and when her artist friends had visited, they'd complimented her on it.

It's my best girls, she'd said. They inspire my best work.

After I'd left home at sixteen, the portrait had stayed there in the living room, propped against the mantel. Pride of place. Once Nora had gone off to boarding school at eleven, Mum had taken it down and handed it off to the National Portrait Gallery. And when Mum died, Nora had inherited it, but had let it stay on loan. Out of convenience, I thought, or maybe a desire to never handle the baggage of the sitting and the creation of the art. I didn't ask her about it. Because Nora and I didn't talk.

Do you know why she gave it away? Richard asked, meaning Ingrid, as though he had heard the color of my thoughts. I shook my head.

Have you been to see it? Since she died?

No. Why would I? I stared at it every day for three years. I know every inch of that painting.

What if you find something new in it, now that she's gone?

I stood up abruptly. I think I've had enough, now, I told him. He stood up, too, mirroring me.

I apologize. I overstepped.

It's fine, I said through my teeth. You're here to do a job, not be my friend.

That's true.

I just don't see much point in raising the dead, Richard, right? I know that to you, and to everyone else, she was this complex, ground-breaking artist. That she was a visionary. A genius. But she wasn't that to me. I didn't see that. I have no interest in her work. I can't extract the genius from it. When I look at *Girls* all I can see is how my sister had to wear a back brace for months to correct her posture after Mum made her sit in that position for so long. All I can hear is Nora crying because her body ached. She was too young. Her bones were too soft.

Richard stared at me, his thumb hovering over the "stop" button on his sleek grey recording device.

She wasn't anyone to me except my mother, I said. I can't offer you anything else.

But that's exactly what I want from you, he gabbled, excited, his eyes wide with the effort to make me understand.

Well, I'm not prepared to give that away, I said with finality.

He snapped the button with a soft click and quietly apologized again before excusing himself. I let him out and closed the door with my forehead. It was cool and hard against my skin.

I hadn't meant to say anything of any substance. I had wanted to keep things as bland, as vanilla as possible. To give as little away as I could manage.

But Mum always brought out the very worst in me.

She brought out the worst in all three of us.

Richard called me a week later to apologize, and offered to take me for dinner—off the record—to clarify how I wanted him to write his book.

I want this to be a collaboration with Ingrid's family, he told me on the phone. I want to work with you, not in spite of you. I want to do right by all of you. And—Matilda—this might be hard for you to believe, but I do want to be a friend to you, as well as getting the job done.

I agreed to dinner and instead of talking about my mother, we ended up talking about me, the version of me that happened after Ingrid. How I had fallen pregnant with Beanie young—far too young—but having her had opened a whole new world to me that was so far removed from the web my mother had spun, it had felt like being born anew myself. I'd moved out of the house in Richmond, leaving Nora behind with Mum, and started fresh on my own. First in a rent-controlled studio above a kebab shop with Gus. And then—when we'd inevitably split up because we'd been teenagers playing house and trying to raise a child—for a year with my old school-friend, Chelsea, before a group home with other young mothers, most of whom had been running from something too. When Beanie had started nursery, I'd worked at a primary school on dinner duty until I'd got some work in the school office. I'd gone to college part time and got a National Vocational Qualification in social work to supplement the five GCSEs I'd

managed to scrape together while pregnant in my final year of school, trying my best to ignore the sneering looks from the other girls when I'd
turned up to the biology exam with a nine-month belly protruding over my
school skirt. When I was twenty and Beanie had started full-time school,
I'd been hired as a teaching assistant specializing in special educational
needs. The hours worked for both of us. Gus had moved back in with his
parents and bartended while he'd studied for his law degree. He'd stayed in
residence halls in Hull Monday to Friday, and come back for Beanie every
weekend. Such a canyon between the way he'd been able to recover his life
from our shared disruption, compared to how I could recover mine. He had
been there, though, in a way I'd never expected that he would.

As Beanie had got older, I'd moved between primary schools, each time
collecting a new local-authority-mandated qualification as the kids got more
online, and new ghoulish problems presented themselves. Anorexic six-
year-olds; kids with dead parents; kids with dead cats; kids who didn't know
how to make friends; kids who feared sex; kids who were far too interested
in sex; kids with knives; homophobic kids; racist kids; kids who fought other
kids because they didn't know how to process what they were feeling; kids
who were being groomed on the internet. All of it made me terrified for
Beanie—who, thank God, had made it through secondary school relatively
unscathed and, due to our being dirt-poor, without access to a home computer or an iPad. I had worked in a range of school mental-health professional roles on account of my social work qualification, which I'd never used
in the way I'd intended. Beanie had got her scholarship and started drama
school, and my line manager had asked if I would take a course in art therapy for children. It had seemed like the obvious next move.

So, you're an art therapist? Richard asked, tucking into his third glass of
wine. We had met at a bar just off Ealing Common for the follow-up "interview," although it had become clear within half an hour that he thought we
were on a date. I was happy to play along. Richard was nice. He made eye
contact with me when I talked, and remembered the things I told him. I was
unsure whether this was because he was interested in me, or he was a journalist. He had this look about him of being beyond delighted with the
whimsy of life, something that I'd lost myself a long time ago.

I shrugged and sipped as I answered his question.

I feel like "art therapist" is too . . . grandiose for what I do. I'm aware of the irony, I told him.

What irony? he asked, his glasses slipping down his face, a face so earnest I wanted to reach out and cup it between my hands. I enjoyed the dusting of freckles scattered across his nose and the apples of his cheeks. I imagined that I could dig each one out with a pinky fingernail.

It makes sense for you to be interested in a career in art, he said. Look at your mother, after all. Your sister.

But I don't get it, I admitted. I don't understand what makes what Mum did so special. What makes people interested in Nora and her performance art. It's all just faffing about, really, isn't it?

Richard looked as though I had spat directly into his wine glass.

Faffing about, he repeated.

I shrugged. I had spent years settling into my no-fucks-given attitude to art, and particularly the art of the women with whom I shared DNA.

You can talk about technique and accomplishment and composition, Richard said, his face now glowing. But, really, it's just about how it makes you feel, on a fundamental level. How does art make you feel, Matilda? What does it make you think of? How does it uncover your darkest desires, your secret aches?

Are you flirting with me? I asked him, and he blushed so deeply I couldn't help but laugh.

In truth, I didn't know how to respond to his statement.

I had a growing suspicion that Mum and Nora felt far too much, and I didn't feel anywhere near enough.

I sort of loved that this was all it was to him. Art was about feeling. It was about history and context and legacy, too, of course. But mostly—and on a fundamental level—he looked at something and he decided whether he liked it or not, and that was it.

It was all so straightforward.

I took pleasure in the easiness of not having to explain myself to him, of not trying to field his questions about my family, telling half-truths and omissions to avoid outright lying about my upbringing. I had only ever dated men superficially after Gus. I didn't want to disrupt Beanie's life by bringing people in who I knew would eventually leave. I had never introduced Beanie to a boyfriend, few that there had been. But with Richard, it seemed easy, and natural.

And if I didn't think too hard about how much he knew about my personal history, and how little I knew of his, I could imagine a future for us.

Now, six months later, he stood in my kitchen, naked, and asked of Nora's whereabouts.

I thought you'd interviewed her twice already, anyway, I said, stretching.

I just need to do a bit of follow-up. She started a new project, did you know that?

I heard something from Beanie about it.

It's interesting. A piece of living art. She's got cameras in an apartment watching her around the clock twenty-four hours a day. Anyone can tune into the stream. She's got a few hundred people watching her every move at any one time.

I see, I said, though I didn't. I had found a coffee grain embedded in the countertop. I took up a spoon and dug underneath it until I pried it away.

It must be her thesis, Richard mused. A take on internet voyeurism, maybe. An interesting subversion of Olssen's work, for sure. A new kind of digital self-portrait. But organic, too. Living and breathing and changing.

He opened his laptop at the table and began tapping something out.

I said, Beanie's going to be back from her dad's soon, so you'd better get moving.

I knew that once Richard had his head buried in a Word document, it could be hours before he resurfaced. And I was handling Beanie carefully. I didn't want her to meet Richard before she was ready—before I was one hundred percent certain about his position in our life. It was something I was still trying to work out, though I felt it might happen soon.

He headed to the shower with a kiss planted affectionately on my cheek, which made me warm. His laptop, still open, was navigated to a website called the Control Room. A live YouTube video took up most of the real estate on the homepage. There she was. My sister. A plain, whitewashed room. With her inside, seemingly too small for its proportions. She sat on a brown sofa and stared at the television. The angle of the cameras meant that the observer could not see what it was that she was watching, but understood nonetheless that she was watching something. Comments flared up on the screen in the top-right hand corner at a speed so swift it was impossible to read what each person was saying before they disappeared. In a banner across the top of the video, the viewer count kept a live tally on the number of active viewers: 198, down to 196, up to 201.

I watched Nora on the computer screen, as two hundred others were doing at that exact moment. She was holding her phone loosely in one hand. So she was contactable, it seemed. Her slight, dark, pixelated figure, poker-straight against the back of the sofa. She looked thin, and tired, and uncomfortable. I tried to reconcile this distorted vision of her with the last time I'd seen her properly, shortly after Mum had died, in a funeral home as we'd picked out Order of Service designs and music and flowers. Before Mum got ill, it had been Los Angeles, just under three years ago, in a hospital bed at Cedars-Sinai, after the second suicide attempt. Her hair was much longer in the Control Room than it had been back then, what had once been a neat, blunt-edged bob now snaking over her shoulders in wild tendrils. Mum had been at the hospital too. She had already been diagnosed with her cancer, and it was metastasizing, but nobody had known yet. Everyone had been arguing about what to do with Nora. Bring her back to London for R&R, or have her stay with Dad in California while she finished her Master's. Maybe find an institution that could look after her better than we could between us, because we could barely look after ourselves. I hadn't wanted to be there. Mum had made me feel like my skin was too small to contain my body. Like I'd been going to fall out of myself and my internal organs would spill across the hospital linoleum.

But it hadn't just been Mum. It had been Nora, too. The fractures of our relationship had splintered into fissures in the gaps between us meeting. When I looked at her now, I saw our shared history, and I saw the gaps in between, and I saw the face of a person I no longer knew very well.

Nora had said back then, Don't you want to know why I did it?

Her voice was a fingernail scratching over the grooves of a vinyl record.

I took her hand and, avoiding the cannula, squeezed it.

The hospital smelled of old potatoes and antiseptic and misery.

I said what I had been trained to say to the self-harming ten-year-olds at work.

If you want to talk about it, if you're happy to talk about it, then you can talk to us. We're here for you.

Nora's eyes closed momentarily.

Everything is too loud, she said. That's the whole point.

Don't be ridiculous, Mum said, the Scandinavian inflection of her accent a little exaggerated, as it always was when she was bored or irritated or put out.

Mum was having a bad spell.

We don't want to know about your bullshit, she said. Honestly, Nora, so dramatic. Anyone would think you've had a hard life.

PARTIAL TRANSCRIPTION OF INTERVIEW NUMBER 2
WITH NORA ROBB [01.04.2020]

N.R.: Everyone wants to know why I did it.

R.T.: Of course we want to know. The whole world wants to know.

N.R.: I think that's a bit of an overstatement.

R.T.: Your—suicide attempt—was covered extensively in the press. When they got that interview with your housemate, the whole thing went international. How did that feel?

N.R.: I can't explain to you how it felt. They had me taking lithium. I wasn't feeling much of anything.

R.T.: Are you taking anything now?

N.R.: No.

R.T.: Why not?

N.R.: Because it turns me into a zombie. Because I can't create.

R.T.: Do you have prescriptions? That you're not taking?

N.R.: I don't see how this is relevant to a book about my mother's work.

R.T.: Sorry, sorry. It's all background, you see.

N.R.: That's a lovely shirt you're wearing.

R.T.: Thank you. So . . . prescription medications?

N.R.: All the usual shit. You know. Olanzapine, fluoxetine, sertraline.

R.T.: And it's something you're comfortable talking about?

N.R.: Sure. Why not. My secrets are yours, Richard.

R.T.: Sorry, to be clear, this is on the record. You know that, right?

N.R.: I thought everything was on the record. I thought there was no such thing as off the record.

R.T.: I just want you to know that I could use anything that you say to me. In the book.

N.R.: I understand that.

R.T.: So . . . what happened?

N.R.: Which time?

R.T.: You're saying this has happened more than once?

N.R.: I'm surprised, Richard. You know so much about me and my family. My mother, especially. I'm surprised you don't know all the details already. Near-death experiences. I've had a few of them. See, there it is. I can tell from that look on your face. You know already, don't you?

R.T.: I've had a few things come up, yes, in some of the other interviews I've done. Everyone knows about Maurice Hoffmann, of course. It's a matter of public record. And some things have been said in my conversations with your aunt. About how you grew up. How you were looked after when you were very young.

N.R.: By my count, it's seven.

R.T.: Seven what?

N.R.: Seven times. Seven times that I could have died.

CHAPTER 3

THIS IS THE STORY OF THE FIRST TIME NORA ALMOST DIED.

In the beginning, there had been nothing, and then there had been me and my mother.

I didn't remember a lot of my early years. As a practitioner, I knew how childhood memory could be skewed and distorted so that what remains in a mind is false, or incomplete, or barely there. Most memories of childhood are stories. They are the stories that are told by parents, and brothers, and sisters, and aunts and uncles, passed through generations in an oral tradition. A shared knowledge, which morphs and ripples like water every time it is retold. In this way, the truth of a child's existence is modified with the input of a collective, familial memory. This is the work of molding a child's character. *You were a bad kid. You were the sensible one. You were a pathological liar. You looked after the animals. You cut off your sister's hair when you were six. At seven, you fell through the glass coffee table and knocked yourself out dancing to Mariah Carey, and we had to go to Accident and Emergency for stitches. At nine, Maurice Hoffmann shot you with a hunting rifle.* If a child has no one to tell them what to remember, to tell them the stories of their first years on this mortal coil, the memory fails to manifest. In its stead is blank, nothing, absence.

I had seen it many times in the children I worked with. Especially the ones who had been separated from biological parents, put into care. Without the storytelling, the space that ought to be filled with memory shrank, until there was nothing there. They had blank spaces where other children had rich and textured legends of belonging. I worked with kids on life-story work, and helped them tell their own stories. I did this work in the small, peeling, windowless store cupboard that served as my office behind the staffroom at school. I kept binders of their handwritten notes, their drawings and paintings and photographs, the things they had collected and manifested to invent their own mythology.

It took me some time to realize I had gaps, too, or rather, the absence of space. There were no family photographs in our house. Only paintings. There were no mementos of childhood that I had taken with me when I'd left. No gentle, nurturing parables of our life together from either of my parents. No stories that were smooth at the edges, worn from being taken out and examined and handled with the pads of thumbs. There was nothing, for the most part, except the sensation of my mother's fingers combing gently through my hair. The smell of her soap—aloe and lavender—on her skin, mixed with linseed oil from the paint, and acetone and old wood from the brushes, and of course stale smoke. The sound of her voice as she mused to herself, and to me, as she worked. She was constantly in conversation with herself, with the work. I remembered things like her bare feet, and the grain of the floorboards, and the dust motes that got stuck in the hallway carpet, which was green and faded.

Mum loved the garden and when she wasn't painting, she was whispering to the lemon tree that bore fat yellow orbs the same color as our front door in the height of the summer. Most of the year, the lemon tree lay potted in a thick-walled terracotta tub that sat in the corner of the conservatory, drinking in the sun through the glass ceiling. In the summer, when it got hot enough, it came out into the garden and went wild with its fruit. Mum cultivated a rosebush that bloomed perfect white roses that hung like teardrops. And in the greenhouse in the far corner there were peas and broad beans and cauliflowers.

And then, periodically, she would disappear. She would stop talking to the lemon tree, cutting through the waxy peel to add slices to her gin and tonic on a summer evening.

There were these snatches of things that my body had recorded, rather than my mind.

The smell of lemon zest on my mother's hands. My mother who taught me how to pour a gin and tonic before I knew how to tie my shoelaces.

The softness of her voice when she sang in Norwegian. The warmth of her body when I had a bad dream and she carried me to her bed with strong, lean arms and let me sleep against her, our chests rising and falling in unison.

Then, the sense of something changing. A telephone call.

Beneath the citrus was something sour and agitated. An anticipation. A clumsiness to her movements. A desperation. Sometimes she would forget to feed me.

Snatches of conversations behind the wall of her studio.

Karoline's voice, pleading. You cannot turn into this person every time he comes, Ingrid, she would say. You have responsibilities. You have work to do. You have a daughter who needs you.

It would go on like this until he arrived. Of my father, I remembered even less: an intermittent shadow in the hallway, one large rough hand on the crown of my head, the briefest of touches before being lifted away. Cigar smoke that left a stale aftertaste in every room he inhabited. Old Spice after-shave, and Brylcreem.

When you are a child, time is elastic. It transforms with the whims of the body and mind. It felt like a lifetime when she disappeared with him, but in reality it would be no more than a few days, a week at most.

And when she was gone, it was Karoline who I remembered. Karoline, who sang show tunes, and served fårikål with sharp pickled cabbage and mutton so thoroughly overcooked that it turned to mush in the mouth. Aunt Karoline who roasted beetroots from our garden in the oven and forgot about them until the whole house was warm and fragrant. Aunt Karoline who walked around the house naked after taking a shower because she didn't trust English towels.

When Dad came, he only came for Mum. And every time he did, the broad beans and the peas and the cauliflowers in the greenhouse were left untended until they were dying.

And when she came back, and he didn't, she smelled of his cigars too, and then, in the days that followed, the smell became that of rot and sweat and an unwashed body.

She wouldn't hold me.

Time was elastic. It went on.

And then, on a day no more and no less conspicuous than any other, she would emerge from the studio, and she would wash her hair with lavender-scented soap, and she would go out to the garden, a cigarette hanging from her mouth, and bring the plants back to life. And she would teach me how to tie my shoelaces and how to make lemon cakes soft and fluffy and sharp with crystallized sugar that got stuck between my teeth. And it was as though nothing had happened. It went on.

Twice or thrice a year, every year, for eight years.

It was unremarkable because I had not known anything else.

It was unremarkable until the year that, months after Dad's last visit, Nora came.

Nora was the thing I remembered the most, and Nora was the thing that anchored me to the surface of the planet.

It was after Nora came that I realized, aged eight—fully and completely for the first time—that there was something wrong with Mama.

Things worsened. She sometimes seemed to forget that Nora and I existed, locking herself in her studio for days at a time. Sometimes she went out at night and didn't come home until the next. She forgot to turn the heating on that first winter. And then the fridge broke and no one thought to replace it. And then the rose-patterned glass in the front door got smashed somehow, and she simply taped some cardboard over it. A problem for another time.

After Nora came, Dad didn't come back for a long time. Strangers, friends of Mama's, began coming to the house. They would stay up for days, their voices filtering underneath the locked door to the studio, sometimes laughing, sometimes shouting, always with the pungent smells of smoke and sweat and champagne—Mama had started drinking Moët by the bottle—seeping out into the hallway and embedding themselves into the old green carpet.

I learned Aunt Karoline's phone number by memory so that, when

Mum disappeared, I could call her from the rotary phone in the hallway and she would arrive hours later with a bag of shopping and a cigarette behind her ear.

Karoline flitted in and out of the Richmond house like a hummingbird. Constantly in motion, constantly restless, always in the midst of a new argument with my mother.

The girls can't be living like this, Ingrid.

What have you been feeding them?

You can't just let these strangers into the house.

Is Matilda going to school?

Time was elastic, and it seemed to speed up as Nora grew. Her baby-head smell, her hair soft golden wisps. When Mum didn't feed her, I did, learning how to make the formula and spoon the mushed-up vegetables out of the jars that Karoline had left in the cupboards for us. Learning the right temperature to bathe her in the tiny plastic baby bath.

And then, on Nora's first birthday, Mum made us lemon drizzle cake, with lemons from the tree.

It was the first good day we had had in a while, in the beginning.

Mum let me and Nora pick out the lemons we wanted from the tree and she plucked them from the branches. Then she sliced them up in the kitchen, adding a new slice to each new gin and tonic I poured for her. Another, please, mixologist, she would call to me, and I—happy that she was happy and that today was a good day—obliged until she was rosy cheeked and soft around the edges. Sun streamed through the conservatory windows. I had grown so accustomed to hearing voices through the walls that the silence of the house, besides the music of her voice, the delighted laughter of Nora, now seemed unfamiliar.

Mum smelled of lavender and lemons; her hair was clean. And she sang in Norwegian as she sliced and drank.

Then, like a haunting, the telephone rang.

Mum froze, and I froze too, the cake batter I had been stirring forgotten. Nora, a baby unaccustomed to the significance of the telephone ringing, burbled and fisted sugar into her mouth, her cheeks round and pink.

Mum, who was a little unsteady on her feet on account of the gin, went to answer the phone in the hall. I turned off the oven and took Nora upstairs to my bedroom.

Moments later, the sound of hard footsteps on the bare wooden staircase, and Mum flung the door open, her eyes bright and shining sharply.

It's a wonderful day, she said, showing me all of her teeth.

I said nothing. The raw cake batter and sugar from the baking was beginning to simmer hot in my stomach. I left Nora on the bed, mashing her hands together, and I went to the bathroom, and I threw it all up.

When I came back, Nora and Mum were both gone from the bedroom.

Mama? I called. I went to the top of the staircase. She was at the bottom of it, Nora balanced on her hip as she tried to pull a comb through her hair.

Mum? I asked again. What are you doing?

Now she was slipping her feet into a pair of high heels, her knees buckling precariously as she did.

Your father is here, she said, a little breathless. She beamed up at me as I stood at the top of the stairs. Your father is in London.

He wants to meet her. He wants to meet his daughter.

I felt my mouth turn dry, the scent of my vomit still burning my nostrils.

But we're making a cake, I said.

Forget the cake, she said. Forget the fucking cake. We're going to go and meet Pappa.

But Nora needs a bath, I tried again, floundering. I need to wash her hair. It's all knotty, look.

I could see now that Mum was swaying a little on the spot, Nora burbling happily in her arms, delighted, it seemed, at the prospect of an adventure, unaware of the danger.

Mum, I said again.

A shadow passed over Mum's face.

Just shut up, will you? she hissed at me, her voice dropping as though someone might hear her. Shut up. You're going to ruin it.

And she flung the yellow door open hard, so that the cardboard that had been covering the broken window panel fluttered to the floor.

Mum only had one high heel on, and she was unlocking the door to the car, an old green Beetle that she had bought second-hand from one of the friends who sometimes came and got locked in the studio with her.

I felt the bile rising again and thundered down the stairs, chasing after her.

Mum, I said. You can't drive.

Shut up, shut up, shut up, she was hissing. I couldn't tell whether she was saying it to me, or to herself, or to Nora who was now crying, writhing around in Mum's arms.

I took hold of her elbow, trying to pull her away from the car.

You're drunk, Mama, I said. Drunk was a new word I had learned at school. The school I'd recently enrolled in, where a kind lady who smelled of nutmeg came and sat us down and asked us questions like: *Does Mummy dress you in the mornings? Does she brush your hair? Does she ever fall asleep during the day? Does she leave you at home alone?* Karoline had coached me on how to answer these questions.

After Nora had arrived, I remembered everything, because it was a question of survival to remember.

I remembered when Nora ate, and when Nora had last been bathed, and what time Mum had left the house, and what time she came home.

So I also remembered, with a clarity that sometimes felt physically painful when I thought of it, how I tugged at Mum's arms, trying to get her away from the car.

How I tried to wrestle the keys from her claw-like grip.

The sound of her voice as she seethed at us, *Shut up, shut up, shut up.*

And the noise Nora made when she slipped out of Mum's arms in the midst of the struggle.

And her skull hit the edge of the pavement with a sickening crack.

Silence.

The crack reverberated up through us, through the open door of the Richmond house.

Through the walls, up the stairs.

Even now, at thirty-three years old, sometimes, in the dead of the night when the apartment was silent and Beanie was at Gus's house for the week, I would open my eyes and hear that crack.

I often wondered how much Nora remembered of it, before she acquired language especially. I wondered whether being there with her, telling her the story, reifying our shared memory, our collective experience, made her remember more.

Perhaps it would have been better if she had forgotten it all. Perhaps if her memory had shrunk like mine, the gaps closed up, the spaces for the stories no longer there, she might have better survived it all.

EXTRACTS [VARIOUS] FROM INTERVIEW TRANSCRIPTS,
QUOTED IN INGRID OLSSEN: VISIONARY BY RICHARD
TAPER (FORTHCOMING FROM ORANGE RABBIT PRESS)

Oakland Frink, art collector:
It was in the mid-nineties that Olssen started experimenting with
the larger portrait work, like *My burial*, which was sold at the
Grift House Art Festival. But you asked about how motherhood
informed her work. I'm not entirely sure that it did, if I'm honest.
Looking at the work between the births of her two children, there
aren't any stylistic points of difference. From what I understand,
Olssen kept her life as a mother quite separate from her life as an
artist. She didn't like to have one inform the other. Her relationship with her ex-husband, however. You could write your whole
book on that alone. The obsession, the glamour! It's an absolute
goldmine.

Edward Robb, ex-husband and actor:
When Nora was born, I just fell completely in love with her. She
looked exactly like my late mother, actually. She still does. Her eyelashes were so thick she looked like a little doll. I was there at the
birth.

Karoline Olssen:
He wasn't there at the birth. He was filming a pilot for *How Many
Hot Dogs*, and he got fired after they caught him drinking on set.

Edward Robb:
In fact, I passed on a very lucrative gig for a series about extreme
eating contests so that I could be there. I had made a mess of parenting Matilda, I'll admit that. But I had a second chance with my
little moonbeam, Nora. And I wasn't prepared to let Ingrid's
behavior hurt our children any longer.

Karoline Olssen:
Please. Edward wanted nothing to do with those girls.

Nora Robb, daughter and performance artist:
I couldn't tell you the first time I met my dad, but if it was when I got dropped on the head, you'll have to ask Mattie, because I don't remember a thing.

CHAPTER 4

RICHARD WAS GONE FOR THE WEEKEND AND BEANIE WOULD BE HOME SOON.

My phone vibrated as I chopped chilies for chicken tikka masala, Beanie's favorite. The caller ID was my aunt Karoline. I rejected it instinctively. For the past few months, Karoline had been trying to put an exhibition of Mum's art together, some sort of retrospective. But she needed my permission—and Nora's—to display Mum's work. When Mum died, Karoline had got the Richmond house—with all the ghosts that hid in the cracks in the walls and behind the radiators, as well as the subsidence that meant it was turning, quickly and literally, into a financial black hole—while Nora and I had got an equal split of the collected works of Ingrid Olssen. We owned all the physical artwork: everything from the huge canvases heavy-laden with slatherings of oil paint, pictures the size of houses, right down to the little doodles in sketchbooks she'd liked to make while sitting on a wicker chair in the conservatory in the summer, chain-smoking and sipping champagne from a water-stained flute until she'd fallen asleep in the sunshine. We owned it all, aside from a few pieces she had sold to different galleries to pay off debts, or loaned out for reasons only known to her. Everything else was ours, including the copyright, the right to reproduce and permission to exhibit.

All of it, a life's work, locked away in a storage facility in Brentford.

Karoline was calling for a third time. I rejected it again with the jab of a thumb, and added some sugar to translucent onions gently sautéing in butter on the stove.

I queued up a nineties playlist and cranked the volume.

I added chopped garlic and chile flakes to the pan. Cumin, coriander.

Another four rejected calls from Karoline.

I tipped in curry paste and canned tomatoes and covered the pan, letting it simmer.

On the fifth call, I answered the phone.

Give it up, Karo, I shouted, over the top of Whitney Houston's "I'm Every Woman." You're not doing an exhibition.

Darling—what is that racket? she shrieked back at me.

Stop calling me. It's Sunday night. Can't you find someone else's blood to suck?

You're such a spoilsport, Matilda, you always have been.

I hung up, and immediately the phone vibrated again.

Fuck off, Karo, I shouted down the phone.

Mum, no, it's me. We've been banging at the door for the last ten minutes; you need to turn your music down. I forgot my keys.

I hung up and let Beanie in. She carried only a backpack. She kept enough of her things at both my place and Gus's that she could travel light when moving between our homes.

She allowed me to pull her into a hug and plant a kiss into her highlighter-orange hair.

Did you have a nice weekend? I asked, taking the music down to a more human volume.

Yeah, we went to the football.

Cooool, I replied exaggeratedly. Gus had instilled in Beanie his deep-seated devotion to Fulham Football Club and she had cried when he'd bought her a season ticket for her seventeenth birthday. Thank God he loved it just as much as she did, so I didn't have to get involved with going to match days on freezing Saturday afternoons in the rain.

Gus was in the doorway now, holding Beanie's headphones.

You left these in the car, you dope, he said.

She grabbed them and immediately slammed her way into her bedroom.

I'm just unpacking, she called back to us, muffled by the closing door.

Well, that's that, then, I said to Gus, and he shrugged amusedly.

This is our life now, isn't it?

Guess it is. Do you want some dinner? I've got curry on.

No, thanks, I've got work to do tonight.

He slid an arm around my shoulders and squeezed the back of my neck, kissed me on the cheek and slumped onto the sofa.

You look tired. Is it a big case?

Not *big*. I don't think we'll spend longer than a few days in court. Just an—emotionally draining one—let's say.

I handed him a beer from the fridge. He dragged a hand across his eyes, pinching the space in between.

I won't ask, I said. Gus worked with a sexual assault victims' charity to bring prosecutions to court, alongside his regular job as a criminal prosecutor. The work exhausted him in more ways than just the physical.

Thanks. How're you, anyway?

Oh, you know. Same old shit. Did you have a nice weekend with Beans?

He sat up a little straighter and set his beer bottle down on the coffee table.

Mattie, we need to talk about something. Did you know that she's vaping?

What? *Vaping?*

I caught her hanging out her bedroom window with one of those battery-powered things while I was taking the trash out.

I wiped my forehead with the back of my hand absent-mindedly.

Vaping, I said again. Flabbergasted. But she's never even smoked.

Yeah, this is what the kids are doing now. I was talking to my neighbor about it. They don't even smoke. They just skip straight to vaping.

What the fuck, I said simply.

Will you talk to her? I confiscated the vape and had a word. But it needs to come from both of us, I think. I've read some articles. Risk of stroke shoots up, apparently.

Yes. Of course, I'll talk to her. I'll do it tonight.

He smiled forlornly.

What else is going on? he asked. How's Richard?

I shrugged, still reeling with the news of my daughter, the vaper. He's—you know—Richard.

We had had dinner last night at some fancy over-the-top bistro in the middle of town. You're not going to propose, are you? I had joked when the taxi had pulled up outside. He hadn't answered. Thinking about it, he'd acted strangely all night. And this morning, with all his talk about Nora. He knew I didn't like him talking about work. It unsettled me, thinking about her. I sometimes tried to picture her but her features were not clear to me, as though she existed to me only through thick glass. I knew I needed to call her soon. Beanie made it too easy for me not to check in; she was up to date with Nora's life via her various social media and her blog. Any developments in Nora's life—like how she had recently moved into her new apartment in New Cross and got a new therapist—came via Beanie, which meant I didn't need to make any effort to obtain the information myself.

I think he's wanting to get serious, I said to Gus, dashing away thoughts of my sister.

Gus stiffened slightly, the rim of the beer bottle hovering at his lips. You've only been going out five minutes.

I know. I haven't introduced him to Beanie, even. I must have been imagining it.

You and your massive ego, at it again.

I know, I know. Not everyone's in love with me, right?

Gus grinned in that way that turned the corners of his mouth down rather than up.

And he keeps asking me questions about Nora. For the biography.

Sleeping with your mum's biographer, Beanie said loudly, announcing her arrival into the living room by bashing the door open with her hip. She carried a tower of glasses in the crook of her elbow, half-filled with orange squash and Coke, collected no doubt from the corners of her bedroom. A therapist would have a field day with that, she said.

Do you mind, I said jokingly. Your dad and I could have been having a private conversation in here.

Beanie rolled her eyes. Yeah. Sure.

God, Gus said, I don't remember raising such a brat, Mattie, do you? Shall we send her to the knacker's yard?

What the hell is a knacker's yard?

Gus and I smiled at one another. What a charmed life you lead, my sweet girl.

Gus finished his beer and said goodbye by pulling Beanie into a hug.

Text me when you know the date of your play, he told her.

It's a showcase, not a play, she replied, grimacing.

Beanie was studying at a central London drama school, and the showcase was her first big performance where family and friends were invited to attend. She had been fretting about it for months, convinced that she was going to embarrass herself, that she was, in her words, a talentless fraud. I could never understand how she, my bright, burning girl who leaked confidence and self-assuredness from every pore, could ever doubt herself. I had never seen her perform myself; it had taken both me and Gus several weeks of persuading to be allowed to attend the showcase. But the fact she'd got into her sixth form on a merit-based scholarship spoke for itself. She took after Nora, I always thought: totally oblivious to her own natural gifts.

After Gus had gone, I served dinner up.

All right, kid, I said, as soon as we had settled at the table. What's this absolutely hilarious news about vaping I've heard?

Beanie rolled her eyes dramatically, her mouth full of curry.

Muuuum.

Don't *Muuuum* me. I'm not having it, Beans. It's just unbelievable. I didn't think you would be such a sheep, that you would be a follower, that just because everyone else is doing it, you should too. I thought you were better than that—

I could feel myself working up into a disproportionate anger. A weekend of Richard acting strangely, and Karoline's phone calls, had me on edge. And now something about Nora's new project, the twenty-four-hour cameras. It made me nervous in a way I couldn't quite articulate.

I just didn't think you were that kind of a person, I told Beanie simply, trying to calm myself.

It was true. Beans loved Nina Simone and Janis Joplin; she often went kayaking with her old scout group even though all her primary-school friends had left several years ago, deeming themselves too old and too cool for organized outdoor fun. She sometimes went to school in men's suits from the seventies that she'd found in charity shops on Pitshanger Lane. She loved herself, and everyone else, so loudly and so fiercely. She wasn't the type to be pressured into anything. So unlike me at seventeen, trying to keep my shit together to raise a newborn, so nervous of how I would be perceived by others that I could barely step out the front door. In wrangling her through her adolescence, I felt painfully ill-equipped.

I don't know what kind of person I am, Mum, Beanie said. And something flickered through her that I didn't understand, that I hadn't seen in her before. Her body so like mine, grown inside me, yet becoming more alien every time I turned away and back again.

I touched her hand across the table. The lightest of touches.

She said, You need to stop worrying about me so much.

I can't help it, kid. It's my job.

We ate in silence for a while, as Spotify cycled through Cher and moved on to Kate Bush.

Nora loved Kate Bush.

Have you heard from Nora recently? I asked Beanie as the thought occurred to me.

Not *recently* recently. I invited her to my showcase, but she never replied to my text.

I nodded and chewed on a piece of chicken.

Nora doesn't go outside, hon, I said.

She goes to work.

That's different.

Why are you asking about Nora?

Just that Richard was saying about her new project. The cameras in her apartment.

Oh, yeah. It's cool, isn't it?

Is it? I don't know. It seems kind of invasive and exposing.

Those are two contradictory ideas.

Are they? You sound like her.

Nora's fine, Mum. I think. You should probably find out for yourself, though, rather than spying on her through me.

I'm not spying.

Really? What else would you call it?

I just haven't seen her in a while, that's all.

Not since Gran died.

No. Not since Gran died.

That was like, two years ago.

I remembered the three of us—me, Nora, and Aunt Karoline—gathered in Mum's bedroom in the Richmond house. Karoline sobbing so loudly and melodramatically that surely the cats in the next borough had heard her. Nora and I, stifled by all the distance between us, saying not much of anything at all.

It had been the center of our shared universe for so long. The Richmond house. Spiders' webs in the corners of draughty, empty rooms. The green carpet. A front door the color of lemons. The sound of the telephone. Mum inside lobbing paint at the walls, trying to find something meaningful in the way the pigments ricocheted across the plaster.

Nora was in another empty place now, the one on the laptop screen. The rooms sparse in a different way. The apartment not old and secretive like the Richmond house, but sanitized and colorless, which almost seemed worst.

I'll call Nora tomorrow, I told Beans, feeling my stomach curl into a tight cone.

Sure, she said.

CHAPTER 5

THE SECOND TIME NORA ALMOST DIED, IT WAS THE SUMMER OF 2001.

I was fourteen and falling in love with Gus Hanson, in that disgusting, all-consuming way only fourteen-year-old girls can.

I was still attending an all-girls school in Twickenham, paid for by my chronically absent father, and Gus was two years above at the local comprehensive.

My best—only—friend, Chelsea Ivanova, was heir to a canned-pineapple fortune. Despite this, she was the most normal-seeming of all the girls at Twickenham Girls', many of whom were boarders and had more than one pony. On my second week at my new school, I woke up, bathed, dressed and fed Nora, before slinking onto the bus at the end of the street via the rear doors to avoid the fare. When the bus pulled up to the front gates of the school, I hopped off and almost got run over by a shiny black BMW that had mounted the curb at speed. On the pavement was Chelsea, two long plaits whipping at the wind as she screamed at her mother.

I DON'T EVEN WANT TO GO TO JOHANNESBURG, she was screeching, her mouth red like blood.

Don't come, then, her mother responded. Stay here with your idiot father in that godforsaken house. I don't want you to come, anyway.

And she slammed on the accelerator so abruptly that she careered into the back of the bus.

Chelsea, her face now as red as her mouth, swung round and stormed through the school gates, not bothering to wait and see her mum throw the car into reverse and zoom off in a frenzy of burning rubber. She slung her blazer over her shoulder when she caught me watching her.

Having a good gawp, are we? she shouted at me. I shook my head hurriedly, my eyes wide. She gave me a once-over with eyes half squinting.

You're Matilda Robb, she said. I know about you.

I felt my stomach turn to lead. I had only been at this new school a week and the whispers about my mother had already started. They were in the new silences that inevitably grew whenever I entered a classroom. They were in the concerned look the school receptionist gave me when I went to the school office asking for a PE uniform from the Lost and Found. They were in the squeeze of the hand my French teacher gave me when I hung back after class to tell her I wasn't going on the ski trip. And they were in the look Chelsea was giving me now. But she didn't have the same malicious bent to her expression as the other girls did.

Stick with me, she said, and that was it. She pulled her socks up to her knees, handed me a cherry-flavored Chupa Chups lollipop from her blazer pocket and linked her arm through mine, and we walked into school together.

Chelsea had grown up with new money and was maligned in a different way to me—but all the same unwelcome among our classmates. We glued ourselves together at school and cycled our bikes to the woods to light fires on the weekends. I already stuck out like a sore thumb: I was scruffy and common-sounding, with a strange Scandinavian lilt to my intonation, picked up from the years I'd spent out of school and rattling around with Mum in the studio at the Richmond house under the loose guise of home-schooling, until someone from social services came and Dad—a shadow cast over the house even when he was out in California—enrolled me. I, with chipped nail polish and greasy dishwater-colored hair and eyes ringed in dark kohl. It was a time of Juicy Couture velour tracksuits and shiny, sticky, apple-flavored lip gloss, and Nokia 3310s. I had none of those things, nor did I want them. I wanted to disappear into the walls as I walked through the corridors and felt the curious eyes of my peers hot on the back of my neck. These girls were the daughters of bankers and CEOs, not socialite tabloid fodder. None of them cared that Mum had recently displayed her first solo exhibition at the Saatchi. A dream of hers for as long as I could remember. In the convenience store we stopped at in the mornings before school, the newspapers lined up on the shelves often had photographs of her slapped across the front, eyes streaming, bruised knees, hands like claws, hanging off some actor or musician like clothes pegged to a washing line. I struggled to reconcile this version of her with the one I knew. The flashbulbs always seemed to illuminate something in her eyes, something wild and angry and unpredictable. At fourteen, I was mostly embarrassed by her.

The other girls called her a slag and a junkie. I knew she was neither—at least, I thought I did.

Just ignore them, Chelsea would say as she dragged me away from another fight.

I had all this rage inside me and nowhere to direct it.

I first met Gus behind the old people's home where local kids went to smoke and kiss. Gus was sixteen and smoked roll-ups, which I thought was the coolest thing I'd ever seen.

More importantly, he went to a different school. He didn't know who I was. He didn't know who my mum was.

Why don't we go for a walk through the allotments, he suggested on the third Thursday Chelsea and I saw him in the alley behind the old people's home. Chelsea was busy sucking face with some sixth former from Gus's school, so I followed him through the gap in the chain-link fence.

We dug up potatoes and carrots and onions, leaving crescents of dark dirt underneath our fingernails. He pulled me by the hand to an abandoned shed at the edge of the property. All that was inside was dust and shafts of light through the holes in the caved-in roof, and scrawled love notes on the bare, brittle walls.

We didn't say much to one another at first. We were too young to express the depths of our feelings fully.

Instead, I told him he could touch me under my school shirt if he wanted to. So he did.

Are you scared of me? I asked him.

Everyone's scared of you, he replied. You're the coolest girl in your whole school.

That sounds like bullshit, I replied, making myself scoff, secretly delighted. I drew a long toke on his roll-up and tried very hard not to splutter in his face. He was very tall, his fingers long and slender, and when he kissed me his whole body leaned over me as though it were a cocoon and I were a caterpillar, ready to be transformed. His eyes glittered when he watched me.

That night, when I got home, Mum was asleep on the chair in the conservatory, an empty bottle of Moët on the floor next to her. I sat on the threshold of the door to the garden and watched her. Her breathing was shallow, as though her lungs were only half filling before she held her breath completely and exhaled, long and soft. Her hair splayed across her collarbones like a caress. In the studio, a commission was half finished. We had been living from commission to commission for some time now. Since the Saatchi show, since Grift House, Mum had been getting requests to paint rich people. Celebrity chefs and minor aristocracy and so on. She was in the press—not just the tabloids when she went on a bender—but serious art magazines too. She had recently been profiled by *Rolling Stone*. Every time she got a new commission she would be on a crazy high for a week or two, not sleeping, rattling round the house singing and talking to herself at four in the morning. She would tell me and Nora, This is it, girls, this is the one that's going to change everything.

And then the sitter would come in for a day or two and after that she would crash.

I can't do it, she would moan to Karoline.

They argued swiftly in Norwegian, my ear only catching snippets of their native tongue.

You have to do it, Karoline would reply. We can't afford for you not to do it.

It's a *sham*, Karoline, she would say over and over again. It's a sham, it's a sham, it's a sham.

What exactly is a sham? Karoline would ask, dragging on a cigarette.

Painting for money. Why are we selling it? It's humiliating. It's embarrassing.

It pays the bills, Karoline would reply, losing patience. You don't want to paint for money? Sell the house. Get a job. Go to work like I do.

Look after your girls, she continued. Perhaps you could ask your moron husband to send some money once in a while.

There was nothing that got Karoline angrier than talking about money. Specifically, how little Mum cared about it.

You are poor, Ingrid, she would say. I am poor. We are poor. And we have responsibilities. Do you want to end up like Pappa?

Karoline worked evenings as a hotel receptionist and sometimes she did Avon, going door-to-door to sell cosmetics to pensioners. And the rest of the time she was Mum's business manager, agent, accountant, anything else she needed to be so that Mum could paint.

It doesn't happen by magic, you know, she berated Mum. Food doesn't magically appear in your cupboards. The girls don't get new clothes and toothpaste and hot water out of thin air. You cannot afford to be idealistic. You cannot afford this ridiculous puritanical ideology of yours. You simply cannot, Ingrid.

Mum never got it.

You're selling me, she would scream at Karoline in the middle of the night.

I'm not selling you, Karoline would laugh back at her, I'm keeping you alive. God knows you can't do it yourself.

And on it went.

And then, instead of painting, Mum would go out. She would put on a sparkly dress and high heels, and spend an hour teasing out her hair and applying elaborate gothic make-up. And then she would disappear.

We had just had all these stages of the cycle and now we were in the final part, where she would crash. Come home and float around the house like a ghost, sleep for twenty hours a day, the canvas white as snow and unspoiled in the studio. The sketches for whoever the subject of the painting was scattered all over the house, sometimes in the bathtub and the kitchen drawers. This time the subject was a cousin of a cousin of the Emir of Qatar.

Mum? I whispered, tucking her hair behind her ear and watching her chest softly rise and collapse.

She didn't stir.

She would be like this, now, for several days, before she would finally pull herself out of the stupor and get the painting done, normally late and in a gasping midnight frenzy. When it was done, she would go out again, to celebrate, and normally bring strangers home too, and lock them all in the studio for days. I pretended that I didn't know what they did behind the locked door.

In between, when she couldn't do it herself, I would take care of Nora. Feed her, clothe her, and when Mum was gone for days, I would call Karoline and she would come to the Richmond house, leaving her little apartment in Hayes, which she shared with two girls who worked cabin crew for British Airways, to fill the cupboards with canned food, to run a vacuum round, to make sure the bills were paid. Sometimes she would call my dad and have a row with him on the phone in the hallway.

They're your children too, Edward, she would moan, late at night when it was lunchtime in Los Angeles. You need to take some responsibility.

Those conversations would inevitably end with Karoline slamming the phone down and lighting a cigarette.

Out in the garden, I could see my little sister, recently turned five, rolling naked in the grass, talking to herself, her blonde hair frizzed beyond any meaningful shape.

Did you do anything with Nora today? I asked Mum. Did you feed her? Give her a bath? Anything?

Mum murmured something unintelligible and her eyes fluttered open.

Hello, darling, she said, lifting a hand up to touch my cheek, her eyes brightening. Will you do me a favor and put Nora to bed? I have a terrible headache today. I just need to sleep a little bit longer.

I pulled a blanket over her as she fell back into sleep, and went into the garden. Nora was smudging her face against the kitchen window, leaving streaks of grease behind.

Come on, we're going to sort you out, I told her.

She came willingly because this routine was not unfamiliar to her. She'd learned not to ask where Mama was, what Mama was doing. She let me pull her up by the armpits, her frame skinny and pliant.

What did you and Mama do today? I asked her. Did you have a nice time?

She didn't answer, burying her head in my neck.

Was Mama working today?

She nodded, a thumb in her mouth.

Did she give you a bath?

A shake.

Did she brush your teeth?

Another shake of the head.

Did you eat anything?

Shake.

Shall we do that now?

Yes, she said quietly, through the thumb.

I found a can of beans at the back of a cupboard—the kind with little sausages in the sauce—and heated it in the microwave, setting the bowl out in front of Nora. She lapped it up greedily, spilling the orange sauce down her front.

I took her to the bathroom and ran a bath, and found her Barbies—my old ones from a lifetime ago—lined up on her bedroom windowsill. I threw them all into the bath with her.

While I bathed her, we pretended that we were the Barbies, going on an adventure.

Where are we going, Nory? I asked her, letting her splash through fistfuls of bubbles.

She thought about it for a long time, while I rubbed a bar of soap into her sticky hair, until eventually she lisped out, We're going to visit the sun.

The sun? Well, the sun's quite hot. We might need some protection.

The phone in the hallway downstairs started ringing. I stared at Nora and she stared back at me. It rang off, and then started ringing again.

We don't answer the phone, Nora said, repeating what I had told her many times.

The phone rang off and started up again, the shrillness of the bell running through the house like a ghost.

Wait here, I told Nora, and trudged down the stairs. It was better if I answered it without it waking Mum, I realized. Because if she answered it, who knew what would happen?

I picked up the receiver and held the cold plastic to my ear.

Hello?

Hello? Who is this? My father, his voice distant, low and crackling, said on the other end of the line.

It's Matilda, I said.

A short pause.

Matilda? Matilda. I need to speak to Ingrid. Is she there?

She's asleep, I replied through gritted teeth. She's not feeling very well.

What's wrong with her? he asked, bewildered. Never mind. Just tell her that I'll be in London at the end of June and I'll visit for a week or two. I've got some paperwork that I need her to sign and my lawyer can't get through. Have you got a pen? Maybe write it down.

I said nothing, exhaling loudly through my nose.

Matilda? Are you there?

Yes, I'm here.

Did you write it down?

Yes.

Good. Will you tell her for me?

Yes, I'll tell her, I said, feeling a strange new rage simmering in my belly.

Good. Good.

He paused, and I thought I could hear him floundering around for something to say.

It's just that I need the divorce finalized, he said, by way of explanation.

Okay. I didn't know you were getting divorced.

She didn't tell you?

I didn't answer. He let out a protracted exhale.

She's dragging her feet, and I've met someone.

Okay.

I'd like to move on with my life, Matilda.

Yep.

And she's making it very difficult for me.

I'm sorry to hear that.

How are you, anyway? How's Nora? Are you going to school?

Yes, I'm going to school, I said.

Grades good?

They're fine.

Good. And how's your mother?

Like I said. She's not well.

He paused. I waited.

Just have her give me a call when she's better. Actually, no, don't tell her to call me. Just pass on the message. All right?

I put the phone down and drove my fist into the wall, grazing my knuckles.

Upstairs, Nora had gone quiet. I climbed the stairs and opened the door to the bathroom and she wasn't there.

Nora? I called, my heart fluttering.

No answer. I ran into my bedroom, where Nora and I slept, and then Mum's. No sign of her. My pulse quickened. I called her name again.

Nora? Where are you?

I slammed back into the bathroom and cast around. Maybe she was hiding behind the door.

No, she wasn't.

She was in the bath.

Her whole body submerged in the water, her head all the way under, her hair billowing out around her like a pillow, stark against the white.

I screamed and launched myself at the bath, grabbing her shoulders and yanking her out in an arc of water. She gasped out for breath and spluttered.

NORA! I shouted, shaking her.

She was ragged, dragging oxygen into her lungs, her face the color of beetroot.

I hit her hard on the back, like they did in the movies when someone was choking.

Ouch, Mattie, she said, her voice strangled.

What were you doing? I asked her.

I was hiding, she said simply, and she started to cry, her face full of fear as she felt the anger radiating off me.

You, stupid, stupid girl! I shouted at her, my heart hammering. I could feel myself beginning to cry too. Don't ever do that again.

Sorry, Mattie, she said, through a veil of tears.

You scared me, I shouted, and I pulled her into a tight hug, soaking my school uniform in the process.

Sorry, she said again, still crying, and I shushed her and lifted her out of the tub, my hands trembling as I wrapped her up in a towel and squeezed her tight.

What about some jimjams? I said, my voice shallow.

She let me dry her hair and pull on her pajamas.

Will you tell me a story, Mattie? she asked once I had tucked her into my bed and wiped my face and hers.

What kind of story do you want? I asked her.

Hector story.

So I told her a Hector story. Hector was the man who lived in the walls and came out at night to protect Nora from the monster in the cupboard under the stairs. He was deeply embedded into our personal shared lore of the Richmond house.

How about the time Hector went on holiday to the sun?

She nodded enthusiastically.

I told her all about Hector's trip to the sun. How it was so big and bright and beautiful that he wanted to stay for ever. He wanted to steal it and bring it home with him.

But he didn't stay? Nora asked.

No. He came back because he knows that he has a very big, very important job to do.

He does?

Yep. He has to look after his best friend, Nory, and make sure the monster doesn't come out. Plus, he ran out of sun cream, and he had to come back and get some more, otherwise he would have crisped up like bacon.

She laughed at that, and the sound warmed me up from the inside out.

Before long she was sound asleep. I drew the curtains and closed the door with a soft click. In the kitchen, I cleaned up and scarfed down Nora's left-over baked beans. I took the stolen vegetables from the allotment from my backpack and boiled them. I mixed the concoction together and shoved forkfuls greedily into my mouth. All the vegetables in our garden were dead now, and they had been dead for a long time. Even if Mum wanted to, there would be no chance of reviving them. As I ate my food, I felt the tears leak and slide down my face until they were under my chin and dripping onto the kitchen countertop. I had never been so afraid in my life, as I was watching Nora under the water, staring up at me, little air bubbles escaping from her lips, her expression blank as though she was waiting for something to happen. I looked out to the conservatory and watched Mum breathing as she slept, counting the in-breaths until the moon hung low in the sky and cast a milky light through the glass ceiling, over the lemon tree.

CHAPTER 6

I didn't call Nora.

I thought about it. I really did. I knew that she had her phone. I had seen it on the computer screen, in the Control Room. Work always seemed to get in the way. I worked on the ELSA team—Emotional Literacy Support Assistance—at a primary school on the west side of Acton—only a ten-minute bus-ride from the common, traffic dependent. There were four hundred kids at the school, and almost thirty of them were in some kind of counseling provided by me and two other mental-health leads. The week after I first saw the Control Room on Richard's laptop, we had three more referrals from Year Five: an eating disorder, a dead grandmother and a bullying case, or what we referred to as "friendship troubles" in front of the parents. I saw Isla (with the dead grandmother) first thing Tuesday morning. I had already forgotten about my promise to call Nora. Beanie was deep into rehearsals for her showcase, so I was driving her back and forth to college most evenings, preferring to have her in the car than getting on a bus or the Central Line in the dark. I had missed calls and unanswered texts from Karoline and Richard coming out of my ears. Karoline wanted lunch, and Richard wanted Nora's phone number for his follow-up interview. I gave them neither. I instead sat in the Wellness Room next to the library and watched ten-year-old Isla carefully select a yellow felt-tip to do her mum's hair on her family portrait.

What about Nana's hair? I asked Isla. What color was her hair?

Isla frowned, her arms crowding over the picture she had spent the best part of forty minutes on. She didn't want me to see it until it was finished. She wasn't a big talker. I always struggled with the quiet ones. I never knew what to say to them to make them feel better.

Grey, she said eventually. Nana's hair was grey.

Let me see if I can find a grey felt-tip in the cupboard, I told her, and stood up to do so. The Wellness Room smelled of pencil dust and old socks, and cheese sandwiches, much like all the rooms in the small, single-storied, sand-bricked building in which I worked. The work was sometimes stimulating and engaging. I had fallen into school counselling by pure accident, swept up in course after course until I had somehow become an "expert" without realizing it. I didn't feel remotely close to anything resembling an expert on pre-teens' mental health. Every time I was asked for an opinion in a meeting, or a parent requested a referral, I felt as though I was playing an elaborate game, that I was performing in some way, like Beanie and her plays. The kids were all so fucked up. I didn't know how to help them and a lot of the time I was afraid I would make their problems worse rather than better. Someone like Isla was a straightforward case compared to some of the others on my books.

I saw my mum crying, Isla said suddenly, as I rifled through the stationery cupboard.

Did you? I asked carefully.

Yes. She was in the bath, crying. I opened the door and saw her in there and she didn't even see me. She just kept crying. Until Daddy came and got me and told me off for barging into the bathroom without knocking first.

She's probably very sad about Nana passing away, I said.

Yes.

Are you sad, too, Isla?

It seemed like the right thing to ask her. Mum and Dad were worried that she didn't understand what had happened, that she wasn't grieving properly. Of course, there was no proper way to grieve. I knew that. I didn't tell them, though. It wasn't what they wanted to hear.

Isla stuck her thumb in her mouth, her hand a tight fist, and shook her head.

Ah, it's okay to be sad, love, I told her.

I'm not, she said through her thumb.

Well, that's okay too. Any way that you're feeling is okay.

I don't feel anything, really, she said.

Her words hit me, unexpectedly, and with all the weight of a sledgehammer. And I was back at the funeral director's clear as day, a week after Mum went. Sat next to me browsing a catalogue of coffins was Nora. She flicked through the pages without looking at any of them.

How are you feeling? I had asked her.

Not much of anything, she replied.

Really? I asked. I find that hard to believe.

I wanted to reach out and touch her. I wanted to pull her into me like I had when we were kids. But so much had happened since then. And it had stretched this canyon of space between us until I couldn't bring myself to reach her.

Why is that hard to believe? she said.

You always seem to be feeling so much of everything, I said, struggling to find the right words.

She put the catalogue down and stared at me directly.

I'm medicated up to the eyeballs, Matt.

I said nothing.

Sometimes, I don't feel like a human being, she said. I don't feel like a real person.

I didn't know how to respond to her, but I understood what she meant. In the days following Mum's death, I occasionally looked at my hands and felt strongly as though they weren't mine, as though they weren't connected to my body, as though they were acting independently and without my authority.

But I didn't know how to say this to Nora. So I frowned and hummed and looked away and pretended that I hadn't heard her properly.

It does ugly things to people. It comes in waves.

Not feeling much of anything at all? I asked Isla. I find that hard to believe.

She shrugged and went back to her drawing.

———————

Beanie had another late night at rehearsals so that evening after returning from school, I made myself a bowl of cereal and settled into the latest reality television show I was binge-watching. There was nothing I enjoyed more than a Kardashian, or a Love Islander, or an implausibly rich Beverly Hills housewife getting pushed into a swimming pool. Richard found my taste in television hilarious and bemusing and perplexing. You come from a family of culturally significant people, he would say, half laughing. Your mother exhibited at the Venice Biennale four times. *Four times*, Matilda. And yet you are the most low-brow person I know.

Hey, I would reply, unsure whether I could be bothered to take offence. There is absolutely nothing wrong with being low-brow.

Tonight, I watched a rich Beverly Hills housewife throw a glass of wine over another rich Beverly Hills housewife at a Greek-God-themed cocktail party. The two women had the same hair and the same vocal fry; it was sometimes difficult to tell them apart. At just gone nine, the intercom buzzed.

We're going out, Richard said on the other end of the line.

I can't, I replied, vaguely amused. I'm doing taxi runs for Beanie. And I'm watching *Real Housewives*.

I'll never understand why you like that trash, Mattie.

Okay, Mister Radio Four.

Come on. Turn it off and come out.

Richard was the type to do this, and it was one of the things I enjoyed about his company. We were the same age but he still had so much spontaneity in him, which offset my pragmatism.

Aren't you going to let me seduce you, Miss Robb? he asked, and I could hear the smile in his voice.

I laughed at him down the phone.

What about my daughter? I'm not letting her get the Tube at night.

When she needs picking up, I'll call a cab for her. My treat.

Oh, such a gentleman, I teased.

Come on, Matt. Let me take you out.

I *did* get my coat, and met him at the front of the building. The April air was cold and moist; I could see my breath in small gusts in front of me.

He pulled me into a dramatic hug when I saw him, lifting me up a little so my feet left the concrete. It made me laugh again. The socks and cheese sandwich smells of school that day—emotionally repressed little Isla—fallen away and forgotten. I had been frowning at the television without realizing it and now felt the tension leave my face. He grinned at me, twin dimples puckering his cheeks.

The words *boyfriend* and *girlfriend* seemed so juvenile to me, even though most of my friends—women in their early thirties—used them. I was the only one among them with a child (who was, admittedly, fast becoming an adult), while the rest of them were taking the first steps into adulthood: engagements, help-to-buy mortgages and tentative gestures towards parenthood. I often felt much older than them.

I imagined introducing Richard to the girls from work on a Teachers' Night Out, which involved getting to a favorite pub on the High Street at four P.M. straight after work, getting shit-faced on two-for-one pitchers during happy hour and being in bed by nine. A lot of the girls brought their partners to end-of-term drinks. They would like Richard, I was certain. He was an incurable flirt, and *those dimples*. But first things first: I needed to properly introduce him to Beanie. And Gus, because if someone was in Beanie's life, he had a right to vet them too. I'd met Gus's girlfriend of a few years, Lulu, also a lawyer, at Beanie's fifteenth birthday and after the initial awkwardness we'd found that we had a lot in common. We saw Queen and Adam Lambert at Wembley together with Beans last year after Gus got food poisoning and had to drop out.

Just as I was picturing Christmas with the five of us, Richard said, Promise you won't be mad at me.

I detached myself from him, suspicious. What?

We're going for dinner with your aunt.

My mouth dropped, the fantasy leaking away. *What.*

It wasn't my idea, he gabbled.

As if that makes it any better? Have you *ambushed* me?

She just wanted to talk to you, and you weren't picking up the phone to her.

Richard, these days, seemed to be closer with Aunt Karoline than any of her own blood relations were.

Did it not occur to you there might be a reason I didn't want to talk to her? A reason I wasn't picking up to her? I asked Richard.

She's your aunt, Mattie. She's blood. I just couldn't ever imagine not being on good terms with any of my relatives. It's sad to see it happen. You know? What could be so bad that you can't even pick up the phone to her?

I opened my mouth to respond but I didn't know where to begin. It had started, I knew, with the Maurice Hoffmann incident, with Nora. And it ended with this new posthumous exhibition that she seemed determined to stage and we both knew Mum would have hated. And mixed up somewhere in the middle of it all was the fact that as Mum got more famous, her work garnering international acclaim, and celebrity, and cultural significance as Richard would put it, Karoline seemed to get richer while Mum just seemed to get more unwell, more alcoholic, more self-medicated, more unstable. It disturbed me in ways I couldn't articulate. There was no way I could explain this to Richard in the necessary detail without him pulling out his tape recorder and scribbling out some shorthand on a legal pad, which was just as disturbing, if not more. Especially as we were standing on the pavement outside the apartment with the siren of an ambulance curving in pitch as it shot past us, and the beginnings of rain bringing up the smell of concrete.

I turned away from him. It was absolutely not your place to do this.

I'm sorry, Matt. I really am. Will you just come to dinner and hear her out?

I don't have a choice, do I?

He grinned sheepishly. Not really, no. It's this way.

We walked in stony silence to a small box-shaped bistro not far from the station, me two or three steps ahead of him. He kept breaking into a swift trot to stay apace with me.

You do realize I'm deliberately walking ahead of you, I said drily.

I know. But I'll still keep up. It won't be that bad, Matt, I promise. She's sworn to be on her best behavior.

You've got it all planned out, haven't you?

We entered the restaurant and I spied Karoline immediately in the corner, typing frenziedly on her phone with a plastic stylus, each tap like a flustered hummingbird at a window. She wore dark satin gloves underneath what looked like some sort of kimono. In one gloved hand was a vape.

Darling, she said, too sweetly. I let her pull me into a hug and kiss me on both cheeks. She smelled of stale smoke and spearmint gum and face powder.

We sat down opposite her.

What do you want, Karo? I asked immediately.

She tsked at me.

Matilda, please. So eager to be out with it. Don't you want to know how I've been? Where is the chit-chat? I haven't seen you properly since the funeral.

At the word "funeral" her voice dropped an octave and trembled a little. She took a hankie from her bag and dabbed at a non-existent tear at the corner of her eye.

You've been hounding me about the rights to Mum's work ever since, I continued, ignoring her. So, I'm assuming it's something to do with that. You're still wanting to put that exhibition together, I take it?

I didn't know what it was about Karoline that made me so furious at the sight of her. It was perhaps every jewel that dangled from her—the necklace that rested gently over her blouse, or the huge garnet on the middle finger of the left hand, over the top of her glove, or the teardrop-shaped amethysts shivering at her earlobes. Her pale hair and the visible Botox in her cheeks and forehead all immaculate, but giving her skin an unnatural, overstretched sheen at odds with the folds on her neck.

You seem to be living well on Mum's money, I said spitefully, and took a sip from the glass of white wine that had been set down in front of me. Annoyingly, it was delicious—and my favorite kind, dry and bitter.

Every pound I earned from your mother's work was earned honestly, Matilda. You know that. It is not my fault that Ingrid mismanaged her own affairs so badly.

She raised her eyebrows—tattooed onto her forehead in the nineties and now competing with the Botox to give her a look of permanent astonishment—and waved a waiter over.

How's Beatrice? she asked.

Fine.

I haven't spoken to her in a while. How are her studies?

She's actually killing it at drama school, I said a little more animatedly. She's got a showcase coming up in a few weeks. Her first big one. The whole family's going. And she's top of her class in everything.

It wasn't entirely true—Beanie's last set of grades had actually been middling, a slip from her usual collection of Bs and the occasional A. But I had got carried away. Any excuse to boast about my kid, who had turned out better than any known previous generation of her family.

A showcase? Richard asked, his eyes large. You didn't tell me about a showcase.

The whole family's not going, because I wasn't invited, Karoline chimed in.

You'll have to talk to Beans about that, I told her.

And what about me? Richard asked quietly. Am I invited?

I glanced at him, feeling something knot in my stomach.

Anyway, Karoline said, placing both palms flat on the table. I wanted to speak to you about this exhibition.

And there it is, I replied.

Matilda, stop being a brat and listen to me.

And then she clicked her fingers in my face. The thumb so close to my nose it was almost touching it. And the noise so crisp. Something she used to do when Nora and I were kids, being naughty. Stealing sips of her sidecar or sticking pins into the heels of her stilettos under the dinner table when Mum, on one of her more lucid days, had hosted one of her salons. The click startled me to attention, so much so that I had nothing to say as she continued.

The exhibition is going ahead, she said. With or without you. We have found a gallery: the Museum of Modern Art in San Francisco. They will be putting it on over the summer. I've spoken to the museum's director, Larry Montague. He's an old friend, actually. He was fond of your mother and very sad to miss the funeral. Anyway, it's going to be called *Ingrid Olssen: A Legacy*. And it's going to coincide with the publication of Richard's biography. So—a *summer of Ingrid*, if you will. A fitting way to round out her legacy.

I groaned loudly and took another large gulp of my wine.

Karoline continued, And if the exhibition goes well, we'll see if we can tour it. I've already had meetings in Sydney and Oslo. Excellent, isn't it?

How long have you been planning all this?

Well—for the past two years, really, darling. Ever since she died. Richard has been wonderful in helping the idea along, picking up some momentum for us in the States. He's got some excellent contacts. I've even spoken to your father, can you believe it.

I thought of my dad then. He had never quite successfully transitioned out of daytime TV and into movies in the same way many of his contemporaries had. After he and Mum had divorced, he'd continued to cast a long shadow over the Richmond house. As a kid and a teenager, I'd known his face better from television than I had in person. Nowadays, he came to the UK once or twice a year and insisted on visiting Beanie and me for a day or two, much like he had with Mum. In his sixties, he was leather-skinned, balding, and plumping round the middle like a turkey destined for slaughter. His Cheshire-Cat smile, which had turned into a grimace when I'd told him I was going to keep the baby. He'd taken advantage of the sausage rolls at Mum's wake.

I don't understand how it's possible, I replied.

What do you mean, darling? Karo said as she popped an olive delicately into her mouth.

What are you going to display at this exhibition of yours? Nora and I have all the rights to the work. Fifty-fifty split. You were diligent with the will, so you'll remember. You need our permission. And *you*—I turned to Richard who was examining the menu with some intensity—you knew all about this and you didn't tell me?

There was nothing to tell until it was all confirmed, he replied. The puppy-dog eyes were back. And that was a few days ago. Come on, Matt. It's a good thing, isn't it? More people than ever will see your mum's work. There will be a whole new generation out there who will discover her for the first time. Appreciate her genius. Don't you want that for her? For her legacy?

Mum didn't believe in *legacy*, I told him. As the *literal expert* on her, you know that better than any of us. I felt the anger rise once again in me. We hadn't really had a proper, full-on row yet. I hadn't shown him how angry I could get, and I didn't want to, but I was struggling to resist the urge to throw my perfect wine in his face, and then smash the glass over Karo's head.

And look at what happened to her, Karoline replied, her voice keening with pity. For who the pity was, I didn't know.

Look how she died. Destitute and swimming in debt, and barely able to hold on to the house. Barely coherent. You know you're going to get your share of the profits of this too, don't you? Lending the art to the museum. That comes with a price tag, of course. Think of all you could do with a bit of breathing room. Think of Beatrice.

Don't you dare, I seethed at her. Don't you dare invoke my daughter in your scheming.

Karoline drew away from me then, a flicker of uncertainty in her face as she registered just how angry I was.

You ought to think about it, darling, she said.

I don't need to, I replied. I've done it. I've thought about it. Mum was difficult. She had her moments. She was a fucking diabolical parent. But there was one thing she never wavered on. And that was art for making money. Art is for art's sake, she said. She drummed it into you, Karo, just as much as she did Nora and me. To do this—to get rich off some exhibition— is like you've just spat on her grave. I don't care how difficult and chaotic she could be sometimes. This is the least we can do for her in death. It's the *bare minimum*. That's why those paintings she left to me and Nora are staying in storage and they're not coming out. *Ever*. Got it?

Now Karo's lip curled up.

A touching speech, darling, she said, a hint of smugness coloring her tone. But like I told you, I have a finger in the game. I'm afraid the exhibition is going ahead with or without your support.

How? I don't agree to it. And Nora never would either.

Well, that's the thing, Matilda. She already has.

I paused, a forkful of ravioli—from a bowl that had been ordered and set down in front of me without my consent in the midst of our conversation—halfway to my mouth.

I—sorry, what?

Richard took my free hand and squeezed it. I yanked it away from him and stood up, involuntarily, fork clattering noisily onto my plate.

It's true, he said.

I met with your sister last week and she signed the necessary paperwork for her fifty percent of the portfolio, Karo said.

I don't believe you.

I can email the documents over to you if you'd prefer. But whether you like it or not, Nora's half of your mother's portfolio is not in storage in Brentford anymore. It's currently—and she glanced at her phone, pulling up a tracking app I wasn't familiar with—Ah, yes. It's about two-thirds of its way across the Atlantic as we speak, on a cargo vessel specially chartered by the museum.

She turned her phone to face me. And I saw it. The little digital cherry-red pindrop that indicated the location of Mum's work. Or the half of it Nora owned, anyway. Tiny in the middle of a vast, cold, blue ocean, approaching the east coast of the United States.

This exhibition is happening with or without you, Matilda, Karoline said, her voice like stone. So you need to get with the program, or you need to sit down and shut up.

———

I met Chelsea for cocktails the night before Beanie's showcase. She was in London to meet with some lobbying group or other, and she wore a mint-green tailored suit to the shitty chain bar on the corner of a leisure complex opposite a budget hotel on the A40. I had realized halfway into my journey on the 95 bus that I was wearing a pair of leggings that had a hole in the crotch. Upon seeing her, perched immaculately on a barstool, I pulled my sweater further towards my knees.

You look like shit, she said cheerfully.

You look like an advert for toothpaste, I replied, and she pulled me into a rib-cracking hug.

How's the pineapple-empire expansion going? I asked her after we had ordered piña coladas and nachos.

Oh, you know, expanding, she said, waving a hand at me. Do you know what's really shit, though?

What?

Brexit.

I mean. We all knew that, anyway.

She rolled her eyes and sipped from her novelty palm-tree-shaped straw.

But, actually, tell me what's going on with you? How's the kid?

Chelsea was Beanie's godparent, alongside Gus's older cousin, Leon, who had moved to Ireland sometime after Beanie's birth and no one had ever heard from again. Beanie and I had lived with Chelsea for a year in a two-bed duplex in the W10 postcode area, immediately after Gus and I had split up and I'd moved out of the studio apartment above the kebab shop, when Beanie was a toddler. I would never be able to pay Chelsea back for what she'd done back then: she'd put her life on hold, aged eighteen, dropped everything, to get me back on my feet. The night feeds with Beanie when she'd been reverse cycling. The days that I couldn't do anything more than stare blankly at the wall unless Chelsea had physically put me in the shower and washed me. The grief over Gus, and then Nora, and then Gus again. Chelsea had folded me into her and, with sheer brute pragmatism and a no-nonsense attitude, and one emergency trip to the walk-in center with a one-year-old Beanie for breathing difficulties, which had turned out to be nothing more than acid reflux, she had turned me back into a human being.

Over the years, unlike Leon, Chelsea visited whenever she was in London, and when she did, I could tell that she felt supremely guilty that she wasn't more involved in our lives. I didn't have the vocabulary to explain in satisfactory language just exactly how much she had already done for me. What I loved about my oldest friend was that, even though her day-to-day involved travelling the world, meeting with CEOs and CFOs and marketing consultants, and managing a workforce of several hundred across three continents, she made me feel that my problems—the fact my kid's grades were slipping, and she was vaping, that my school had just had its Ofsted rating downgraded—were just as important as hers. It seemed silly that

I ever felt inferior to her, but I did. Chelsea and I had started out in the same place—at our obnoxious suburban rich-girl school—and had ended up at wildly different destinations. The difference between us was, of course, inherited wealth, and to a lesser extent teenage pregnancy. But she never talked down to me, never made me feel small, never assumed that I couldn't relate to her. Maybe it said more about me than it did her, that my default position was that she should, or would, condescend.

We talked about Beanie's school, her friendship dramas, the fact that she didn't talk to me the way she used to. The way that I didn't know the minutiae of her life anymore.

That's just teenagers, though, isn't it? Chelsea said. Not that I've ever interacted with any teenagers other than Beatrice.

It's not *my* teenager, though. It's different. We've been through so much, we're best friends.

Chelsea widened her eyes at me, and her eyelashes, coated in waterproof mascara, became spider-like. Okay, she said. Your first problem is that you think that you can be best friends with your child. It doesn't work like that, Matt, we both know that better than most.

I grimaced at her. She knew all about my mother, and I hers—crashing a Beemer into a bus outside Chelsea's secondary school was just the beginning. An Azerbaijani gymnast who, when Chelsea was seventeen, had walked out of the family mansion one day and never come back. A year later, Chelsea had been having dinner in a Mayfair hotel with her father, the original canned-pineapple millionaire, and had spotted her mother on television in the audience at the Athens Summer Olympics.

We talked a little about Chelsea's new boyfriend, a Canadian semi-pro ice-hockey star who enjoyed some light choking in bed.

Would you choke someone? she asked me.

I don't know. I've never been asked. I feel like it depends on the person.

I imagined, briefly, choking Richard in bed, and cringed away from the mental image.

I don't think I want to choke Luca, Chelsea mused. I feel like it's anti-feminist, or something. I know that doesn't make any sense.

Are you serious about Luca?

She shrugged and shoved a salsa-coated corn chip into her mouth.

I wasn't at first. It's only been a few months, she said. But I'm thinking about asking him to come to New Zealand with me.

This is very typical of you.

What is?

You meet someone and after five minutes you're moving in and going to New Zealand.

We're not moving in! Yet.

Maybe you need to decide on that sort of stuff first, before you choke him?

That's very conservative of you, Miss Robb. Surely first comes choking, then comes moving in. Which reminds me, she said, taking out her phone from a Prada cross-body. I've had correspondence from your gentleman caller.

Chelsea exclusively referred to Richard, and anyone else I had ever dated besides Gus, as my gentleman caller.

Why does choking your boyfriend remind you of my gentleman caller?

She slapped my arm and pulled up an email.

He wants to interview me, she said.

He what?

She handed me her phone and I scanned through the email. *Dear Miss Ivanova, please forgive the unsolicited . . . hope you don't mind . . . would like to invite you to interview . . . working on a book on Ingrid Olssen . . .*

I didn't reply, because I wanted to check with you first, Chelsea said as I read.

He didn't tell me he was going to contact you, I said, puzzled.

That's kind of weird, Matt.

Yeah. It kind of is. I think I've only mentioned you once or twice to him, in passing.

I'm offended.

You know what I mean, though.

It's to do with the book he's writing on your mum. But I never really knew Ingrid, apart from when we were, like, fourteen.

Yeah, I said again.

Are you going to talk to him about it?

I was still reading and I didn't answer her immediately.

Yeah, I'll talk to him, I said, handing her phone back to her and feeling the beginnings of a disquiet in my capillaries.

I still think you should have stayed with Gus, TBH, she said, provoking me.

Are you ever going to get over him? I asked her.

But he's so *fit*, Matt! Have you seen his profile recently?

Gus is in a loving and stable long-term relationship with a loving and stable long-term woman named Lulu, I said flatly.

She blew a raspberry. I wouldn't be so sure, she said, having already pulled one of his socials up, and attempting to turn her phone to show me. I batted her hand away.

Stop it! That's the father of my child you're ogling.

Bet he wouldn't send me unsolicited correspondence, she said, wiggling her eyebrows. Unfortunately.

You're insufferable.

She grinned and sucked up the rest of her cocktail through the straw until the ice rattled. She picked out a cube of pineapple and popped it in her mouth.

Hawaiian sugarloaf, she said. And it's fresh. Not bad.

Missed you, I said.

Missed you, too, she replied. Hey, how's Nora getting on?

I felt my shoulders slip down. I don't know, I said honestly.

I explained, briefly, the Control Room.

Aw, mate. She took my hand across the table.

I'm so shit when it comes to Nora, I said. I'm so shit at it. I want to reach out to her but I can't seem to bring myself to do it. I'm such a shit person.

There's a lot of baggage there, she said. With your mum and leaving and stuff. It's hard.

That doesn't excuse it, I replied.

Well, maybe it doesn't, she said. But it doesn't make you a bad person.

Then why do I feel like I'm rotting from the inside out, Chelse?

You're not rotting. You're just ripening, like a big peach.

What she was saying made no sense, but I let it soothe me anyway. We said goodbye on the corner of the car park. Chelsea had to be up at the crack of dawn for a call with New York before her flight back to Portugal, and I wanted to be home to make sure Beanie got back from late-night rehearsals okay.

I walked from the Tube station in the rain, feeling curiously heavy, and let myself into the dark, empty apartment.

CHAPTER 7

BEATRICE GRACE HANSON-ROBB WAS BORN IN THE
AUTUMN OF 2002, ON THE STICKY SHOP FLOOR OF KEBABZ
4 U ON SOUTHALL HIGH STREET.

It all happened very quickly.

Gus and I weren't calling ourselves boyfriend-and-girlfriend, as teenagers were wont to do. We thought we were above it.

Even so, every Friday night, after I got home from school, I changed out
of my uniform, bathed and fed Nora and put her to bed. Then at about ten I
would slip out from under the duvet, making sure that she was fully asleep,
her chest rising and falling softly, her breathing deep and heavy, and dress
in something inappropriate—often raided out of my mother's wardrobe—
and shimmy down the drainpipe leading up to my bedroom window, into
Gus's cousin's waiting car.

We were just children. We didn't know what we were doing.

We went to kids from Gus's school's house parties and sat at the back of the
garden with Chelsea and Gus's friends, chain-smoking on someone's trampo-
line and stealing gulps of the Christmas wine out of a suburban kitchen
cupboard. I liked to snoop around those houses. I felt a thrill run through
me going through the parents' things in the master bedroom. Soft, clean
pajamas folded neatly into chests of drawers; a school photo secured to the
radiator with a novelty magnet from a family holiday to the Scottish High-
lands. The mother's perfumes lined up on the windowsill in the en suite.

Gus and I went from kissing in the front seat of his cousin's car, to fucking in the back, with a remarkable seamlessness.

I told myself I didn't love him. When he wrapped himself around me so tightly and whispered things to me that made me want to explode with happiness, like the sky was fizzing up with sherbet, I told myself I didn't love him. When I woke up and saw the streetlamps dappling his hair the color of autumn leaves and the way it got all messed up when he was excited or frustrated or happy; the way that when he smiled, the corners of his mouth went down not up, but you could tell he was smiling because of how his eyes changed. And when, one night, a few months into it, I came home and found Mum on the kitchen floor and thought she was dead, and I couldn't get through to Karoline for help, I called Gus instead, trying not to cry, and he came to the house and waited with me until the ambulance arrived, playing dinosaurs with Nora and letting her ride around on his back and making pterodactyl noises so that she would laugh instead of cry. How, after that, without any kind of conversation, he decided that Nora would come out on the weekends with us too. And he let her ride in the front seat of his cousin's car, and he took us for ice cream and to the movies and to the park to play cops and robbers, and when Nora was so exhausted she fell asleep in the car, he would come with me back to the Richmond house to help me bathe her and put her to bed, and check her breathing once or twice in the middle of the night without asking why I needed to. And when he brought me round to his parents' house, a house that looked like the other ones we'd been to for his schoolfriends' house parties, with perfumes lined up in the bathroom, and working clocks, and a second set of crockery that was for only special occasions. How Gus's mum, Grace, got the special plates out for dinner, the first time Gus brought me round. How his dad asked me questions about school and cooking and gardening and growing food, the things I liked to do, and not my mum, who they knew about, and had seen in the gossip pages of the *News of the World* earlier that very same week. And the look on Gus's face when his mum took my hand and said, come out into the garden and have a look at my cauliflowers and tell me what you think's wrong with them. I told myself I didn't love him then, either.

When I told him I was pregnant and that I wanted to keep it, and he cried and then looked up at me and said, I promise you, I'm happy, I believed him. And still I didn't tell him I loved him.

When I told Mum about Beanie, who was a tiny little chicken nugget in my gut, and she walked silently into her studio and slammed the door shut and locked it. When Gus dropped out of college and took a job stacking shelves in a warehouse, because I didn't want to take his parents' money. The nights he spent swapping saucepans out from under the leak in our kitchenette in our new studio in Southall above a kebab shop, because I didn't want to live with his parents either, and staying in the Richmond house, with Mum the way she was, was out of the question. With the unearned bravado of overconfident teenagers, we decided that we would be doing it our own way.

It all happened very quickly, and I knew in my bone marrow that I loved him, but I didn't tell him, and I didn't tell myself. It would make it easier when things inevitably self-destructed.

When my water broke, I was watching *Coronation Street* on the black-and-white television in the apartment above the kebab shop, eating a whole cucumber to satisfy my pregnancy cravings. Gus was ninety minutes into his night shift. I dialed the warehouse's landline, over and over and over, but no one picked up. I waited, and dialed and called and dialed and called until *Coronation Street* was over, and the sky became black outside, and the contractions seemed to come in waves that merged into one long, never-ending tension that coiled my body around itself like a snake in a chokehold of its own making. I couldn't stop burping.

I finally got through to the warehouse but by then it was too late.

I made my way downstairs to wait for Gus, but I only got as far as the takeaway's shop counter before I realized it had been a terrible mistake to avoid the ambulance. It took two hours from then for her to slip out of me, wet and mottled-pink and demanding to be heard by the world.

My little girl.

By the time she was out, there were paramedics. Constantine, who worked the cash register and had become a friend since we'd moved in, had graciously taped menus over the large shop-front windows to stop passers-by staring in as I screamed and writhed on the floor and pushed her out of me.

By the time Gus arrived, our girl was latched onto my breast, feeding quietly, her tiny fists punching at nothing.

The little puffs of air she made through her nose. The startled way in which she stared out at the lightness of the world around her, her eyes almost black. It was as though the universe was an inconvenience to her. It was as though she demanded more of it, and more of everyone living in it. Her nose. Her smell. Her soft, perfect head tufted with dark wisps of hair.

Gus could only say, Oh God, oh God, oh God. And all I could say was *shhhh*.

She was ours, and she was the most perfect thing we had ever known, and nothing else could ever matter to us as much as she did.

After we made it to the hospital in the back of an ambulance, a nurse asked whether we would like to call anyone. Gus called his parents first.

Do you want to call her? Gus asked me when he put the phone down to his father, who promised to be there within the hour.

I grimaced at him. My mother and I had not spoken since the day I left home. I had told her that the baby was going to be a girl. Not another one, she said in Norwegian. *Stakkars tispe.* The poor bitch.

I took the phone and dialed the landline, my hands a little shaky from adrenaline and exhaustion and sleep deprivation and the thought of speaking to her. The call rang on for what seemed like for ever, and I was almost ready to hang up.

But then came a quiet, Hello? barely audible over the static.

I hardly recognized her voice, though I had been gone barely six months. She sounded small, as though she had curled in upon and around herself and was talking into her chest. I had missed her birthday. She was seven years old, now.

Nora? Is Mum there?

Who is this?

Don't be an idiot. It's me. Mattie.

Mattie? she said with more urgency, more strength in her voice. Where are you?

I'm in the hospital. I had the baby, Nora. We have a little girl. You should see her. She's so perfect. She's the most perfect thing in the entire world. I can't wait for you to meet her.

Will you come and see me? Will you bring her to visit?

I paused, hesitating. The last place I wanted to take my baby was the Richmond house.

Yes, I lied. We'll come, soon. Is Mum there?

No, but Aunt Karo is.

Can I talk to her?

There was some scuffling on the line as the phone was handed to Karoline.

Matilda? Where are you?

I'm in hospital. I had the baby.

Congratulations, darling. Is all well?

Yes, she's fine. She's perfect. I can't believe I did it, Karo, I—

Do you have any idea where your mother is, Matilda, darling?

What? No . . . no, I don't know where Mum is, I replied, feeling my whole body squeeze. I don't live there anymore, remember? I moved out.

I heard some scuffling on the line as Karoline moved the receiver away from her face to say something to Nora.

Then, to me, she said, She hasn't been home for three days and I've been here with your sister, like the social worker mandated, but there's no food here, Matilda. And I'm meant to be going to Montenegro next week, with a popular Puerto Rican pop-star whose name I can't disclose.

I don't know where Mum is, I said stonily.

Well, if you hear from her—

I don't think I will.

More muffled conversation on the other end of the phone.

I just wanted to tell her first, I said quietly. I haven't spoken to her in months.

Tell her what?

About the baby.

Karoline sighed on the other end of the line.

Oh, my darling, she said.

I felt a tear slide down my face, unprompted.

If you hear from her, please let me know, won't you? And congratulations, again.

A soft click indicated the end of the call. The look on my face, I think, told Gus everything he needed to know. He pulled me into his chest and I exhaled all the bad out of me.

It's all right, he said.

I know, I replied, but I couldn't stop more tears leaking down my face. Humiliating relics of the power she held over me; the power she held over us all.

It's just me, you, and the baby, now.

The hospital room smelled of disinfectant and sleep and blood. Gus's fingernails were short, bitten down to the quick. I looked over at Beanie, not Beanie yet, just a brand-new human being. Completely unspoiled by the world around her.

That's all that matters, I told them both. Just the three of us.

———

Two Wednesdays after my fight with Karoline, I stood in a corridor adjacent to an auditorium in Hackney Wick, that smelled not dissimilar to my own school: a potent mix of socks and sawdust and pubescent bodies. I checked my watch again. Gus was running late. Everyone was running late.

Against my protestations, Beanie had invited Karoline to her showcase after all. A series of pointed texts from Karo after I'd let slip about it at my dinner with her the other week, no doubt. I hadn't spoken to her since, and things between Richard and I were strained after he had ambushed me with her.

The news of the exhibition had filled me up with something rotten and spoiling.

But I didn't know how to fix it. I had finally gathered the courage to call Nora and had been dialing her number daily since the revelation that she had signed release papers for Karoline. Never an answer. Beanie kept an eye on her blog but she wasn't posting. She checked in every now and then on the Control Room. I sometimes looked at it, too. It was never anything more exciting or stimulating than Nora moving listlessly through the rooms of her apartment. Bare white walls and minimal furniture. The simple meals she prepared. Sometimes she was there, and sometimes she wasn't.

I still don't understand how this is art, I'd told Beanie again.

She rolled her eyes at me.

The more I watched the Control Room, the more I noticed things. Nora only ever drank water and sometimes bottled lager. She had meticulous personal hygiene. Sometimes, she looked directly into the camera lenses, which, judging by their positions, seemed to be mounted in every corner of every room, except the bathroom. At night, in bed, a square of blue light from her phone illuminated her face. There were people who watched her sleep. I shut the laptop with a firm snap when I saw that she was starting to drift off. Her phone tumbled from her hands and landed somewhere in the duvet. The next morning, she spent five minutes burrowing around in the bedding to retrieve it. She seemed to become more angular, more pixelated, with every day spent in the Control Room. I didn't recognize her on the computer screen. I imagined that I knew how the apartment smelled: sterile, but lived-in. The smell of a body that has spent too long wrapped up in soft furnishings. The smell of a body that has been asleep for too long.

Now, as Gus arrived outside the school auditorium and muttered, Sorry, sorry, under his breath and we made our way into the slowly filling theater, I saw that there was a seat reserved for Nora—her name scrawled on a single sheet of A4 pasted to the back of it. And I felt my fingers flutter against my legs with nervous energy. I knew that Nora wasn't going to turn up. Beanie knew that too. We had talked about it.

I don't want you to get your hopes up, I'd said to her gently the night before.

Nora leaves the Control Room sometimes, Beanie said. She leaves to teach her classes and get food and stuff. She can leave her apartment to come to my show.

Her overbite became more pronounced when she was feeling stubborn, and I saw it now.

I don't think she's going to come, Beans, I said simply, with as much tenderness as I could.

We'll leave space for her, anyway, Beanie replied.

Gus and I climbed the steep theater steps to our allocated seats, our own names scribbled onto printer paper in Beanie's handwriting.

Is Nora coming? he asked, narrowing his eyes at the piece of paper stuck to the chair.

I grimaced at him by way of answer, and he squeezed my elbow.

How're your parents? I asked him.

Much the same. I invited them, but . . .

I nodded. With Frank's dementia and Grace's recent stroke, neither of them was much up to an evening out at the theater. This time last year, Gus had made the decision to sell his childhood home—the beautiful terrace with the perfumes lined up on the windowsill and the second set of china—and put Frank and Grace into residential care. Beanie loved them to bits. I did, too. A little while after Gus and I had broken up, they'd become closer to me than my family. Every year without fail, an invitation to their caravan in Colchester for the annual two-week Hanson family summer holiday had been extended to me too. I had taken them up on the offer a few times, especially in those early years as a co-parent, when money had been tight and I couldn't afford to take Beanie anywhere else on holiday. Frank had been coming to the seaside since he was a boy, and had insisted that we visit the nudist beach, because it was the *best in all of the east coast of England*. The five of us had spent afternoons building sludgy sandcastles out of clay-mud at Walton-on-the-Naze, shielding Beans's eyes from, and trying not to giggle too much, at the nudists. I'd stopped going on the Colchester holidays once Gus had got serious with Lulu. It had felt too strange to be the third, fourth, sixth wheel, depending on how I thought about it. Now, it was startling to realize that Frank and Grace would probably be gone soon.

A seat was reserved for Karo, too, but none for Gus's other half, Lulu.

Is Lulu not coming? I asked him over my shoulder, indicating the signage.

Oh . . . it's a long story, he replied cryptically. Where's Karo?

I shrugged and tried my best to keep my face clear of expression. What expression would appear there, I wasn't so sure. But Gus knew me too well.

Matt? What's up? he asked.

Before I could muster an answer, the lights dimmed and one of Beanie's teachers—one I recognized from last term's parents' evening—stepped out onto the stage below with a flourish, to a smattering of polite applause. He launched into an involved monologue then, thanking the teaching faculty, congratulating the Year Twelve class on all their hard work. I got the impression he was congratulating and thanking himself, truly. A touch of reminiscing about his own years on a West End stage as a puppeteer in *Avenue Q.* He was quite clearly enjoying himself, while an audience of restless parents had no choice but to listen and silently will him offstage so they could get on with seeing their own kid perform and sneak out during the intermission. Gus and I raised eyebrows at one another, fighting to stifle our snickering.

After the teacher left the stage, we launched into the first scene. I checked the program that had been placed on my seat. There were twelve of these little scenes to get through. Each of them a different vignette from a play or film or musical, each of them chosen by the students. The first was a group of boys doing a number from *Moulin Rouge!* in drag. I couldn't tell whether their can-can line in giant bustle skirts was meant to be funny or sexy. They couldn't tell, either. Next was a scene from a Harold Pinter play, which seemed to go on for ever. Then another from *Abigail's Party*, which I thought was the most impressive so far, the kid playing Beverly perfecting the drunken boorishness, the Estuary English accent slipping and sliding all over the place in an unnervingly accurate imitation. I started to wonder what Beanie would be like. She had always been a theater kid, and we'd encouraged her by signing her up for drama club and attending the endless school plays she had parts in. She'd always seemed quite good but I didn't have the discernment to tell how good an actor she ought to be as a twelve-year-old. Since winning the scholarship to sixth form at this fancy drama college, she'd barely done anything else in her spare time but rehearse. Sometimes she hadn't left rehearsals until midnight on the weekends.

A few more performances came and went and finally—after what seemed like an age—the intermission came. Gus and I shuffled out into a lobby and took a glass each of warm white wine from a steward.

How do you think she'll be? I asked him. Will she be good?

He frowned at me as though he was annoyed that I'd asked the question.

Of course she will. She's on a merit-based scholarship.

The night before, Beanie had come through the door and it had been very obvious to me that she had been crying and was pretending she hadn't. I told Gus this.

Do you think it's nerves about the performance?

I don't know. Did you not ask her?

I didn't want to impose on her.

Lately, Beanie was less interested in me being a friend to her, listening to her problems and helping her solve them. It wasn't just the vape thing. I didn't get to hear about every aspect of her day anymore when she came home from school. I used to pretend to listen, to be interested in the minutiae of her friendship dynamics. *Lizzie is pissed off with Dami because Dami invited everyone to a party except Lizzie.* I couldn't relate—when I was Beanie's age I'd been preoccupied with being pregnant, and at school I'd been a loner, besides Chelsea and Gus. I was happy that Beanie had friends coming out of her ears, and that at seventeen all she had to worry about was school and who got invited to which thing. She had turned out so well that I had always trusted her to figure things out for herself, to make good choices. Now I wondered whether that was a mistake.

She doesn't want to talk to me about that stuff anymore, I told Gus.

What stuff?

You know. Emotional stuff.

You're literally a children's counsellor, Matt.

Yeah, and she's my kid. It's different when it's your own kid. Do you think she'll talk to you?

Gus shrugged. I doubt it, he said.

What do we do, then?

You're the therapist. You tell me.

I took another sip of shit wine and felt myself deflating. I felt like she was slipping away from us, our girl. I always thought that I would know every single part of Beanie. That I would know all her hopes and fears and idle thoughts and joy and heartbreak. That she would volunteer those things freely. I was afraid of the parts of her that I would never know. The parts that she now was choosing not to share with me.

I felt for the first time as I imagined my mother had felt when she'd realized that her daughters were slipping away from her.

I thought then of Nora, and I wanted to cry, too.

We're losing her, I told Gus.

No, we're not, he replied, bemused, not understanding me. Losing her to what?

The auditorium lights flashed then, and we joined a slow-moving queue back into the theater. As we waited in line, I saw the unmistakable figure of Aunt Karoline striding down the corridor, a decorated silk kimono billowing out behind her like bat wings. She spotted us immediately and joined us in the queue.

Matilda, she said. *Darling.*

If you were going to insist on coming, you could have at least turned up on time, I hissed.

Ah. And he's here, too, she said, turning her attention to Gus.

Hello, Karoline, he replied pleasantly.

Goodness. He's really still rattling around, isn't he? she said to me.

Well, I'm actually here to see my daughter, he said.

She ignored him and lit a cigarette, realized we were indoors, and promptly put it out on the carpet.

Have you been in touch with Nora? I asked her.

There's no point trying, darling. The papers are signed. The art is already at the museum. There's no reneging on this. Nora knows that. You can't talk her out of it. Even if she wanted you to. I didn't do anything.

You can't just steamroll this, I said, feeling the anger from the restaurant seething inside me again.

The fact is, I can, darling, said Aunt Karoline dismissively.

We filed into the theater, finally, and took our seats. As we settled down for the second half of the show, another familiar figure appeared at the door. Karoline waved him over to us and he climbed the stairs lankily, shadowed by the stage lighting behind him.

My bus was late, he said, grinning at the three of us.

Oh, for fuck's sake, I said.

I don't think we've met, he said to Gus. I'm Richard. Mattie's boyfriend.

He held his hand out to Gus who, clearly amused, shook it. At the word "boyfriend" I felt my fingers curl up into my hands.

Gus. Beanie's dad, Gus said. Obviously.

Richard squeezed into Nora's empty seat between Karoline and me.

Richard is writing the most wonderful book about Ingrid, you know, Karoline said loudly to Gus.

Yes, I heard about that, Gus replied, and then he turned his attention back to the stage. Karoline folded her arms and glared in the opposite direction.

What are you doing here? I whispered at Richard as he settled into his seat.

Your aunt invited me, he replied, his freckles visible even in the darkness.

My aunt wasn't even invited herself, I said. She barged her way in. Did it not occur to you that there's a reason I didn't invite you?

I'm sorry. I didn't think it would be a big issue. Karoline asked if I wanted to come and I thought it would be a good opportunity for us to talk, anyway.

I don't want to talk to you. I'm very angry at you. Take a hint, Richard.

What if I don't want to take a hint, though? What if I want to fix it?

I elbowed him hard in the ribs as the lights dimmed again and the first act came on. I barely registered what was happening onstage.

I bristled through a handful more scenes until finally it was Beanie's group's turn. They had chosen the opening to Act 5 from *Macbeth*—or, as she had insisted upon calling it to anyone who asked—the Scottish play. Beanie was in the starring role as Lady Macbeth and her co-stars were playing a doctor and a gentlewoman.

We watched her as she performed, the lights trained on her as she became Lady Macbeth. She was magnificent. The way her body moved, the way her face contorted into expressions I had never seen on her before. The careful handling of the lines made it seem as though the words were coming to her spontaneously. In front of us she became an entirely different human being. She was magnetic, the whole audience hushed to silence as they watched her perform her character's madness brought on by subconscious guilt. I glanced over to Gus and saw that he too had the same expression on his face: one of complete bafflement, and wonder, at our kid.

The scene ended and Beanie and her group took a bow at the front of the stage to applause, which to me seemed more enthusiastic than it had been for the other performances. Gus and I stood up and hollered. She spotted us in the seats and grinned shyly, her face pinkening, as she bowed deeply.

Did you know she could do that? Gus asked me. I shook my head, awed.

That's our kid, he said. We made that.

As the applause died down and we took our seats again, I noticed Beanie scanning the rest of the audience as she prepared to leave the stage. Her eyes slid over the seat where Nora ought to have been, and she saw Richard instead. A shadow passed across her face and she disappeared behind the curtains.

CHAPTER 8

After the show, Karoline announced that we were all going for dinner.

We stood in the foyer of the theater, waiting for Beanie to get her stage make-up off and meet us out front.

Actually, Gus and I were going to take her out to eat, I told Karoline. Just the three of us.

Nonsense, she replied, waving a hand at me and fishing around in her handbag for one of her vapes.

Richard was still there, hovering. He slid a hand across my shoulder. I resisted the urge to shrug him off—so juvenile—but I felt myself freeze when he touched me.

The more I thought about it the more I couldn't keep the anger from bubbling out of my mouth, like a reaction to a potent poison.

You know that Mum never wanted money made out of her work, I told him in a whisper as Karo and Gus argued about who should pay for dinner.

He sighed exaggeratedly. Are we still talking about this?

Yes, we are still talking about this, you brick.

But don't you want to see her celebrated? See her genius opened out to the world, Mattie?

Genius is an arbitrary concept, I replied, almost spitting.

Think of how important a show like this is for her legacy.

If you mention the word legacy to me one more time, I'm going to put a chair through a window.

He squeezed my shoulder then.

Just . . . forgive me, please?

I glared at him, but his stupid soft face made my lip curl. He was so utterly clueless, so bashful, his eyes wide and innocent and pained at the idea that he had upset me. I knew that he would never hurt me. Not intentionally.

And it was the intention that mattered, wasn't it?

I'll think about it, I said reluctantly.

He planted a swift kiss on my cheek. Then Beanie arrived and I remembered the other reason I was angry at him.

Hugs and another round of congratulations and a fair amount of very obviously embellished, and typically Aunt Karoline soliloquizing about how she'd introduced a certain Shakespearean actor who transitioned from stage to screen, to a certain beloved English-rose-type actress, and now Dame, back in the eighties.

Then, with some trepidation, I said, Beanie, this is Richard. I didn't know he was coming.

Richard held out his hand for Beanie to shake, the same way he had done with Gus, making her narrow her eyes at him suspiciously.

A truly glorious performance, Lady Macbeth, he said, grinning. He even curtseyed to her a little bit.

Ha ha, yeah, cool, thanks, Beanie replied, touching his hand for the briefest of moments. Her eyes darted to mine from under her highlighter-orange fringe, half amused, half incredulous.

Shall we eat? Karo announced.

We walked to a Sri Lankan restaurant on Dalston High Street, Karoline and Gus in front as Karoline, tottering in her high heels a little, told Gus all about the time she'd almost been cast as Fanny Brice in *Funny Girl* for a UK production tour. Gus, bless his heart, listened attentively, flinging a grin over his shoulder at Beanie and me who walked behind them. Richard trotted along further back, pretending to be engrossed in his phone. I considered making Beanie slow down so he could walk in step with us, participate in the conversation. But I suddenly felt embarrassed by him.

I guess Nora couldn't make it, then, Beanie said, her arm linked through mine.

I'm sorry, kid, I said, and I truly was. I know you wanted her here.

I sent her the invitation weeks ago. She said she would come.

Nora doesn't go outside much, I reminded her.

I know. I just thought she would make an exception. For me.

I know. I thought she might, too. Maybe we can try to call her together later.

We both knew that I didn't mean it; I would make Beanie place the call alone. That I would chicken out, again.

You know who would have really loved today? I said eventually.

Who?

Your grandfather.

My dad, Edward, now mostly lived in Hollywood with his new wife, Marnie, filming various bit parts for American daytime soaps or reality television cameos. But sometimes if he was working in London, he would visit us unannounced for a weekend. The last time he had visited, late last year, he'd bought Beanie a push bike sized for an eight-year-old, left a fist-full of cash in my microwave, and was gone within the hour.

I would say you get your talent from him, but we both know you're a thousand times better.

Ugh. Mum, shut uuuuup.

We arrived at the restaurant—deep red walls and statement light fixtures in bamboo cages—and were seated at a large table in the center of the room. It was quiet—only one or two couples elsewhere, and a waitress standing at the cash register lazily scrolling on her phone with one thumb. A giant oblong glass tank, teeming with tiny silver tropical fish, was embedded into the wall.

Am I lying, though? I continued, bolstered. Where's the lie, Beans? You were fucking amazing up there. I'm not even saying that because I'm your mum. You were seriously impressive.

She blushed again and smiled into the collar of her coat as she sat down between Gus and me.

It is true, Richard said, piping up from across the table.

Yeah, *a truly glorious performance*, Beanie said, mimicking him from earlier.

And I haven't got any skin in the game, Richard said, apparently oblivious to her tone. So I've no reason to lie.

Well, you do, don't you? Beanie replied.

I do what?

Have skin in the game. 'Cause you're shagging *her*. With a flick of the wrist, she indicated me.

The table fell silent for a moment.

Beatrice, I said, shocked.

What? It's true, isn't it? Are you or are you not smashing uglies with my mother, Richard?

That's enough, Beanie, Gus said firmly.

She stood up.

I don't know why you invited him, she said to me.

I didn't, I replied, still trying to process the etymology of *smashing uglies*. Sit down, please, Beanie.

I need a wee, she said, and promptly left the table.

An absolute silence settled over the four of us. I stared after her, feeling my mouth hanging open. Beanie was sarcastic and sardonic, and her wit was often more cutting than blunt, but this behavior was unprecedented. I felt something twist and tighten in my throat.

So, drinks and starters, then? Aunt Karoline said brightly.

No one responded.

I'm sorry, I said to Richard, after a moment.

Oh, it's nothing, he replied, his smile wobbling a bit.

This is why I didn't want you to come, I said, my voice an octave lower. She's not ready.

But I was beginning to wonder, silently, whether I was ready, either.

Let's talk about it later, Richard said kindly.

I'm going to give it a minute and then check on her, Gus said.

No, let me do it. I don't know where this has come from, by the way.

You don't? Gus asked, incredulous.

No. What do you mean?

Well . . . Gus paused. She's made it quite clear what she thinks of Richard, Matt. No offence, Richard.

None taken, Richard replied, his voice squeaking.

She's never met Richard, I said. Until tonight.

But, I mean. Come on, Mattie. Gus looked at Richard pointedly.

I'm just going to go and look at that fish tank, Richard said, and scraped his chair back noisily and walked across the restaurant, hands in pockets.

Karoline, oblivious, examined the menu.

I gritted my teeth.

So it's fine for you to be with Lulu, I told Gus. But I have to stay single forever? Is that her logic?

I had never really had a serious boyfriend. Not since Gus. And even Gus and I hadn't been that serious, just thrown together by circumstance and teenaged lust, or that's what I told myself. I'd never introduced any man—who, admittedly, had been few and far between—to Beanie. I told myself that if she ever met someone I was seeing, it would be because it was the real thing. That I wouldn't have a stream of men parading through her life, our home, in one week and out the next, like my mother had after she and my dad divorced. I wouldn't put Beanie through that. But now I wondered whether I had been too protective. That I had kept her so oblivious to the fact that I was an adult human woman who occasionally liked to experience romance, and maybe even have sex from time to time, maybe find someone with whom I would one day want to grow old, that the idea of me having a partner had become unfathomable to her.

Well . . . actually, Lulu and I broke up, Gus said. A few weeks ago.

I stared at him.

What?

I didn't want to tell you. It's stupid. I'm sorry, Matt.

I felt my mouth open and close and open again.

I never liked that woman, anyway, Karoline piped up, abandoning her menu. Far too jolly for my liking. That awful hair.

You never met Lulu, Karoline.

Why didn't you tell me? I interrupted. Does Beanie know?

Yes, she does. I asked her not to tell you.

Gus . . . *why?*

It's . . . complicated.

I stared at him then, trying to extrapolate something from his face to explain. Gus and I were exes, yes, but we were best friends. We shared everything with one another. We knew about all of the dirtiest parts of one another's lives. There was nothing I felt I couldn't tell him. Looking at him, all I saw were tired, sad eyes, and a hard-set mouth, and the shape of an apology that I didn't understand.

You asked Beanie to lie to me, I said.

I asked her to keep a secret, he admitted, rephrasing, shame writ across his face.

Gus . . . what the fuck.

Mattie, just . . . listen for a second.

No. I need to get my daughter.

I stood up and marched towards the restroom, my pulse hammering. It felt, very acutely, as though there was water rushing into the restaurant and we were all about to drown.

A paradigm shift. Why would Gus keep something from me, something as frivolous as this? Why would he ask Beanie to lie?

I got to the bathroom and knocked gently on the locked cubicle door. To my horror, I could hear Beanie sniffling behind it.

Beans?

No reply.

Listen, kid, I'm not angry at you. Will you come out and talk to me and we can sort it out? I know Richard shouldn't have come without your permission. I know that. It was all a big, stupid mix-up.

Silence from inside the cubicle.

Come on, Beans, I said quietly.

It's not that, Beanie replied.

It's not what?

It's not Richard.

What is it then?

The cubicle opened with a soft click. And she stepped out, eyeliner streaked down her beautiful angel face, orange hair sticking out in all the wrong directions. She was holding her phone in a trembling hand.

It's Nora, she said.

And she thrust the phone at me.

Confused, I took it and squinted at the screen.

It was the Control Room. The livestream of the Control Room, anyway. The shape of Nora's bedroom was on the screen, dark and pixelated as it was. I had been watching far too much of the livestream in recent days and even though I had never visited Nora's apartment in New Cross myself, I felt I knew it as well as my own. There were lights illuminating the doorway to the en suite, and shadows diffusing that light. There were people—yes, multiple people, moving around inside the open door of the bathroom.

What's going on? I asked no one in particular.

Look, Beanie said through sniffs, jabbing a finger at the phone.

Then, as I watched, I saw the back of someone.

A big person, dressed in a dark padded coat and matching trousers, as though they were about to go skiing.

There was writing on the back of the jacket.

I squinted at it, pinched the phone screen to zoom in on the video.

The word PARAMEDIC emblazoned across the back of this person.

They were coming out of the bathroom backwards.

And then, following them. A stretcher.

They were carrying a stretcher out of the bathroom.

On the stretcher, there was a figure. Slight, unmoving, one arm dangling over the edge.

A slash of dark hair obscuring her face.

I dropped the phone.

Oh my God, I said.

I looked at Beanie and saw the same expression of abject horror on her face as was surely on my own.

And my mouth was suddenly so dry it felt like my tongue was made of sandpaper. And I could feel my heartbeat thrumming in my fingertips.

Oh my God, I said again.

I could feel whatever knot was in my throat tightening, tighter and tighter and tighter now. Like I was about to lose my breath all together. Like I was going to drown.

There was a knock on the door, the exterior bathroom door, then.

Beans? Matt? You okay in there?

It was Gus.

Mum, Beanie said.

I couldn't speak.

Mum, your phone's ringing.

It was. Vibrating in the back pocket of my jeans, still on silent from the theater.

Gus opened the door a fraction.

Can I come in? he asked.

Mum, answer the phone, Beanie said, wiping her eyes, her voice urgent. Dad, something's happened to Nora.

I took my phone from my back pocket and stared at it. No Caller ID.

What's going on? Is Nora okay? Gus asked, letting himself into the cubicle and sliding an arm around Beanie. She picked her own phone up from the floor and handed it to him. The livestream of the Control Room was still open on the screen. He watched it and said, Oh, no. Oh, Nora.

The three of us were now standing in the toilet cubicle while I stared at my phone uselessly, still vibrating with an incoming call.

I tried to say something to Gus, but my mouth was still dry. Like a desert in July. I croaked at him instead.

He gently took my phone from my hand and slid the bar across to answer it himself.

Matilda Robb's phone, he said into the receiver.

He listened quietly, nodding and making small "mmm" sounds, "yes," "right," and "okay."

Then he handed the phone to me.

They won't tell me what's going on, he said. They need to talk to Nora's next of kin.

I took the phone and lifted it to my ear and slipped my free hand, trembling, into Beanie's, while the medical professional on the other end of the line told me what she had done.

PARTIAL TRANSCRIPTION OF INTERVIEW NUMBER 2
WITH NORA ROBB [01.04.2020]

R.T.: Tell me about the new work.

N.R.: It's not ready yet. I haven't untied the knot, but I can feel it loosening. When I'm ready to try something new I feel it brewing inside me. I can feel my blood, my bile getting hotter. Like humors, right? I've felt this work, the Control Room, cooking itself up inside my body.

R.T.: A lot of your work involves the body and its limitations. Why did you choose to call it the Control Room? What's the relationship with control there?

N.R.: You just said it yourself. The limitations of the body. The control that an individual has over their own body—not just their body, though. Also their identity. How they might be perceived by others. How they choose to formulate an identity for an audience. The slippage between that identity and a person's true self. Whether the *true self* even exists.

R.T.: And what exactly is the Control Room?

[N.R. takes a long pause here]

N.R.: It's a feeling. And, of course, there will be a physical aspect to it. A work of several dichotomies. Total exposure versus complete isolation. An objective point of view versus a subjective one. Visibility or otherwise. Performance versus authenticity. Where does the performance begin and end? Is anyone not performing in most aspects of their lives in the contemporary moment? That's what social media and the internet has done to us. Is all identity digital, and performative? Is it affirmed and re-affirmed only through the perspective of others?

R.T.: I find it interesting that your mother Ingrid's work almost completely erased the artist from participation in the experience of creating the art. Even in her self-portraiture she is never quite present. She blurs her own features or morphs her body. Inverts and contorts the figure. Whereas in your work, you're almost doing the opposite. Your work is hyper-focused on the artist as the subject. Your thumb-print is visible all over it.

N.R.: I don't know why you find that interesting. I am a wholly separate person to my mother. I'm not the same artist. We ought to be treated as such.

R.T.: But what about *My burial*—

N.R.: I don't want to talk about *My burial*.

R.T.: Sorry. Okay. But I do think it's worth thinking about how she treated meaning and subtext in her art.

N.R.: Mum—*Ingrid*, sorry—wanted to render the truth of the world, of other people, in her art. She hated these kinds of analyses that centered her. When I was finishing my post-grad at UCLA, one of my professors devised a block of work on Ingrid Olssen, I think—truthfully—because she was a bit starstruck to be teaching me, her daughter. It was extra-curricular. The professor asked me to speak in the class. I couldn't. I have nothing to say about her work. Mum had nothing to say about it either, besides the tech-nicalities of her process. She would have hated that they were teaching classes on her. She would have hated your book, I'm sure.

R.T.: I'm sorry to hear that.

N.R.: Don't be. You've already been paid, haven't you?

R.T.: It's interesting to me that Olssen was so intent on being anonymous, but became something of a celebrity in her heyday. Away from the art world, I mean. She courted scandal, the paparazzi, she dated famous men, including your father. She made herself something of a socialite with her antics.

N.R.: There are two arguments here. One is that she didn't make herself anything at all. That she didn't have any say in how the tabloids painted her, and that she was a victim of a cruel and deeply misogynistic press.

R.T.: What's the other school of thought?

N.R.: That she was doing what most creators are always trying to do, through their work or—otherwise—in my mother's case.

R.T.: Which is what, exactly?

N.R.: She was trying . . . trying to make herself immortal. She was trying to make something beautiful and infinite before she was dead.

R.T.: We've veered off a little here. Let's return to the Control Room. Where do you see the work going?

N.R.: I'm not certain yet. But I know that I need to make myself the subject and object of the work.

R.T.: Can you tell me any more?

N.R.: I don't know. I don't think so. There's a piece of work that Abramović proposed to a gallery in Belgrade in the late sixties. It involved her dressing entirely in clothes that her mother picked out for her in front of a live audience. She would take off her own clothes, make herself naked, and then re-dress herself in her mother's clothes. Were they chosen by her mother or owned by her? I can't remember. You'll have to look it up. Then . . . she would take a gun with two chambers and load a bullet into one of the chambers and turn it. One chamber empty and one loaded. Then she would put the gun to her head and pull the trigger. The gallery rejected the proposal.

I don't know what's going to happen next. I know that I need to make the audience participate, to give them collective responsibility, in the work. To blur the lines between art and reality, between the digital space and the physical.

Whatever it is, it's going to be big.

CHAPTER 9

SOMEONE WATCHING THE CONTROL ROOM HAD NOTICED NORA'S FOOT POKING OUT OF THE BATHROOM DOOR AND DIALED 999.

His name was Benny Montgomery. He was a sixteen-year-old A-level Art History student from Stoke-on-Trent. His parents had recently divorced and he hadn't seen his younger sister or mother in seven weeks. He had been writing an essay on Ingrid Olssen's silkscreens for his final project at school and had fallen down a rabbit hole into Nora's work instead. Her early stuff when she'd been a student herself in California, with the concrete and the bathtub. The short film. Then the performance art that she had turned to since moving back to London and starting her PhD at Goldsmiths.

Benny had been watching the Control Room near-constantly for weeks. He had all of Nora's social accounts bookmarked, and every time she posted something new he would watch her compose the photograph live on the stream in the Control Room, her iPhone twisted in her wrist. The multiple takes. The way she contorted her body for a selfie. He would watch her sit in quiet thought on his computer screen while she composed a caption. He imagined that he knew what she was thinking in those moments. He thought that she seemed so sad, all the time. Then he would receive the notification to his own phone once, seconds later, it was posted.

Benny knew something was wrong with Nora when she went into the bathroom and didn't come out of it for over forty minutes. He knew, because he read Nora's blog, that Nora had made the decision to spend as little time as possible in the bathroom because there were no cameras there. To remove herself from the digital eyes that were dotted around her apartment was to undermine the integrity of the performance. Benny knew that to not have cameras in the bathroom was a decision that she'd regretted after she'd begun the performance. If she could go back and start again, she would put cameras in the bathroom and expose every part of herself, her life to the audience. That was the purpose of the work, after all. Total vulnerability in total isolation. A reflection of our modern times.

It was after ten when Benny decided to call it a night, closed his laptop, rubbed the blue-light particles from his eyes and rolled into bed.

He couldn't help but look again, though.

It was Day Thirty-Two of the Control Room.

Nora, and the Control Room, were taking up more and more space in his life, his brain, every day. Sometimes when he closed his eyes, he could see it. The pale white walls and sparse corners of the set of rooms she inhabited. Her, a dark figure moving through that space. His art class had moved well on past Ingrid Olssen; they weren't even covering performance art this term. His friends were getting bored of him finding ways to bring her up in conversation. But he couldn't close the tab and put Nora Robb away. He felt as though she were haunting him. Sometimes he direct messaged her on one of her social media profiles, but she never replied. He imagined her as an angel that had fallen out of heaven and become trapped in that set of rooms. He pictured himself in there with her. He imagined being in her, not in a sexual way, though. Just inhabiting her skin and wearing her body like clothes. But that would spoil it, he knew. He lay in bed and took out his phone and opened the Control Room on that device instead; his bedroom—soiled laundry and textbooks and dried-up paint covering the carpet—dark and still and warm with the air of a human body spent too long in it. He felt a strange sense of calm settle over him when he opened the stream and loaded up the now deeply familiar landscape of her bedroom. The walls and corners and bed. The door to the en suite. It was like white noise, like how some people play whale calls to fall asleep. He felt his whole body relax into the Control Room as his head hit the pillow, phone held aloft. That's when he saw her foot.

I didn't know about Benny Montgomery, or the foot, yet. I was stomping into the Accident and Emergency waiting area at Homerton University Hospital. It was raining outside, and I didn't have an umbrella, so my hair was wet and slicked to the back of my neck. The restaurant was a lifetime and an hour ago. I felt rainwater trickle down my neck into the small of my back, underneath my shirt, between frantic exchanges with the nurses, and corridors that seemed to go on forever.

The hospital was exactly the same as every other hospital I had ever been inside. It made me feel carsick, without the motion.

My sister, yes, Nora Robb, she was brought in not long ago, I told someone, my fingernails tapping out an agitated rhythm on the concrete wall.

If you could just take a seat, my love.

If you could just calm down a moment.

That's right, nice deep breaths.

What was the name, my love?

No, your name.

Someone will be here to talk to you soon.

Oh, my love, that's it, nice deep breaths.

Any seat over there is fine.

Yes, don't worry, we've got your name. And hers. Have a seat.

I thought back to the last time Nora and I had been here—same problem, different hospital—as I sat in a plastic chair and waited. I waited for something to explode. I waited to vomit up my organs all over the floor. I knew it was coming. I could feel the bile gathering, like a storm. My organs rallying. Ready to make the jump.

Something smelled dead and everything in the hospital was blue.

I opened the stream to the Control Room on my phone, ignoring the texts and missed calls from Karoline, Richard.

Maybe she wasn't here at all. Maybe she was on the screen, still in her apartment. Ready to jump out from behind a door and shout *SURPRISE! Fooled you!*

I felt the bile rise further up as something struck me.

The idea that perhaps she'd done it as part of the art. Perhaps it was all in service to the performance.

I didn't know whether that was better or worse than the alternative.

I didn't know for certain whether she was still alive. I reasoned that if she wasn't I would know by now. Someone would have found me and told me she was dead. Someone would gather me into a private room, not let me sit out here in the blue, and smell the death, and fester. More than that, I was certain that when Nora would eventually die, that something intrinsic and biological and mythological inside me would snap and I would know.

I would know, wouldn't I?

In the hours before Mum died, I'd developed a terrible itch. Across my whole body; I couldn't stop scratching at myself. At work, I'd excused myself to the bathroom so I could strip in a toilet cubicle and run my fingernails all over my skin. My chest, my belly, my arms. I'd thought it was an allergy to the fabric of the dress, or our washing detergent, recently switched out for a new brand. That afternoon, shortly after the itch went away, Mum had died.

If Nora was about to die, perhaps it would be the same kind of itch.

I counted the shades of blue and waited.

Someone pressed a too-hot black coffee in a polystyrene cup into my hand sometime around 3 a.m. I burned the tip of my tongue on it.

I called Gus, who was waiting back at the apartment with Beanie.

No. No news yet.

Can I get you anything?

No, just, stay with the kid, please. Is she okay?

I can't tell.

When weak sunlight turned the concrete outside blue too, I found a restroom and ran calcium-rich, hard London water across my wrists. Splashed it in my face and dragged a brush through my hair. My skin didn't seem like my own; it was the wrong color. My teeth were coated in an unpleasant-tasting slick film. I realized I hadn't urinated since before dinner last night, and as if on cue my bladder was suddenly unbearably full. I sat on the toilet and let my eyes trace the black crust of the tiles, and cried.

When I got out of the bathroom a doctor was waiting for me.

Nine o'clock. She's not going to wake up.

Nine thirty. Okay, I misunderstood. She's going to wake up. Just not yet.

At eleven o' clock, unclear whether a.m. or p.m., Gus was pressing a toothbrush and a packet of baby wipes into my hands. I stared at them. So strange for such things to exist in this space, toothbrush and baby wipes, in the blue dead space, when Nora wasn't breathing independently.

Will they let you see her yet?

No, not yet. They haven't woken her up. Did you bring toothpaste, too? Ah, shit.

Tell me another Hector story, she'd asked me, when I was sixteen and she was seven.

You're getting too old for Hector, I told her. I loved her so much that I sometimes cried about it, I was so worried something terrible was going to happen to her. That Mum would do something terrible.

It was autumn and the trees in the garden were on fire. I was pregnant with Beatrice. I would have to abandon Nora soon. I had just walked in on Mum in the kitchen inhaling deep and long from an old rag that we kept under the sink for cleaning the grime from the windows. She was thinner now than she had ever been. When she walked, she walked lopsidedly. When she talked, she did the same. Lopsided. She pressed the cloth to her nose and mouth, and sucked all the air out of it, her breath a rasp.

What the fuck is that, I said.

Don't you dare, she replied, pointing at me. Strange bruises on her arms and wrists. White-grey summer dress. Don't you dare.

Outside, it was the golden hour. Nora's hair was spun straw in the sunshine. I told her the story of the day Hector saved all the elephants.

He went to the circus and he stole the keys from the evil ringmaster and he let the elephants out, one by one by one, until they were all free, and then he led them back to the jungle where they lived happily ever after.

And what did he do after that, Mattie?

Well, obviously, after that Hector came home and climbed back into the walls so he could watch out for his best friend, Nory.

I'm going to kill you, Mum had said. If you don't leave me be, I swear to God I'll kill you.

Nora had the most distinct of Nora smells, even when she was filthy. She smelled of talcum powder and jasmine and milk. She could still fit into my lap if she made herself small enough. She folded herself in half, into quarters and eighths. As though she was trying to make herself so small that she would disappear. The skin on her face was soft and her hair was fine. She sometimes sucked her thumb.

We heard the front door slam shut downstairs.

Nora crawled into bed with me.

Love you, kid, I told her. We're going to get out of here.

Do you promise?

Yeah. I promise.

And can Hector come?

I nodded and pulled her closer.

And can Mummy come too?

I don't know. Maybe.

Talcum powder and jasmine and milk and the soft sound of her breathing, her shoulders rising and falling, the gentle snores. Black mold spores under the windowsill made her skin cold and damp.

We didn't see Mum for ten days after that.

Once she was asleep, I slipped out from under the duvet, and climbed out the window to the car waiting below. When I got back in the small hours of the morning, giddy with the feeling of being thought of, Gus's hands on me in a way that made me feel like a real-life human being, she was still asleep in my bed.

———————

At school, the Friday after it happened, the deputy head Lindsey gently suggested that I load off some of my casework to one of the other counselors. I don't want to presume, she said, but I'm going to take a stab and suggest that you're not going to be in the right headspace.

Just the hardcore stuff, she said. The self-harm and the eating disorders, and we'll see how you go.

I thanked her. My limbs didn't feel as though they were connected to my body.

———————

By Saturday it had broken to the press.

BBC News 24 in the hospital waiting room, with the volume all the way down: ARTIST NORA ROBB HOSPITALISED.

An image of Nora flashed up on the screen: the same one Beanie had glued to the photo-collage on my living room wall. Her university faculty portrait.

She'd hate that, I said to no one in particular.

The subtitles read: *Nora Robb, daughter of the actor Edward Robb and the late artist Ingrid Olssen, is in a critical condition after she was found in her London apartment unresponsive on Wednesday. Miss Robb is also a well-known artist whose work has been exhibited in the United States, Brazil, the UK and Germany.*

Richard texted me a photo of the *Mirror*. A little scrap of page twelve, a four-sentence article. Had these people nothing better to do? The headline: TROUBLED ROBB IN CRITICAL CONDITION AFTER OVERDOSE.

In the hospital car park, someone was filming me on their iPhone as I unlocked the Civic.

I called Richard. This is unbearable, I said, on the verge of tears.

I'm so sorry, he said. I'm so sorry.

———————

Visiting hours were between nine and eleven, and five and seven. Beanie said, Whatever you do, Mum, don't look at social media.

––––––––––

I had stopped keeping track of what day of the week it was.

In the soft hum of the dead blue night, the air was unusually close and humid. There had been so much rain, but it still felt like something in the atmosphere needed to break. I had strange dreams where I didn't know whether I was awake or sleeping.

––––––––––

Richard turned up at the hospital, with flowers—unclear whether they were for me or Nora—brandishing his iPhone.

I don't know if you should be here, I told him quietly in the waiting room, my stomach tying itself into a tight knot. There was something in his face that made me feel ill. Perhaps it was the sleeplessness that made me nauseous. And then he showed me what he had done.

A statement from the family, he said, showing me a *BBC News* alert on his phone. Asking for privacy during this difficult time.

I glanced at the article. I saw the words *beloved sister* and *daughter of famed portrait artist Ingrid Olssen* and then I saw *mental-health episode* and *manic depressive* and *exhibition slated for the summer* and *forthcoming biography* and *spokesperson for the family*.

I made an involuntary noise in my throat.

Who did this? I asked, mortified. Who is calling themselves a spokesperson for the family?

It was actually—

These people are fucking *shameless*, I said, standing up.

Richard caught me by the shoulders.

Matilda. Listen. It was me. I'm the spokesperson.

I stared at him. My face—my eyes—were so tired I could feel the muscles beneath the skin twitching. I thought I could see his face morphing into worms and silverfish and woodlice. His whole complexion crawling with them. I pressed the heels of my hands into my eye sockets.

Why did you do that? I asked him levelly.

He looked at me quizzically.

I was trying to help.

I glanced over his phone again.

Where did you get *manic depressive* from? You didn't have any right to put out a statement for us.

Karoline mentioned it might be a good idea and I took the liberty—

You have no idea what her diagnosis is.

I was trying to help—

And you didn't *think*, I continued, seething, That you ought to check with me first?

Matilda—listen. He smiled at me, pleading. I didn't mean to—

I looked at him properly then, and I saw a hint of something behind the veneer of the smile. A disguise for someone who knew too much about me. Someone who seemed to have become inextricably intertwined with every aspect of me. Who was privy to the most intimate details of our collective history. And I wasn't sure how it had happened, but it made me a little bit disgusted.

I stood up and walked out of the hospital, leaving him shoehorned into a plastic chair, gaping after me.

———

I let myself into the apartment and found that it was immaculate. Gus had always been such a slob in his teens; his adolescent bedroom in his parents' house was a hellscape of towering book stacks, the faint but unmistakable pong of marijuana, and half-drunk mugs of tea. Beanie took after him. I had expected to come home to stacks of pizza boxes and dirty laundry, as I often did when Beanie was left home alone for more than twelve hours. He had offered to stay at mine while I zipped back and forth between school and the hospital. My place was closer to both Beanie's school and West Middlesex Hospital, where Nora had been transferred Saturday night. A pair of sneakers were in the washing machine on a spin cycle. Beanie was back at school for the time being. No use rattling around in the apartment waiting for news, and she needed to focus on her exams. She insisted that she was seventeen, she didn't need to be *minded*, she could take care of herself. But I felt reassured knowing Gus was here when I couldn't be. The crescent moons suspended under her eye sockets were just as dark as mine. She slept with the Control Room open on her phone, though no one was there now. I texted her: *Didn't know Dad was a neat freak?! How are you holding up? No news on Nora yet. Whose sneakers are these in the washing machine?* She replied: *Miss you xxx*

I ran a bath and saw that someone had put out fresh towels. Not even from the airing cupboard—brand new ones, a bath sheet and a hand towel, with the tags snapped off, Egyptian cotton, a deep emerald green. I ran my hands over them while the bath filled up. They were soft under the pads of my fingers. A key turned in the front door and there was some shuffling as shoes were taken off, and then Gus was at the bathroom door, filling up the frame with his arms and shoulders, hair the color of liquid amber in the dappled evening light, laptop satchel slung across his back, two days of stubble dusting his chin.

You got new towels? I asked him.

Yeah, I did, he replied.

I hugged the larger one, folded into a neat square, into my chest, and stared at him. The noise of the bath filling with water overwhelmed me momentarily. The smell of coconut-scented soap, the steam rising from the tub became thicker with each passing second.

I don't know why I got them, he said, joining his hands together in front of him. I just thought it might be nice to have something fresh and new.

It is, I replied. It is so nice.

I cried, then, and he drew me into him.

In my dreams, I saw her sleeping in the single bed in my bedroom in the Richmond house, all bones and softness and fear. Sometimes she was her and sometimes she was Mum and sometimes she was Beanie. I climbed out of the window over and over and over again, and every single time I left her behind. I changed my mind then, tried to pull myself back up to the window, panicked and clumsy. But the century-old brickwork crumbled beneath my fingertips. I couldn't find the right foothold, the right purchase. The whole house was falling down, in fact, and she was inside. And there wasn't a thing I could do about it.

———————

Then, on the tenth day, they woke her up.

CHAPTER 10

Karoline and I were the first to see her.

Close family only, they said. We were the closest family Nora had, living on the same continent as her at least, so we nominated ourselves.

We met outside the entrance to the ward. Karoline was late. When she arrived, we gave each other an awkward, angular hug.

How are you managing, darling?

I threw my arms out in front of me, half shrugging. Somewhere underneath the shock of Nora, which was as though we had been dunked into ice-cold water, I knew that I was still angry at Karoline for the exhibition. But in the hangover of Nora's almost-death, everything else was insignificant.

How about you? I asked her.

Much the same, she replied, and lit a cigarette.

A man in a yellowing denim jacket approached us.

Excuse me, are you Karoline Olssen? he asked.

I am, Karo replied, her eyes narrowed, her lip quirked up.

Any update on your niece's condition? I'm reporting for the *Mail*.

I'm sorry, what? I interjected. Can you kindly fuck off, please?

Sheepishly, the reporter backed away, arms up in surrender. Our readers would like to know, when you're ready, he said.

It's like Ingrid all over again, Karoline said as we entered through the revolving doors. You know, the press were *vultures* back then. *Vultures.* The things they printed about your mother.

I remember. I was there. But, who the fuck even cares about Nora? I asked, indignant, spitting it out before realizing too late how bad the words sounded when spoken aloud.

We checked in at the front desk and were ushered to a waiting area.

How did she do it, darling? Karoline asked as we sat down in blue plastic chairs. Blue, blue, blue. She didn't try to hang herself again? What was it, pills, this time round?

I stared at her. Blue, bad smell, rancid.

Karoline, I said, shocked, hands fluttering, feeling the rot on the inside.

She waved a hand at me, rolled her eyes.

I love that girl just as much as you, darling, she said. Don't you dare think anything otherwise.

Please don't talk like that in front of her, I replied, my voice quiet. Don't talk about pills.

We waited in silence, then, until a nurse with a nose too small for her face told us Nora was ready for visitors.

Her medics had moved her from the ICU to the main ward, now that she was awake, and hers was one of six beds divided by blue papery curtains. The other bays were swimming with relatives, all chattering over one another. The patients in the beds looked so much older than her. Their skin papery-thin and folding over on itself. Nora was at the end of the ward, by the window.

She lay flat on the bed, without a pillow to prop her up, staring directly at the ceiling.

Hello, darling, Karoline said matter-of-factly, as though she had just popped by for a cup of tea.

Wires going in and out of her. Tubes. A tube in her nose. Her skin was damp-looking and blueish.

Every hospital looks and feels and smells the same.

Hello, she said, her voice flat, staring at the ceiling.

It was the first time I had seen her, I realized, since our mother died.

It's been a while, I said, quietly, and my voice wavered. I wanted to climb onto the bed with her and wrap my arms around her and never let her go. But she looked as though the lightest touch might shatter her into sharp fragments. The sun streamed through the slatted blinds and made her face shiny.

The room was too warm and I was beginning to sweat. Machines beeped rhythmically. On the bedside table was a pile of her jewelry. Rings and earrings and necklaces and bangles. So much of it. Nora loved to wear jewelry.

You look old, she said, without looking at me.

Want to tell us what's been going on, kid? I asked her gently.

Tears, pooling at the corners of her eyes and sliding horizontally down her cheeks.

I don't know where to start, she said.

You don't have to start now, I replied.

Where've you been, Matt? she asked, finally turning to look at me, meeting my eyes for the first time.

Twenty-four, now. Still so young, but she felt older too. The beginnings of the finest lines around her eyes. Less freckles than I remembered. Paler eyes, with their new knowledge reflecting back at me. A more angular face. The dusting of grey hairs at her temples. Olssen women always went grey young. The rest of her hair a shade darker. The passing of time was written across her.

But very suddenly, as I stood at the edge of the hospital bed, it was as though no time had passed at all. I felt like I was sixteen years old again, saying goodbye to her for the first time, dragging my things out the door of the Richmond house in trash bags into Gus's waiting car. I'd told her I would come back for her.

I'm sorry, I said now, in the blue. I'm so sorry, I'm so sorry.

It's been years.

Two years, I replied. Since Mum died.

It's weird. I was half expecting her to walk in with you.

I smiled tightly, acknowledging the strange déjà vu of our meeting here, in a hospital, visiting Nora.

It's been a lifetime. It's felt like a lifetime.

I know.

Aunt Karoline took out her vape and inhaled on it deeply, ignoring the fact that we were in a hospital, contemplating something.

I wanted to ask her why she did it.

I wanted to know whether it was part of the performance, or whether it was real.

I didn't know which answer would scare me more.

But I couldn't bring myself to ask the question. I had nothing else to say, and neither did Nora, so we sat together quietly, the three of us, until the visiting hour ended and the small-nosed nurse asked us to leave.

———

We're looking at moving Nora to Park Royal, the doctor told me, at the next day's visiting hours.

I was there alone. Nora was there, too, but the doctor spoke only to me, as though Nora was a child who couldn't understand, or couldn't hear us, or both. She was sitting up today. She drank orange juice from a sippy cup. Wires everywhere, though less of them now.

You're sectioning me, she said matter-of-factly, between sips.

They were sectioning her.

I called Gus. They're sectioning her, I told him.

He sighed heavily down the line.

I thought so, he said, and I heard the lawyer brain in his voice. The grounds for a Section Two are pretty much overwhelming. I'd have been surprised if they *didn't* section her, to be honest.

I called Karoline and told her the same thing.

That's preposterous, she replied. There's nothing wrong with her.

It's for her own safety, the doctor said. She was still talking to me, and not Nora.

Nora is in crisis, Miss Robb. We're concerned that she might try to hurt herself again if she leaves our care. We're going to monitor her for up to twenty-eight days. I am convinced that this is absolutely the best thing we can do for Nora, and Nora can do for herself, right now.

I asked questions, and got answers involving treatment plans and mental-health assessments and counselling services and medication.

Medication? I'm not taking any medication, Nora said passively.

I heard the tapping sound of pills rattling down the plughole of the kitchen sink in the Richmond house. Heard something of Mum's voice in Nora's.

One step at a time. Let's get you assessed first, the doctor replied.

Beanie and I tasked ourselves with collecting things from Nora's apartment: fresh clothes, underwear, toiletries, books, a blanket.

You don't have to explain it to me, Beanie replied, as we drove to Nora's apartment near the university in New Cross. I know what sectioning is. I'm not a kid, Mum. I remember the last time.

But if you want to talk about it, I said carefully. I was starting to worry about how well Beanie was coping, how much she knew and how very young she was to know it. I thought of little Isla with her dead grandmother at school. Isla who didn't feel sad, Isla who didn't cry. I hadn't seen Beanie cry since the toilet cubicle.

I don't want to talk about it, Beanie said stiffly. There's nothing to talk about. It's just a fact.

I unlocked the door to Nora's apartment with her key. She had given me a list of things to pack. Much like Beanie, she came across as unbelievably calm about it all. It was only me who seemed to have a low-level constant hum of panic running through me.

A headline earlier that week had read: NOW NORA HEADS TO REHAB. The subtitle read: LIKE MOTHER LIKE DAUGHTER: ARTIST'S TROUBLED OFFSPRING CHECKS INTO FACILITY AMID LATEST CRISIS.

I had started rejecting calls from unknown numbers. Richard's statement pleading for privacy had done nothing to assuage journalists from camping outside the hospital and dialing the house phone so often that eventually I disconnected it from the wall.

I had never been in Nora's living space before. It was sparse, much like my own apartment. The opposite of the Richmond house, which was overflowing with hoarded goods. Mum had had a taste for expensive and impractical furniture. It was a habit to find myself comparing things to the Richmond house, and I scolded myself for doing it again now. We had grown up trying to fit ourselves into the spaces around the abandoned canvases and sketchbooks piled up in the rooms. The art had been in the middle of everything, so Nora and I had had to slide around it, hugging the walls and folding ourselves into the corners. It was no wonder we had ended up owning as little as possible once we could choose. Nora's apartment was simple: bare white walls and minimal furniture. A living-kitchen area, two bedrooms, an en suite and a bathroom. Still, it seemed too big for one person, though truly it was a sanitized space-saver new-build, the fifth floor of an enormous pool noodle of a development that punctuated the skyline of south-east London. Going up in the elevator felt like we were driving directly into the ozone layer.

It's like no one lives here, Beanie said.

But the smell was a giveaway. It was human, was Nora's.

We walked through the rooms, our socks slipping on the vinyl floors, frictionless.

Mum, look, Beanie said, pointing at the corner of the kitchen. There it was. A large, globe-shaped camera secured to the ceiling. The kind that could swivel on the ball and socket joint to track movement across the room. I scanned the rest of the ceiling and saw that the cameras were mounted in every corner. They looked expensive, sophisticated. Shiny white plastic helped them camouflage against the walls.

Fucking hell, I said.

The feed's still up, Beanie said, now checking her phone. Look.

It was. The Control Room website was still online, and there on the feed were Beanie and I, standing in the middle of the empty room, looking at her phone, looking at us looking at the phone looking at us.

Two dark figures, an infinite loop.

How do we turn it off? I asked.

Shouldn't we ask Nora first?

Are you joking?

Well, it's her project. It's an installation, Mum. We can't mess with it without her permission.

I pointed to the viewer count which, sitting at eight when Beanie first opened the stream, was now rapidly rising. Fifteen, twenty-two, twenty-eight.

Someone's probably posted that we're here, Beanie said, matter-of-factly.

Sorry, *what*?

There are fans who keep an eye on the stream twenty-four-seven, Beanie explained. There's an account posting updates. I think they're waiting for her to come back. To finish the work.

I felt the bile rising then.

I think she made it pretty clear that the work was over, don't you? I said, an unnecessary spike of venom in my tone.

I'm sorry, Beans, I said when I saw her face, taken aback by my anger. I'm just trying to get my head around it.

All my primary-school counselling courses, away days and training certificates hadn't prepared me for this. Couldn't help me to articulate what had happened, process it or understand it. Nora wanting to die was one thing. The Control Room—the art and the cultish following that had sprung up around it, almost organically, an alien lifeform that made Nora this kind of morbid internet darling—was something else entirely.

Do you think she should come back? To the Control Room? I asked Beanie, managing now to keep my voice neutral.

Beanie looked at me and, again, I saw something pass through her that I didn't fully comprehend. A piece of knowledge or understanding in her from which I had been excluded.

No, she said. I don't think she should come back.

Nor do I, I replied, through gritted teeth.

But it's not up to us, Beanie continued. It's up to her.

Not if I've got something to do with it.

We moved through Nora's apartment, searching for the items she had listed. Her phone, which had not been picked up by the paramedics, was on the kitchen counter, the battery drained. Her laptop and chargers. Clothes from her wardrobe, which hung in neat rows ordered by color so that the different fabrics made a pleasing soft gradient. Fresh socks. A handful of books from the shelves in the spare bedroom. Some papers from the desk, academic journal articles. In the fridge, the food was rotting. I bagged all of it up and left it at the front door to be thrown out as we were leaving. Finally, her toothbrush and soap and wash things, all in the en suite.

I stood at the door to it, which was closed, and willed myself to reach for the handle. Glanced up at the camera in the corner of the bedroom. I knew they were watching me. Whoever they were.

Mum, Beanie said, worried.

It's fine, I replied. Wait here.

I took a long, shuddering breath. I let myself in.

As we were leaving the building, arms laden with trash bags and a duffel of Nora's stuff, a teenager on the side of the courtyard in the center of the complex approached us. She had bad acne and wore her hair in a long plait that reached the bottom of her back. She was holding a bunch of sunflowers in the crook of her arm.

Is Nora okay? she asked, her voice so small that I thought for a moment that I'd misheard her.

I stopped. So did Beanie.

Excuse me?

Nora Robb. She lives in that building, doesn't she? I'm one of her students. From Goldsmiths. She nudged her head in the direction of the university, which was a ten-minute walk towards the city.

She was teaching the first-year abstract expressionism block, the girl said. Before she . . . before it happened.

I stared at her. She looked only a little older than Beanie.

I saw you guys on the Control Room feed, she continued, her face now flushing. I thought I'd run over and see if I could catch you.

How many people know that she lives here? I asked the girl.

Oh—well—everyone on my module, I think. Most people on the course. It's not really a secret, I mean. Nora didn't make a secret of it.

For fuck's sake, I said.

Mum, Beanie said.

Can you just give her these? the girl said, shoving the sunflowers at me. From everyone on Abstract Expressionism, please tell her. We're all thinking of her.

Beanie took the flowers and balanced them on top of one of her trash bags. Thanks, she said.

We're all thinking of her, the girl repeated.

Please don't come here again, I replied.

EXTRACTS [VARIOUS] FROM INTERVIEW TRANSCRIPTS,
QUOTED IN INGRID OLSSEN: VISIONARY BY RICHARD
TAPER (FORTHCOMING FROM ORANGE RABBIT PRESS)

**Angelica Hoffmann, wife of the late Maurice Hoffmann
and Director of the Hoffmann Trust:**

Ingrid worked at Maurice's print shop for the first three or four
years she was in London, until she sold her first big commission.
During that time—it was the early eighties—she acquired some
English, apprenticed as a screen printer to Maurice, and he taught
her everything he knew. He was her patron, you could say. She was
a sweet girl, really. Very timid, slip of a thing. Maurice saw something in her and he wanted to shape that. He did the same for
others. I suppose, yes, it was strange that a man in his fifties at the
time was spending so much time with a teenager. I suppose it
looked quite strange to anyone on the outside looking in. But it was
the eighties, you know?

Karoline Olssen, sister and manager:

Oh, Maurice Hoffmann was absolutely a predator.

Angelica Hoffmann:

He saw the natural talent in Ingrid. He knew that with work he
could help her become something brilliant. That's why he let her
live with us for a year, rent-free I might add, above the shop. She
slept on a cot in the kitchen and folded it up every morning before
she went downstairs to work in the shop. She paid him back by
drying the serigraphs and cleaning the stencils in between series.
And, of course, he spent hours with her in that shop, sometimes
well into the middle of the night, teaching her how to do it herself.
She had a knack.

Edward Robb, actor and ex-husband:

I never met Maurice Hoffmann. By the time Ingrid was a part of my life, they had lost touch and she wasn't working with silkscreen any longer. She got into portraiture, and that introduced her to a whole new crowd. Hoffmann trained at some fancy-schmancy college himself, and Ingrid, as you know, was almost entirely self-taught. She was better than him. She outgrew him. It's just a fact.

After she got a commission from some old client of Hoffmann's, she made a couple of connections. She was sleeping on the floor of a warehouse in Peckham by that time. Then, someone knew someone who knew someone and, all of a sudden, not long before we met in eighty-three or eighty-four, she had her first little show at the Whitechapel Gallery. Pete Burns turned up, or so they say. I don't think he even knew her, who she was, anything about her. It was pure coincidence. He was probably just in the area shopping or something, and he walked into Ingrid's little show, her linocuts and her thumbnail portraits, the Rauschenberg knock-offs. Rumor has it she didn't even meet him. She was out back smoking a bowl the whole time he was there. Within ten minutes he'd bought the whole show. He loved the work so much that he purchased the entire collection, right there on the spot. They'll be worth a fortune now, but he won't have paid more than a couple thousand. Anyway, it caused enough of a stir that the press picked it up—Pete Burns was hot shit then. Dead or Alive had just put out "The Stranger."

She could have had five minutes in the spotlight and faded back into obscurity, then. It was a make-or-break moment for her. But she had bigger plans for herself. She leveraged the Pete Burns story, started talking her way into all the night spots in Soho. She got Karoline over from Oslo, where she was working as a typist, and got her in on it, too.

Karoline Olssen:

Life began when I was sixteen and Ingrid flew me over to London with her Pete Burns money. I told everyone I was a typist. I wasn't an idiot. I knew it wasn't very *fashion* to bring up the pig farm. That's why we never did. Ingrid got me out to all the clubs with her, and she rented a little apartment on Dean Street where she could work and I could be her assistant. Manage her diary, arrange her social commitments, when things started getting too busy for her to look after on her own, and so on. My English was a lot better than hers, you see.

Edward Robb:

The two of them were a force. They made sure they were photographed adjacent to the right people. I think the fact that they were sisters made them more alluring to the gossip rags. Two gorgeous, young, talented Scandinavian bombshell starlet sisters from the middle of nowhere. Legs that went on for days and perfect spun-gold hair. And suddenly they were the hottest gals on the scene. Of course, though, Ingrid was the real star.

Karoline Olssen:

I was the real star, but Ingrid was older, so I let her have the glory.

Edward Robb:

They knew all the people. The *shiny* people. Out of nowhere, Ingrid was this overnight celebrity, this London It girl. The shiny people became her friends. She was photographed getting out of cars with Mick Jagger and Naomi Campbell. All the tabloids were reporting on her. Who she was with, where she was going, who she was fucking. Karoline was there too.

In between, she was putting together a portfolio, more ambitious work, finding her way towards what you might call a *signature*. She started on the huge oil work; the stuff people remember her for. She got another show, and then another, and then she ended up doing some modelling for Tony Snowdon and *that* ended up as part of a *Rolling Stone* long read about club culture, and then suddenly she was some kind of a national superstar.

I met her in the middle of all of this. I was in London doing a screen test for some *Star Wars* rip-off that never got made. I bumped into her in the kitchen at Earl Slick's New Year's Eve party. Turned out we were both there because we thought we might get a chance to meet David Bowie. Well, Bowie didn't show up, but by the end of the night neither of us cared. We put enough coke in us to power a family home for a week. It was pure love.

Karoline Olssen:
It was around this time that I was approached for the lead role in a nationwide tour of *Funny Girl*.

Edward Robb:
We spent most of our nights at the Jinty or Billy's, and most of our days sleeping it off on the floor of Ingrid's studio. When she woke up in the middle of the afternoon she painted, she worked, and then by midnight she was on the town, ready to do it all over again. I liked that about her, when I met her. She was just like me. She worked hard—that's why she got famous so quickly—but she also knew how to cultivate an identity that was exciting and mysterious and enchanting.

New people, new idols, new parties, new drugs to play with. She was an alcoholic by twenty-three—I ain't judging her, we all were. We got married in Vegas in 1985, and we drove to the Grand Canyon in my Mustang for the honeymoon. She had a coke problem that she had to cold-turkey when she fell pregnant with Matilda. I don't think Hoffmann fit in with that lifestyle. He had old-fashioned ideas about who could and couldn't be successful in the industry. He reminded me of a director, who I won't name but I will say has had two Best Picture nominations and who you will definitely know, who told me on an audition in 1988 that I would never make it in Hollywood without acting lessons. Well, who's laughing now? Shortly after that audition I was cast in my first major role in a three-episode arc on a little old show called

Quantum Leap. Ever heard of it? And look how we ended up. Ingrid outgrew him, that's what it was.

Karoline Olssen:
The only time I ever saw Maurice Hoffmann after my first year in London was when he turned up at the Richmond house with a double-barrel hunting shotgun in 2004 and almost killed Nora.

CHAPTER 11

Nora had been moved to a psychiatric ward at the new hospital.

It was sixteen days since It had happened. Gus had sort-of moved into my apartment. Beanie was in the final throes of her first year of drama school. Exams hung over us like a bad smell. When she wasn't at school, she trapped herself in her bedroom for whole evenings, only coming out to pour herself pints of Coke from the fridge. Gus and I shared the cooking and she often ventured out to grab a plate of carbonara or green curry before disappearing once again to eat in her bedroom.

I'm worried about her, I told him.

It's exam stress, he replied.

Are you sure?

No, I'm not.

Have you told her any more secrets?

Now that the shock of Nora had bedded itself in a bit, I returned to his betrayal, his forcing Beanie to withhold his break-up with Lulu.

No, I haven't told her any more secrets, he said. Matt, it was so stupid, I can't begin to—

Just, don't. Not yet.

We were going to talk about it soon, I knew. Now wasn't the right time. Beanie needed us, I needed Gus, and I was afraid of understanding the reasons for the lie. Afraid to begin to disarticulate the feelings it had brought about in me. Gus was sleeping on the sofa bed in the living room, working on his laptop from the kitchen table. I conceded that his presence in the apartment, the way he had slotted so easily into that role in our lives, catalyzed an overwhelming sense of calm and comfort in me. I wasn't prepared to examine the other things his presence brought about in me any more than that. In the evenings, I found myself falling asleep on his lap in front of the television. We shopped for groceries and ran errands and arranged Beanie's schedule.

One night I dreamed again of the Richmond house and woke up, shaking, cold sweat pouring down my back. It was the same dream as before. The house was falling down and everyone I ever loved was inside. I would survive them all. I didn't want to. How would I live without them?

Gus was at the bedroom door.

You okay? he asked. I heard something—it sounded like you were crying.

Can you come here, please?

I felt the hot tears tracking down my cheeks, pooling at my chin.

He climbed into my bed and pulled me into his chest and placed one hand upon the crown of my head. He buried his face in my hair.

It's going to be okay, Matt, he said. I promise you.

And we were teenagers again, wrapped up in sheets on a mattress on the bare floorboards above the kebab shop, when we'd had nothing and no one except each other and we'd been terrified, yet still I'd felt safer with him there than I ever had alone.

I let myself into Beanie's bedroom one night and found her scrolling her phone in bed.

You won't sleep if you keep that up, I said.

I know, she replied. She relented and put her phone, face down, on her bedside table.

How's Nora? she asked. A question she posed now multiple times a day. I hadn't let her come to see Nora in the hospital yet. Nora wasn't ready and Beanie was just a kid. The psychiatric ward was eerie, unnerving: Nora's room was all smooth corners and picture frames bolted to the walls and televisions locked in glass cabinets. I guessed so that no one could hurt themselves with the cables. It felt too extreme for Nora to me, and I was scared for her being there alone, in a place she so clearly didn't belong. But then I reasoned that what Nora had tried to do warranted those precautions.

Bringing Beanie to that place would cement the reality of Nora's illness, in my mind and in hers.

I couldn't answer her. I knew about as much of Nora's mood as I did my teenage daughter's. I felt as though I were on the beach and the tide was sucking them both out, away from me. I couldn't reach them. I had seen videos of the ocean disappearing before a tsunami hit. The disturbance underneath wasn't visible, but it caused so great a displacement of water, that the tide could be pulled out for miles. I felt as though I was waiting for my own tsunami to hit. That the water had gone and I could see the monstrous wave on the horizon, coming for me.

I visited Nora most evenings, for an hour or two. She had a regimented schedule—group therapy, solo counselling, activities, mealtimes—which gave a small window for guests to come to the unit. She was surly and difficult and unresponsive. Sometimes she cried. Sometimes I cried. Sometimes Karoline came and pretended we were on a social call.

I can't stay long, darlings, she always said. I've got a dinner/show/business meeting with Richard Curtis/Graham Norton/Miley Cyrus.

Have you spoken to Dad? Nora had asked me on one of my visits.

I shook my head.

I had left the news of Nora's hospitalization, and the contact information for the ward, with Dad's housekeeper, Polly. But Dad hadn't called me back.

Have you? I asked Nora. She shook her head too.

I looked at the carpet and imagined punching Dad in the stomach over and over, until he folded himself in half.

Girls, Karoline said, setting her vape purposefully on the table and steepling her fingers. Nora's room was plain, with white walls and blue (blue) curtains and a view of the hospital car park from the window. In one of the bolted-on picture frames was a photograph of a seascape with a lone figure walking on the sun-drenched beach. Underneath the photograph was the word FAITH in block-capital serif font.

That's a bit sad-looking, isn't it? I asked Nora, pointing out the picture. For a psych ward?

She shrugged. I think it's a Jesus thing? One-set-of-footsteps-type bullshit?

Weird.

Definitely going to cure my psychosis, isn't it, a reminder that we're all alone in this world except for the voices inside our heads.

I snorted.

Girls, Karo said again, louder this time. I'm going to meet Larry Montague next week.

Who the fuck is Larry Montague? Nora asked.

He's the director of the MOMA in San Francisco.

Nora looked away.

I think it's very important that you are both there at the opening of your mother's exhibition, Karoline continued. This is a significant time for all of us, as a family. And a milestone in our endeavor to honor her legacy.

Your endeavor, Nora said.

I can't throw this party without Ingrid's daughters there. The original *Girls*. Especially as we only have half the portfolio available. She shot daggers at me.

I won't speak for Nora, I said, glancing at her. She was still looking away, out into the car park, where a couple were having a loud argument about what sounded like something to do with the recession.

I continued. But you know how I feel about it. I think Mum would have hated it. And I think that the whole thing is, like, a little bit despicable.

Complex mortgage bonds, the man outside shouted at the woman. Unregulated investment banking.

Well, I'm sorry, but the fact is there's nothing you can do about it, Karoline said.

You keep saying that.

That's because it's true. Swallow your camels, Matilda. I'm flying out next week and we'll open on the second week of August. I would like to see you both there.

I'll try my best, Nora said, deadpan. But they might not let me on the flight seeing as, in case you hadn't noticed, I am literally locked in the loony bin.

Karoline said her goodbyes and swept out of the hospital room with a swish of her pashmina. I couldn't bring myself to argue with her about the exhibition. I felt as though all the water had left my body and, exhausted from the last weeks, I was shriveling up. I thought of Mum, in the final days, in the Richmond house, shriveling up too as the life had left her body, as stubborn as she ever had been. Throw it all away, she'd said, talking about her paintings. I don't want anyone making money off me after I'm gone. Especially none of *you* awful fuckers.

I said this to Nora, gently. She wouldn't look at me.

Do you remember Mum saying that? I asked her, aware that now—amid a mental-health crisis and a suicide attempt—was probably not the time to be antagonizing Nora about her decision to let Karo have her half of Mum's portfolio for the exhibition. I couldn't help myself, though.

I thought we were together on this, I told Nora. We never talked about it, but I thought we had kind-of agreed not to do anything with Mum's work.

I pictured my half of the portfolio stacked neatly in a climate-controlled steel box. It felt like a shadow hanging over me, watching me though I couldn't see it myself.

We never talk about anything, do we? Nora said quietly, spitefully.

No—we don't.

I wish you'd picked me up, Matt, when you left. I wish you'd taken me with you.

I knew that she was talking about the Richmond house. Her, eight years old, stuck in that house with our unstable mother who sometimes drank herself catatonic and sometimes disappeared for days at a time.

I wish I had, too. I *tried*. I should have tried harder.

It had happened so long ago but the memory was so clear to me, it could have been yesterday. Nora had been picked up by the police for sleeping in the park when Mum had gone on a binge and locked her out of the house. After that, a new social worker had started visiting. Started asking questions, like why wasn't Nora in school and where were the other family members and what was the nature of Ingrid's substance abuse and why were half the windows in the house smashed through and boarded up. Nora could have lived with me, Gus and the baby. Above the kebab shop. She was only small; there would have been room for her. It was shit and cramped and Gus and I argued incessantly, but it would have been better than that house. We'd tried. But we'd been too young, and too unstable, barely feeding ourselves on Gus's wage and welfare handouts. The council inspection of our studio had lasted less than ten minutes before a woman who'd looked like an owl had told us that the accommodation wasn't appropriate for foster carers and we couldn't have kinship custody. Dad was filming a war epic in Beirut and wouldn't pick up the phone. We hadn't seen him for over a year. They'd appointed Karo as a secondary guardian instead. Nora would stay living in the Richmond house on the understanding that Karo would live there, too, and be responsible for her welfare.

I could have run away, Nora said. Maybe I should have.

I don't know. Maybe.

It worked out okay for you.

I looked at her then. She seemed a little better, a little livelier. Her skin wasn't so pallid, her features not so gaunt, her eyes had some of the color back in them. But she still wasn't good. I detected a hard edge in her when she spoke. Even when she cracked her morbid jokes. She held her body as though it were a knife. She chewed at her fingernails until they were raw and bleeding. I felt the chasm of space stretch out between us in that moment. The gulf so wide that it seemed impossible to cross over to her and take hold of her.

Nora's doing okay, I told Beanie now. Could be better, could be worse. What's new with you, anyway?

Beanie shrugged, staring at the wall. Picked her phone back up from the nightstand and began to scroll again.

Hey, kid, look at me when I'm talking to you.

She huffed and rolled her eyes and stared up at me, a defiant look on her face.

What the hell is going on with you? I asked, exasperated.

What do you mean *what's going on with you*? she countered, mimicking my tone.

This attitude, I replied, waving my arms at her. The dirty looks. Don't think I've forgotten your tantrum at the dinner after your play. What's happening, Beans? Is it the exams? Are you stressed out about them?

She shrugged noncommittally. I dunno.

Help me out, here.

I don't know, Mum, she said finally, putting her phone down again. Maybe it's that you don't tell me *anything* about Nora. I probably like her more than you do. You didn't even bother to know anything about her until she tried to kill herself. I'm not a kid anymore, you know. I'm the same age you were when you had me. But you treat me like I'm five.

She dragged a pillow over her face, her orange hair sticking out over the top.

First of all, I said evenly, to the pillow. I absolutely do not treat you like you're five. You get a lot of allowances that your friends don't have. You barely have a curfew, Beans, you get treated like an adult. And that's because I trust you to make good decisions for yourself and behave in a responsible way.

She didn't move the pillow.

I want you to have a better life than I did, Beatrice, I continued. I don't want you to make the same mistakes I did.

Mistakes like me, you mean.

Oh my God, *no*, of course not. I didn't mean that—you know I didn't.

Whatever.

Beanie. I meant that I want you to have a good life—a life where you don't have to struggle so hard to get the things you want. That's why I make certain decisions. It's because I'm trying to look after you.

She was quiet, then, under the pillow.

You're so annoying, she said.

I'm annoying because I love you.

BORING, she shouted into the pillow, but I could see now that her body had relaxed and there was a note of amusement in her voice. I patted her leg and left her bedroom, feeling myself becoming more unsettled.

CHAPTER 12

She's already almost died seven times, Richard said over dinner, frowning. Though she only told me six of the stories.

I'll have to play you the tape sometime, he continued.

He was talking about Nora again. He shoved a forkful of spaghetti into his mouth as he spoke, and the sauce slid down his chin.

I watched him as though he were an alien, baffled that I had even let him come over after what had happened. Richard had a way of making everything seem okay, better than it was. And it was easy being around him. I felt truly myself with him, all of the ugly parts as well as the good. Here too was a man who knew everything there was to know about my personal history, my family and the mess of my life as the daughter of Ingrid Olssen. If Richard could look my flaws in the face—my spikiness, my secretiveness, my nightmarish family, an overbearing personality and a barely concealed rage—then surely he was my person.

Nevertheless, something had changed between us.

We sat at the kitchen table in my apartment. Beanie was at her friend Dami's, studying for her media exam. Only two exams left to go and she was free for the summer. My own school was breaking for the summer soon, too. I wanted to do something special with her to celebrate finishing her AS levels—a trip, maybe, somewhere far away like Edinburgh—but I worried about Nora. And I worried that Beans would say "no," that she would want to spend the summer with Gus, who had moved back into his own place now that my schedule was becoming a little more regular. I couldn't imagine how it might feel if that happened. How it would feel for my heart to break in two.

Karoline was now gone, to San Francisco, and Nora's twenty-eight days at Park Royal were going to be done within the week. She had a final evaluation and a medication plan scheduled, meetings I had been asked to attend, as her next of kin, and then she would be free. Things were about to change.

Why would you play me the tape? I asked Richard.

What? he asked, glancing up from the hastily-thrown-together Bolognese I had prepared for his arrival. We hadn't seen each other in a while—not since the hospital when he had shown me his press release—the statement that no one had asked him to write but he had felt entitled to do so anyway.

Since then, I had made excuses not to see him. I was busy with visiting Nora; work was overwhelming me. Beanie was stressing out about her exams. There were so many reasons at my fingertips, ready to deploy until I could understand the disquiet thrumming through me every time his name flashed up on my caller ID.

After a while, after the disquiet had subsided some, I realized that I was being a coward avoiding him, and relented, and now he was in my apartment eating my food.

Why would you play me the tape, of your interview with Nora?

Well—I just thought you might be interested.

Why?

I don't know, Matilda, he said, sighing. It's going in the book, so you can read it there, anyway.

Oh, I won't read the book, I said flippantly, dismissively, half laughing.

Richard paused.

Sorry, what?

I looked up at him and saw hurt written across his face.

I lived Ingrid's life, I said, feeling hostile. I lived it with her, alongside her. I'm still living it now. I know all of it already. I don't need a biography to tell me what happened.

I see.

I don't see how you can't understand that. It surprises me.

I just thought you'd be interested in what I've been working on the whole time we've been together.

I rolled my eyes. Well—yes, of course I'm interested.

I ask you about work, don't I?

Yes, you do.

Right.

But, like, I'm not massively excited to read salacious gossip about my sister's suicide attempts.

Salacious gossip. Fine, okay. It's not, but even if it was? You watch all that awful trash TV.

We ate in silence for a while.

I know it's important to you, I said eventually. The book.

He slid out of his chair and came over to me, pulling me into his chest and kissing the crown of my head. It made me flinch a little.

But you also need to realize that it doesn't hold weight for me the way it does for you. It feels kind of unpleasant, actually. Voyeuristic.

His hands froze in their position on my back.

I'll keep apologizing about the statement until you forgive me, he said.

I know, I replied, my mouth muffled by his shirt, thinking, *But it's not about the statement. Not really.*

And he *had* apologized. By text, by handwritten letter, by an obscenely large bouquet of flowers sent to my school, which made the girls in the front office coo like moorhens.

I'm not some tabloid journalist chasing an ambulance, Mattie. I'm not trying to get a scoop here.

I know.

I worry that sometimes that's how you see me.

Well, historically, my family has not had good relationships with journalists, I replied. I pointed to Beanie's and my photo collage on the living-room wall. The tabloid snap of my twenty-something-year-old mum falling out of a nightclub, and her dress.

This is an important, serious project. Not sensationalized claptrap—not *that.*

Then why does it sometimes feel like you're looking at me as though I'm an exhibit in a museum?

It's fine, he replied, flashing me a strained smile.

But what's fine? I asked, frowning, feeling the rage bubble. What exactly is fine? None of this is fine.

He smiled broadly and benevolently at me.

Everything is fine, he said.

He sat down again, and I watched him as he ate. His face became more and more alien, more inhuman, with every bite.

I visited Nora that evening. She seemed a little brighter, the shift nurse told me, as though she were a dog at the vets. A little brighter. What could that mean?

But when I walked into the small room with short electrical cables and a window in the door to the en suite and the TV set locked inside a cabinet, I kind of understood. Nora had the window open—the sliver of it that was allowed, that is—and the spring air rushed into the room. She was playing music on her laptop. George Michael's "Freedom."

Oh, I love this one, I told her.

I know, she said, glancing up from her spot on the bed.

Bit on the nose, or?

Nah.

I sat on the bed next to her and we listened together. Nora was an excellent sitting-down dancer. She rolled her shoulders and mimed George—even all the "uh's and "oh yeah's—so well that it was as though she were singing.

Are you ready to go home? I asked, raising my voice to be heard over the music. She grinned at me, ignored me, and carried on sitting-down dancing.

What happened to you? I asked, bewildered. Last time I saw you, you were ready to punch someone.

Nora shrugged.

Maybe the meds are kicking in, she said, and I detected a hint of spite in her words.

I'm just ready to be out of here.

I bet.

How am I, the depressed one, more excited about life than you are? Nora asked.

Wait till you have kids, I replied, grinning.

How is the old Bean?

I honestly don't know, I said, feeling my stomach clench, feeling the lightness leave my body. She's a teenager, mainly.

I'll come visit when I'm out.

Will you? I asked her, an eyebrow raised, before I could stop myself. I could already picture what was going to happen when Nora got out of hospital. She would lock herself back up in her skyscraper, her Control Room, and another two years would go by before anyone saw her again. That was if she even survived.

I'm getting assessed for discharge in a couple days, Nora said, and I could see the color leaving her face too.

Do you feel ready?

To be discharged? No, of course not. But that doesn't mean I shouldn't be.

The world is a scary place.

That's no good reason not to experience it. Can't wait to take a shower without someone checking in to make sure I haven't topped myself in between shampoos.

You *do* have a bit of a track record with bathrooms.

She laughed at that, and it was a genuine laugh. Not sardonic or backhanded or dripping in sarcasm. The sound of it made my heart squeeze.

I don't want you to go back to your apartment, I said quietly.

Explain.

The music had stopped and the room suddenly felt stifling. Even the wind through the trees outside, the cars pulling into the car park, heard through the cracked window, felt imposing.

I think the Control Room needs to go offline, I said. I don't think it's healthy.

She considered me for a second, her dark eyes, the pupils seemingly too large for her storm-colored irises, sliding over my face.

That's my art, Matt. My thesis.

I know, but it scares me.

It scares me, too.

So, stop it. Come and stay with me and Beans instead. We'll go to Edinburgh over the summer. I wanted to take Beanie to the Fringe, treat her for finishing her exams.

Edinburgh?

Yeah. Why not?

Can't you dream a little bigger, Mattie?

Edinburgh's lovely.

You're an incredibly incurious human being.

Well, that's rude. To me *and* Edinburgh.

Where am I going to sleep, on Beanie's bedroom floor? Haven't you got Gus on the sofa?

We'll work something out. I promise I won't check on you in the shower.

Even as I said this, I wasn't certain whether I was telling the truth.

I just don't want you alone in that place, Nora. All those blank walls. I don't trust you not to do something silly.

Do something silly. God, Mattie, you're literally a therapist. Don't say shit like that. Don't talk about trusting me like that.

She was right. I knew this as well as she did. Language that made her the villain in the story of her illness only made things worse.

I felt I was watching her on the edge of some precipice, trying to grab on to her to stop her from tipping over into the abyss. I never could get a good purchase.

I'm sorry, I said. I just want to help you. I don't know how. I need you to tell me what will help.

Let me think about it, she said.

I was always snatching on to a scrap of her sleeve or a coil of her hair. That fear ran through me like a low-frequency electrical current. It was always there.

PARTIAL TRANSCRIPTION OF INTERVIEW NUMBER 2
WITH NORA ROBB [01.04.2020]

N.R.: I was at university in Los Angeles, studying for my Master's in Art History. I was working at a bar in Inglewood where they screened international sports games all night.

    This was when I tried to kill myself. In 2017. The second time. This would be the fifth time I almost died.

    Nothing in my life felt good. I couldn't muster joy for anything, you know? Not even the most special important things. Graduating college. When my niece was born. I just felt . . . like . . . super numb all the time.

    I had school, and work, which cascaded from one shitty bar to the next. I would work one bar until I got so burned out that I convinced myself *any* job would be better than this one, so I would quit and find another, and it would be the same thing all over again, rinse and repeat. At the same time, I was going to school and working on my first big installation piece. You know, with the concrete? Yeah, well, that was my whole life.

    I started having a lot of *meltdowns*. I wasn't coping very well. The installation happened, and it was this huge success. Too successful. Mum came to California to visit it. Strangers became interested in my work. I found it . . . difficult.

R.T.: What was difficult about it?

N.R.: Being—uh—scrutinized. All I ever wanted was to be alone. To sit quietly, you know.

R.T.: But the stuff with the concrete exposed you.

N.R.: Yeah.

R.T.: I suppose it's like what happened to Ingrid, early in her career, at a similar age to you.

N.R.: That's true. But, you know, I'll tell you something about my mum. Something you can put in your little book, Richard.

R.T.: Please do.

N.R.: She fucking *loved* it. She *loved* the attention. I mean, who doesn't? I loved being loved too. But Mum—she was a whole different breed of person—a different species, even. She pretended that she didn't care. But, truly. She wanted *everyone* to love her, the *whole world*. And they did, for about a second. And then she had to come down, and it ruined her.

R.T.: Are you talking about her relationship with fame?

N.R.: I'm talking about her relationship with everything. Everyone.

R.T.: I'm not disagreeing with you, but I wonder . . . how do you parse that with her behavior in later life? Her reclusiveness? Her decision not to exhibit? To not make money from her work?

N.R.: Like I said. She had to come down from it. Everyone does.

R.T.: And the same thing happened to you?

N.R.: I took one little step towards it. I got shortlisted for the Herb Alpert award, and I won a couple of others.

Everyone said I was like a new version of Mum.

Which I think is possibly the worst thing anyone could have said to either of us.

Around the same time my social media blew up in a big way. I went from less than a thousand followers, to like forty thousand, and then three hundred thousand, in the space of about a month. People began asking me questions and wanting my opinion on things, like it mattered. At school, during my third year of my undergrad, people stopped me on campus to talk about the concrete. People treated me differently. People got my email address and sent me deeply personal stuff. They DMed me their problems like I could help solve them. It was overwhelming.

And I was sad, and spiky, and exhausted, all the time.

I was afraid of what was going to happen to me. Afraid

of what it meant to have three, four, five hundred thousand followers on the internet. Afraid of what my mother would think.

She never believed that performance art was a real discipline, you know? Which is funny, because Maurice Hoffmann never thought she was a real artist because she didn't have any training. Well, guess what, I *did* have training. And people loved me. I just didn't know how to love them back, how to love myself.

So that's why I did it.

Of course, I fucked it up, and they put me in hospital.

I was always some kind of problem to everyone. No one has ever wanted to be responsible for me, in my whole life. My mum, my dad, my aunt. Even Mattie left as soon as she could.

When they came to see me in hospital, it was like they were itching to leave. Mum *did* leave. She was here for a few days and then she made some excuse about the humidity fucking with her head, or whatever, and then she left.

As soon as they let me out, Mattie dropped me off on Dad's doorstep and left too.

CHAPTER 13

RICHARD AND I LIVED THE MIDDLE-CLASS DREAM FOR THE WEEKEND.

The Sunday afternoon before Nora's discharge meeting, we drove to a farm in Esher to pick our own vegetables. We trudged through stretches of thick, muddy fields to find rows of zucchinis, summer squashes, deep-burgundy-colored globe-like beetroots. I let my boots sink into the soft ground as I pulled each vegetable from its roots, relishing the crisp air, the perfect blueness of the sky. Richard's presence in my peripheral vision made me a little uneasy. I wasn't sure what I had to say to him. He mostly asked questions about Nora, her health and the discharge. Beanie's exams. My work. It felt as though the space between us was widening, so that even standing next to one another, his arm sometimes grazing mine, I couldn't reach him.

Of all the things in my mind, I kept thinking of the press release. And then, of how he had emailed Chelsea and never told me about it. Every time he opened his mouth to speak, I was expecting him to mention it. Something simple, nonchalant. *Hey, you know your old friend, Chelsea? I was thinking of interviewing her for the book. I got in touch with her, actually. What do you think? Would it be okay with you?*

But he never said it.

What will happen with Nora when she's discharged? he asked instead.

I've asked her to move in with me and Beanie.

That'll be a squeeze.

We'll make it work, somehow. I'm not sure how yet.

Haven't you ever wanted to start your own little garden? he asked, abruptly changing the subject.

I shrugged and looked away. I don't know. Maybe.

You've always been good with this sort of stuff.

What sort of stuff?

I don't know. Cultivating plants, I guess. Nurturing growth. You've got all those tomatoes on your balcony. And the leeks. You could do a lot more, you know. You love doing it, I can tell.

He was right. I did love it.

And you had all the vegetables in your mother's garden, didn't you? In Richmond? Do you think that's why you like to grow things? Where it came from?

I shot him a look, warning him.

This isn't an interview, he said, smiling earnestly. I promise, Matt. Just a conversation.

I squeezed his hand apologetically. Sometimes it was hard to tell the difference.

I don't have a garden.

You could get an allotment.

I could.

I imagined it now. Carrots and pea shoots and bronzing onions in damp, dank soil. I liked the thought of it.

You know who does have a garden? he asked, grinning.

Who?

Me. Listen.

He plucked a gooseberry from his basket and popped it into his mouth. I want to explain something to you.

Okay . . .

He inhaled deeply, as though bracing himself.

I'm in love with you, Matilda. I have been since almost the first time we met.

I stared at him, the cauliflower I had been examining nestled in my limp hands. I seemed to be suddenly sinking further into the mud.

Erm, I said.

I don't expect you to say anything back. I don't want you to say anything you don't mean. But I need you to know where I stand on things. Where I stand on this. Us. And after the summer, maybe after the exhibition's open and Nora is settled a bit, I want you and Beanie to move in with me.

Guiltily, I struck down the internal wash of relief that he wasn't proposing marriage.

He watched me expectantly, his face aglow with boyish hope.

Oh God. Richard . . . I thought of the press statement again.

I don't know about that.

His face fell a fraction, but he recovered and kept his sheepish smile in place.

Just, think about it, all right? Talk to Beanie about it. Maybe after you're back from Edinburgh and I'm back from San Francisco, we can make a decision.

San Francisco?

For the opening. Your aunt invited me. It makes sense for me to be there.

Yeah—yeah, I know, I just hadn't thought about it.

I do think you should consider it, Mattie. Consider coming to the exhibition.

And what will I do with Beanie? Nora?

Beanie can stay with your ex. And Nora—well, I don't know. Bring Nora with you. She was the one who made the whole thing happen, after all.

I grimaced.

He reached for my hand but I was still holding the cauliflower, so he sort of patted my shoulder instead.

I love you, Matilda, he said again. I really do.

I couldn't answer him. I felt my insides squirming as I looked at him.

That night, in bed, I traced the outline of his lips with my thumb. His eyes glittered in the darkness.

What if I hurt you, I whispered, more to myself than to him.

I don't think you will, he whispered back.

I wanted to say, But that's what I do, that's who I am.

I'm the kind of person who hurts other people.

I'm the kind of person who leaves people behind, to deal with the wreckage alone.

But I stayed silent instead.

I closed my eyes and, inexplicably, I saw Gus at seventeen, in the back seat of his cousin's car in the middle of the night. The way the universe was expanding in his dark irises, the way he looked at me. Like his existence depended on mine. It was terrifying. It still terrified me now, that strength of feeling.

I don't think it's possible for you to hurt me, Richard clarified, resting a hand on my cheek.

I sighed and pulled him closer to me.

This is it for me, he said. This is the end goal.

I drove to Gus's place to pick up Beanie on Monday night. She had spent the weekend there with him. Gus lived in the basement apartment of a terraced Edwardian mews house of beautiful proportions just off Ealing Common. All original oak floors and high ceilings and sash windows, it was a world away from our ten-year-old sand-colored shoebox in Acton. Gus had made his money as a lawyer and, though he still had a long way to climb on the career ladder, and often forsook his salary for pro bono work with charities, he had done well for himself in the years since our grimy start in our kebab-shop studio. His parents had been well off in his youth, and the financial stability in early life had paid off for him. I often thought about how different things could have been for me and Gus. What might have been my life if Mum hadn't spent all her art money on mind-altering substances and ludicrous chaises longues, and handed off large swathes of it to her friends as loans that were untraceable because she'd never written anything down. Gus was probably going to fund Beanie's university expenses, outside of the tuition loan. Something I could never dream of doing on my school salary. It was a given that Beanie would go to university, after Gus and I both had had our own schooling disrupted—with him delaying his degree and my smorgasbord of adult education—there was no discussion that Beanie would ever not be undertaking higher education. Luckily, Beanie was just as excited to go to university as we were for her.

I felt an incredible stab of jealousy as I let myself into the wide, bright corridor with a beautiful ornate mirror on one wall above the shoe rack. Lulu's taste seemed to be impeccable. I noticed telltale suitcases stacked by the kitchen door.

In here, he called from the kitchen, and I walked in to see him slumped over his laptop at the breakfast table.

Your posture is terrible, I told him.

It was evening, but the equinox was approaching, and golden-hour sunlight filtered in through the French doors, flung open to the shared garden, at the back of the room. Beyond it, a cherry tree with ripe fruit leaned over the fence.

Lulu's stuff? I asked, cocking my head at the suitcases.

He nodded grimly.

Do you think you'll redecorate?

What do you mean?

Well, I assume she had a hand in all of this, I said, sweeping an arm at the kitchen. The mint-green tiles gleamed, and the AGA range looked like it had barely been used.

She was hardly here, to be honest, Gus said. She worked more than I did. None of this was her doing. I've barely seen her in the past six months.

I nodded and picked up an apple from the fruit bowl and examined it, and then placed it back down.

Beanie will be through in a sec; she's just on the phone to some boy, Gus said. Then, as though the thought had just occurred to him: Should we be worried about that?

It's probably Dami, I said, shrugging. I think they're just friends, but, who knows? She's going to be eighteen soon. We need to deal with the fact that . . . that she's going to be on the phone with boys.

Beanie had never had a boyfriend, and was more interested, it seemed, in cultivating friendships rather than romance. That suited me fine. My recurring fear was that history would repeat itself and she would be a teenage mother like I'd been. She had almost gone too far the other way, though.

Her lack of interest in finding a boyfriend seemed to be obstinate: she was aggressively anti-romance. Whenever I asked her about it, she shut the conversation down completely. I wondered whether I had set a bad example there, too.

Are we too hands-off with her?

I slumped into the seat next to him, and pressed the heels of my hands into my eyes. I suddenly felt exhausted.

I don't know what to do, I said. She's changing so quickly, Gus, I can't keep up. We keep having these silly arguments. We *never* argue—*ever*. I don't know what I'm doing wrong. I feel like she's leaving me behind.

Suddenly, embarrassingly, I felt like I was on the verge of tears. He squeezed my shoulder.

I feel like I don't know how to parent my own kid.

Of course you do. You're an amazing mum. You always have been.

And it's no surprise, I mean, I continued, ignoring him. Look at how me and Nora were brought up. It's no wonder I'm total shit at this.

Beanie poked her head around the door and shouted a hello at us. I gathered myself, flinching away from Gus's hand.

Hi, babe, I called back, feigning cheerfulness.

I'm just grabbing my school stuff, she yelled, disappearing back into her bedroom. And then we can go.

How's Nora? Gus asked, to change the subject.

She's . . . a bit better. It looks like they're going to discharge her this week. I'm thinking she'll come and live with us for a bit.

Nora's coming to live with us? Beanie said, appearing again, now with her rucksack stuffed and overflowing.

I think, maybe, for a little while. Until she's back on her feet.

Beanie threw her hands up and sing-songed *yasssss* at the ceiling.

In the car on the way home, I said, There's something else I need to talk to you about, kid.

Yeah? What? she asked, not lifting her eyes from her social media feed, her thumb poised to scroll.

Richard has asked if we would like to move in with him.

She stopped scrolling then, and looked up. Not at me, but at the road ahead. We had paused in a queue at some red lights, a mile or two away from home.

Say that again, she said.

Richard wants us to move in with him. Not for a little while, with Nora coming to stay. But maybe in a few months' time. He lives in Putney, not far from—

Stop talking, she said loudly. Just stop.

I did. And I waited while she brought her hands up to her face and rubbed her forehead.

I don't get what's wrong with Richard, I said.

Have you *seen* Richard?

He has his faults, I said. But so does everyone. Nobody's perfect.

I don't trust him.

I shuddered, because by saying it out loud she had hit something in the base of my gut, something that asked me whether I trusted him, too. And I didn't immediately know the answer.

I thought of all the hope he'd had in his face when he'd been talking about my hypothetical garden.

Do you love him? Beanie asked me, her eyes shining.

Yes, I said. But for some reason the way I said it made it sound like I was asking a question.

There's not many people who are willing to take me on, I added, feeling a little ashamed to admit it to her.

What?

With my family history. All of the baggage. This is a chance for me to be, well. Happy.

You're settling, Beanie said. You're settling because he's a safe bet.

I couldn't help but laugh.

Old Bean, I said. You are so young. There's so much you don't know yet.

Stop patronizing me.

I tried a different tack.

It's not like I was going to be single forever, I said. I was always going to meet someone eventually.

I know. I don't care about that.

One day I might want to live with someone, Beanie. One day I might even want to get married. And you need to accept that.

Listen, Mum, I'm not going to stop you from living your life. I don't care about you having a boyfriend. I know you've had them before. I'm not stupid. And I'm not a kid anymore. I don't know what you've been trying to protect me from, but you never needed to. If you want to live with Richard, go and live with Richard. But you can't make me live with him, too.

I would never force you to do anything you don't want to do, Beans, I replied, pulling into the car park underneath our building and killing the engine.

Good, she said.

I think we need to talk about this some more.

It's fine, she said tonelessly. I'm done.

She opened the car door and let herself out, then paused and leaned down to talk to me.

So, once you move in with Richard, I'll go and live with Dad. Like, full time.

We stared at one another momentarily, as though ready to draw pistols, her eyes as hard and stubborn as I knew mine were.

Fine, I said, refusing the bait. You can go and live with Dad.

It'll just be for a little while before I go to uni, she said, backtracking.

I understand that.

So, you agree? That I should live with Dad?

If that's what you want, Beanie, there's literally nothing I can do to stop you.

Fine.

Fine.

She slammed the car door.

CHAPTER 14

Nora got out of the hospital two days later.

I picked her up from her ward with the single duffel bag that Beanie and I had packed for her in her apartment, what seemed like a lifetime ago now. Beanie hadn't spoken to me since our disagreement, and my stomach churned with the uneasiness of it. I hated that she wasn't talking to me. I hated that I could feel the distance between us. So many times I had thought to knock on her bedroom door and offer an apology. But I couldn't bring myself to do it.

They've got me so medicated I'm rattling, Nora said as we signed paperwork.

The nurse handed me Nora's prescriptions and a bunch of other leaflets and booklets.

Make sure she takes these at the same time every day, the nurse said.

I know, I said. We went through it with the doctor.

Just make sure.

I wanted to say, do I look like an idiot to you?

How are you feeling? I asked her in the car.

I'm okay, I'm good. Matt, I'm going to tell you now that you can't be asking me how I feel every five minutes, okay? It's going to drive me fully crazy.

All right, I won't.

Don't therapize me.

I won't. I'll try not to.

Cool. I just don't think this is going to work otherwise.

I get it. Don't worry.

We got to the apartment and unloaded her one bag from the boot.

So this is where you live, she said.

I can't believe you've never visited us.

You never visited me, either, remember.

This is going to be weird, I said.

Yup, she replied.

We walked up the narrow staircase to the front door of the building and I fiddled with the keys to get the door open. I saw the building, the apartment, through Nora's fresh eyes as we walked in. The corridor and stairwell were tired, with crappy, cheap carpet tiles. One of the fire escapes was jammed shut and had been for several weeks. The vibe, I realized now, was not far off that of the secure unit. Inside the apartment, Beanie and I had kept the walls white, opting to hang photos and drawings and art rather than paint them. Nora examined each framed item carefully, holding her body strangely as she stood in the living room. I could see that she felt awkward, unsettled, out of place. My apartment wasn't so different from hers, except that there seemed to be nothing personal in hers while ours was overflowing with idiosyncratic touches, the pieces of my and Beanie's shared life in this place. I realized then that I had been foolish to ever consider Richard's offer. He lived in a spacious terraced house, inherited from a grandparent, in a fashionable west London suburb teeming with yummy mummies and smoothie shops. But this place—which I had rented for four years before scraping enough pennies together to afford a deposit for a forty percent share—was our home. I felt a tug on my heart as I watched Nora examine our things. She came upon the framed photo collage.

Hey, I remember this, she said. From Beanie's calls.

I came over to her to look at the collage too. I noticed that the photo of Nora—the university faculty picture—was gone.

Beanie and I made this together, I said.

Look at that. Nora pointed at the postcard tucked into the bottom right-hand corner of the frame. The *Girls* postcard Beanie had picked up from the National Portrait Gallery. I felt Nora let off a shudder, the anxiety coming off her like ripples in a still pool of water.

I'll throw it away, I said instinctively.

No, don't, she replied. I'm *facing up to the reality of my existence.*

Therapy talk?

She nodded, and shot me a sly, playful look that I didn't understand.

At that moment, we heard the key turn in the door and Beanie arrived in the living room.

Auntie Nora?

All right, Old Bean, she said.

Oh my GOD, Beanie screamed and rushed into Nora's open arms. I turned to the kitchen and flicked the kettle on, embarrassed to disturb their moment of reunion. Beanie hadn't visited Nora in the hospital—I had emphasized how important it was that she focused on her exams, but, really, I was worried how seeing Nora so vulnerable would make her feel. I hated the idea that Beanie knew mental illness so acutely at such a young age.

Tea or coffee? I asked Nora. I don't remember what you drink.

Nora didn't hear me over her chatter with Beanie. Tell me everything, how's school? How are your friends? What are you working on at the moment? Are you dating anyone? What are you thinking for uni? Oh, you're going to love it, Beans, you'll be amazing. Are you still thinking of stage acting? What's the vibe? Wait till you get to move out—it'll be the best thing you've ever done.

I felt myself stiffen as they chattered away as though there was nothing wrong, that Nora hadn't just come off a psychiatric ward, wasn't up to her eyelashes in antidepressants, anti-anxiety meds, mood stabilizers. And that Beanie hadn't spent the last two days pretending I didn't exist.

Guys? Tea? Coffee? I said, a little louder.

Tea, please, Nora said.

Yeah, same, Beanie added, not making eye contact with me.

I made the tea and brought it over to the sofa.

So, the plan, I started.

Can we not have the plan yet? Nora said petulantly. I just want to chill for five minutes. I've only just sat down. It's so nice to drink from something that isn't a plastic beaker or a polystyrene cup, you know. It smells really nice in here.

Thanks.

Where can I put my stuff?

Well, that's all part of the plan, but you don't want to hear the plan yet.

Just, let's have an hour, shall we? Let's have some peace.

So we did. We sat on the sofa, the three of us, curled around one another, and we listened to the ticking of the clock and the heating of the hot-water tank and the sighing of the traffic outside the window and the electrical cicada-esque hum of the fridge.

We settled into a rhythm. Nora slept in Beanie's bed and Beanie slept on an airbed in the living room. Beanie went to school. I went to work. Nora spent most of her time in Beanie's bedroom with the door closed.

I hated to leave her there, alone again. But I was also aware that she had been living alone for a long time. That she had gone straight from the Richmond house at nine to a boarding school, then more boarding for college, funded by our father, to university in California, and then back to London for her PhD. It had been a long time, I realized, since she had relied on another person for anything at all. She seemed more comfortable in her own company than she did in mine. I found that she avoided eye contact, as one might do with a stranger in line at a coffee shop. She couldn't relax around me. I understood it. She was not at home in mine.

So, I tried to stay out of it. Her therapist, who she video-called three times a week, had warned against me hovering, overwhelming or stifling her so that she became resentful and closed off. At least here, I could keep an eye on her. I tried to stop myself from counting her tablets, checking the day-labelled dispensing boxes to make sure she had taken the correct dosage. I stopped myself from hiding all the razorblades in the bathroom, from letting myself into the bedroom while she was taking a shower to search her things for potential weapons of self-destruction.

I felt myself becoming exhausted in my obsession with my sister's mortality.

I took the bus home from work and watched the oncoming cars from the top deck. The air was warm, the school year almost over, the summer equinox upon us. Beanie's last exam. New beginnings for all of us as we charged headfirst into this unknown.

With each in-breath, each car that passed by us in the traffic, I thought of Nora's hair and her picked-at fingernails and the way she wrapped her arms around herself as though she were holding all her body parts together, stopping her organs from falling out. The way, as a child, she would find corners to disappear into. With each in-breath, I thought, *please don't die, please don't die, Nora, please don't die.*

And every time I got home and she was still alive, all the breath I was holding, so that my lungs were full to bursting, left my body all at once.

———

On the day of Beanie's last exam, Gus and I took her to an ice-cream café in Shepherd's Bush and we ordered banana splits. And then, because it was a special occasion, we each had a coffee with Tia Maria.

How do you feel? Gus asked her as he sipped his coffee. Feel any lighter?

Beanie shrugged.

I don't feel any different, she said. I've still got a year of college to do, haven't I? So, nothing's changed, really.

She took a deep breath, as though she was going to say more, something else, something important. But she stopped herself and exhaled slowly instead.

I caught Gus's eye.

After the ice cream, she left us in the café to go and meet Dami and a couple of her other friends. Someone was hosting an end-of-exams house party and she wanted to find something to wear before the shops closed.

Stay safe, Gus said, kissing her orange head.

We're proud of you, kid, I said, squeezing her shoulder. And she looked up from underneath her hair and rewarded us with a beaming smile.

I'm proud of me too, she said, as though she had surprised herself with the knowledge.

Once she was gone, Gus sat back down and stretched, content.

You did a good job with her, he said. You've got nothing to worry about.

It was a team effort, I replied, and we clinked coffee mugs.

I felt all the stress leaking out of me as we talked.

Remember the time she found a dead bird in the park and thought she could bring it back to life if she cycled home fast enough? Gus asked, chuckling.

And when she decided she was vegetarian for all of five minutes until you cooked chicken fajitas and she changed her mind?

Our memories were not collective, but independent of one another, because she had lived two separate childhoods. One with me and one with Gus. But our stories had been retold and intertwined and evolved, over those years, that they each felt like a shared experience.

He had undone the top button of his collar, now. And he leaned across the booth, his arms long and corded beneath his shirt.

I missed this, he said.

Missed what? I asked.

He blinked. Banana split, he said eventually.

He picked up our empty bowls and took them over to the counter at the front of the café, and ordered more coffee. I watched him as he did and when he was back, we sat in a contented silence for a little while, sipping.

So, what happened with Lulu? I asked him eventually, surprising myself.

I thought he wouldn't answer. I was taking a risk, asking him. It truly wasn't any of my business. Gus had been with Lulu for several years. I'd always assumed that they would stay together for ever. Maybe even have children.

He shrugged, drawing his hands around his coffee mug and staring down at the table, lost in thought.

I just sort of . . . he started, then stopped himself before continuing. I realized that she wasn't what I was looking for anymore.

What do you mean? She was great.

Okay, rub it in, he said, laughing. No. I don't know. I can't explain it very clearly. We were growing apart and we wanted different things, and I just . . . realized that I didn't really love her anymore. You know? Does that sound bad?

No, it doesn't. It sounds honest.

She felt the same way, if that makes it any better.

You don't have to justify yourself to me.

He smiled a silent thank you.

It wasn't any one big thing, he said. It just happened gradually, over time. But I think it had been there, maybe even from the start. I think I was kidding myself that she was what I thought I needed.

I thought of Richard, and what Beanie had said in the car.

You're settling because he's a safe bet.

And do you know what you need, now?

He glanced up me.

I think so, he said.

That doesn't sound very certain of you, I said teasingly, poking him in the chest. He laughed.

I think I know what I need about as much as you know what you need.

Okay. Sure.

Or maybe a little bit more.

You're a very assertive person, Gus. I think it's maybe a little bit more.

Fine.

I grinned at him and he grinned back. I wasn't entirely sure what we were smiling about.

I wished you'd told, me, though, I said, referring to Lulu. I still don't understand why you didn't.

I don't know if I understand it either, he said.

Want to try and explain?

He cleared his throat. And went to say something. And then thought better of it.

I can't explain, he said. Not yet.

You, I said indignantly, are just like your daughter.

I checked the time and was surprised by how late it was.

I need to get back and look in on Nora, I said.

Be good, Matilda, he said as we hugged goodbye outside.

He said it low and quietly, close to my ear, and I felt his breath on my neck. I broke away from him quickly, not wanting to acknowledge the way his lips so close to my skin made my heart jump. Unexpectedly. I felt my fingertips fizzing on his back.

He pulled away and looked at me hard, as though he was trying to answer a question that nobody had asked. Although maybe the question was in my face, and I didn't even know it.

I thought for one obscene moment that I would reach out and take his collar in my hands, which were still fizzing, and kiss him.

But then a police siren wailed past and the first spatter of rain landed on his nose and the moment passed.

Be good, Gus, I replied, repeating him, and I turned towards the Tube station, trying to ignore the disquiet in my limbs.

I forced myself to not look back.

———

In the middle of the night, Beanie shook my shoulders, whispering softly, Mum, Mum, Mum.

I rolled over, still half asleep. I had been dreaming of the Richmond house, of all of them dead inside again. Felt the tears leaking down my cheeks, not crying, not properly, just the unconscious expression of grief my body made in sleep.

Mum, Mum, Mum.

I woke up with a start and Beanie stood over me.

It's Nora. I don't think she's well.

I flung the covers away from me and let Beanie lead me across the hall to her bedroom. Inside, Nora was crying, wrapped in a duvet, cross-legged on the carpet with her iPhone placed carefully on the floor in front of her, perpendicular to her body. Karo was on speakerphone.

It's four in the morning, I said blearily, as I registered the scene before me. What's happened? Is someone hurt?

Nora looked up at me, her eyes shining, her face a mask of despair.

She won't let me take it back, she said, through sobs that wracked her entire frame.

Take what back? Karo, are you there?

Yes, darling, I'm here, she crackled on the other end of the line.

What's Nora talking about?

I told her, darling, and I'll tell you now, too. I knew this would happen if she moved in with you. That you would poison each other against what I'm trying to do.

She took a prolonged drag of a cigarette between clauses, so that she sounded like this: No respect (drag) no gratitude (drag) nothing (exhale).

Can someone tell me what the fuck's going on? I asked again, now losing patience. I've got to be up for school in two hours.

You can't just ring me in the middle of dinner without warning, darling.

Why not? You do it all the time, I snapped back.

Beanie sat down on the single bed and placed a hand on Nora's shoulder as she dissolved once again into sobs.

Your sister wants her paintings back, darling, said the iPhone.

I leaned against the doorframe and sighed deeply.

Let me guess, I said. She's already signed off on them being used, so nothing can be done.

Nothing can be done, darling, Karoline said at the same time as I spoke the same words.

Nothing can be done, I repeated, this time to Nora.

Mum would've hated it, Matt, Nora told me.

I know she would've, I replied. I don't know why you even let them go in the first place.

Maybe, she said, her voice rising an octave, maybe it was because I was in the middle of a *psychotic fucking break.*

Beanie shushed her and pulled her closer to her.

It's all right, she cooed. It's okay.

Nora, darling, Karoline said on the speakerphone. Nora, I don't want to keep bringing it up, but you signed off on the licensing rights in sound mind. It's not my problem if you've had a change of heart. And it's frankly disturbing that you would suggest that I took advantage of your—

Karo, I'm going to hang up now, I said, and I ended the call while she was still mid-sentence. Nora flopped backwards on Beanie's single bed and dragged the duvet over her head. She made no noise but the duvet shuddered with her sobs. Her dark hair snaked across the cream-colored pillowcase. Beanie sat on the end of the bed and took hold of Nora's left foot, tenderly.

It's okay, she said soothingly. It's all right. It'll be all right.

I sat down on the bed too, next to Beanie, and wrapped an arm around her. In the hospital, Nora had been stoic, emotionless, sardonic and distant. Now it was as though all the feelings she had been holding in for God knew how long all spilled out of her at once. I wanted to hug her, but it felt over-familiar. I couldn't remember the last time I had hugged her, whether she would respond to it, whether it was at all what she wanted or needed. I felt the humiliation that I didn't know whether my sister liked to be hugged, that I didn't know whether she drank tea or coffee, embed itself deep. I felt the knowledge that I had been failing her—over and over again for years—boil away inside me. But I found that I couldn't blame myself. I blamed Karoline instead.

She can't do this, I said quietly.

She can, Beanie replied. You just said that she could.

We're going to stop her, I said, more to myself than to either of them.

We're going to stop her, I repeated. I yanked the duvet away from Nora's face and leaned close into her tear-stained cheeks, so that our noses were almost touching. Her eyes like dinner plates. She flinched away from me.

Listen to me, I told them both. We're going to stop her. We're going to stop this exhibition. We're going to fix this.

I knelt on the floor at their feet and Nora reached out and placed one hand, long fingers and round knuckles, on my head. I felt that I was praying to them both, repenting on the floor of Beanie's bedroom, asking for salvation from the two women wrapped around one another in their pajamas on the single bed. The headlights from the cars on the road outside flickered through the slatted blinds and illuminated our faces sporadically, with pale white light.

Yes, Mum, Beanie said, grinning, encouraging, proud.

We both turned to look at Nora, who was still lying back on the bed, her face parallel with the ceiling. Now she propped herself up onto her elbows.

Okay, she said. Let's fix it.

———

I guess we're here then, I said exactly one week later, as we stepped through the last of the security checks. Border control, the stern-faced guards eyeing us for signs of errant terrorism, a particular death wish. We had lied on Nora's visa about the state of her mental health, but she had been waved through the passport inquisition without issue.

I'd felt my heart in my throat.

Don't say anything stupid, I had thought as I'd approached the desk. Nora had been ahead of me, having already passed through. *Don't say anything stupid, don'tsayanythingstupid.*

What's the purpose of your visit? A woman with one nostril bigger than the other asked, as I peered at her through the grimy security screen.

Cultural? I said, grinning.

She leaned a fraction closer.

Excuse me, ma'am?

I stared into the larger of the two nostrils and, for a moment, thought I could see hell.

I'm visiting an exhibition in San Francisco, I said. Sorry.

And why have you flown into Phoenix?

I stumbled over the words. Last-minute flights. They were a lot cheaper than flying direct so we've rented a van—

Are you planning on working while you're here? she interrupted.

No.

Do you have paperwork showing your onward travel plans?

She sifted through my documents slowly, taking her time, her long pearlescent acrylics catching the edges of the papers. She examined each hotel and Airbnb booking that I had meticulously printed and filed, the camper-van hire agreement, the insurance certificate.

Are you planning to engage in any criminal behavior while you're in the United States? she asked, gazing down at me with eyes that seemed overly suspicious.

What? No, of course not, I gabbled quickly.

She spent another lifetime examining my visa until eventually she stamped my passport and waved me through the Plexiglas gates to the beige-toned Arrivals lounge at Phoenix Sky Harbor International Airport. As soon as we'd stepped off the plane, the air hit us like a slap in the face. Hot, dry, salty to the tongue. Desert air.

This is it, Nora replied as I joined her on the other side of the border control. She still looked a little shiny; she had thrown up a sausage roll during the turbulence on the descent into Arizona.

The exhibition was opening in less than two weeks. I had booked a camper van that would drive us across the Mojave and then a car that would take us up the Pacific Coast Highway. I felt the anxiety crackling like electricity around us. I could tell that Nora was thinking the exact same as me: is this a terrible idea? Have we made a mistake? Can we fix it?

I squeezed Nora's shoulder and grinned at her. Her skin was warm under my hand. Her hair was shiny and clean. It was something. It was better than nothing.

If we were going to fail, we were going to fail together.

My mother's ashes, stowed in a Tupperware container in my backpack, a last-minute addition to my packing, spur of the moment. They had been tucked into the bottom of my wardrobe for two years, but now they seemed to glow red-hot, like newly minted embers. I felt them singing through the layers of fabric, the heat radiating into my skin.

This is it, I agreed.

Beanie skipped up to us having bought a Diet Coke from a nearby vending machine. She wore a pair of novelty heart-shaped sunglasses—eyewear I had never seen and did not know she owned until this very moment.

This is fucking it, she agreed.

EXTRACT FROM CHAPTER 12, INGRID OLSSEN:
VISIONARY BY RICHARD TAPER (FORTHCOMING
FROM ORANGE RABBIT PRESS)

Grift House Art Festival is known today as one of the most exclusive art fairs in the world, with millions of dollars exchanging hands in the buying and selling of the world's most coveted pieces. Once a year in September, the iconic purple Grift House marquee overtakes the banks of the Serpentine in Hyde Park, London. Desirables from the world over are invited to the festival to browse the crème de la crème of contemporary art. The festival's origins is in *Grift House*, the magazine known as the first word in contemporary art criticism, with a particular specialism in Western European oils.*

Opened for the first time in 1996, the Grift House Festival represented a shifting dynamic in the contemporary art landscape in the West. No longer was this high prestige culture reserved for the elite: it was accessible to anyone who thought to turn up to the box office at Marble Arch on a Wednesday morning and buy themselves a general admission ticket for £5.50, as it was in 1996. These days, the price of entry to Grift House will set the layman back around £49, while VIP entry—with its own private drinks receptions, private lounges, and, of course, access to the notorious fleet of complimentary Mercedes Benzes, which will whisk passengers to any destination of their choosing in the Greater London area—can run into the thousands. VIPs tend to number European aristocrats, Chinese investment bankers with billions of liquid dollars ready to be tied up in assets, the occasional celebrity, and representatives of multinational hedge funds looking to diversify investment portfolios for their clients. While Grift House is ostensibly for everyone, it is only those with a net worth of several commas—from Charles

* Incidentally, my own first profile, as a newly fledged culture journalist, was on the late Ingrid Olssen in 2006, shortly before her father died, and it was published in *Grift House*.

Saatchi to Roman Abramovich to Jeff Bezos to Beyoncé—who can truly treat the fair as a marketplace, a place to buy and sell. Otherwise, the Grift House Art Festival serves as a bizarre yet beautiful spectacle for those who are just browsing, interested in whatever is new and exciting and fashionable on the scene.

The 1990s represented—through the inauguration of Grift House and other festivals of its ilk—a new frontier in the contemporary art space. Gone was the high culture approach, the gatekeeping of the likes of Ingrid Olssen's mentor, Maurice Hoffmann, whose meticulous linocuts were sold in the smoky members' clubs of Mayfair and Bloomsbury in auctions to exclusive audiences of five or ten. The democratization of art ownership came too with its inevitable commercialization. Olssen experienced this herself for the first time in 1982, with the purchase of the entire collection by Pete Burns of the Eurodisco synth-pop band Dead or Alive at her debut show in London, *Ingrid Olssen: Neighborhood Book*. In the intervening years, the price of commercial art exploded. Pieces that were worth tens of thousands in the sixties and seventies frequently sell for tens of millions at Grift House today.

The landscape of contemporary art was in a state of flux when Ingrid Olssen was invited to exhibit at Grift House for the first time in its sophomore year, 1997. Olssen was a working artist maneuvering a landscape that was entirely divorced from her own apprenticeship under Hoffmann. As a purist, Olssen had rarely brought her work to auction. She had sold *Edward and me on a bed of lies* (egg tempera, 1986) to the National Gallery in Oslo a year or two before she exhibited at Grift House. *Girls* was loaned indefinitely to the National Portrait Gallery upon Olssen's receipt of an undisclosed stipend in the early 2000s. It's not clear why Olssen (who infamously spat at the art collector, Oakland Frink, in a Soho strip club when he asked whether she would be willing to sell to him) chose to sell one of her most famous works to the Norwegian National Gallery. Her eldest daughter, Matilda Robb, speculates that by the end of 1995, Olssen was in a state of severe debt that effectively amounted to her living in high-functioning poverty. Friends from the period recall that, when visiting Olssen at her studio in her Richmond home, they would often find that the electricity had been shut off and Olssen was working by candlelight, or that there was no hot water.

That year, Olssen had given birth to her second daughter, Nora Robb, with her estranged husband, the television actor, Edward Robb. Weeks after Nora's birth, Robb had returned to the United States without his wife and two young daughters, and had filed for divorce at a Los Angeles County courthouse, in a legal battle that lasted years as both Olssen and Robb underwent lengthy court proceedings to determine the distribution of their shared assets. The divorce was not finalized until early 2000. Notably—and unusually—Olssen and Robb were fighting over their two young daughters. Not, as one might assume, to haggle over custody. As recently uncovered civil court documents reveal, both parties were asking the court that the other person took custody of the girls. Bizarrely, neither Robb nor Olssen wanted to take responsibility for the care of their children.

Matilda Robb, who at the time of her parents' separation was eight years old, recalls that Olssen's drinking had increased to worrying levels around the same time. We also know that at this time, following reports in the British tabloids, Olssen's night-time pursuits—which mainly took place in the company of her clique of models, musicians and photographers at popular nightclubs the Jinty and Billy's—increased in both frequency and intensity. Four weeks after Robb filed for divorce, Olssen was exposed in the *News of the World* for attempting to buy cocaine from an undercover reporter in an Islington squat. Meanwhile, her daughters seemed to be left home unsupervised for hours and days at a time.

"No one ever asks where my dad was, why he wasn't looking after us," Nora points out in our interview when I put this to her. "People are only ever angry at my mum." At the time of writing,

neither Nora nor Matilda are aware that Olssen was actively trying to relinquish custody of her daughters during this period.

On the state of her finances, Matilda notes that Ingrid Olssen
had a habit of lending money to friends and losing track of who
owed her what.

"When I was ten, my mother took me to the bank with a photographer friend of hers, withdrew two thousand in cash, and
handed it all over to him," she tells me. "I never saw him again. All
I remember is that his name was Pinky and his two front teeth were
missing. I once asked her about it when she was in her fifties, dying
of cancer, and she denied that it ever happened. I've always wondered how many more Pinkies there were in her life. Probably far
more than any of us ever knew."

It was against this backdrop of financial chaos, the breakdown
of her marriage, and the most intense press scrutiny of her career,
that Ingrid Olssen made her debut at Grift House. At thirty-four,
Olssen was too old to be a prodigy and too young to be a safe
bet. Grift House represented more than an opportunity to stabi-
lize her career and—if things went well—her finances. It was a
chance for Olssen to reinvigorate her image, to remind her audience of her undisputed genius in oil, and to draw the attention of
the world's media back to her work, rather than her personal life.

"Suffice to say," her sister and manager, Karoline Olssen,
remembers, "Grift House did not go well."

Olssen entertained the great and powerful at Grift House that
year. She had much working in her favor. She was a master of oil
portraiture, an evergreen medium, which, at the time of her debut,
was notably popular and performing well in European markets. It
was common knowledge that Olssen had a problem with both alcohol and stimulants, but in the VIP lounge she was reported as
seeming cogent, articulate and sober. Contemporaneous reports
even called her lively and witty.

"The problem started when someone from Associated Funding
approached us," Karoline tells me.

Associated Funding, today known as one of the largest financial services and investment banks in the world, headquartered in
Denmark with equity of around sixty billion euros, was relatively
unknown to Olssen when a representative from the bank offered
to buy some of her work.

The work in question is *My burial*, an oil on canvas from 1995,
which is now a typical example of Olssen's mid-career portraiture
style. The piece, printed on page 92, incorporates elements of
Olssen's imperfectly depicted backgrounds, her aggressively
anti-symbolic approach to self-portraiture, which challenges
viewers to establish personal meaning, to become an active par-
ticipant in the articulation of the work's purpose. Olssen never
spoke of the intention behind her compositions. Nevertheless,
My burial is clearly a deeply transgressive piece of work. It is
often interpreted by critics as politically motivated and steeped
in the edicts of second-wave feminist thought: anti-motherhood,
a rejection of biological essentialism and an attack on the
patriarcho-capitalist familial establishment, all in one. The grave
depicted in *My burial* was constructed in the living room of Olssen's Richmond house with the help of two carpenters and a
gravedigger from nearby Mortlake cemetery. Olssen—heavily
pregnant at the time the painting was completed, and visibly so in
My burial—suspended a full-length gilt-framed mirror from the
ceiling of her studio, and painted while lying flat on her back, and
naked, in the grave. After the painting was complete, Olssen
buried all of her preparatory drawings for the piece, including
sketches and studies, as well as the mirror, in the grave, and had
it re-filled with cement and the floorboards replaced.* Karoline
Olssen attempted to recover these studies after Ingrid's death, in
2019, but found that the vibrations from the pneumatic drill used

---

* Nora Robb's 2015 performance piece, also titled *My burial*, was conceived in direct response to
Olssen's oil on canvas. *My burial* (2015) developed for Robb a degree of notoriety on the California art scene—where she was studying at the time—that ultimately catapulted her to international renown, a curious echo of her mother's career trajectory at a similar age.

to break up the concrete had destroyed the fragile cartridge paper embedded inside.

According to Karoline Olssen, the representative from Associated Funding offered six hundred and thirty thousand dollars (approximately one million sterling in 2020) for *My burial*. The offer was made to Karoline, rather than Ingrid, as is customary at Grift House and other similar art fairs. As Ingrid's representative—her manager and agent—Karoline was charged with not only managing the finances of the Ingrid Olssen machine, she was also the conduit through which all business dealings travelled to Ingrid.

"It is not unusual for an artist's management to accept an offer of purchase without first consulting with the artist themselves," Karoline Olssen notes, though in my fifteen-year career as a culture writer, conversations with other artists suggest the contrary. Karoline nevertheless insists that it was completely ordinary for her to accept Associated Funding's offer to purchase *My burial* without having a conversation with her client.

Associated Funding and other banks like it use art as an asset for its near-guaranteed appreciation in value over long periods of time. For cautious hedge-fund managers, contemporary art—if one knows what they are looking for—is a solid, worthwhile and reliable investment. Most of the work purchased in this way never sees a gallery floor: it is stored away in bank vaults, until a time that its valuation appreciates so much that it is sold at a profit to benefit the bank's clients.

"I don't know what Associated Funding wanted to do with *My burial*," Karoline tells me during one of our conversations in her kitchen garden as she lights another cigarette with the click of an oven lighter. "It's not my business. All I wanted to do was my job, which on that day was to sell Ingrid's work to the highest bidder, so she could clear her debts and keep the lights on for her children, since their American trash father was about as useful as a cheese teapot.

"My own father often said to us this: don't sell the hide until you've shot the bear. That night I told Ingrid that we had sold *My burial*, that her financial problems were over. With all the ugliness around her divorce in the press, the photographers camping out on the green opposite her home, trying to catch a picture of her in an unflattering state—which they often did, because she was very often off the wagon—this was what we needed to take control of the narrative that had been building up around her for some time. Ingrid was about to become one of the most well-regarded, critically beloved modern artists in Europe. The sale of *My burial* was going to be the thing to cement it for us. It would drive up the price of all her other works. It would give us many, many opportunities to build her profile and improve the value of her portfolio.

"But things went wrong."

There are several accounts of what happened at Grift House that year. Oakland Frink, who insists he was in the room on the night in question (though this cannot be corroborated by any third party that I have interviewed about the incident), tells me that Ingrid Olssen was "tripping balls" when her sister-manager-agent announced to everyone that *My burial* had been sold. Another source tells me that Raymond Callow, star of the blockbuster war epic of that summer, *Four Hundred Chariots of Men*, had just propositioned her in quite rude terms, and she had thrown a nearby candelabra at him in response. I've also heard reports of a bomb scare and a rabid dog that had somehow been let loose in the VIP suite. These also cannot be corroborated.

What everyone who was definitely there that night agrees on, is that Ingrid Olssen, upon hearing the name of the buyer of *My burial*—Associated Funding Investment Bank—lifted the thirty-eight kilogram frame herself and put her foot through the canvas.

"She didn't just destroy that painting," Karoline Olssen reminisces. "She also ruined any chance of ever being taken seriously as a contemporary artist, ever again."

"No one thought it was cute," Oakland Frink tells me.

"Everyone thought Ingrid Olssen was batshit insane. And, by the way, she absolutely was."

Raymond Callow, star of *Four Hundred Chariots of Men*, did not respond to my request for comment.

Ingrid Olssen left the VIP tent immediately after destroying *My burial*, and did not return to the festival. She was not seen for several days.

"Six hundred thousand dollars, gone, just like that." Karoline snaps her fingers dramatically as she recounts the story.

I ask her what she said to Ingrid when she finally saw her again the following week, returning to the Richmond house in the same clothes she'd worn at Grift House.

"I shouted at her. I said to her, 'You seem to be hell-bent on assuring your own self-destruction.'"

And what did Ingrid say in response?

"I will never forget it. She said, 'Darling, this is not self-destruction. This is self-preservation.'"

CHAPTER 15

We spent our first day in the Sonoran Desert
disoriented.

We collected our rented camper van from the kiosk at the airport. Everything was yellow: the walls, the furniture in the waiting areas, the marble-
esque super-shiny floors with flecks of brown flintstone. Even the sky outside,
seen through a window crusted with dirt, though the most crystalline blue
directly above, diffused into a haze of yellow particulate pollution the closer
the eye drew to the horizon, and the city sprawled out like an oil spillage
through the trough of the Salt River Valley, the mountains from the South
range ominous distant grey obelisks.

Did you ever visit Arizona when you lived out here? I asked Nora as we
waited in line at the car rental desk.

She shook her head.

I still don't understand why we couldn't have flown straight to San Francisco, Beanie said, narrowing her eyes as she glared at her phone, trying to
access the airport Wi-Fi to check her DMs, or whatever.

Because it was about a third of the price to fly to Arizona, I said. And
because of this.

I yanked my backpack open to let the Tupperware peek out through the
open zip. She glanced up and registered it.

Is that . . . *Grandma*?

I nodded grimly.

Is that, like, even legal, Mum? Transporting human remains into the States?

I shrugged. I don't know. I didn't check.

Nora was staring at my bag, too.

She *did* tell us to throw her into a canyon when she died, Nora said.

I know, I replied. I guess it wasn't clear which canyon she was talking about.

No. Nora put on Mum's accent then: Throw them in a canyon. I don't care. Just as long as you don't take me back to that shit hole.

I shot her a look. Her imitation of Mum's voice was uncanny, unnerving, in its accuracy. It made my stomach flip.

What shit hole? Beanie asked.

Ringerike, Nora and I replied at the same time.

Best avoid the whole of the Scandinavian peninsula to be on the safe side, I said.

Best avoid the whole continent, Nora agreed.

And here we are, I concluded.

Put it away, Beanie said urgently, shoving her hands over the opening of my bag to obscure the grey soot inside the translucent plastic.

When we got to the front of the queue, an attendant—a girl who must have been no more than seventeen with acne blossoming across her cheeks—took us to our camper van. The van was a five-seater camper, a Ford E-150 with a sofa that folded out into a queen-sized bed in the back, and when the rear doors were opened, there was a miniature camping kitchen including a tiny sink, a water tank and a gas-cartridge stove. It was just about big enough to sleep the three of us, but only because Nora and Beanie were both five feet three.

Do you think we could maybe get one that's a bit less ostentatious? I asked her, eying the custom paint job on the side of the van. Wrapped around the edges of the vehicle were tendrils of bright orange and red flames against the original black paintwork.

You can upgrade to a different model. We have a T-350 available for an additional six hundred dollars, the girl replied, bored. But that one's got a Jessica Rabbit paint job on it, sooo . . . The girl trailed off expectantly. I noticed then that Beanie had gone bright red.

Mum, just leave it, she said, stage-whispering to me. I'm so sorry, she said to the girl, blushing deeper.

What are you getting so weird about? I asked her, confused. She threw up her hands and walked away. Are you *sure* you haven't got anything without the flames on it? Or Jessica Rabbit? I asked again.

Nora opened the side door and climbed inside.

This is fine, Matt, she said.

Ma'am, I've got customers waiting, the girl replied. If you're not going to upgrade, I just need a signature on your paperwork.

Mum. Just sign the thing.

I shrugged and signed the paperwork, while Beanie, apparently mortified, climbed into the passenger seat and slumped down, as though she were hoping to disappear from view.

The car-hire girl gave me a quick run-down of the rental rules and showed me how to fill the water tank for the sink. We would drop the van off in Los Angeles, switching it out for a rental car for the final leg of the trip.

You're so embarrassing, Beanie said, after the attendant had disappeared. She popped a piece of gum in her mouth.

Chew with your mouth closed, kid. That's gross.

She slid her headphones on over orange hair.

I felt all the breath leave my body with a long exhale as I walked round to the other side of the van and climbed into the driver's seat.

The multistorey parking lot was covered over with thick concrete, dark and echoey. I put the van into reverse and shot it across the car park, almost smashing it into a pillar before slamming on the brakes at the last moment.

Fuck, I muttered. Nora, who had been in the back section of the van, shoving all of our luggage underneath the seats, now appeared at my shoulder.

Do you need a hand? she asked. I've driven automatics in the States before.

It's not that it's an automatic, I snapped at her. It's the size of it.

Are you sure?

Yep. It's all fine. Put your seatbelt on, please.

I bunny-hopped out of the parking space, my foot tentatively nudging the gas pedal.

The accelerator's really sensitive, I explained to Nora and Beanie.

Yeah, okay, Beanie replied. She had pulled her headphones off and was now clutching the passenger-side handle with both hands.

You don't need to be so dramatic, I said.

I finally got us out of the parking lot. The van bounced up and down with each touch of the throttle. No one said anything about the clattering of cutlery and crockery that could be heard in the mini-kitchen at the back of the van.

I'll replace those, I said quietly, as we heard the distinct sound of something smashing.

At the first set of traffic lights, I forgot how to brake, forgot there was no clutch, and came to a screeching halt that threw all of us forward. Nora's head bounced off the back of Beanie's headrest.

Mum, Beanie said loudly, urgently.

I really can drive, if you want, Nora said, pretending not to clutch at her forehead.

I felt my hands gripping the steering wheel, my fingernails making indentations in the plastic skin of it.

Fine, quickly, I said, defeated.

We hopped out of the van and swapped places, just as the lights turned green and a queue of cars was forming behind us. As soon as I opened the door, the heat hit me like a slap in the face. Oppressive, close, claustrophobic. I was momentarily stunned.

What the heck are you doing? a man in the car behind shouted from his open window, his hand firmly on the horn.

I waved an apology and strapped myself into the back of the van. Nora put the vehicle into drive and pulled away smoothly from the lights.

Thanks, I said, feeling my own face glow hot from the desert sun. Sweat dampening the backs of my ears.

Where are we going? she asked.

She drove us into downtown Phoenix while I pulled up the motel information on my phone.

I thought that we would want a proper bed for the first night, I explained. It was four p.m. local time but around midnight in the UK, with all of us having been awake for at least twenty-four hours, if not longer. The flight had been turbulent and I could still smell the sausage-roll vomit on Nora's breath, mixed in with the dusty air-conditioner scent of the van.

We pulled into the motel and Nora parked the van expertly. I felt my pulse slow a little as soon as the ignition died. Outside, in the lot beside a busy multi-lane highway, the sun was relentless: on the concrete, on the van, on the walls of the buildings. There were no people, only cars, speeding past us at sixty miles per hour, huge American cars with thick tires and aggressively large hoods with sparkling paint jobs that demanded space and attention. I had only been to the United States once before, visiting Nora in hospital after her second suicide attempt. I had spent much of that time inside the walls of Cedars-Sinai. I hadn't thought to take a walk in the city and observe anything at all. Now, I let the bigness of Phoenix—the vastness of it—settle over me. I realized my sunglasses were packed somewhere deep and inaccessible in my hold luggage. My ears still hadn't popped from the flight and I couldn't remember the last time I had drunk anything.

We're here, I said.

Yep, Beanie replied.

Twenty minutes later we clambered into our room—two doubles and a single bed with dated décor and the distinct smell of decades of stale smoke. The carpet—a swirly brown pattern—looked like it hadn't been vacuumed in twenty years. The air conditioner, which was rattling ominously, had been screwed into the ceiling with bolts that looked like they might give at any moment. Beanie followed me into the small, green en suite. I pulled back the shower curtain to inspect the bath.

Ugh, spider, Beanie jabbered, pointing down at the edge of the bathtub.

I looked down at it. No, not a spider. But a pair of used and discarded false eyelashes, clumpy with mascara. Beanie gagged.

Let's get another room, I said.

No—don't, Beanie answered. Just leave it. She took a tissue and plucked up the eyelashes, which were stuck to one another, and flushed them down the toilet.

That's what you get when you book literally the cheapest room in the whole city, Nora said slyly, observing us from the doorway.

We each showered quickly and tried our best not to touch anything at all. Then, with the gunk of international air travel washed away, teeth brushed, hair washed, we stepped out onto the street. Our midnight-thinking, sleep-deprived eyes squinted up at the bright sky.

God, Nora said. In the desert heat she seemed even paler than she did back in London. She slotted a pair of enormous bug-eye-shaped sunglasses onto her face and didn't take them off for the rest of the day.

We walked the broad sidewalk, past an abandoned gas station, a super-market, and a cream-colored apartment block built in the style of a Mediter-ranean villa. We walked north towards the central downtown area. I felt sweat pooling in my lower back.

Where is everyone else? Beanie asked offhandedly.

She was right. There were no other pedestrians on the street. Only cars whipping by on the multi-lane road to our right. We continued walking and the scenery began to change: still the broad, flat streets and wide sidewalks, but now in addition to colonial-style white mansions with signage indicat-ing university buildings, schools and government departments. Still, we saw no one.

Everything was so big, there was too much space between the buildings.

We got to a newly built mall, with a metallic, angular façade.

Great, let's eat, I said. I'm starving.

We walked through the mall, which had mostly shopfronts facing out-wards into a concrete plaza with a water feature. Juice bars, clothing shops and package-vacation providers intermingled. A few teenagers—just out of school, maybe—hung around outside a frozen yoghurt hole-in-the-wall. Most of the other shops and restaurants were closed.

What is this place? I asked Nora, as though, having lived in California, she might know the local idiosyncrasies of central Arizona. She just shrugged.

Can we find somewhere else? Beanie asked, glancing nervously at the frozen yoghurt teens. There's nothing here.

There's something there, I said, pointing to a restaurant at the edge of the complex, which clearly had clientele. I could see them through glass panes, perched on the barstools and tables on the pavement outside. Through the glass, an American football game played on flatscreens mounted on the dark mahogany-paneled walls. On the door a sign read: NO FIREARMS ALLOWED, with a big red circle and slash through an illustration of a revolver.

Why don't we just go here? I said, striding towards it. Come on.

Mattie, Nora said, that's a Hooters.

I stopped and looked at her, trying to weigh up her expression.

So? I asked.

She held my gaze a little longer. Beanie was quiet.

You know what a Hooters is, right?

Yeah, I said, sounding—I realized—a little petulant.

Fine, Nora said eventually after a weighted pause. Let's go.

We ate burgers. Nora picked at her food like it was trying to poison her, and left most of it on her plate. We were served by an exceedingly polite, beautiful, tanned, athletic-bodied woman named Casey.

Beans, I said quietly, as Casey took our orders and sauntered back to the bar in hot pants that looked as though they might be cutting off her circulation. It's rude to stare.

Beanie's cheeks bloomed red. *Mum* . . .

She went to the bathroom and didn't come out for twenty minutes.

Let her chill out a bit, Nora said quietly when Beanie disappeared.

What do you mean, *let her chill out*? What is that supposed to mean?

Nora raised her eyebrows behind her sunglasses and took a sip from a glass of Coke the size of her head. The Hooters was fairly empty, despite the initial impression it had given from the outside. It was early afternoon on a weekday, I supposed. Only a couple of men in their forties, both wearing flannel, sat at the bar, and a family of four in a corner booth.

Who's taking their kids to Hooters? I nudged Nora, pointing out the couple with the ten-year-old-looking twins.

She gave me another pointed look.

You're rolling your eyes at me? I accused Nora, a hard edge to my voice.

She ignored me, and I felt an immediate stab of guilt. The lack of sleep was getting to me.

I'm sorry, I said quietly.

Yeah, okay, she replied. She flipped her hair back, away from her face.

We've got two weeks sleeping together on one bed in the back of a van, she said.

I know, I replied, glancing over to the bathroom door.

Who the fuck's idea was that?

It was yours, actually.

My phone buzzed in my pocket. It was Richard. Nora saw the caller ID.

He's probably in San Francisco already, with Karoline, I said. He doesn't know what we're doing. That we're here. I didn't tell him.

Why not?

I thought about it as I took a bite of my cheeseburger.

I don't know, I said eventually.

She grinned, as though that was the answer she was expecting me to give her.

I do, she said, her voice weighty with meaning. Do you remember Guernsey Steve?

God. How could I ever forget Guernsey Steve.

He had been one of Mum's boyfriends after she and Dad had finalized the divorce, sometime in the early aughties.

There had been a lot of boyfriends after the divorce. They'd paraded in and out of the house like a police line-up. All of them smelled of cigarettes. Some of them had been okay. They'd bought me and Nora candy and had filled the cupboards with food and gave us stuffed toys that we were too old for, and Disney VHS videotapes for a TV that didn't work. Others had liked to pretend that we didn't exist. They'd not been there for us, after all. They'd been there for Mum and whatever had gone on behind the locked door to her studio. If we'd left them alone, they'd left us alone. Most of the boyfriends had been around for a week or two before they'd gone, and we would never see them again. After the first few, Nora and I had learned to stay away. The short term ones hadn't been the problem. I was fourteen and Nora six when Steve had moved in for four months.

I liked Mum with him, though, I said, and Nora nodded. Those months had been the most normal time we had spent together as a family since before Nora was born.

We went to the zoo.

Steve liked to take photographs of Mum. He made her go to the dentist's and fix the tooth that had been slowly rupturing and rotting in the back of her mouth, sending spikes of pain into her skull, since Dad left. Steve wasn't into the club scene. He liked to go to bed at ten o'clock every night. So, Mum went to bed at the same time as him.

Guernsey Steve's specialty was lamb ragu with homemade pasta. He had a special machine for it. He taught me how to make a tomato base from scratch. None of that jar sauce shit, he would say. Here's how you get the most flavor out of your tomatoes, he would say, joint hanging from his mouth as he smooshed the fruit beneath the flat blade of a knife so that the flesh and pulp seeped out from beneath it. The first step, he said through his teeth, is to buy them on the vine. Or even better, grow your own.

Mum wasn't disappearing so much, both from the house and from her head, wasn't dropping wine glasses on the bathroom floor and forgetting to clean up the shards of glass.

Nora was six, and she knew what was about to happen. She knew it better than I did, and I should have known better. Should have known not to get too invested, not to let him embed himself into the fabric of our lives. Nora had started to pull out her own eyelashes.

The day Guernsey Steve disappeared, we woke up one morning and came into the kitchen to find Mum wrapped around a bottle of champagne, in the conservatory. She was asleep, shivering, cheeks wet with tears.

I had grown to have no patience for it by the time I was fourteen. It was a pattern that had repeated so many times that it had lost all meaning to me. I had thought that this one would be different. I liked Guernsey Steve. I wondered what she had done to drive him away.

I knew that it must have been her fault, because, well, look at her.

I loved her with all my heart. But I knew what she was.

I smoothed her hair and wiped the drying tears from her cheeks, and got Nora dressed for school—she was still going at that time—and walked her right up to the gates with a backpack stuffed with peanut butter sandwiches and loose watercolor pencils.

Mum didn't come home that night, or the night after. I remember because I lost my virginity to Gus in the back of his car the same weekend, in the car park for Chobham Common, and he gave me a pressed flower, delicately held between the pages of a 1920s edition of *Wuthering Heights*, and I told him he was being a little on the nose and that I never wanted to see him again. Of course I didn't mean it. I couldn't stop smiling and running my fingers across the binding, as though it were a sacred object.

That Sunday, after Guernsey Steve disappeared and Mum not long after, Aunt Karoline was hammering at the front door of the Richmond house. I rolled out of Mum's bed, where Nora and I slept when she was gone, and answered it.

Where is she? she said, pushing past me.

I don't know, she hasn't been home since Wednesday, I said, rubbing sleep out of my eyes. Can you keep your voice down? Nora's sleeping.

Karoline placed a loaf of bread and a pint of milk—the glass-bottle kind that gets delivered by the milkman—on the kitchen sideboard. She was holding a newspaper, folded over on the gossip pages.

Let me see that, I said, snatching at the paper. Did you steal that milk off someone's doorstep?

She let me take the newspaper from her hands.

It wasn't the first time Karoline had burst into the house with a paper tucked under her arm, with something salacious to do with Mum in the newsprint inside. This time, two pages were dedicated to MY WHIRLWIND ROMANCE WITH INGRID. There were pictures, too, of Guernsey Steve and Mum. At the beach, holding hands on the pier, in the garden on a picnic blanket, her head delicately nestled in the lap of his jeans, glowing up at him with all the force of her being. She had put on a little weight, and her skin was sun-dappled, her hair clean and combed. She had started to eat a little more and drink a little less since Guernsey Steve had arrived, and she looked healthier for it.

When Karoline finally found her days later, catatonic in the upstairs bathroom of an opium dealer's apartment off New Kent Road, we learned that he'd taken money from her, too. Just like Pinky with no front teeth had.

Yeah, I remember Guernsey Steve, I told Nora.

Richard reminds me a bit of Guernsey Steve.

I stared at her.

That's a horrible thing to say, I said, a little shocked.

Don't you think there's something about him? You told Gus—your ex—that you're coming here, what we're planning, didn't you? But you didn't tell your actual boyfriend? What does that tell you about how much you trust him?

I scoffed. Yes. But that's different.

How is it different?

Gus isn't just an ex, is he? He's also the father of my daughter.

And what else?

What do you mean, what else?

Don't pretend like you're an idiot, Matilda.

I went to say something further but Beanie arrived back from the bathroom then, and as we sat there staring at our half-eaten onion rings, our nose hairs burning with the potent scent of highly sugared BBQ sauce, sleep became inevitable.

Beans, let's toast the end of your exams, I said enthusiastically, and she relented, let the sullen look on her face slide away. She picked up her own Coke and we clinked our glasses in the center of the table.

And let's toast Nora being out of the secure unit, Beanie said, and I glanced at Nora, worried that this might have been the wrong thing to say. But she shrugged and clinked again, took a long drink.

Yep, fully cured and mentally stable, that's me, she said. Smuggling my dead mother into another country. Having a completely normal one.

Have you taken your meds? I asked sincerely, and she spluttered into her Coke.

Shut up, Mattie, fuck.

I'm serious.

I couldn't keep track of her pill schedule, now that we had changed time zones.

Remember what I said, she replied. Just chill.

We walked back to the motel, dazed, over-full with red meat and caffeine, blinking in the eighty-six-degree heat, and fell asleep in our clothes, on top of the bed linen, in the stale-smoke room. The air conditioner unit rattled its way into our dreams.

CHAPTER 16

Beanie wanted to go to Target.

Insisted on it, in fact.

We'll stop at one on the way to the Grand Canyon, I said, as we loaded the van up with our luggage the next morning. None of us were functioning on the right amount of sleep. I'd woken up at 4.30 a.m. to the sound of the air-conditioning unit relinquishing its tenuous grip on the ceiling and narrowly missing turning Nora's head into coolant-flavored soup. After that, all of us were too awake, too wired to go back to sleep. I complained about the murderous AC to the twenty-four-hour front desk while Nora showered and Beanie scrolled lip-sync videos on her phone. The receptionist apologized and offered us a free breakfast, which turned out to be a cellophane-wrapped pain au chocolat out of a vending machine. It had been treated with some chemical that meant it would never spoil, like a fast food hamburger. I wondered how long it had been in the vending machine, waiting to be purchased or offered as consolation for a near death experience, as I chewed on the artificially sweet brioche.

Got Mum? I asked Nora. She reached behind the passenger seat and patted the car-company-issued cooler.

I thought it was more dignified to put her here, rather than stuffed into your backpack next to your panty liners, she explained.

Do you think there are drug dealers here? Beanie asked, eying the sign for the motel suspiciously. It was a piece of thick vinyl tarpaulin declaring

VALLEY B&B 24 HR CHECK IN, draped over another, older sign, which was illegible under the thick plastic.

We pulled out of the motel, with me behind the wheel this time, having done a few practice turns of the parking lot. I just about had the measure of the gas pedal, and the bunny-hopping was gone.

We chose Foo Fighters for the 140-mile drive north to our first stop. As we left the city limits, the flatness of the valley basin gave way to rugged orange-and-brown hills speckled with different species of cacti, which softened the edges of the hard desert landscape. Even this early in the morning, the sun was hard and hot, and though the van was air conditioned, Beanie insisted on having the windows down. The sky was bright and broad and effortless, just like everything else in Arizona, bigger than any equivalent landscape in London. The scale was incomprehensible to me, someone who had spent my whole life maneuvering myself around terraced houses and squat, square public housing blocks. The glorious concrete vista of the A4, the Great West Road, was visible or at least audible from the open window of any place I had ever called home. It seemed impossible that there could ever be so much of the sky. The van whipped up tan-colored dust as we put stretches of asphalt between us and downtown Phoenix.

Beanie hung out of the window to catch the breeze. She let her arms loose, away from the van, so that the velocity of the wind threaded through her fingers and kept her hand elevated like a parachute catching the upthrust. She smiled into the morning sunshine eating at us. I worried that she hadn't put on enough SPF. On the sofa in the back, Nora slept with a copy of *Fear and Loathing in Las Vegas* over her face, the spine cracked to fan the pages across her pale cheeks.

I felt some of the tension leave my body.

Do you know, I said to Beanie, I think this is the most relaxed I've felt in ages.

What, even though the air conditioner fell on Nora? Beanie asked.

Yep, even though, I replied. Nora wouldn't be Nora if she wasn't facing a near-death experience on the reg.

She slid on her heart-shaped sunglasses and kicked her feet up on the dashboard. Her hair whipped around her face, blended with the desert beyond.

I could see us being from here, she said, and she took my hand and squeezed it.

We arrived in Flagstaff before most of the shops had opened for the day. As we drove further north, the landscape became marginally greener, with juniper trees and firs and spruces lining the streets, the soft fuzz of dry desert grass dusting the loose slate-colored stones beyond the sidewalks. There seemed to be more people around than there had been in Phoenix, and the temperature was about ten degrees cooler too—though still in the low eighties even at breakfast-time. Temporary LED signs advertised overflow parking for a graduation at Northern Arizona University.

Target, Target, Target, Beanie shouted urgently, pointing at the huge brown-bricked building to the right of us as we drove through the central street. Nora stirred and knocked her book off her face with an errant hand.

Beanie dragged us into the supermarket and filled our baskets with American candy that I'd never heard of, but that she insisted was the most delicious thing we'd ever eat. Nora picked up a crate of beer and loaded it onto her trolley.

Are you sure? I asked her, eyeing the alcohol warily.

She rolled her eyes at me.

I am going to be stuck in a van with you for the next two weeks, Matt, she said. Please, for the love of God, let me have this.

Ashes? Beanie asked in the car park as we loaded our treasures into the van. I checked behind the passenger seat for the cooler and thumbs-upped her.

We stashed the food and drink into our mini-kitchen, the storage overflowing with nutritionless junk food—luminescent hard candies, lollipops, American chocolate and Cheetos—and a lone bunch of genetically-improbable bananas that I had added to the checkout as an afterthought. I avoided the curious gaze of early-bird shoppers eyeing our stupid flames paint job on the side of the camper van. Beanie had started calling our transportation the

Flamesmobile. We stacked the bottles of beer in the mini-fridge, though none
of us could figure out how to turn it on.

We're going to die, Nora said, staring at the stash.

At least we'll die caffeinated, Beanie said, grinning as she pulled a vacuum-
wrapped coffee-flavored cake from a plastic bag, like a magician pulling a
rabbit from a hat.

None of us are going to die, I said with a certainty I didn't truly feel, as I
slammed the doors shut.

———————

As we drove on, Beanie became quietly engrossed in her phone, just as
Nora did.

Who's looking forward to the Grand Canyon? I asked cheerily, fiddling
with the stereo after "The Pretender" started up on the aux cable connected
to my phone for the fourth time that morning. I found a local FM station,
which was playing some sort of hybrid country-hip-hop music with lyrics
about freedom, guns and God.

Oh, to penetrate the psyche of Lil Gashy, Nora said ruefully as the song
finished.

Is everyone ignoring me? I asked.

No one's ignoring you, Beanie replied, not taking her eyes off her phone.

Can you put that down for a second? We're on holiday.

Wouldn't exactly call this a holiday, Nora commented from way back by
the mini-kitchen.

This was literally your idea, I said loudly, hearing my tone begin to
prickle.

Erm, no it wasn't, Nora replied.

Then why the fuck are we doing it? I asked.

Because you're on a crusade, Mum, Beanie said. And sometimes it's just
easier to go along with it.

I touched the brake and stuck the hazard lights on, pulling over to the
side of the road on the northern stretch of street leading out of Flagstaff.

You can't stop here, Nora said.

I'm not on a crusade, I replied.

Sure.

I don't go on crusades. What are you talking about?

Yeah, you do. All the time. See exhibit A: we're currently on your crusade.

I thought we'd all agreed to go on this trip together.

Well, we agreed, said Beanie. But only because you would've been impossible to live with if we hadn't.

No, I said firmly. I don't accept that.

Mum, whatever, it's not important, we're here now. Can we just keep driving, please?

Do you think I'm on a crusade? I asked Nora, trying to make eye contact with her via the rear-view mirror. She wouldn't meet my gaze.

Does it matter? she asked, looking back down at her phone.

Have you two been talking about me behind my back?

No, Beanie lied.

Why don't I drive for a bit? Nora said. You can take a nap back here.

She looked at me now, her own eyes ringed with dark shadows. She had a pleading note in her voice.

Okay, I said. I could do with some sleep.

I climbed into the back of the van and lay down on the grey corded sofa cushions that Nora had been lying on moments before. Nora slid into the driver's seat and as we pulled away, started a hushed conversation with Beanie. I let the deep vibrations of the engine lull me to sleep.

It seemed like only minutes later that Beanie was shaking me out of a dream in which Mum was getting married to Guernsey Steve in a minidress and the house was falling down. Mum, she said. Wake up. We're here.

We were. "Here" was a shingled RV park, with picnic benches and electrical hook-ups attached to each oblong pitch. There was space in this park for ten or twelve vehicles, though there were only two parked up on other sites. I sat up swiftly and smacked my head on the lip of the van door. The air was far cooler than it had been down in the desert basin. It felt thinner too, as though we had increased our altitude. Despite this, the sky was still enormous and crystalline, the sun hot and heavy hanging in it.

Disoriented, I rubbed sleep from my eyes and dragged myself out of the

van, running my tongue across the slick film over my teeth. The RV park
was uninteresting. The flat stones were warm against my socks. The signage
towards a smoothly asphaltked road to our left pointed to SHOWER
BLOCK, RESTAURANT, SHUTTLE BUS STOP, HOTEL, GIFT
SHOP, DELI, and SOUTH RIM.

Oh, I said. We're here.

The orange flames of the Flamesmobile winked at me.

My whole body aches, Beanie said, shielding her eyes as she watched a
family on the other side of the campground unload picnic equipment from
their RV.

Tell me about it, Nora replied. She climbed out of the driver's seat and
into the back of the van, into the spot I had just crawled out of, and pulled
her blanket over her head.

What are you doing? I asked her.

I don't feel like doing anything right now, she said, her voice muffled
underneath the blanket.

Don't you want to go and see it?

She didn't reply.

Nora? I asked, a hard edge in my voice.

Mum, leave it, Beanie said, tugging on the strap of my tank top. I had
dressed for the desert, and the sudden change in temperature as we'd moved
through microclimates had sent goosepimples up my arms. I rifled around
in my backpack for a cardigan.

No, let's not *leave it*, I said to Beanie quietly, so that Nora couldn't hear me.
It's the fucking Grand Canyon. She doesn't want to see the Grand Canyon?

She's allowed to *rest*. She just did all that driving so you could go to sleep.

Beanie was right, I realized, a little ashamed of myself.

We need to get rid of Mum's ashes, I said after a while. I dragged the cool
box out from behind the passenger seat and extracted the Tupperware con-
taining the cremated remains of Ingrid Olssen.

Nora muttered something under the blankets.

What? I asked her, and I pulled the blanket covering her mouth back,
reaching over and plucking it from her face.

It's the sertraline, she repeated. It makes me drowsy. It knackers me out.

Oh . . . I said. Okay. That's fine. As long as you're taking it.

I'd rather not be, but.

OK, let's go, I said quietly to Beanie. She gave me a look that suggested I was monstrous, her hair catching snatches of sunlight and glittering in it, and I felt all of the air come out of me.

I'm sorry, I said to her quietly. I'm just. Tired.

Yeah. Me too.

Let's do the ashes later, Beanie said. We can just go and have a look at the South Rim now.

She took my hand, the hand not holding the Tupperware, with a claw-like grip, like she used to when she was a little girl. I didn't have a car back then, when she was tiny, so every morning I walked her to the Church of England primary school, a mile away from the apartment. Her shiny black school shoes and white socks. Knobby knees that were always inexplicably scabbing and bruised. The burgundy sweater with the points of the polo-shirt collar peeking out over the top. Every morning for three years, I wove her long fine hair into one long plait that hung down her back, and every afternoon when she arrived at the school gate, the plait was gone and in its place was a mass of twigs and knots. She was so precious to me. She looked up at me with her enormous brown eyes and said, Mummy, can I hold your hand? And I sang the Beatles to her walking to Gus's parents. I resisted the urge now to do the same. I felt nostalgic for her even as she stood next to me.

We can't leave her here, I told Beanie.

I think the point is that she wants to be alone, Beanie replied.

We walked to the bus stop at the edge of the campsite, where it adjoined the main through-road. The air was still and quiet. Evergreen trees lined the concrete like eyelashes. I had always thought the Grand Canyon would be a tourist trap, but it was eerily empty on the campsite. And no Canyon in sight.

You can't just pretend that it's not happening, Beanie said, as we climbed onto the bus moments later.

Can't pretend what's not happening? I asked.

Because it is, Beanie said, ignoring my question. It is happening.

I have no idea what you're talking about, I lied.

The bus journey was barely a few minutes. It dropped us off at the visitors' center at the top of a slight incline. There were more people now. We dismounted in silence and followed a couple in serious-looking hiking gear through the visitors' center, stopping to read placards about wildlife and sedimentary rock.

Ready? Beanie asked. I nodded. We exited and followed a tour group up through unnecessarily complex roped-off queue management systems.

We got through and came upon a small observation deck, with dark iron bars fencing it in. People everywhere, now.

Let's go and have a look, Beanie said.

I was still holding Mum's ashes.

We walked up to the edge of the rim and I allowed myself to look out at it. I had been expecting to feel some sort of biblical awe, but still I was shattered by it in a way that took me by surprise. The vastness of it, like everything else we had seen since we landed, seemed impossible. It was big, and brown and orange and hot and dusty. It was as though we had shrunk ourselves to the size of pinpricks and we were observing the deep, magisterial and physically improbable complexities of a crack in dry ground. It felt like a microcosm of the universe, the entirety of human experience. In a moment, it was the Big Bang and the history of the world and yet it was foretelling, too. It was beautiful.

What do you think? I asked Beanie.

She ignored me. She stared out at it, the North Rim on the horizon, ten miles away, her jaw unhinged.

Big, she said, her eyes darting around to drink it all in.

Yeah, really big.

We walked around the edge of it on the designated pathway, avoiding the trailheads that led hikers down into the basin on trips that would take them days. We stopped and read placards. We visited a geology museum that sat squat and new on the edge of it, so close that it seemed as though it might topple into the ravine at any moment. We found a big-jutting-out bit of it, flat and smooth, eroded from millions of years of existence on a mortal plane. Hundreds of millions of rubber-soled hiking boots smoothing it out into what it was now.

Do you want to stand at the edge? I asked Beanie.

Oh my God, can you get a picture of me?

Here there was no railing, no bars separating the *up here* from the *down there*. She got as close to the edge as she dared and threw her arms up. A huge beaming smile splitting her face in two.

Now you, she said, after she had posted the picture.

I stepped right up to the edge and looked down. I thought I might see the bottom. But there was no bottom. It seemed to go on forever, as though it might reach the center of the Earth. I smiled tightly while Beanie snapped her photograph.

Did you look down? she asked as I joined her back at the safety of the middle of the ledge. I nodded grimly.

We wandered some more, exclaiming at the size of it, the birds, the few sparse trees clinging onto the sheer drops with slithers of roots. They looked so frail.

We walked back to the entrance to the South Rim, with its restaurant and gift shop. And idled for half an hour, browsing key rings and fridge magnets.

Hey, I said, holding up a fridge magnet with an illustration of the Grand Canyon, and words that exclaimed in bold yellow letters, IT'S SEDIMEN-TARY, BABY. Who would love this?

Beanie examined the fridge magnet. Dad, she said, grinning.

Let's get it for him.

I paid for it and met Beanie outside, thumbing through the likes on her Instagram post.

Eighteen effing dollars, I told her, counting the ones back into my money belt, feeling more like a tourist than ever before.

Dad's worth it, though, Beanie said.

He sure as hell isn't worth an eighteen-dollar fridge magnet. Who is?

She glanced up at me and I saw something hard come into her expression.

Is Richard worth an eighteen-dollar fridge magnet? she asked slyly.

I stared at her, the warmth of the morning we had spent together now gone from her. As though it had never been there.

Like I said, I replied, weighing my words. No one is worth eighteen dollars.

She raised her eyebrows.

Except maybe you, I added, winking at her.

Whatever, she said, but her lip quirked up.

We bought plastic-wrapped sandwiches from the deli and ate them on a park bench that overlooked the Grand Canyon.

Do you feel like this is a completely out-of-body experience? Beanie asked me as we ate.

What do you mean? I asked.

I mean, like, we're *here*. This place actually exists. I never thought I would ever get to see it.

Nor did I, to be honest. Your grandmother talked about it. I get what you mean. It felt like she had made it up. But we're here, and it's real.

Beanie knew the story well. In 1985, my father had taken my mother to Vegas for a shotgun wedding that had scandalized the newspapers and made the pair of them more famous than ever. Then he'd driven them from the chapel to the Grand Canyon in a soft-top Mustang, once they had sobered up. Mum had called it the most formative experience of her life. *More formative than becoming a mother*, she'd often told journalists, which had always been nice to hear. She'd liked to tell me, when I was a child, that I had been conceived somewhere along the Bright Angel Trail halfway down to the Phantom Ranch. I'd believed her at first, before I'd become old enough to know better. I'd realized that Mum had never been one for hiking, even in health. And I'd been born more than a year after her honeymoon.

It's still a nice story, Beanie said.

Yeah, and it's at least forty percent bullshit. I hope she appreciates her final resting place, though.

Excuse me, ma'am, a Park-Ranger-looking type in a broad green hat with a walkie-talkie affixed to his breast pocket said. He wore a shiny gold-colored badge with the name HERNANDEZ printed on it in an official-looking serif. He had approached us quietly from behind our picnic bench, and neither of us had noticed him until he was directly adjacent to us.

I'm sorry to disturb you, he said. He was young-looking, maybe in his mid-twenties, with an enthusiastic expression across his suntanned face.

How can we help you? Beanie asked, for some reason making herself sound more British. I glanced at her, baffled.

I couldn't help but overhear your conversation and I was wondering whether there are ashes in your tub, there.

His walkie-talkie crackled with static. I glanced down at Mum's ashes, and then at Beanie. In a moment I was envisioning the TSA woman at Phoenix Airport, eyeing me, with her ginormous nostrils.

No, I said, at exactly the same time Beanie said yes.

What I meant to say was, Beanie corrected herself quickly, floundering, and then failing to finish her sentence.

Yes? Hernandez asked.

I'm sorry, can I just ask, what exactly is your authority here?

I too found myself now also inexplicably becoming more British-sounding.

I just thought I ought to let you know, Hernandez continued, ignoring my question, that it's illegal to scatter human remains here at the Grand Canyon National Park.

I narrowed my eyes at him.

Well, thank you for that. But these aren't human remains.

I stuffed the Tupperware into the underside of my cardigan, doubling down on the inexplicable lie, while Hernandez rifled through his pockets and produced a comprehensively-folded leaflet.

Park byelaws, he said, by way of explanation. You'll see that there's no ash-scattering allowed, here, or in any of the National Parks, without permission.

Thanks.

Have a good day, ladies, he said, smiling in way that told me that he didn't believe a word of what we had told him. Nevertheless, he tipped his hat to us like a cowboy, and strode away like a cowboy.

I glanced at Beanie, whose eyes were wide like dinner plates, a piece of lettuce hanging out of the corner of her mouth.

Fuck, she said. And then, Why is he walking like he's constipated, though?

CHAPTER 17

We arrived back at the campsite, Mum's ashes stuffed safely down the front of my top.

My ankles ached from the walking and I thought of bathing. There was a shower block a ten-minute walk away and I imagined cool, clean water on my back. But as we approached the van, I saw that there was a second, more ostentatiously painted van pulled up next to our own. Nora had rolled out a blanket on the hot asphalt and was engrossed in her book. She had changed into a sports bra and shorts. Still, she was as pale as the refracted light off the windshield. She looked like perfect trash. Beanie called out to her and she waved us over, shielding her eyes.

I found a friend, Nora explained.

The van that was not ours was the same make and model, even possibly the same year. The two vehicles were identical, besides the fact that the other van had a giant-sized artist's rendering of Abraham Lincoln holding an AK-47 on the side of it.

Oh my shit, I said quietly, involuntarily, to Beanie.

Rounding the corner of our own camper we now saw that Nora was accompanied by a man who looked as though he might be in his sixties, though it was difficult to tell, because he had skin the color and texture of leather. He wore a red baseball cap and a khaki-colored shirt, which was open to the belly. From the sides of his hat sprang snow-white mutton chops, which contrasted starkly with the yellowing tint to his moustache. He was lying on a blanket of his own, and his body jutted out in the opposite direction to Nora, his belly a mound sticking directly up and out. His and Nora's feet faced one another sole to sole. As we approached, he propped himself up onto his elbows, dark sunglasses obscuring most of his narrow face.

Randy, this is my sister and my niece. Mattie, Beans, this is Randy, and this is his van.

Nice to meet you, Randy, I said levelly. I shook his hand, which was rough and calloused. Beanie shot me a what-the-fuck look and crawled into the back of the van. I saw that he too had been reading a book when we returned: his was Victor Hugo's *Les Misérables* and he was reading it in the original French.

Looks like we hired our vans from the same company, I commented, eyeing it up warily.

Only because mine's in the shop, he replied in a thick Southern accent. To be honest, I don't love the paint job.

I laughed, in a way that might have sounded a little too relieved. I've been complaining about ours but I think you might have got it worse, I said.

Beanie banged on the window of our own van, from the inside. I slid the door open a fraction.

Yes? I asked gently.

That man, she hissed, her voice a whisper, looks like he is going to murder us. He looks like he is going to take out one of his guns from the back of his van and one-shot each of us in the head.

I think you're being a bit dramatic, I said.

I think you're being *way too fucking chill* about this, she replied.

God—which is it, Beans—I'm too uptight or I'm not uptight enough? You two need to make up your minds, for crying out loud.

I went to the back of the Flamesmobile, feeling a little defiant, and pulled out Nora's beers.

Randy, can I interest you in a light beer? I asked him, clinking the glass bottles together as I pulled them out of the mini-fridge.

Light beer? he asked, incredulous. What the heck is that, toilet water?

I showed him the cardboard-box crate for the twelve-pack. Oh, honey, he said, laughing.

He opened the door to the Abraham Lincoln camper and yanked out the cool box from behind his passenger side seat, same as ours. He opened it to reveal two unlabeled, plastic, four-liter bottles of a nondescript dark yellow liquid.

What is *that*? Nora asked, lifting her sunglasses with interest.

This, ma'am, is my own special brew.

So . . . it's moonshine?

Sure is. I'm on my way to visit my sister in Vegas. She always asks for a batch of it when I visit. It's the only thing that'll get her to sleep. Same as my wife.

I glanced at Nora as she shrugged and reached out to take the bottle from Randy's proffered hand. She swiftly unscrewed it and took a sip. The jug was so big and so heavy it looked as though her arms might snap under the weight.

We both waited as she assessed the moonshine, swallowing and smacking her lips thoughtfully as she brought the bottle away from her mouth.

Eventually she said, Fuck, that is *stronk*.

Randy was already taking out tin cups from his own mini-kitchen.

I'm going to find a shower, Beanie said loudly, exiting the Flamesmobile with a toiletry bag and a towel.

Want me to come with you? I asked her.

Mum. It's fine, she replied. She gave me another wide-eyed, meaningful stare that, I thought, was supposed to mean *this guy*? I smiled patronizingly back at her. I didn't understand what kind of argument we were having. I took Randy's offered tin cup.

———

It took an hour and a half to realize, drunkenly, that Beanie hadn't come back from the shower. I texted her as, around the picnic bench between the two vans, Randy told us the story of how his sister had won a state award for mukbang. You might know of her, he said. *Teresa Eats*?

Oh my God, Nora said, alert. I actually do know her. She's the one who did the macaroni thing?

Yeah. The macaroni thing. That's her.

I went through a phase of binge-watching her YouTube videos.

I made Nora explain to me again what mukbang was, as I checked my phone for texts from Beanie. I felt as though my body was moving with the same intention and consistency as the trees. Into the wind, and out of it again. The leaves moving with the branches.

A reply from Beanie came: *I'm fine, just went for a walk.*

It was still daytime—too bright to be this day-drunk. Obscenely bright. It wasn't even close to supper.

I would love to talk to her, Nora continued. Teresa, I mean. I'd love to know more about her process.

Her *process*? I asked, incredulous. Isn't it just eating stuff on camera for fetishists?

I still hadn't quite fully grasped the concept of it but that was what it sounded like to me.

I just think there's something inherently vulnerable-making, Nora said, between hiccups. About putting yourself in a position like that on the internet.

I stared at her as Randy shrugged and topped up our drinks with the moonshine, half a bottle down now.

Teresa's going to be mad at us, I said to him, pointing out the moonshine's negative space.

Randy shrugged. Eh, she's got mukbang money, she can brew her own.

What made her want to do it? Nora asked.

What, mukbang? I don't know. I think she just wanted to be famous.

She wanted to create something permanent, Nora agreed. Something that would go on after she left our mortal coil.

No, said Randy. I don't think that's it. I think she just wanted to get sponsored by a fast food chain.

Well, that she did, I said with finality. And we toasted Teresa's success, clinking our tin cups together ceremoniously.

Do you know, Nora said. I'm also kind of famous on the internet.

Nora was swaying with the trees too. On top of the booze, the jetlag was beginning to get to me once again, I thought. I wondered vaguely about the effects of alcohol when mixed with sertraline. The sun baking the dusty concrete we were parked on. The unrelenting heat. The colors around us were all wrong—too luminescent—and the smell of everything was too strong. If I concentrated hard on the particular sensation of the hairs on the backs of my kneecaps, it felt for a moment like I had temporarily left my body.

Oh, really? Randy said, humoring her.

Well, I was. My therapist made me delete all my social media apps from my phone. So I don't know what I am now, she said. The cameras are still running, though. The cameras in my apartment.

She had suddenly changed, the easiness around her conversation with Randy about Teresa the mukbang queen now gone. I thought that she might have forgotten that I was there with her.

What did you do on the internet? Randy asked, curious.

Oh, performance art, she replied. Her voice had a hard edge to it as she spoke. But. You know. I tried to kill myself again. So, I had to stop.

She said it matter-of-factly, as though it were the most normal thing in the world. Like getting fired for being caught stealing paperclips from the stationery cupboard. Oh well, her sigh seemed to say. Them's the breaks.

Nora, I warned. And she blinked at me, confused. What?

I'm sorry, I said to Randy. Maybe we've all had enough to drink. I'm sure you don't want to hear this.

What are you sorry for? he asked me, his face as soft as it had been all afternoon, his eyes sparkling, the corners folded over and unfolded many times so that the lines stretched all the way to his ears. Then he looked at Nora without waiting for me to answer. Why did you try to kill yourself again?

Nora, taken aback that he had asked the question, when so many including me rarely did, shrugged.

I think, she said, that I was trying to prove that I was still a real person. That I still existed.

He nodded as though he understood completely.

My wife shot herself in the neck in our barn in 2009, he said, matching Nora's tone.

God, I'm sorry, I said, again.

Young lady, stop apologizing for things that don't need an apology, he replied.

I resisted the urge to apologize for apologizing. Nora sat very still, despite her alcohol-sway, and waited for him to continue speaking.

I think that she was trying to prove the same thing as you, he said. That she still existed, that she was still a real person. Or what have you. She was a beautiful woman. We got married when we were seventeen in Jackson County, Missouri, and her parents thought I was a bad choice for her. She came from a good family and I came from dirt. But we worked hard, the both of us, and we scraped money off the walls and we made it. But we lost a baby, and things were never quite the same after that.

That's awful, Nora said, sniffing.

Stillborn, he explained. All I wanted to do was make her happy, but I don't think I could. Not after we lost our daughter. It took me a long time to realize that, but I do now. The world was too hard on her. The problem is, she wanted to feel something, and to make everyone else feel it too. And she did. She got everyone feeling something rotten when she shot herself. But she couldn't take it back, see? That was the problem. She couldn't take it back.

He looked into Nora's eyes, making a point to catch her gaze while she avoided his.

You exist just fine, he said. You're a real person just fine.

CHAPTER 18

THE YEAR BEANIE TURNED THREE, 2005, I MOVED BACK INTO THE RICHMOND HOUSE FOR THE SUMMER.

Nora, almost ten years old, was home from school. Instead of coming to the UK and parenting her after another incident of Mum going AWOL, Dad had paid for her to board at some Montessori place in the Hertfordshire countryside. I still didn't believe that I was in love with Gus, and I knew that he couldn't keep his education on hold forever. I knew that he wouldn't go away to university when Beanie and I were so present in his life, so helpless and pathetic and dependent on him being able to work.

It will get easier when Beans is in nursery, he would say in the tent of our duvet in the middle of the night, whispering so as not to wake her.

And then what? I would ask him.

Then you could get a job. We'll both work. We can move out of this apartment. Find somewhere else. Maybe live with my parents for a bit before we find a place of our own. They would love to have us.

I felt my stomach turn.

You know I can't live with your parents, Gus.

He sighed heavily through his nose. We had tried it once, when I was pregnant, and their charity, though well intentioned, their pitying looks, the way they handled me like soft clay, made me want to scream.

Yes, he said. I know.

He threaded his fingers through mine and ran his thumb across my knuckles.

I'll get a better job, he said. And you will, too.

We don't have qualifications.

I've got A levels.

I haven't. What's the best job I'm going to get?

We'll make it work.

He was trying to convince himself as much as he was me. I could see it.

One day, the August after the Maurice Hoffmann incident, I was leaving the big Tesco in Greenford, my two-and-a-half-year-old daughter in the thrifted buggy that had become a little too small for her over the summer, and a bunch of stolen bananas shoved into my backpack, when I saw Nora in the car park.

I wouldn't have recognized her if it weren't for the leg brace. And the way that she moved, which was quite distinctive. As though she—with a frame that barely reached over five feet—were trying to make herself smaller.

Nora? I called out uneasily.

Her arms were scrawny and her hair slung back into a messy ponytail.

She glanced up when she saw me, and then her eyes slid away from me, pretending that she hadn't.

I marched across the road to meet her.

Nora, I said again, firmly.

This time she said, Oh, hello, Mattie.

What are you doing here?

She looked like a ghost.

Well, she said, speaking slowly as though deciding there and then whether she was going to lie.

If I offer to put the trolleys away for people, she said, they let me have the pound coin in the slot. So I've been doing that.

I stared at her, feeling my stomach turn to lead.

Why would you do that? I asked her quietly. Beanie gurgled happily in her buggy, chattering away to herself. Nora, instinctively, lifted her out and swung her around, making her scream with delight.

This is Beatrice, she said.

Yeah, Beanie, I replied.

She's cute.

Nora, what are you doing here? Why are you taking pound coins out of trolleys? Where's Mum?

Nora shrugged, distracted by Beanie.

I don't know.

What do you mean, *I don't know?*

Mum's gone.

I pressed my fingers to my forehead.

How long has she been gone? A week?

Nora shook her head. No, I think it's been a couple of months. She was gone when I got back from school and that was in July.

I felt my hands beginning to tremble.

Where's Aunt Karoline, then?

I don't know.

Nora.

She said, like, Croatia, or something.

So, you're on your own?

Nora shrugged again. I felt something that could have been fear or rage or both, cold and spiky in the base of my spine.

Has the social worker been around?

Another shrug.

I was eighteen years old. Nora was nine.

Are you still going to school? I asked her, trying to tamp down the rising panic in my voice.

She sniffed.

The other girls hate me, she said. They call me rats' tails.

I stared at her. She cradled Beanie so tenderly, as though she were a precious piece of ceramic. Beanie, in her arms, screaming with delight as Nora blew raspberries on her cheeks. She had odd scratches on her arms. Her skin pale and the hollows of her eyes dark like bruises.

Will you come back to my apartment with me, Nory? Come and stay with me and Gus for a bit?

Her face hardened as she looked up at me.

I'm fine, she said. You don't need to look after me. I'm not a kid.

She placed Beanie gently back in the buggy and kissed her tiny hand.

But you literally are a kid, I said, feeling my stomach fizzing. Beanie was starting to get restless, now, taking personal offence at being back in the buggy, screwing her face up until it turned pink, and letting out little wails, which meant she was hungry.

I'm actually doing pretty good without you, Nora said, trying to make her voice sound casual.

Nora, *please* come back with me.

Her face flickered then, and beneath her impassive gaze I saw something that I had never seen in her. A mixture of fear and desperation and deep-set, barely suppressed rage.

It reminded me of how I felt.

I'm not coming with you, she shouted then, loud enough that one or two of the shoppers in the car park turned to look at us.

Okay, fine, I gabbled, but let me come over? To the house? Just to see how you are?

She had already turned away from me and was hobbling out of the car park towards the main road, dodging cars as she went, dirty blonde hair streaming out behind her. She had been white-blonde as a toddler. But since I'd left the Richmond house, her hair had deepened until, as she ran away from me now, it looked like a thick dark slash across her back.

I didn't tell Gus what I had seen of Nora. I knew what he would say. Call social services. She needs to go into foster care. She needs someone who can look after her properly. His parents would say the same thing, *had* been saying the same thing ever since I'd known them.

But the idea of it made me more terrified than anything she had said in the car park.

I realized that she had been falling apart like the Richmond house, crumbling at her foundations, and I had run away.

I had already made up my mind but hadn't realized it yet. I was going to fix things, and it didn't matter what I would have to give up. All that mattered was Nora.

In a way, once I had decided, everything became easier.

Earlier that week I had found a letter from Hull University stuffed down the back of the passenger seat of Gus's cousin's car. He had been accepted to study his undergraduate LLB law degree, an unconditional offer based on his grades, straight out of college. But he had deferred twice already. The letter was to tell him that, if he didn't take his place this year, it would be rescinded entirely. I took the letter out and smoothed it down, my palms flat across the paper.

I knew what I needed to do.

I would break Gus's heart, I would run away, with Beanie, back to the Richmond house. And in the process I would save Nora, and save us all.

I would do it in a way that would make it impossible for him to change my mind.

I thought of him as a firefly under an upturned jam jar. It was time to let him escape, before the oxygen ran out for him.

I packed Beanie's and my things while he was at work and called his mother, told her to expect him by the end of the day, and that I would bring Beanie to see him as soon as we were settled.

I didn't leave a note, but I placed the acceptance letter from Hull University squarely on the kitchen counter, weighing it down with the kettle so that it wouldn't flutter away.

———————

Returning to the Richmond house was the last thing I wanted to do. When Nora opened the door to me, skinny, leg brace, hair in knots, she sniffed.

What are you doing here?

I'm staying here with you.

I set about cleaning the house and mending the things that had been broken in the years I had been gone. I boarded up the windows, pulled all the broken furniture into the garden. I moved into Mum's bedroom, and I coaxed the vegetables in the greenhouse back from extinction. Fresh soil and water and sunlight over that long hot summer. Nora and Beanie playing in the garden. Clean hair, dirty hands, laundry that smelled like daisies.

I managed to get hold of Karoline. It turned out that she was touring an amateur production of *The Vagina Monologues* in the Balkans.

You left her here alone, I growled down a crackling phone line.

I thought she was at school. And your mother was fine when I left.

Mum's not here, I said, feeling my voice harden.

Have you spoken to Edward?

I snorted by way of reply.

I heard muffled noises on the other end of the line as Karoline spoke to someone else.

I'll book a flight tonight, she said, when she came back on the line. I didn't realize. I would never have gone abroad if I'd known.

I heard the agony in her voice. I chose to ignore it.

It doesn't matter, now, I replied through gritted teeth, letting myself sneer at her. Stay where you are. I'm here. I'm looking after her.

Gus wouldn't speak to me at first, when I brought Beanie to his parents' house.

I told myself that the pain in my chest was because I missed Beanie when she was gone for the weekend. And because I was worried for Nora, who spoke mostly to herself in soft whispers, and didn't like to eat, but had at least stopped pulling out her eyelashes. And it was, partly.

Is he going to accept the offer? I asked Grace at the front door, as Beanie ran between her legs into the hallway, searching for him. I couldn't bring myself to stay for breakfast. Not yet.

He hasn't rejected it yet, Grace told me. But he has responsibilities here, now, Matilda. Things change.

He needs to go to university. It's his dream, I said, steadfast.

But what about *your* dreams? she asked me, her eyes full of sadness as Beanie tugged at her leg, urging her into the house to come and play.

I don't have dreams, I replied, surprised at the truth behind the words.

I had spent my life so far watching my mother dream—dream so big that sometimes those dreams were too heavy to be held up. They couldn't support themselves independently, and so Mum propped them up, held them, until her arms couldn't take the weight of them anymore, and sometimes Karoline could help her bear the load, and me and Nora too. But in the end, they always came crashing back into the ground.

I just want to exist, I told her.

Things have changed, Grace said meaningfully, her eyes drifting to Beanie's heart-shaped face. She was two and a half years old, and she was in love with dinosaurs. She balled her hands up into claws and demanded that Nanny be the T. rex.

After we said goodbye, and I kissed Beanie on her strawberry-colored nose, I took the bus back to the Richmond house and cried until it felt like my whole body was choking.

A few weeks into it, after the dust from the immediate wreckage had cleared, Gus came to see us. Nora answered the door and flung her arms around him. His eyes met mine over her shoulder, where I stood at the top of the stairs. There was nothing in him except unspoken, unconditional forgiveness. I felt the love flood through my lungs then, and it was like I was drowning.

I'd realized it too late.

And now, if I told him, I'd ruin him.

I couldn't drag him down with me. I had to let him go.

We sat in the garden, the four of us, and dug holes in the soft soil, pulling out the worms to show Beanie and re-planting pansies in the flower beds. It was almost, for one day, as though Mum didn't exist, and nothing hurt, and everything was as it was meant to be.

Then Gus said, I decided I'm going to take the university place.

I looked up at him. He had Beanie slung across his back, pulling on tufts of his hair and trying to shove fistfuls into her mouth. Gus's hair, like his daughter's, turned the color of copper coins in the evening sunshine.

Good, I forced myself to say. I'm glad.

It will pass, I told myself silently.

I've worked out a plan, he continued. If you have Beanie here, Monday to Friday, I'll drive down and be with you every weekend. That way I'll still get to be Dad. And I'll call you every night for bedtime. And by the time I'm back I'll be able to get a proper placement in a law firm, and I'll earn some real money, and I'll make it work.

Okay, I said, because I didn't trust myself to say any more.

He was twenty years old but behind the eyes he looked old, and sad, and resigned.

It's three years, Mattie, he said. Give me three years to get it done, and I'll be back for you. And I'll be back for her.

In bed the way he touched me, on my back, the inside of my thigh, the soft part behind my ear, felt like worship.

We had gone from a juvenile, fledgling first romance that was barely flickering into its own flame, to parenthood, in a matter of months. We were still blinking into the overhead lights, catching our breath, understanding the new feeling of our skin on our bones. And there had been no space for love in the gaps between. All of our love was saved up for our daughter.

I had never told him I loved him, and he had never told me.

But on that day, he didn't have to say it. I found it in the intention of his body, his hands on my face.

In the cold light of morning, I turned to him, and through gritted teeth said, You shouldn't wait for me.

What? he asked, his face strangely bare without his glasses.

When you go away, I lied. I don't want you to wait for me.

He propped himself up onto his elbows, and I saw a thin vein of devastation across his face. I made myself not care. I made my face impassive, impenetrable.

Why don't you want me to wait for you? he asked, eyebrows knotted.

The choice had become clear to me in the days I had been back at the Richmond house. If I chose Gus, if I chose myself, who knew what would happen to Nora?

I thought I was going to die.

The cut was surgical, the words came out bitter and grainy and they stuck to my teeth. Sometimes I can still taste them on the underside of my tongue.

Why do you think I left? Because I won't do the same for you, Gus. Because I won't wait.

———

By September, Mum was still missing, Karoline was in North Macedonia, Dad hadn't called the house phone once, and Gus had gone to university. And my heart had broken into a million pieces.

Beanie, Nora and I rattled around the Richmond house like the last three jellybeans left in the entire world.

Beanie started nursery, and I helped Nora get ready to travel back to school while I applied for jobs.

Mum came back.

She did it without ceremony, and as though nothing had happened, and as though it was completely normal that I had moved back into the house with a toddler.

The morning that I woke up to find her in the kitchen flipping eggs on the frying pan, she looked up at me and said, Oh, hello, my darling, a warm smile spread across her face.

Nora was already up, folded into the armchair in the corner of the room and staring at her as though she were an apparition.

I thought you were dead, I said, and realized as soon as I said it that I truly had thought she had died. I had been subconsciously expecting a phone call or a police officer's knock on the door to tell us they had pulled a body out of the Thames.

Don't be silly, Mum said, laughing musically. I just went on holiday. I was on a research trip.

I looked at Nora quizzically, but she wasn't watching me. She was watching Mum. Or rather, she was watching the scattered stack of brown glass bottles with prescription labels on the counter next to Mum. Each pill bottle half-full with white dots of medication. Later, when I examined them closer, I would see that none of the prescriptions were in Mum's name. They were the names of strangers.

You left Nora here on her own.

Nora's a big girl. She should also be in school.

Mum said it in this faux-condescending way, finger-wagging, with a raised eyebrow and a disciplinarian's smile. As much a mother as she could muster. I'm disappointed but I love you.

I thought that I was going to be sick. The house suddenly felt tiny, so small that I couldn't squeeze through the doorframes, that the ceiling might fall in and crush us all, Beanie and Nora and Mum and me, at any moment.

Nora's ten years old, I said evenly.

Mum pretended she hadn't heard me.

So I walked over to her until my lips were level with her ear. She was still staring down at her eggs, which were burning in the pan, the acrid stench burning at our nostrils.

NORA'S TEN YEARS OLD, I shouted at her. So loud that her eardrum must have ached with it.

Get away from me, she whispered, the spatula in her hand. She turned, still holding it.

Mattie, stop it, Nora said, from the armchair, pleading.

Mum brought the metal spatula down on my forearm, where I was holding on to the kitchen counter. Her breath smelled of rotten meat. The spatula hissed against my skin and the burning was instant. I yelped and backed away.

The look in Mum's eyes wasn't one I had ever seen before.

Beanie, oblivious to what was going on, waddled over to Mum on unsteady legs and picked something up from the floor by her feet. Before I could move, Nora was up from the armchair and had shot over to her and wrestled it from her hand, making her cry out in surprise. Nora threw the tiny white pill into the sink and washed it down with water from the tap.

Mum didn't explain herself, instead locking herself in the studio while I ran my scorched arm under water, my insides boiling. She emerged only to head out to the wine shop and return with three bottles of Moët at lunchtime. She sang to herself, humming softly as she worked. We could hear her through the door.

It was like waiting for a tsunami to hit. In a moment, the patterns came rushing back in a flood of memory. Who knew how long this manic episode would last, before Mum came crashing down again and started throwing plates at the wall? Tried to get behind the wheel of a car while drunk? Said something vile and unforgivable unprompted, like how she wished we were both dead? I wasn't entirely sure whether she was even up or down, and it frightened me.

The garden seemed to be the safest place for us so we stayed out there, playing with Beanie in the grass, until the sun went down.

Mum came out of the studio at midnight. Nora and I waited up for her, sitting in the conservatory watching the door as we shared a bowl of sweet blueberries picked from the greenhouse.

Girls, she said, sighing slowly and smiling as she came upon us. You're still awake? It's so late. You should be in bed.

Neither of us answered her. She stretched and yawned and tucked a pill bottle from the kitchen counter into the front of her dress, pretending that she couldn't see us watching her.

I think I'm going to lay down, she said. I've been staring at a blank canvas all day. I've such an awful headache.

Come on, Mum, Nora said softly, with the gentleness of a mother bird, and she stood up and took Mum's hand, and Mum let Nora lead her up the stairs. I followed and watched in the doorway as she undressed Mum and wrapped her in pajamas, Mum's eyes dilated and unfocused and the features of her face soft.

Nora wrapped the duvet tight around her, as though it would make her stay.

You girls, Mum said, sighing softly, just as she closed her eyes.

I moved my things into Nora's bedroom and slid into my old single bed. Beanie was asleep in a drawer on the floor.

Beanie can't be here, I said, more to myself than to Nora.

I know, Nora replied.

I stared up at the ceiling in the black.

You're going to leave me again, Nora said, stating a fact rather than asking a question.

No, I'm not, I replied.

The tablets are really bad, Mattie. *Really* bad. The worst ever. Worse than the drinking.

She sounded afraid.

I'm not leaving you.

Yes. You are.

You'll go back to school, for this term at least, I said, formulating the plan as I spoke. And I'll find somewhere for me and Beanie to live. And when you come home for Christmas I'll come and get you.

Do you promise? she whispered. I could hear it in her voice. The desperation. Her life in the Richmond house had become a question of survival.

Her cheeks shone.

I promise, I replied, cradling my blistering arm.

Don't make me go back to that school, Mattie, she said. I hate it.

You have to, I whispered. Just until I can find somewhere for us. Just until I can get settled.

And then you'll come for me?

Next door, Mum was talking in her sleep. I could hear the soft murmurings of her whispers through the wall.

Yes, I said. Then I'll come for you.

CHAPTER 19

I COULDN'T REMEMBER THE CIRCUMSTANCES OF US GOING
TO BED.

Beanie got back from her walk a couple of hours later, took one look at Nora
and me and Randy, all of us splayed out across the picnic bench, loopy with
homemade alcohol of an unknown percentage, and got in the van and
closed the door. After that I remembered climbing over her, and stage-
whispering to Nora to be quiet. But she was already quiet. She'd gone super
quiet all afternoon.

I don't remember what I dreamed of, only that Beanie was calling for me.
It was disturbing, until my semi-conscious body realized that she was calling
for me in real life, in the stuffy airless van too. It was our first night asleep in
the van and we had more-or-less fallen into it, after Beanie had had the good
sense to turn the seats into beds earlier that day. Now, Beanie was dragging
me out of the heaviest sleep of my life.

Mum, she said—a whisper at first and then louder—Mum, wake up.

I groaned myself awake, disoriented. Everything was too close to us: the
roof, the walls of the van.

What's up? I asked her.

It's Nora. I can't find her. She's gone.

I was awake then, and I sat up quickly, my heart immediately starting to
hammer. I yanked the door of the van open to a dark, silent night.

Where the fuck is she? I asked.

I don't know, I can't find her anywhere close by. I've checked all around the campsite and in the woods.

I stared at Beanie and willed myself to hold it together for her.

Okay, I said. First things first. Let's check Findyr.

At the start of our trip, we had all agreed to sign up to an app that tracked one another's phones, in case one of us got lost on a hike or left their bag somewhere. Beanie pulled out her phone and opened up the app. Bizarrely, her clock told us that it was just past eleven. I'd been asleep for several hours already; my body told me it was five in the morning. The app pinged our phones to locate them. There were the two of us, our red dots nestled together on the screen at the campsite. Beanie tapped at the screen to navigate to Nora's dot. It was farther north, close to the spot where Beanie and I had eaten our sandwiches earlier that day, near the entrance to the South Rim.

Do you think she's okay? Beanie asked.

I'm sure she's fine, I lied. There had been something about Nora earlier, the hardness in her as the day wore on, that frightened me.

Let's go and see her just to make sure, though, I said to Beanie.

I pulled on my walking boots and a coat. The temperature had dropped rapidly and now the air was chilled. We walked to the bus stop at the edge of the campsite and found that the shuttle service had stopped for the night.

What are we going to do? Beanie wailed.

I pointed at the Flamesmobile. We'll drive, I said.

We threw our stuff in the van and fired up the ignition. The noise of the engine was rude in the quietness of the night. We drove the ten minutes up to the car park at the hotel, and I parked badly in a spot that was far too small for the girth of the van.

Where is she? I asked Beanie.

She's gone into the park, Beanie replied, monitoring the red dot on her phone.

Come on, I said, trying to keep the franticness out of my movements, the urgency out of my voice.

We walked through the same entryway as we had earlier that day. It seemed like a lifetime ago now. It seemed that we had been here for years already. The park, and its entrance to the South Rim, was quiet too, despite the twenty-four-hour opening times. We couldn't see much—just the white dots of stars scattered across the dark sky above us, the air so clear and crisp, the Milky Way glowing.

We followed Nora's dot to the east, along the trail, our boots crunching quietly in the dust.

And we found her.

She was standing at the very edge of the soft, rounded platform.

Beyond her it seemed really as though it were just the black of the night, night-time for as far as the eye could see. Even the great, dark obelisk-like shapes of the sand-colored rock formations were invisible in the indigo. Above us, the stars were pinpricks. The air was cooler still.

Nora? I called to her. She didn't turn around. Beanie wasn't far behind me, dusty grey walking boots trudging through the red soil. Her feet soft on the ground. She put a hand on my shoulder.

Nora looked out at the black.

Mum? Beanie asked quietly.

Go back to the van, kid, I replied, my voice matching her own hushedness.

Is . . . she okay?

I don't know. Go back to the van, Beans. I mean it.

Beanie—of course—didn't listen.

Auntie Nora? she called.

We stood on the edge there, waiting for something to happen. We were all waiting for something to happen.

I had been trained for this. I knew exactly what to do. I knew the exact right words to say. I had the tactics at my fingertips for talking a suicidal person down from the—literal or figurative—edge.

But in that moment, I couldn't move.

Beanie, ever softer on her feet, walked slowly towards Nora.

Auntie Nora? It's me.

Nora gave no acknowledgement that she had heard us, or even knew that we were here. I willed my feet to work, and finally they did, and I followed

Beanie, quietly, behind, both of us magnets in compasses dragged towards our true north. The burning twisting of something rotten in my belly. The feeling of something terrible about to happen, moments away from being split off into a new timeline.

What are you doing there?

Nora snapped her head round now, hair like black ink slitting her face into ribbons. Her eyes found mine in the dark. Face the color of the moon.

Dirt on her kneecaps and her sharp, angular elbows and the palms of her hands. Dirt darker than the night sky, even.

The wind made strange noises out in the canyon, as though it were crying out for something.

Nora's eyes glittered, pinpricks reflecting the starlight.

What is it? I asked her, but I already knew.

I knew it in her face. The disquiet.

I knew that look on the face of our mother, over and over and over again.

She said, Every time I think it's gone, it comes back stronger.

Oh, Nora.

It's so *loud*, Matt.

She was crying very suddenly, a low keening sound I had never heard come out of her. A noise that was frightening in its animalism. She stared at her hands as though they had committed a despicable act without her consent.

Beanie, go back to the van, I said again, teeth clenched.

Mum, she said, ignoring me, her voice urgent. Look down there.

I edged closer to the precipice of the ledge and saw then the tiny white dots scattered over the edge, strewn through the shrubbery, pinpricks as bright and as white as the stars. I couldn't see them, but I knew somewhere down there would be a fistful of tiny brown glass bottles, too, and pillboxes, perhaps cracked against the rocks, or half buried in the dust. There were enough tablets down there to amount to Nora's prescription for the entire trip.

Instinctively, I grabbed her by the wrist, yanked her backwards.

I can't take them anymore, Nora said, referring to the flurry of pills dusting the ground below us.

It's all right, I replied, struggling to keep my tone neutral. I understand. Just come away from the edge.

She let me pull her gently back towards the rope partition delineating the pathway.

You don't understand, though, Nora said, all of the strength gone from her voice. Do you? You don't get it.

Beanie, come on, I said again, louder, yanking Nora by the wrist now.

Just wait a minute, Beanie replied. Stop for just a second, Mum.

Get away from the edge, Beatrice.

Mum. Stop!

I stopped then, wheeling round to stare at my child, who'd never spoken to me with such anger barely masked in her voice. She glared at me, her hands balled up into fists.

Can't we just let her be for a second?

She meant Nora, who was still crying.

Beanie stepped over to her and wrapped her arms around her waist, like she used to do with me when she was a little girl, her cheek pressed to Nora's shoulder. I dropped Nora's wrist and it fell limply to her side.

Don't be sad, don't be sad, she whispered to Nora, who now lifted her hands and pressed the heels of them into her eye sockets. She pressed and pressed so hard, as though she was trying to get her brain to swallow her eyeballs. I stared at the two of them, Nora shuddering with her emotions, her whole body quivering with sobs, and Beanie saying soft and gentle things to her, so quiet I could barely hear them.

I can't do this without you, you know, Beanie said quietly.

Nora shuddered once more, burrowed fists into eyes once more, and sighed as she nodded into Beanie's orange hair, her face wet and shining with tears. The wind had stopped for a moment and we were there alone. It felt as though we were the only people to exist in the entire world.

I can't do it without you, Beanie said again, and I realized then that, no—I didn't exist either. Not to them, not in this moment.

I know, Nora mumbled. I know. I'm sorry.

Let's go, Beanie said, and she walked with Nora, hand in hand, ahead of me, back to the van.

I woke up with my face pressed against the dashboard, my body folded in on itself. I remembered, vaguely, driving back to the campsite, putting Nora to bed, letting Beanie curl up next to her under the blanket like she used to do with me when she was just a toddler. I felt such a swell of love and hope for them there. The stars lit them up. My girls. I don't know how long I stood there, watching their chests rise and fall in unison, their fingers and toes twitch with their dreams. I couldn't disturb them so I slept in the front passenger seat instead with my coat over my shoulders. Now, in the milky light of the morning, I glanced back to see only one soft shape of a body under the blanket. The air smelled musty. I heaved the door open and stepped down into the scrub, linking my hands behind my shoulders to straighten my back out. Every part of my body ached, the kind of deep-vein-thrombosis ache of the very worn down. As I shuffled out to the picnic bench, I saw movement ahead. Randy's Lincoln-painted van next door to ours was gone; there was only one other camper on our patch, and a quick glance at it confirmed that, all quiet with the curtains drawn, its inhabitants were still asleep.

I heard Beanie's voice, musical, from some distance behind, towards the dirt road. She was on the phone.

She was saying, Well, Nora's just yeeted all her meds over the side of the Grand Canyon so I don't know whether we'll even make it to San Francisco at this rate.

More movement in the trees.

I waved my arm at her frantically, shushing. She stopped in her tracks, Doctor Martens stuck in the dust, toothbrush hanging from her mouth.

I put my finger to my lips, holding her gaze, and with my other hand, beckoned her over.

Slowly, I warned, my voice low.

She obeyed, and came level with me just as a large, thick-necked, russet-brown elk emerged from the pine trees at the edge of the campsite.

What? What's going on, Beans? came Gus's voice from Beanie's phone, her FaceTime call still active. She flipped the camera to show him too.

Overhead, the birds were waking up. I checked my watch: it wasn't even six a.m. yet. The jetlag made it feel like late morning. It felt as though it would never end.

Look at him, Beanie whispered quietly, linking my arm in hers.

We watched the elk—easily twice the size of a deer—nose around in the brush with a round dark snout, kicking at the undergrowth with gnarled legs, before huffing out a breath of steam and disappearing back into the tree line.

Holy shit, Beanie said.

I know, right?

Amazing.

We stood there for a moment in perfect silence, with only the birds and the gentle breeze winding its way through the trees for company. Beanie wandered off to finish her call with her dad, and I turned back to the van to see Nora leaning out the window, eyes crusted with sleep, her arms hanging over the door limply.

Did you see it? I asked her.

Yeah, she replied. I saw it.

And we grinned at one another, instinctively, that look of knowledge of something special, something beyond our known universe existing inside of it. And it felt—for just a moment—like Nora was there, *really* there, for the first time since I'd got to the hospital. Present, and ready to be alive.

But then I saw the way her fingers curled up around her elbows. The dark crescent moons underneath her eyes. Last night at the edge of the rim. Suddenly it was all there, and in the stark daylight it was so much uglier.

Nora . . . I started.

I don't want to talk about it.

Please.

No.

I just want to know, I said. And I steeled myself to say it out loud. I walked over to her, dangling out of the window like a loose thread. I said it quietly, as though it were a terrible secret. In some ways it was.

I need to know if you were planning to jump, I told her.

She snorted. Please, she said.

You realize this isn't unreasonable to think, I said steadily. What with—

What with my track record? Yeah. I know.

I leaned against the door of the car so that my left ear was next to her right one. We both watched Beanie on the phone to Gus, her voice ani-mated, big wide arcs of the arms, musical laughter.

You've got a good one there, Nora said, nodding at her.

Yeah, I replied. I don't know how I deserve her.

You don't, she said, a little spitefully.

I felt the warm metal of the van against my back and despite the whirling fear in my body, which started somewhere in my lower abdomen and rose like floodwater up to my throat, the tide felt momentarily calm.

I wasn't going to jump, Nora said, after a while. At least, I don't think I was.

Okay, I said slowly.

I just can't take the tablets anymore, she said.

I nodded, half understanding. I felt the beginnings of a hangover-induced migraine coming on.

There were so many things I wanted to say to her in that moment. I felt the weight of our shared history bearing down on us. I knew that she wouldn't take the pills because she, more so than me, had watched Mum spend most of her life getting medically upped and downed until she'd become a wholly different kind of person, until she couldn't function with-out being in some species of chemically altered state.

I knew that she was afraid of what Mum had become, whether she would become it too. I knew she saw the rest of her life mapped out in front of her, and all the mistakes she felt doomed to repeat. I wondered whether to her it was easier to choose no path at all than the one that would hurt.

I wanted to say, Sorry, Nora. Sorry I left you there with her. I wanted to say: every day I wonder what you might have been if I'd taken you with me. What *we* might have been if we were born to different people.

I wanted to say, I don't know how to help you. And that scares me the most.

I wanted to say, Please, for the love of God, please don't die.

But nothing came out when I opened my mouth, and eventually she slid back into the van and pulled a blanket over her face, feigning sleep.

What the fuck am I supposed to do? I asked Gus, having stolen Beanie's phone to explain the details of what happened over FaceTime. On the other end of the call, he was in his office, hair messy and face tired, tie askew.

What time is it there? I asked him, frowning.

You don't want to know, he replied. I haven't left this building for eighteen hours.

God, what's going on?

You don't want to know, he said again.

Gus. I do want to know. Is everything okay?

He sighed, took off his glasses and rubbed his eyes. It's a horrible case, Matt. Really vile, disgusting, workplace sexual assault. Sustained abuse of power, coercion, and . . . I just can't put words to it.

I wish I could help you, I said. You shouldn't be pulling all-nighters like this. It's not healthy.

If you and Beans were around, I wouldn't be, he said, smiling ruefully.

You need someone to temper you, I agreed, thinking of Lulu. Now that she was gone, Gus didn't have anyone to hit his off-switch.

You're going to run yourself into the ground, I said. You need to remember to stop sometimes. And eat. And sleep. And drink water.

He shrugged and put his glasses back on. Just look after the kid for me, he said. And get back to me in one piece.

What do you know about getting prescriptions for mood stabilizers in the States? I asked.

He laughed humorlessly.

I can make some calls for you. Text me your stopping locations and I'll see if I can get something sorted.

Thank you, I said. I don't know what I would do without you. I felt tears pricking at the corners of my eyes unexpectedly.

His eyes widened a little, the angled edge of his jaw tensing.

Be safe, he said, and he hung up the call.

I wandered back over to the van. Beanie had the back doors open and was trying to get the gas stove lit to fry some bacon that she had bought from the deli. I took the lighter from her and got the flame going underneath an improbably small frying pan.

How's Dad? Beanie asked as she laid the rashers down in the pan and I buttered some bread.

Working himself to death, I replied ruefully. How're you?

Me?

I squeezed her arm. I worry about you. There's a lot going on. With Nora, school, this trip.

She shrugged and flashed a quick smile at me.

I'm fine. I'm always fine, she replied.

I squeezed her arm again and felt the keen hurt of how much I loved her well up in me.

You know I'm here, I said. To talk about anything.

She rolled her eyes. I don't need you to therapize me, but thanks.

I'm just saying. If you want to talk. I'm here.

Do you miss Dad? she asked, unexpectedly.

I frowned at her and rooted around in the mini-fridge for ketchup.

I suppose so, I said. We see him every other day, pretty much. So it's weird that he's not here with us. Why, do you miss him?

Yeah, she replied. I wish he was here, too.

We finished the bacon sandwiches and Beanie went to rouse Nora from her sleep. We ate on the picnic bench in a contented silence.

Okay, Nora said, a blanket wrapped around her shoulders, once she had finished her sandwich. I noticed that she had left the crusts of the bread. I picked them up from the flimsy plastic plate and gobbled them up. Like we were six and fourteen all over again. She smiled at me as the same flicker of remembrance passed across her face.

Okay, she said again. I'm going to text my therapist and take a shower. And after that, what do you think about lobbing Mum into the Grand Canyon?

I choked a little bit on her sandwich crusts.

Sounds like a plan to me, said Beanie, holding her hand up for a high-five.

CHAPTER 20

I PULLED THE COOLER OUT FROM BEHIND THE PASSENGER
SEAT, WITH MUM'S ASHES STASHED INSIDE.

We added protein bars, bottles of water and bananas to our backpacks, and
tied our walking shoes up tight. Nora wore a cap low over her eyes and had
her hair slung into a loose ponytail. She looked so small under the bulk of
her rucksack. Beanie and I carried the cool box between us.

Let's keep her in here, I said, until we get to the spot. Keep the park rang-
ers off our backs.

We boarded the shuttle bus and got off at the same spot as the day before.
The air was crisp and clean, with the faint scent of woodsmoke.

We queued at the entrance to the trail and once again were confronted
with the size of it, the impossible distances that it stretched, the secret
depths. I watched for Nora's reaction, her first time seeing it, in the daylight
at least. She pulled a face which said, *not bad.*

Good, innit? I said, grinning, and then she smiled back at me.

We took the western path this time and walked up a slightly elevated section, which curved northwards. There were more hikers on the trail now—it
was the weekend—and the sun bore down on us. We walked for an hour or
so, before coming to an outcrop dusted with dry and brittle brushes of salt
cedar and arrowweed. The section of rust-colored rock, eroded smooth over
millennia by rain and wind and river and sand, jutted out into the nothingness of the canyon itself. Beanie and I sat down as close to the edge as we
dared, the cool box between us, our legs dangling over. I watched Nora

stand and stretch her arms out at the nothingness, her whole body tensed to receive it. I felt a sudden anxiety then, at seeing her so close to the edge, *I wasn't going to jump, at least, I don't think I was* ringing in my ears. I resisted the urge to snatch her away from the abyss.

I knew what she was feeling: the universe, expanding and shrinking at the same time, the knowledge of the smallness—the insignificance—of the human experience of life.

Beanie took a selfie.

I've been thinking about the Control Room, Nora said.

Oh, yeah? I replied, my stomach churning.

I think I need to finish the project. Like, I need to see it through.

I stared at her long and hard. She wouldn't meet my gaze. Instead she looked out at the landscape.

Why? I asked hopelessly.

Because of this, Matt, she said. She threw her arms out again at the impossible nature before us. Because I need to take this and distil it down into its smallest possible form. Because the smallest possible way to express it is with my own body in a small space. That's it. I've been working on this for years; everything has led up to it. I can't finish my thesis without it. And then what am I? A postgrad dropout? A cliché? Failed daughter of the great Ingrid Olssen? I can't be that.

You're not a failed anything, I replied, reaching up to take her hand. You're a genius, maybe.

Thanks, she said, laughing hollowly.

But you're going to hurt yourself. You're literally going to kill yourself, if you go back to it.

At least I'll have made something beautiful before I'm dead.

You're going to drive yourself crazy.

Bit late for that, she said.

You know what I mean. I don't want you left alone.

I'm a grown woman, Matt.

You are. But you're still my sister, and I still want to look after you.

The unspoken bit hung between us. The bit where I did leave her alone, when I shouldn't have.

I should have tried harder, I said, feeling my throat catch. Back then, to keep you safe. I should have come back for you.

Yeah, she said. You should have. But there's no point raking over it. It's done. You can't fix it.

I can fix it now, though, I thought.

The damage has all been done, she continued.

I can fix it now swam around in my head on an infernal loop until I couldn't hear the wind, or Nora's voice, anymore. My brain and my body dominated by that one thought. *I can fix it now.*

We ate our bananas on the edge of the abyss with Mum still in the cooler.

A familiar voice sounded from behind.

Good morning, ladies, Park Ranger Hernandez said cheerily, joining us on the outcrop, leaning down to pick up a discarded cigarette butt in the dust and pocketing it.

Good morning, Hernandez, Beanie replied, matching his jocularity.

Just wanted to drop by and give you a quick reminder to take your trash home with you when you leave.

Of course, I said.

Perhaps he had forgotten us from yesterday.

Then he said, I take it you haven't brought any human remains out on the trail with you today? His smile was looking a little strained now. He gave an unconvincing chuckle.

No, Beanie and I said in unison, too quickly, too urgently. Beanie's eyes darted conspicuously to the cool box, which was still unopened. At the same time I saw her do this, I saw that Hernandez had seen her do this, too.

Say, what's in that cooler, there, ladies? Hernandez asked, eyes now hard, his tone markedly shifted.

Nothing, I said, just some protein bars. Trail mix, that sort of thing.

Mind if I take a look? Hernandez asked, already striding towards it. Before any of us could say "no" he had popped off the lid and was peering inside. I felt my heart in my mouth, and Beanie let out a strange garbled throat noise that I'd never heard her make before. Nora looked like she might kick the whole cooler off the edge of the trail down into the canyon below.

But Hernandez frowned at the contents of the cooler, and then, perplexingly, looked up with a relaxed smile on his face.

I'm sorry to disturb you, ladies, he said, tipping his hat like a cowboy in an old movie. You have a nice day out on the trail, now. Make sure you drink plenty of water; it's going to be another hot one.

And he strode away.

I glanced at Beanie, frowning.

Beanie scrambled over to the open cool box, muttering, *What?* to herself.

She bent her head over it and then shot a look of pure horror at us.

What is it? Nora asked, walking over to the cooler.

Inside were two almost-empty plastic gallon jugs of moonshine. And nothing else.

Oh, *fuck*, I said.

The presence of the moonshine bottles could only mean one thing.

The remains of our dead mother were currently en route to Vegas, squished in our cooler, under the passenger seat of a camper van with a paint job of Abraham Lincoln holding an AK-47.

CHAPTER 21

ALL I COULD SAY, OVER AND OVER AGAIN, ON THE BUS
BACK TO THE CAMPSITE WAS, FUCK.

A dad made his two kids move further down the bus, away from us.

How the hell are we going to find Randy? Beanie asked.

We arrived back at the campsite and I felt all the air coming out of me,
like I was deflating.

Nora held her own elbows in the opposite hands, as though she were trying to hug herself, and squeezed.

We're in big trouble, she said.

I sat down on the hot asphalt, my legs out in front of me. The dust in the
air stuck to my skin, giving the appearance of a suntan. But I pulled the
band of my sock away and saw the sickly pink skin underneath. My legs had
turned to lead.

Let's think about this, I said. We're not in big trouble. Mum's dead
already. She's not going to come back from the dead and kick off. She doesn't
know that her post-corporeal form is currently in Randy's van.

That depends on whether you subscribe to Plato's theory of the tripartite
soul, Beanie said matter-of-factly.

Nora and I both stared at her.

Oh my God, if Mum knew, though, said Nora.

I think she'd find it funny, Beanie replied.

Yeah, she would either find it funny, I said. Or she'd—

Go on a three-day bender, Nora finished.

I nodded.

Well, I guess she'll have her bender in heaven, Beanie said.

Or hell, I replied glibly.

Nora walked away.

———————

There was nothing else for it. We packed all our stuff up into the Flamesmo-bile and drove away from the campsite, out of the Grand Canyon National Park, and onto the road to Nevada.

I was driving. Nora went quiet again. Beanie sat up front with me and fiddled with the music, while Nora pretended to read her book in the back.

I knew there was something off about that Randy guy, Beanie said quietly as she concentrated on finding a station that wasn't either hard-right talk radio or country and western. In the end she found a Spanish language CD in the glove compartment, and shoved that into the disc slot instead.

There wasn't anything *off* about Randy, I said. He was a nice man.

Whatever.

I've met a lot of not-nice men in my life and Randy wasn't one of them, I insisted.

Well. You never truly know, do you? Not until you leave your mother's ashes in someone's van and have to chase them across state lines.

It's our fault for getting wasted and losing track of things, I continued, ignoring her.

You know what? You're right, Beanie said. It *is* your fault.

The dense mass of hopelessness weighed heavy on me.

There's simply nothing we can do, I said. Except drive to Vegas and comb the streets for a van with an Abraham Lincoln AK-47 mural on the side of it.

I've seen three of those since we left Phoenix, Beanie said.

We drove in silence, climbing steep hills and rugged terrain, and the micro-climate changed again. Now it hailed, hard, and the edges of the road changed from soft dust and sand to slate-colored mountainous rocks. There were even the remnants of snow in some places. I felt the van straining and sliding beneath my hands as we climbed further, the air thinning and the altitude increasing. Sparse coniferous trees of the Kaibab National Forest lined the road. It was a four-hour drive to Vegas.

I can do this in one go, I told Beanie. She ignored me. She was DMing.

And then, with a quickness that seemed to defy logic, we were once again descending, away from the huge crack in the earth, and back into the desert, flat and open and dry and nothing.

We listened to Janis Joplin, Led Zeppelin, Lynyrd Skynyrd, Jefferson Airplane, Kate Bush, Jimi Hendrix, and Fleetwood Mac on Beanie's phone using the aux cable. Nora got up and propped herself on the front seats, making requests of Beanie who was playing DJ. We sang through the whole of *Rumors* faultlessly.

My phone rang, and Beanie answered it.

Hi, Richard, she said, her voice dripping in sarcasm.

What? No! I shouted, veering into the next lane as I grabbed the phone from Beanie and ended the call. My heart was suddenly pounding a sickening rhythm.

Mum, what the hell? Beanie asked.

I quieted as I righted the camper back into the correct lane.

I, erm, haven't told Richard that we're here, I said, a little confused with myself.

Why not?

I don't know, I said uselessly.

Aren't you like, moving in with him soon? Beanie asked, and I felt the hostility then, radiating off her. The old argument from back home bubbling up between us. She had been prickly all morning about Randy. She was right: we had been irresponsible, and now we were on a madcap car chase in the desert. I felt her disapproval of me palpably. I felt myself rising to it.

Beans, you're my only child, I said. I love you with all my heart. But you need to stop thinking you can dictate what I can do with my own life.

I'm not telling you what you can and can't do, she said. I'm telling you that Richard is a moron. And I think you know that he's a moron, too.

Richard is . . . I started, and found myself grasping for words. Richard was *what*, exactly? I realized that I didn't know.

I thought of what he had said in bed, not long before he'd left for the

States, his hands cupping my face. *I don't think it's possible for you to hurt me.* There was something deeply comforting in knowing that that was true.

Nevertheless, when the phone rang again with his number, him on the other end of the line probably assuming Beanie had dropped the call by mistake, I rejected it swiftly.

I don't understand you at all sometimes, Beanie said after a moment's pause.

Nora scoffed lightly.

What? I said.

It's like watching Mum, Nora said, smiling ruefully.

I felt my fingers tighten on the steering wheel and my foot slacken on the accelerator.

Don't you *ever*—

Yeah, Nora said quickly. That was out of order. I'm sorry.

I wanted to say to her, sometimes I look at you and see Mum too.

I wanted to.

But I knew it would hurt her just as much as it did me.

Rumors finished its second run-through and no one moved to change the music, so instead, we drove in stone-cold, heavy, impenetrable silence.

––––––––––––

The desert seemed to go on forever. The roads straight as a knife, carving lines in the dust. We wove between fifty-feet-long haulage trailers and RVs and soft-top sports cars. The air was heavy and musty, but the open windows sent blasts of wind into the cabin, upsetting the bags and the bottles of half-drunk water perched on the fold-down table, so we left them closed.

I thought of Mum in the thick quiet of the van. Mum in the Richmond house, when the cancer had eaten her all up from the inside out. She'd still been painting, horizontally. It had been something she had done before, something with which she'd been familiar. Sometimes the paint had dripped on her face, slick and viscous oils of cerise and violet. She had stopped smoking but she'd drunk, and drunk, and drunk. No one could begrudge her it; we'd all known she was going to die.

We can let her have this one thing, I'd said. Nora and Karoline were there, too, and we kept a strange somber vigil at her bedside, the ghost of the nights Nora and I had slept in that bed when Mum had gone away hovering between the three of us. The memories stank up the house. We could hardly bear to sit in it—in them—because it felt as though they tainted us.

We let Mum paint, the canvas suspended above the bed, because it made her calm and quiet and comprehensible. I arrived one morning after Nora had spent the night there. In adulthood, an uneasy friction stuttered and staticked between us. She was very much a stranger to me, though she loved Beanie and spoke to her often. Before Mum deteriorated, I had last seen Nora in hospital in Los Angeles, after the second time she'd tried to kill herself. And before that, it had been at least a couple of years since I had spent time alone with her. I knew nothing of her personality, her wants and hopes and fears. I knew that she had had a boyfriend in LA and it had ended badly. I knew that she was working on something new. And that was all I knew.

How is she? I asked Nora quietly as I came into the bedroom.

Nora shrugged. She seems okay. She slept for most of the night.

It'll be any day now, I said, a statement of fact rather than of curiosity.

Yeah, Nora said, her voice free of feeling. Any day now.

In the middle of the morning while the great Ingrid Olssen undertook the task of dying, I searched in the cupboards for fresh linens, and pulled open the door to the cupboard under the stairs. The stairs were made of thickly varnished mahogany, rickety and old. The cupboard underneath was small, yellowing and smelled of animals that had crawled in between the floorboards and died decades ago. I opened the door and the memory hit me like a punch in the face. Nora and I hiding between the coats on the hooks. Nora and I falling asleep to stories under the dim-flickering bulb. Nora and I listening to Mum's parties, and Mum's rages, through the crack underneath the door. There was a universe inside this cupboard that I had forgotten. I crawled inside and closed the door and cried.

Mum, in the bed, skin yellowing and paper-thin, tubes from the nose and wrists, eyes watery and rheumy, lips cracked with dried saliva at their corners, a smell I could not describe signaling the oncoming end for her, the way her fingers stuttered against the bedsheets as she slept.

In life, we had been afraid of her, though neither of us would admit it to one another, to her, to ourselves. She was like an asteroid, burning so bright and hot and turning everything she touched to ash. Later on, after I'd left for the second time, I had hated her viciously.

Now we held her existence like a baby bird in our hands. Soft and delicate. It would be so easy to do it. No one would ever know. A press of the thumb would snap the neck like a twig.

I sat down on the ottoman at the end of the bed. Everything in the room seemed to have a slight moistness to it. We had been told that under no circumstances could we open the windows. The bedsheets writhed around her like coils.

I took Nora's hand in mine.

It went on. Mum became barely awake. She couldn't paint anymore. She couldn't lift her arms to the canvas. Sometimes she spoke in meaningless, half-formed riddles that no one could decipher. Sometimes she ranted in Norwegian and I wished I had bothered to learn more of her first language. Eventually we took away the paint and the palettes and let the morphine do its work.

Girls, Mum said, simply, her voice barely a whisper—a rasp.

We couldn't help but lean into her, closer and closer and closer. She drew us into her orbit, less an asteroid and more a star in its final evolutionary state, a white dwarf infinitely dimming, its matter forever degenerating.

Girls, she said again. And she told us what she wanted done with her body. And what she wanted done with her work.

The rest of it, she said, can burn.

I watched her and thought that there would be no more burning on the site of her existence. No thermal energy. No fusion. Only endless cooling.

I caught Nora's watchful eye.

And now, Mum whispered, you can tell us all a Hector story, Matilda.

I snapped my eyes to hers, surprised. Hector belonged to Nora and me. He had watched over us as children, over the house, when Mum had gone away.

But I had no energy left to question it, to rage at her, to refuse to forgive her for the mess she had made of us all.

So, I told her a Hector story. An old one that had somehow imprinted itself into my memory in a way I had not registered until the moment that I could deliver it one more time. A story of the day Hector freed the birds from the zoo and let them all fly away into the blue.

I didn't want to tell it. I didn't want to give her any further pieces of us. But I did it anyway. I told the story because she asked, and because she was dying.

And by the time I had finished, she was gone.

———

In the third hour, Beanie yelped at her phone, which she had been staring at steadfastly ever since Richard called.

Mukbang girl messaged me back.

What? I asked, not fully understanding what she was saying.

Teresa Eats. Mukbang girl. Randy's sister. I messaged her on Instagram.

Oh my God, I said. Beans, you're a genius. What did you say to her?

Beanie read out the message: *Dear Teresa, you don't know me but my name is Beatrice Hanson-Robb and I'm currently in the Grand Canyon National Park on a road trip with my mum and my aunt from London. We met your brother Randy yesterday and, long story short, we think that Randy may have inadvertently driven away with the ashes of my dead grandmother in his cool box, which is actually our cool box. My mother and aunt have also drunk your moonshine, for which I apologize. Please can you ask Randy to return our human remains at earliest possible convenience or provide details of drop-off point. Yours sincerely, Beatrice Hanson-Robb.*

Then I sent her a picture of the moonshine as proof, Beanie added.

And what has she replied? I asked, impatient.

Beanie glanced over the message, her eyes moving rapidly.

She's mad about the moonshine, she said.

Okay. And?

Teresa says that Randy hasn't got to her house in Vegas yet and he turns his phone off when he's travelling so she can't call him.

I slammed both hands on the steering wheel, exasperated.

But, Beanie continued, he always stops at this restaurant in Boulder City for lunch before he gets into Vegas.

Great. We'll go to Boulder City. Done deal.

I really, *really* do not want to go to Teresa Eats's house, Nora said.

Mum, what's your PayPal login? Beanie asked.

Why?

I'm buying a T-shirt off her website, Beanie said. As a thank you. Shall I get the one with her eating a triple hot dog or the one with her eating a raw potato?

Obviously the potato, Nora said.

I couldn't pinpoint the exact spot on the road where it stopped being Arizona and started being Nevada. The landscape barely changed, besides the brown mountains ahead of us becoming marginally larger and closer with each mile we put behind us. We pulled into Boulder City through the deep crevice of a road shorn into the rocks, past the turn-off for the Hoover Dam, which was just outside the city limits, to the south-east next to a huge artificial-seeming lake, where boys with no shirts raced on Jet Skis. The heat was once again dry and perfect and very, very hot.

I had never seen anything like Boulder City, and I couldn't find any analogue for it in my knowledge of British towns and cities. We passed huge multistorey casino hotels on our way in. But inside the city limits, the roads were empty, wide, and the sidewalks were sparse. The area of the city proper was smaller than I had imagined. The houses were single-storied with vast gaps between one another like tombstones. It was as though barely anyone lived here: there were gas stations, RV parks, convenience stores and the Historic District. The Historic District looked less than thirty years old, and as though someone had taken a model village of a flat Mediterranean town, sized it up and dropped it in the desert. The grass on the public landscaped land was unnaturally green. There were bars, a florist, a movie theater with a whitewashed arched façade, whose showings simply read "GOD BLESS

AMERICA" in carefully placed lettering. There were also two 7-Elevens and too many antiques stores to count.

We found the place that Teresa had told Beanie Randy would be stopping at for lunch: a microbrewery styled as an Irish pub. I crawled the van along the road while Beanie leaned out the window and searched for the Abraham Lincoln paint job.

I can't see his van, she said, her shoulders slumping as she got back into the passenger seat.

He's probably already been and gone, Nora said. He must have left the Grand Canyon hours before we did.

I hit the back of my head against the headrest in frustration.

Jesus, Mattie, calm down, Nora said, alarmed.

We're fucked, I said. We've lost her. We're going to have to go to that mukbang girl's house in Las Vegas.

We're not going to the mukbang girl's house, Nora soothed. It'll be okay.

We decided to eat at the microbrewery while we decided what to do. We sat in the garden under a table umbrella, which kept most of the white-hot sun off our scalps, and ordered cheesy fries and burgers, and deep-fried pickles, which Beanie ate three helpings of.

I asked our server—a bespectacled teen with greasy hair—whether a man in a camper van decorated with Abraham Lincoln holding an AK-47 had been here that day.

Oh, you mean Randy? he asked, his round face dawning with recognition. Yeah, he comes here once every couple months. He left an hour or so ago, though.

What do you think, shall we try and chase him down? I asked Beanie, ignoring the concerned look on the boy's face.

Well, we need to find Nora first, unless you want to leave her in Boulder City.

What do you mean, we need to find Nora? I asked, scoffing.

Erm, because she's not here? Beanie said sarcastically.

I turned around and, sure enough, the garden chair Nora had been sitting in while unenthusiastically pushing cheesy fries around her plate with a fork was empty.

Why didn't you say anything? I said to Beanie, borderline shrieking.

I thought you'd realized, Beanie said, defensive. She was sitting right next to you, Mum.

FUCK, I said loudly. The bespectacled teen server flinched. Beanie raised her eyebrows.

Should I come back later with the check? he asked.

No—no—I'll pay it now.

I tapped my card to his machine frantically, trying not to think about the currency conversion fee my debit card had just been charged, and gathered up my bag and the car keys.

For crying out loud, I muttered.

Mum, chill. It's a tiny little town in the middle of the desert. How far could she have gone?

I didn't answer her with what I was thinking, which was: *she's off her medication, and I have no idea what that means for her.*

We power-walked down the main thoroughfare through the Historic District. I resisted the urge to call out for her by name.

Where the hell is everyone? Beanie asked, pulling on her heart-shaped sunglasses.

I don't know, I replied, nervous. It was the middle of the day, waves of heat rising off the sun-baked asphalt. But Boulder City—a city in nothing but name—had the aura of a ghost town. No people on the streets, no signs of life in the few windows through which we peered. There seemed to be not enough people here to accommodate the number of businesses lining the street, and certainly not the number of antiques' stores.

Up ahead, the automatic doors of a convenience store dinged open and out came Nora. I screeched her name, too high, too shrill. She looked up at us, startled.

What the fuck, Nora? I shouted, again not able to modulate my tone, as we jogged over to her. Don't ever do that again.

What? she asked innocently. I was literally just getting cigarettes.

I stared down at the carton of Marlboro menthols she held in her hands alongside a receipt and a Clipper lighter.

For the second time that day, I felt all the air leave my body, this time with relief.

You're smoking again? I asked, finally able to bring my voice down to a regular volume and pitch.

Nora shrugged.

If I'm going to get through this trip in one piece, I'm going to need some mind-altering substances, she said.

You had some mind-altering substances, remember? I said, frustrated. Your prescription medication. You know. The pills you doofed into the Grand Canyon.

She ignored me and opened the packet, sliding her long fingernails under the cellophane. I grabbed one for myself and lit it.

Since when did *you* start smoking again? Nora asked. I thought you stopped at like, seventeen.

Beanie was staring at me with eyes the size of dinner plates.

You told me that you've never had a cigarette in your life, she said accusingly.

No, I replied, as I inhaled deeply and remembered, with the nicotine hit, exactly why I had loved it so much. I said I never had a cigarette in *your* life. I stopped when I got pregnant with you.

We leaned against the wall outside the 7-Eleven and smoked, staring out into the road.

Anyway, I said. I'm starting to think that I need some mind-altering substances to get through this trip, as well.

Nora snorted. Really, she said. With Mum's track record, it's a Christmas miracle that neither of us ended up junkies.

I was put off drugs for life, I agreed. After seeing what they did to her.

She literally died of lung cancer, you idiots, Beanie said, staring at the both of us with such a piercing look of disapproval, I almost gave in and stubbed my cigarette out on the wall.

Okay, Miss Vape Queen, I shot back at her. She huffed, and a heavy-sounding engine whooshed past her on the road, a blur of red, white, blue and black.

I would have barely noticed it, had it not been for the fact that a familiar set of piercing, devilishly handsome, ocean-colored eyes glittered in the rush of color and metal as they flew by.

I recognized those eyes.

I knew the baby blues of Abraham Lincoln holding an AK-47 anywhere. I knew them like the back of my hand.

RANDY! I yelled at the top of my lungs, and took off in a sprint after the camper van down the road.

Nora and Beanie weren't far behind.

I had never been much of a runner. In cross country at school, Chelsea and I would finish half a lap and then hide behind the trees at the far end of the field and smoke, or hop the fence and play truant for the rest of the day, haunting the allotments or the alleyway round the back of the old people's home. As a result, I had about as much physical stamina as a soggy twig and before we'd sprinted more than fifty yards, I felt the beginnings of a stitch in my side, tasted blood in my mouth. Nora was even more out of shape than I was, with no discernible sign of a muscle on her body, and she lagged further behind me, barely able to conjure up more than a jog.

But Beanie—wonderful, gorgeous girl that she was—had spent most of secondary school on the girls' football team at Acton Comprehensive. She had taken the team all the way to the regional knockouts in Year Eleven and they'd placed second in the league table before she went off to drama school for her A levels. She missed playing football, I knew it. Though she pretended that she didn't. She'd played a midfield position. I didn't really have much of a clue what that meant, but it clearly had something to do with running. She sprinted down the road, right in the middle of it where the camber was at its highest, flames of orange hair billowing behind her. I'd never seen her move so quickly outside of football cleats. She was wearing her silver Docs and her feet slapped heavily against the concrete.

RANDY, she screamed, mimicking my tone.

But even Beanie couldn't keep up with him. There were no traffic lights on the main stretch of the Historic District. The vehicle was receding fast, Abraham Lincoln's sparkling eyes beginning to fade from view, in the midst of the brown fine dust the tires kicked up.

We were back at the microbrewery, level with our own camper van.

Quickly, I shouted, my breath catching as I fumbled with the keys. The van didn't have central locking, so I unlocked the front doors, my hands trembling as I did, and Beanie and Nora both bundled into the passenger side, while I launched myself into the driver's seat. The ignition stuttered because I was being too heavy-handed with it in my efforts to get us moving and behind Randy.

MUM! Beanie shouted urgently.

I KNOW, I shrieked back at her.

The engine finally roared to life and I immediately squealed forward, the car in Drive instead of Reverse. Beanie had somehow managed to get all four of her limbs but not her head or butt up onto the dashboard and was now stuck. Nora was trying to pull her out of the gap between the plastic and the glass of the windscreen.

What the hell are you doing? I screamed as I finally got the van going and into Reverse.

It seemed heavier and more cumbersome than it ever had before, the 120,000 miles on the clock and the engine light that had been flashing on and off and that I had been ignoring since we'd left the Grand Canyon now both making themselves known.

We groaned down the road in the direction Randy had been driving, breaking the speed limit of every neighborhood through which we drove.

As we approached the city limits once more, the roads began to clog up with more cars, and still no sign of Abraham Lincoln and his gun.

We're fucked, Nora said matter-of-factly. I eased my foot off the accelerator. We'd lost him.

I'm sorry, I said quietly. I noticed then that Beanie's Spanish language CD was playing again.

Tengo un gato. Tengo un perro.

Don't worry about it, Nora said, and she looked suddenly exhausted. She climbed through the middle space in between the driver's seat and passenger's seat, and tucked her whole body under the blanket in the back.

Sorry, Nory, I said again, quietly so that she couldn't hear me.

Beanie was in the process of disengaging herself from the dashboard, while I did a three-point turn, when she grabbed my arm urgently. Mum, look, she said.

Further down the road, which led out into the desert and towards Vegas, the Lincoln AK-47 van sat, engine off, in the forecourt of a small, rusting gas station.

Oh my shit, I replied.

Let's go!

I eased the van back into Drive, up the road and then, once I had turned in, crept up into the gas station, as though if I went too fast or too loud, I might spook the other van. Randy's vehicle was quiet and empty, with no Randy in sight.

What shall we do, just wait? Beanie asked.

Nora had already fallen asleep.

I guess we just wait.

I'll go and stand by the van, Beanie volunteered, letting herself out of the passenger door.

I killed the ignition and watched as she leaned up against the van, popping a piece of chewing gum into her mouth.

The Spanish CD said: *Tengo una familia hermosa.*

We waited for what seemed like for ever. The CD finished and started again from the beginning. I watched Beanie, and Beanie watched the interior of the store through the grimy windows. Outside, propane and firewood and engine oil were for sale. Inside, a queue had formed at the checkout.

We watched and waited.

It seemed to be taking too long. The queue to pay had fully completed and refreshed itself with new customers, and none of them were Randy.

What's going on? I asked myself quietly. Nora rolled over in the back of the van.

Then, he seemed to come from nowhere, though realistically it was the door at the side of the building. Probably the door to the lavatory.

He saw Beanie leaning against his van, and disappeared back through the same door.

Beanie glanced at me through the windscreen, baffled. I was the same.

What is he doing? I said out loud.

Moments later he reappeared from the bathroom with—to my sickening horror—a shiny metal baseball bat, and now he was striding purposefully towards Beanie.

With a yelp, I let myself out of the van and sprinted over to him. Beanie, now standing rigid, seemed to be unable to move, her eyes glued to the baseball bat.

Uhhhhh, she said, her eyes wide.

Trying to hot wire my van, Randy said, clearly mid-rant. I've had it with you fucking kids trying to fuck with me, need to learn some respect—

Uhhhh, Beanie said again.

Randy! RANDY! I screeched out to him, sprinting over. Hey Randy, remember me? This is my daughter.

He squinted at me, baseball bat still poised to swing, and stared. Then he stared again at Beanie.

I'm sorry, sweetheart, he said. I don't remember your name. I do remember you, though, even without my glasses.

I gulped down a ragged, metallic-tasting breath.

It was Matilda, I said, feeling sweat pool in my lower back. And this is my daughter Beatrice; I think you only met her briefly last night.

Randy walked away. And Beanie and I glanced at one another frantically, at sea.

He walked back to the door at the side of the building once again and went in, disappearing from view for a handful of seconds. And then he reemerged without the baseball bat. He walked back over to us, relaxed and purposeful. I felt the tightness on my heart ease just a fraction.

Want to tell me what in the hell you're doing here? he asked, suspicious. Are you following me? Are you trying to rob me?

No, no, I said, still trying to catch my breath.

You've got something of ours, Beanie clarified, looking small next to him.

You've got our cool box, I added. And we've got yours.

I ran back to the van and yanked the passenger-side door open, and dragged out Randy's cooler.

See? I said, opening it to show him the two almost-empty moonshine bottles inside.

The heat of the car exhausts moving in and out of the gas-station fore-court was a different kind of heat to that of the desert. It was close, slick, cloying, unbearable.

Randy peered into the cooler and registered its contents. Then he looked up and eyed me suspiciously.

Are you running drugs? he asked beadily.

No! I replied quickly. No. Just on a road trip.

He looked unconvinced, and made no move towards his truck.

I realized that Randy wasn't going to move until I told him everything.

It's my mum's ashes, okay? I gabbled. It's my mum. We didn't declare it when we came into the country. She asked us to scatter her in a canyon, which was a bit abstract and non-specific, but we decided to scatter her in the Grand Canyon. That's what we were trying to do.

Randy said nothing, still didn't move, sized the pair of us up.

Please, I said pathetically.

He chewed on his moustache.

Wait here, he said. He opened his own van up—the back door this time—and climbed in, sliding the door shut behind him.

And then he was back.

You're a very silly pair of girls, he said.

Okay, misogynistically charged language, Beanie replied.

Shut up, I hissed at her. Randy was holding our cool box.

You can't scatter ashes at the Grand Canyon, Randy said, his voice finally softer. It's illegal and it messes with the ecosystem. But there's a few smaller canyons in the desert that aren't patrolled. You can take a hike and find a nice spot for her.

He plopped the cooler on the ground and picked up his own. I ran over to it and opened the lid. Inside, nestled between two bottles of lager, was Mum in a Tupperware.

Thank you, I said, the gratitude spilling out of me. Thank you, thank you, thank you.

Y'all be safe, now, Randy said. And with that he climbed into his van and fired it up. Within thirty seconds he was dust on the road up ahead. I felt my bones turn to jelly.

EXTRACTS [VARIOUS] FROM INTERVIEW TRANSCRIPTS, QUOTED IN INGRID OLSSEN: VISIONARY BY RICHARD TAPER (FORTHCOMING FROM ORANGE RABBIT PRESS)

Karoline Olssen, sister and manager:

Ingrid's work in the latter part of her career certainly seemed to have a preoccupation with death. I would say that it started around the time Matilda left home, and it continued—really—right up until her death some fifteen or so years later.

Oakland Frink, art collector:

There were rumors that, after her father died sometime in the winter of 2006, Ingrid visited her birthplace in Ringerike, with her sister, and produced a series of line drawings portraying her father's dead body. It was *quite* transgressive, though of course we've seen other artists do the same thing. Lucian Freud's mother was his subject many times in life *and* death. There's also the Victorian tradition of post-mortem photography, which is more of a celebration of the dead rather than a ritualistic approach. It's unusual for Olssen to be influenced by the Victorians—it's not consistent with the rest of her body of work. But the nature of the portraiture is very much in the vein of the gothic, and her thematic interests: the body as monstrous, the disarticulation of artist and subject, a preoccupation with the macabre. Nevertheless, those line drawings of her dead father—if they exist—are something of a blip in her portfolio. She never used dead people as her subjects at any other time in her career, though she played with death as a concept in her work. I often wonder why she bothered to do them. I once offered her a substantial amount of money for those drawings and she—can you believe?—*spat* directly into my face.

Sadie Nelson, bassist for Acid Rain and close personal friend:

I know all about dead dads. I wrote a fourteen-track concept album about mine while I was in rehab.

Karoline Olssen:
Oakland Frink is a leech and I'm pleased that Ingrid spat at him.
I now barely remember the details of the Vivienne Westwood col-
laboration we lost when the news broke to the press.

Chad McCloy, journalist and host of *McCloy Who's Talking*:
It was truly a shame that someone leaked the spitting story to the
press. From what I've heard, the behavior was justified. I wasn't
there, but my close personal friend, that fella from the movie adap-
tation of *Ubik* whose name I can't remember, was. According to
him, Frink—who is known for being something of a provocateur—
made some derogatory comment about Olssen's father, who had
recently passed away. Of course, the press ran with "out of control
Olssen is at it again." None of it was helped by the fact that whole
affair took place in a strip club and Ingrid was photographed later
that night passed out in an alleyway.

Sadie Nelson:
Ingrid and I both knew about how to channel pain into our art,
you know? And that's why she decided to do the drawings of her
dead dad. I've never seen the drawings, actually. I'm not one hundred percent sure that they exist.

Matilda Robb, daughter:
I haven't seen the drawings, no. I didn't know she did those. She
did go to Ringerike in late 2006, though, when my grandfather Lars died. She and Karoline both went; they had to make
arrangements for the funeral, and this bank was trying to repos-
sess the farm.

Sadie Nelson:
Ingrid told me herself that it was someone from a bank who'd found
Lars Olssen's body in the pig shed. The bank guy had been around
to take stock of collateral, and ended up evicting a dead man.

Nora Robb, daughter and performance artist:

Yeah, she went to Hønefoss to bury our grandfather. It wasn't just organizing the funeral. It was the estate—it turned out that Olssengården wasn't making money. It hadn't been for years. And Lars Olssen, my grandfather, was basically waiting for the bailiffs to come knocking or to die, whichever came first. Turns out those two things happened at exactly the same time. Did Mattie tell you that? Because I told her about it. Mattie wasn't really around then. She was off with her new family. But I was there. I was there when Mum got the call to say her dad was dead. I was there to help her pack. To book her flight. To call Aunt Karoline. When it turned out that the farm was drowning in debt, I was there to help Mum arrange the selling-off of all the assets, to make sure the debts were paid properly. She couldn't do it herself, she was so bad with money. I was eleven years old, by the way. I did all of it, and when she went off to Norway to deal with our grandfather's estate, I spent Christmas alone.

CHAPTER 22

THE NIGHTS IN THE MOJAVE DESERT WERE JUST AS HOT AS THE DAYS.

We booked the van into another campsite on the edge of a small range of rocky terrain called Bootleg Canyon. The campsite was flat and quiet, with a drab swimming pool behind a locked gate next to the reception building. I parked us up in a corner of the site, and opened all the doors to the van. It was mid-afternoon now, and the sun was relentless. We dragged folded garden chairs out the back of the van and set them up in a loose triangle on the edge of the pitch. Then I took off my walking boots, my toes throbbing, and slid into a pair of flip-flops and took a towel over to the shower block. And then I had the best shower of my life.

When I got back to the van, Nora was awake and leaning back in one of the folding chairs, her arms and legs tilted towards the sun. Beanie sat in the back of the van with the sliding door all the way open, silent tears sliding down her cheeks.

Oh my God, what's the matter? I asked her, immediately panicking.

It's nothing, she said, wiping her eyes. I'm watching a most heart-warming sporting moments YouTube compilation.

I rolled my eyes at her and slid into one of the other chairs.

Oh my God, I said quietly, to no one in particular, to the desert.

Yeah, Nora replied.

We got Mum back, I said.

Yeah, Nora said again.

She brought a hand to her brow and pinched the skin on the bridge of her nose hard.

Nora said, You can feel the universe expanding into itself.

What, here?

Yeah, here.

We watched the sun make its way across the sky slowly and methodically. Beanie got Pink Floyd playing out of a Bluetooth speaker she had brought in her luggage.

I checked my phone and saw that I had another missed call from Richard. A text from Gus with details of a pharmacy in Vegas and another in Los Angeles that would be able to prescribe Nora's medication if we showed them her insurance and got a letter from her clinic in the UK. Gus had already arranged all the details. The letter would be with us by tomorrow as long as Nora got on a video call with her doctor and confirmed the situation.

I texted him a quick thank you and watched Nora as she picked up her book from the ground next to her and turned the pages contentedly. She seemed to be okay—stable, even—if exhausted.

How're you feeling? I asked her.

She looked up at me warily.

Fiiiine, she said, suspicious.

How's your mood?

Matt, she said. Shut up. I'm not going to throw myself onto the highway while you're looking the other way.

I'm just worried—

Don't be.

I pouted a little, inadvertently.

God knows how you look after all those kids, she said. I thought of little Isla and her dead nan.

They're kids, I said. They're a lot easier. And they're not related to me.

You can stop with this. Just let me be.

Okay, I said reluctantly. I resolved to talk to her tomorrow about getting her medication.

I felt the weight of the day heavy on my chest, and slid into a chair opposite Nora. It was the best time of the day. Nora lit a cigarette and returned to her book.

I woke up two hours later, a flaky patch of dribble dried at the corner of my mouth. The temperature hadn't changed at all. The evening approached, and the sun was about ready to dip behind the mountains. On the other side of the RV park, someone had unlocked the gate to the fenced-off swimming pool and there were kids divebombing into the water from the edge. A Labrador was chained up outside the reception building and every time one of the kids screamed or laughed with exhilaration, the dog started barking.

Nora and Beanie were both gone, and so was the van.

Immediately I felt the claw of panic crawling up the inside of my ribcage. But I looked at the ground. Nora's book and flip-flops, two empty beer bottles, and a mess of potato chip bags and banana peels. I checked my phone and saw a text from Beanie. *We went exploring, back in a couple of hours! Let me know if you want anything.*

Fine, fine, fine, I thought, and relaxed back into my chair, trying to ignore the gnawing at the back of my mind that said, *She's not on her drugs, what if she's not stable.* I noticed how my skin was starting to crisp. But all the SPF was in the van, and the van was gone. I maneuvered my lawn chair into the shadow of the RV in the pitch next door, dark and quiet as it was. I willed myself to believe what Nora had told me plainly, with her full chest, while maintaining eye contact, that she was okay, that I should trust her.

I thought I would wait and, when they got back, be petulant about the fact that they didn't wake me up and ask me to join them. But I knew that it made sense that I didn't. I chastised myself. *You're her mother, Matt, not her friend.*

When I was a little younger than Beanie, *I* was the one leaving *Nora* behind. Climbing out the window in the middle of the night to drive out to the Surrey Hills with Gus and snog in the back of his car until the sun came up. Nora, seven or eight, not understanding that she couldn't come with me, that I was outgrowing her.

Her face, pressed up against the window as I left, had stayed smooshed to the pane of glass until I'd got home hours later and slid into bed with her to share the warmth.

The small whisper of her voice in the middle of the night, making me promise to come back for her.

Now, I was the one with my face pressed against the glass.

It made sense, but it still hurt.

I decided to call Richard, because I knew he would make me feel better.

Hey! he said, his voice colored with surprise as he answered my call.

You'll never guess where I am, I said, mustering a conspiratorial tone.

Hmmm . . . I don't know. Can you give me a clue?

Okay . . . I looked around as though inspiration would pop out from behind the shower block.

It's uhh . . . very hot, I said lamely.

Are you at Champneys? I thought we were going to do that together at Christmas.

No, I'm not at Champneys.

Oh.

There was a long and awkward silence.

I'm in the desert, I said eventually, giving up. Just outside of Vegas.

Oh—wow!

We're on a road trip.

We?

Me, Beanie and Nora.

Oh, *wow*.

There was something about Richard's tone that made me think that it was very not *wow* that we were, all three of us, in the same country as him.

We're going to come to the exhibition, I said, testing for his response.

Oh, *wow*, he said once more, in the same dead-behind-the-eyes tone.

What? I asked him.

What do you mean, what?

Well, it sounds like you're not very happy to hear that we're coming. You were the one who was encouraging us.

You. I was encouraging you.

So? What's the difference? What's wrong with the only living descendants of the late, great Ingrid Olssen coming to her show? Aren't you the one always harping on about legacy?

It's just . . . he paused. Hold on, let me go somewhere quieter.

I could hear background noise. The noises of a restaurant or a bar, maybe. Multiple voices, cutlery against crockery, glasses clinking. I thought I could hear the distinctively shrill tone of my aunt Karoline, even, though I might have been imagining it.

I don't think you should come, Richard said finally, once the noises had died down. He was slurring his words a little and I realized he was tipsy.

Why not? I asked, annoyed.

I just . . . really don't think you're going to like it, Matt. I don't think you're going to like what they've done.

What *you've* done, you mean. You and Aunt Karoline.

I had nothing to do with it. I've just been holed up in an Airbnb finishing the book while I'm out here. I've barely been to the gallery space. I don't get a say in this stuff. I just don't want to see you upset. I know how difficult it is for you, with all the history with your mum and stuff.

I stewed, a little shocked, momentarily lost for words.

I'm sorry, what the actual fuck are you talking about, Richard?

I just—don't think it's a good idea. You're going to upset yourself. And Nora and Beanie will get upset, too. God knows how Nora will react with the state she's in. I'm not sure how responsible it was of you to take her out of the country.

I seethed a little more as he fell silent on the other end of the phone.

Matilda? You still there? he asked eventually.

Yeah. I'm still here, I said.

So, what do you think?

I exhaled heavily. What I think, Richard, I said carefully, is that just because you're writing a book on my family, it doesn't mean you know what is best for me, best for Nora, and sure as hell what's best for my daughter. And I don't appreciate you suggesting otherwise.

I heard him sigh. I know. I'm sorry, he said, a pleading note in his voice.

The second thing, I continued, on a roll now, is that this is my fucking mother. My mother's *legacy*. Remember? It's got nothing to do with you. And you're not allowed to fuck it up.

Matilda, listen—

So I'll see you in San Francisco, I said. In six days.

And I ended the call.

I sat in the desert dust and listened to the kids screaming euphorically, the noises so far removed from the churning I felt inside me. I wished that Nora was here with me. I knew that she would understand why I felt such anger. I stared at the cool box, which had been left out in the sun. And then I heard the sound of an engine I recognized, as the Flamesmobile pulled into the campsite and Nora expertly guided it through the lanes to the parking spot on our pitch. Relief washed over me.

She threw the door open and climbed out.

We have got to get rid of it, I told her, pointing at the cool box.

Our mother? Sure. Okay, but don't be mad, she said.

What do you mean, don't be mad?

Beanie had walked around the front of the van then, a sheepish look on her face.

What's happened? I asked. And then I saw it.

Beanie had a bar of metal through her left eyebrow. It sparkled in the sunlight. I stood up, feeling the look of horror sweep across my face before I could mask it.

What do you think? Beanie asked, grimacing.

Show me, I said, reaching for her chin. She obliged and came over to me, rested her chin on my fingers so I could turn her face this way and that.

The bar had a little rhinestone-encrusted ball on either end of it to keep it secure. And the skin around where it had punctured her face—her beautiful, perfect face—was angry and red and swollen.

I sat back down on the chair, all of the air gone out of me. My mouth couldn't form words.

Mum? You're scaring me. Say something, please.

I have nothing to say, I said finally, my voice flat.

Muuuum. Come on. I'm seventeen. It's not illegal.

And *you*, I said, finally turning to Nora. You. I'm going to fucking kill you.

Not before I do it first, she said sardonically, punching at the air.

Stony silence fell between us.

Sorry, she said. Too soon?

I locked myself in the van out of spite. And then, annoyed at my idleness and restless with unspent rage, I cleaned everything. I tidied discarded clothes back into suitcases. Cleaned down the table and righted the furniture back into the upright seated position. Folded Nora's blanket and cleared away the trash that Beanie had discarded back here while working her way through a share-size bag of Haribo as we drove across the desert.

Call your father, I told Beanie after she'd been pounding on the van window with the flat of her hand for ten minutes. And she had the good sense to follow my instruction. Nora had gone quiet again, which was infinitesimally worse than her joking about being suicidal.

After the interior of the van was spotless and smelled of lemon-scented disinfectant, I sat stoically at the table and watched through the blackout windows as Beanie paced back and forth a hundred yards away, talking on her phone to Gus who I was certain, on the other end of the line, was just as furious as I was. Meanwhile, Nora eased herself back into one of the lawn chairs and promptly fell asleep with a T-shirt over her face. Just as I did, she slept quickly and deeply.

Eventually, the sun slid all the way down and the sky turned indigo. My phone buzzed.

Matt, I think you should get out the van and talk to her, Gus said when I answered it.

I know, I replied. But now I'm in here. I've made a statement and I've got to stick by it.

No, you don't, he said soothingly. She's technically not done anything wrong, you know.

Gus, you should see it, though. Her *little face*. And it's got a big bit of metal sticking out of it.

I think you're less bothered about the piercing and maybe a bit more upset that she didn't tell you she was doing it. Or that she didn't invite you along with her.

I slumped further back into the chair. Shut up, I said.

Just talk to the her, please, Gus urged. You're all sleeping in one bed tonight. Don't make it more painful than it needs to be.

I sighed deeply. You know I hate it when you're right, I said.

I know, he replied, and I could hear the smile in his voice. Now, go and make up with the kid.

We signed off the call and I suddenly very acutely felt like I was the child throwing the tantrum, and Nora and Beanie were the rational adults, and Gus was being called in to *handle* me, which was of course preposterous.

I slid the door open with a sharp screech of metal on unoiled metal.

Well? I asked Beanie directly, as her head snapped up from her phone.

I'm sorry, Mum, she said earnestly.

Fine, I replied. Let's get some dinner.

We slept rough, the van too hot for comfort, but the fear of mosquitoes and lizards and other sorts of bugs preventing us from keeping the windows open overnight. At four in the morning, I walked through the dust, illuminated by floodlights, to the shower block. I took a shower and fell asleep under the water for ten minutes.

The next morning, Nora slept in late again. Beanie—a light sleeper like her father—cracked eggs on the travel-sized frying pan while I brewed the camping kettle.

I poured us coffee in a silence that wasn't wholly comfortable.

I'm sorry again, Mum, Beanie said eventually, her eyebrows scrunching together, which only served to highlight the ugly metal stuck in there.

I exhaled heavily. I had spent most of the night trying to reason with myself.

It's fine, I replied. I overreacted. It's your body, and you should be able to do what you want with it.

She smiled and hugged me round the waist as though she were a child again.

Thank you, she whispered.

You know you're going to have to take it out for auditions, though, don't you?

She shrugged. I'll work it out. It looks cool though, doesn't it?

I didn't think that it looked cool. I thought that it overpowered the rest of her delicate features, the freckles on the bridge of her nose and the paleness of her mouth.

I nodded. Yeah, it looks cool, kid.

She grinned at me and flipped an egg.

An hour later the van door slid open and Nora joined us in her pajamas, her face tired and her hair a fuzzy mess. She looked ill. I resisted the urge to ask if she was okay.

Instead I said, Thanks a lot.

For what? she asked.

I pointed at Beanie's face.

Didn't think to ask me first? I said, my voice hostile.

Nora stared at me, her face blank.

Yes? I asked. I was waiting for an apology.

She's basically an adult.

She is *not* an adult.

She's seventeen.

I know.

Remember what I did at seventeen?

She rolled her socks down and exposed the twin tattoos that I had almost completely forgotten about. On her right ankle, the word *fuck*, and on her left, the word *off*. Stick-and-poke, self-inked so that now the neat cursive script had begun to bleed and had turned a lukewarm blue as the ink had slowly rejected itself from her skin.

Oh God, I said. Yes. That.

I had received a call from Karoline one Saturday morning. I'd been living on my own by then, recently out of Chelsea's apartment and finally working so that I could rent our first tiny studio on the Great West Road in a building that had been condemned to demolition due to asbestos and mold. Beanie was ten years old. She had recently placed third at her first ever cross-country meet.

You won't believe what she's done, Karoline had said dramatically.

I didn't know whether she was talking about Mum or Nora at first.

What? I asked, distracted. I was wrangling with laundry at the time, only half listening.

She's come back from school—ah, so Nora, then, not Mum—with *fuck off* tattooed on her ankles.

I snorted involuntarily.

Matilda. This isn't a joke. It's permanent!

And what do you want me to do about it? I asked her.

Call her. Talk to her. She needs a bit of guidance, darling.

Isn't that Ingrid's job?

Mum had recently disappeared for a month while Nora was at school, and had turned up on the south coast of Italy. She had joined her friend Sadie's band on tour and the pair of them had decided to rent a chalet in Naples and get high indefinitely, until Karoline somehow found her and flew over and fetched her home.

You and I both know your mother can't, Karoline said darkly. I need *you* to talk to her.

By then, I hadn't spoken to Nora for two years.

I can't, I said, my stomach knotting.

Karoline groaned and hung up the phone.

Do you hate them? I asked Nora now, meaning the tattoos. You were so young.

She narrowed her eyes at me, as though she wanted to say something more. But instead she just shrugged.

A body is a body, she said simply.

Good, you're up, I've got something to tell you both, Beanie said with some gusto, emerging from the back of the van and handing her a plate of eggs on toast, and Nora and I both fell silent, the rest of the conversation dying on our lips.

What? Nora asked.

I found a place for Grandma's ashes, Beanie said, proud of herself. And you need to get ready, because we're going in half an hour.

———————

I could tell that Nora didn't want to go, that every effort she made to move was like dragging her nails across a chalkboard, like she was walking uphill with a pickup truck tied to her waist, and she was dragging that up too.

You good? I asked her as we walked to the shower block together. I couldn't help myself. The look she shot me told me to shut up.

When I got back to the van, clean and dressed, she wasn't there.

Beanie was getting restless. We were running late for whatever it was that she had planned.

I think she's still showering, she said.

I'll go and get her, I replied.

I walked back to the shower block, the dust I kicked up from the ground settling on the skin of my newly-soaped shins.

Nora? I called inside the sparse, tiled, square room.

There was no reply.

One of the showers behind the plastic curtains that separated the cubicles from the changing area was still running, steam rising above it and mushrooming across the ceiling.

Nora, are you in there? I asked again.

Yes, came the small-voiced reply.

Can I come in? I asked, beginning to panic.

She didn't answer me.

I slowly pulled back the curtain.

She was on the floor of the cubicle, letting the water run over her, down across her face and eyes and off the bridge of her nose. Her hair soaking wet and slicked to her back.

I can't move, she said.

I couldn't tell whether or not she was crying, on account of the water.

Okay, I'll help you, I said, feeling my heart hammering.

I unlaced my shoes and took off my socks, and once the automatic water timer ran out, I stepped in.

She had a towel hanging up on the hook on the wall, and I took it and wrapped it around her as though she were a child. A curious déjà vu of all the times I'd bathed her as a child at the Richmond house. Except she'd been a child, then. Now, I could see the damage the years had done to her body, though I tried not to look. The notches on her spine strained against her skin. A burn mark on her shoulder, or that's what it looked like. On her upper left thigh, a gnarled and bruise-colored scar was the evidence left behind by Maurice Hoffmann's shotgun. I shuddered when I saw it. It seemed to me like the shadow of another existence, one in which there was Mum and the circus of her life, which sucked us in too.

And on Nora's hips and belly and the tops of her arms were rows and rows and rows of neat silvery-white scar tissue, straight, perfectly formed lines going all the way up her like the rungs of a ladder.

Oh, Nora, I said.

She was crying properly then, wracking sobs making her whole body judder with the effort of them.

I stood her up, letting her lean her whole weight on me, and guided her out of the cubicle and made her sit on the bench next to the sinks while I dried her off and dressed her slowly. By the time I was done she had stopped crying for the most part, and was staring ahead at the shower curtain, a faraway look in her eyes.

I wiped her face with a baby wipe from her toiletry bag, and combed her hair back out of her face, gently working out the knots. Then I sat down next to her.

Just let me know when you're ready, I said, feeling the fabric of my heart ripping as I looked at her.

I don't think I'm ever going to be ready, she replied.

Okay, I said, that's fine. We can wait here for as long as you need. But I think you will be, Nory. I think you're much stronger than you think you are.

They were words that I trotted out to kids at school all the time. I was aware of their fraudulence even before they'd exited my mouth. But I also knew in the bottom of my stomach that for her, they were true, too.

I knew now wasn't the time to bring up medication, the prospect of Nora taking it so she might curb the edges of these jagged swings of her mood, so instead we sat in silence as slowly Nora's breathing turned to normal.

After ten minutes Beanie was standing outside the shower block calling for us.

Guys, we're so late, she was saying, her voice urgent.

I'll tell her we're not going, I said quietly, standing up.

No, no, Nora said quickly. We're going.

Are you sure?

We need to get rid of her.

I felt the same way. I nodded, feeling my own body turning to lead.

Okay, let's go, I said.

It was a zipline company. Beanie made us walk for twenty minutes along a road with no pavements to a different part of town, a little further to the north and closer to Vegas. To get to a zipline company.

What are we going to do, send her off down a zipline with the lid off? I asked as we signed waivers on a too-small bench in a dingy storefront. We had watched a safety video, had been given helmets, and were now waiting to be loaded into a school bus with no doors.

No, Beanie replied patronizingly. We're going to scatter her at the top and then zipline down.

At the top of what?

Bootleg Canyon. It's still a canyon, isn't it? Just not quite *the* canyon. It's the best we've got unless you want to drive back to Arizona.

And we're paying seventy dollars a person for the pleasure, I confirmed.

Beanie rolled her eyes.

We got in the bus with a couple who had been on honeymoon in Vegas and had decided to daytrip to this zipline. Apparently it was quite the attraction. There was also a group of girls in their twenties on a bachelorette party, and a solo German traveler who got chatting to Nora—who was too quiet to indicate either way whether she was into it or not—and showing her pictures of supercars on his phone. The guy was a supercar enthusiast. He had just been to a big meet in the desert and now he was heading back to Vegas to fly home. Nora's lip curled as he spoke to her about the Nissan Skyline that had crashed into a dune. I watched her closely—so closely that she turned and frowned at me pointedly. It was becoming clearer and clearer to me that I was in no way equipped to deal with Nora's illness. In my training we had been taught to distinguish between mental illness and mental ill-health. Mental illness was a disease, which needed a robust treatment plan, often medication and therapies. Nora had a treatment plan, sure, from her doctor and her therapist. I had no idea what it was. All I knew was which pills she was meant to take at which times and in what sorts of volumes and frequencies. I had taken her out of the country when she was fresh out of a mental breakdown and a suicide attempt, and she had abandoned her medication. I was hurting her. But there was no turning back, now. We had come too far already.

The bus was being operated by a surfer-looking dudebro type, and his colleague, another bleach-blond ultra-tanned kid. Both were probably on summer break from college. They wore red polo shirts, board shorts and worn-out Converse. One of them navigated the bus up dirt tracks of increasing altitude, tracks that seemed too narrow to accommodate a school bus, while the other spoke into a microphone and delivered quippy facts about Bootleg Canyon and Boulder City. The bus careered wildly from side to side as we ascended. It didn't seem safe at all. I looked out of the open gap where the door was meant to be and tried not to think about being flung against the rocks.

Where did you find this place? I asked Beanie as the bus continued to jerk and sway, taking hairpin bends up the mountain with what seemed to be way too much speed.

She shrugged, grinning. She was an adrenaline junkie, and she was enjoying herself. Don't know, she said. Dad sent it to me. Then quietly, she said, Is Nora okay?

Nora was still being talked at by the German man. She still hadn't said a word, and he hadn't taken the hint.

I sidled over to them and caught his eye. *Beklager, hun snakker ikke engelsk,* I said in Norwegian, shaking my head at him vigorously, my eyes wide.

Comprehension dawned on him and he apologized in German and sidled away.

Now, no one say anything in English in front of him for the rest of the trip, I said as I squeezed into the seat next to Nora, dragging Beanie with me. I nudged Nora. *Er du ok nå?*

Yes. I'm fine, she said quietly, looking away from me.

We finally stopped at an inlet in the rock, and we filed out of the bus. Each of us was handed a large and heavy metal contraption that looked like something that might be used to connect pieces of railway track together.

The bleach-blond instructor—Andrew—explained the rules of the zipline.

We strapped on our helmets and got started. I had prepared for a difficult hike, with steep climbing and uneven terrain. But it turned out to be fairly relaxed. The equipment we carried was heavy, but not restrictively so. As we climbed, the desert came into view, as did the Colorado River that cut through the middle and ended with the Hoover Dam. The desert seemed to stretch on for ever, and the water in the dam was black and still and perfect. It was peaceful. I looked up to Beanie and Nora, who were walking side by side ahead of me on the trail, and I saw that they felt the same. They looked out to the desert, which was never-ending, and their faces were unspoiled, apart from that fucking piece of metal hanging out of Beatrice's eyebrow. Nevertheless, the exercise felt good. The feeling of blood moving through the heart and the body. The feeling of being alive.

We reached the destination of our climb, a little breathless, our pulses quickening. In front of us, much larger, higher, and longer than what I had been expecting, was the first of a series of ziplines, with three cords running from a large metal platform far down the mountain to a destination point a couple of hundred meters diagonally below us. The function of the contraptions now became evident. Andrew showed us how they fitted onto the cords and, once secure and clipped to our body harnesses, would carry us all the way down to the next checkpoint. He showed us how to lie backwards to make our bodies more aerodynamic.

Shall we do it now? Beanie asked, as he talked. At the top?

I shrugged and looked at Nora, who shrugged too.

Let's go this way.

Beanie found a gap in the rocks and we slipped through it as Andrew continued his safety demonstration. We climbed a little more, gripping on to rocks and handholds as we did so. Ahead, and further up, was a viewpoint on a shaved-down platform, with a bench and a little pedestal with some information about the canyon and the adjacent Red Mountain on it. To the east was the lake we had seen when we'd driven into the city, still and flat and perfect. And to the south was Boulder City itself, sprawled out flat in the basin. In every direction there was hot, dry desert the color of rust.

Here? I asked Nora.

She looked around, kicked at the stones on the ground, squinted into the sun, sniffed a little. Took off her sunglasses, cleaned them with a corner of her shirt and put them back on.

Yeah, here, she said.

Beanie got the Tupperware out of the waistband of her shorts.

Oh my God, *that's* where you've kept her?

She shrugged. They said no bags. What else was I supposed to do?

I scoffed. She hesitated as she held the box out to us.

Who wants to do it then? she asked.

I raised my eyebrows at Nora, who grimaced.

You do it, she said. You're the eldest.

I rolled my eyes. Bullshit. You knew her better than I did, anyway.

Okay, it's not a competition, she said spikily.

Why don't we do it together?

I unsnapped the lid and removed it. She took one side of the box and I the other. Mum's ashes were grey and fine and unremarkable. It seemed almost a science fiction that the dust in this box had once been her body. It was no more distinguishable than the dust on the ground.

'Kay, ready? I asked her.

As I'll ever be, she replied.

We walked to the edge of the viewing point with a strange ceremonial gravitas. And when we got to the edge, we gently tipped the tub and let the softness of the wind carry the dust away into the desert. Slowly, the ashes dissipated. Slowly, slowly. Until there were none left, and they had already disappeared on the wing of the breeze.

And that was it.

I looked at Nora and she looked at me, both of us a little confused.

Anticlimactic, Beanie commented.

I laughed. And then Nora laughed. And then we couldn't stop laughing. She slapped me on the back as I doubled over with a stitch. I couldn't stop. Every time I tried, it bubbled back up in me. Beanie stared at us, bewildered and offended, as though we were madwomen.

That was it, I said, repeating myself out loud.

That was fucking it, Nora agreed.

And we laughed some more.

Beanie pulled out her phone and took a photograph of us.

We returned to Andrew and the group of honeymooners and bachelorette party-ers, the giggles still bubbling at our lips. Andrew didn't seem to have noticed we'd gone.

We waited for our turn to be strapped into our runners, and our runners attached to the steel cords running down the mountain. And then we lay back and Andrew let us loose.

And we screamed. And we flew.

CHAPTER 23

AFTER THE CATHARSIS OF GETTING RID OF MUM'S
ASHES DISSIPATED, I COULDN'T STOP STARING AT
BEANIE'S EYEBROW.

It bothered me as we walked back to the RV park, having been guilt-tripped
into leaving Andrew and the other guy an extortionate tip in an envelope
alongside a comments form at the zipline's storefront once we'd been ferried
back down the mountain in the school bus.

It bothered me as we stopped at a gas station for beers (Nora), ice cream
(Beanie) and bananas (me).

It bothered me as we crammed together in the small space of the camper
and slept restlessly for one last night in the desert.

It bothered me as we loaded up the camper van the next morning and
pulled into yet another gas station to fill the tank before we hit the road.

And it bothered me as we walked slowly around the Hoover Dam gift
shop, and climbed the memorial bridge to watch it from above, the great
white vertical plane of it, the Depression-era art-deco architecture with
relief sculptures of workers that seemed vaguely Soviet in their design. There
was something utilitarian about the whole thing that I found unnerving.
The water below was a deep and rich dark turquoise.

I looked over to Nora and thought of how easy it would be for her to
jump. I wondered whether she was thinking the same thing.

Everything on this trip seemed to involve looking down at the world
from a great height.

We climbed back into the van and started on our way to Los Angeles, skimming the edges of Vegas as we did so.

I saw the bar of metal in Beanie's eyebrow catch the light again as I got behind the wheel. She was fiddling with it, digging her fingernails under one of the balls.

I think it's getting infected, she said when she caught me looking.

It will do if you keep picking at it like that, I replied, feeling my stomach turn.

She rolled her eyes, but relented, moving her hands away.

Why don't you put something cold on it? I suggested. She pulled a pint of Ben and Jerry's out of the mini-fridge and held it against her face.

Could've been worse, Beanie said sheepishly.

What do you mean, it could've been worse? A lip piercing, maybe? Double nipple piercings?

Beanie smiled enigmatically, and I did as much of a double take as I could while keeping one eye on the freeway.

Please, I said. For the love of God, don't tell me you've got a nipple piercing.

Beanie laughed. No, I haven't got a nipple piercing, Mum.

I breathed out. To be fair, I said, even you're not that stupid.

As I said this, Beanie deliberately caught Nora's eye in the rear-view mirror and smirked.

She's not that stupid, Nora said, laughter in her voice, but I am.

And she yanked up her T-shirt and bra, and flashed two small silver nipple rings at me in the rear-view mirror. I had been so preoccupied with getting her out of the shower yesterday that I must have missed them.

But there was something else about Nora's boobs. Something eerily familiar.

And then it hit me.

Oh my God, I said, struggling to keep the giggle out of my voice. Do you know whose boobs you've got?

Don't, Nora said, turning pink, pulling her shirt down.

What? Beanie said. Whose boobs?

Aunt Karoline's, Nora and I said at the same time. And Beanie actually gasped.

You've got Aunt Karoline's tits, I told Nora.

Shut up, it's the worst thing ever, she replied.

I held my fist hard on the car horn and let it blast long and hard as I laughed. Visions of Aunt Karoline swam in my head. She'd had a penchant for drip-drying when she'd got out of the shower, looking after us as kids in the Richmond house when Mum had gone missing for days on end. As a child on the cusp of puberty, it had mortified me. Aunt Karoline had always been a woman very comfortable in her own skin. And apparently visions of her naked form had permanently imprinted themselves onto my psyche.

I rolled down the window and waved at the woman in the car sitting in traffic in the next lane over, with her own window rolled down and a golden retriever hanging out of it.

She's got Aunt Karoline's tits, I told her, throwing a thumb over my shoulder to indicate Nora.

Good for her, she shouted back.

No, it's bad, Nora shouted out of her own window in the back. Really, really bad.

Have a great day, ladies, she shouted back, waving and smiling and pulling away.

Nora took off a Croc and smacked me round the head with it.

And with that we were on our way to the west coast.

———

The landscape became less dusty and more scrubby and brittle as we crossed from Nevada into California. Nora fell asleep on the back seat again. Beanie played "Wanted Dead or Alive" by Bon Jovi eight times in a row on the aux cable until I unplugged it and shoved it under my seat. So we listened to the Spanish language CD instead. Yuccas and Joshua trees lined the craggy rocks of the freeway, flat and straight. The drive was five hours long. Beanie and I practiced our Spanish in hushed tones while Nora slept, windows down and the air conditioner blasting us with lukewarm air. I ran my fingers over my lips. In the sun and the dust and the dry, they had split into cracks.

Beanie's had too. The pain felt a little bit like vindication, though I wasn't sure what for.

Once the Spanish language CD finished once again, we drove in silence and Beanie scrolled Instagram.

Have you spoken to Dami? I asked Beanie, to make conversation. Beanie normally chatted about her friends in a stream-of-consciousness type of way which meant that, without realizing it, I had a lot of pointless information about these kids that really had no bearing on my life. For example, I knew all about Dami's recurring back acne, which had flared up over exams season. I knew the intricacies of the friendship dynamics in Beanie's classes from breakups to perceived slights to who had embarrassed themselves at the most recent house party. I knew about Lizzie's secret abortion, which only Beanie and Lizzie's mother knew about. I was happy that Beanie felt that she could talk to me about her friendships, that she trusted me with their secrets. I prided myself on being the kind of parent who stayed cool about underage drinking (in moderation) and had had several frank birds-and-bees conversations with Beanie since she'd hit puberty. At this point, I was convinced she could stick a condom on a cucumber blindfolded with one hand tied behind her back. But recently she hadn't been telling me so much about her life, her friends, and their dramas.

Yeah, we've chatted, she said, answering my question. And Lizzie, too. She sent me some places we should go to eat in LA.

I nodded, waiting for her to say more. But she didn't.

Is everything, like, okay, kid? I asked, testing the water.

Yeah. She glanced up from her phone, frowning at me, confused. Why?

You've just gone a bit quiet on friends and school and all that, I said.

I haven't really been thinking about it, she said. We're on holiday.

So we're back to it being a holiday, now, I said. Not my crusade.

I didn't know why I was being so prickly. I just wanted to get something out of her. I didn't know what it was I wanted, though.

Mum, leave it, yeah?

I know, I know.

She went quiet again, back to her phone. I felt the silence, the space, stretch out between us.

You know, Dami hasn't been over ours for a while, I commented.

Well, his place is bigger than ours. His dad has a pool table in the garage now.

But it would be nice to see him every once in a while.

Yeah, I'll invite him over for dinner or something when we get back.

I dipped my toe a little bit further.

It would be nice to see him, I said. Especially if you two are . . . going out?

She dropped her phone in her lap and stared dead ahead.

I'm not going out with Dami, she said.

Okay, fine, fine, I said. I was just checking. I don't hear anything from you these days. I have to guess.

Well, you guessed wrong. Her voice was a monotone, dead and emotionless.

Fine, I said, stonily.

We drove in silence once more.

But if you do start going out with someone . . . I said, unable to help myself.

Mum.

I'm just saying. Let me finish. If you *do* start going out with a boy, I'd like to be the first to know, and I'd like to meet him. Properly. Okay?

Sure, whatever. Fine. Can we stop talking about this now?

Yes, we can stop talking about this.

She squirmed in her seat and stared pointedly out the window.

No one says *going out* anymore, she muttered under her breath.

I shrugged and poked her in the arm.

Anyway, she said, you'll be living with Richard soon, won't you? So I guess it won't matter.

What do you mean, it won't matter? I asked, taking the bait.

Because I'm not going round Richard's like, ever, so there's no point even having the conversation.

I groaned in exasperation.

We stopped at Barstow, a small featureless town roughly half way between Vegas and LA on the I-15. Beanie wanted burgers, and, after a moment to think about it, I realized that I was also ravenous and desperate for junk food. We parked in a huge lot next to a shopping center and walked over to a fast-food burger chain on the other side of the road.

We sat in a plastic-upholstered booth with a sticky table as Beanie went to find a menu. We were the only people sat down inside the place. Everyone in the queue of six or seven was ordering to go, and the drive-thru queue round the back was even longer. I didn't care. I was hungry and irritable, and my muscles were sore and cramped up from the driving. I cracked my back against the booth and tried to stop the smell of deep-friedness emanating from the kitchen from making me salivate.

I'm so ready for this burger, I told Nora.

You need to stop asking Beanie about her love life, she replied in a hushed tone, ignoring me.

Sorry, what? I asked, glancing over at Beanie, who was completely oblivious to us, chatting to one of the servers behind the counter about whether fried or raw onions were better.

Stop asking her about it.

I'm sorry, are you trying to tell me how to talk to my own child? I asked, feeling the bewilderment and hurt building up in me. How *dare* she? How dare my childless, fuck-up twenty-something sister who was *still at uni*, for fuck's sake, tell me how to look after my—

She's trying to work out how to tell you something. And you need to stop pushing her.

I gawped at her.

I have absolutely no idea what you're talking about, I said, my voice dripping with sardonicism.

Oh, Matilda, Nora said, unbearably condescending in her tone. You big, stupid idiot.

Can you stop fucking talking in riddles? I asked, anger building.

Can't you see, Matt? Nora said, pity in her eyes. Can't you see your kid is like, the queerest little girl on the planet?

I stared at her again.

Sorry, *what?*

And then I looked at Beanie, again, where she was, her elbows propped on the counter, chatting easily with a beautiful girl with shaved green hair and a tattoo of a butterfly on her neck.

Beanie was wearing her iridescent silver Doc Martens, her denim cargo shorts cuffed to just above her knees. Her teeth gleamed brighter than her highlighter hair; adolescent braces and daily flossing made them perfectly formed and pearly.

Oh my God, I said, feeling my mouth drop open.

You're such a fucking millennial, Nora said.

Oh my God, I repeated.

Of course she is.

In that moment I felt such a swell of love for her that I thought I would have to go over there and pull her into a hug. I felt the tears pricking my eyes.

And then came the guilt. The guilt that I hadn't known, hadn't realized, hadn't even had an *inkling* of what was very clearly in front of me that it might as well have slapped me on the butt and told me to giddy up. How could I not have known? And, infinitely more importantly, *why* did she feel like she couldn't tell me?

I can't believe you've done that, I said, turning back to Nora, trying to stop the tears from spilling over. Easier to redirect my anger towards her than at myself.

What do you mean?

You just outed her to me. If she's been trying to work out how to tell me, you've taken that moment away from her.

Nora stared at me, calculating, and then her face sagged, realizing that I was right.

Please don't tell her, she said. That you know. That I've told you.

Of course not, I replied, grabbing her hand across the table, conspiratorial. It felt good that it was Nora and me sharing the secret for once, not Nora and Beanie with me left on the outside of their whisperings and secret body piercings, looking in. I felt a coil of satisfaction at it.

She breathed out slowly. Thank you.

But you can drive the rest of the way to Los Angeles, I added.

I . . . feel like that's a fair trade, she said.

Beanie returned with the menus, bouncing on the heels of her feet. She sat down next to me and said, Whew, it smells like a fryer in here.

I pulled her into a hug, dashing my tears away before she could register them, but she did anyway.

Wha . . . Mum? What's the matter?

Nothing, I just . . . I love you, kid. I'm not moving in with Richard, okay? And I'm sorry I said that I was. Because you're the most important person to me. You and Nora and your dad. You're the only people that matter. I'm sorry if I ever made you feel like you weren't.

I realized wholeheartedly then the truth of what I was saying. It didn't matter what I thought of Richard, whether I would be able to forgive him for the small things he had been doing—going to the press, reaching out to Chelsea behind my back, and apparently allowing some bastardization of Mum's work to happen in San Francisco?—which, when all added together, became one very big problem.

It didn't matter that I couldn't hurt him. It didn't matter that he was stable, and safe, and caring and generous. That he was—I had convinced myself—my only chance at a healthy adult relationship.

Nora's face was suddenly abnormally alert.

You're not moving in with Richard? she asked.

No. I'm not moving in with Richard.

Why not?

I hummed into my Diet Coke.

You don't trust him, I told Nora. Neither of you do. And I guess, well, I don't trust him either.

Beanie and Nora exchanged twin looks.

Oh, shut up, I said. Both of you.

They did, thank God.

Our burgers came and the onions were perfect.

CHAPTER 24

Dolly Parton was sticking out a thumb on the side of the road in Barstow.

I gawped at her from the back seat as we drove past.

Did anyone else just see that? I asked.

What? Nora said, her eyes on the road ahead, her hands resting on the steering wheel. Beanie had her headphones on in the passenger seat.

I leaned out the window.

There's a Dolly Parton impersonator hitchhiking back there, I said.

The Dolly Parton impersonator was wearing a white catsuit covered in tiny fragments of mirrors. The mirrors were reflecting so much light it looked as though she were glowing like an angel on the side of the road. The trademark platinum hair was piled high on her head. The thumb that she was sticking out had an acrylic nail so long that it curved like the talon of a bird of prey.

Oh my God, can we pick her up? Beanie asked, pulling her headphones off and gawping out the window.

Absolutely not, I said, at the same time Nora said, Yeah, sure.

She guided the Flamesmobile to the side of the road and honked to get Dolly's attention. Dolly—or the Dolly impersonator—tottered over to the van at a quick trot in stiletto heels that seemed like they shouldn't be possible to walk in. Nora rolled down the window.

Where are you going? she asked.

Beverly Hills, darlin', the Dolly lookalike replied in a perfect imitation of a Southern Belle drawl. Up close, she had the whole look down to a perfection: the make-up, the thinly-drawn lip liner and the immaculate, straight white teeth.

We're on our way to LA, Nora replied. Do you want to hop in the back?

Dolly blessed us all and I reluctantly slid the door to the side of the van open. As she heaved herself in, I noticed for the first time the slimness of her frame, the paperiness on her hands. I realized that this was a very, very old woman. Possibly in her seventies or eighties. In the most impractical shoes I'd ever seen.

Can I offer you a hand? I asked, concerned.

Oh, no, sweetie, don't be silly, I've been doing cartwheels on stage all weekend. Little step up won't hurt me.

I glanced at Beanie with a confused frown, but her face was plastered with a look of sheer delight.

We set off, back on the 15, towards LA.

What had you stuck in Barstow? I asked Dolly.

Well, I've been doing a few gigs in Vegas, she replied, as she snapped open a compact to reapply lipstick. But my crew left me at a truck stop by accident. They'll have realized by now. They'll be going loopy, I expect.

And how long have you been doing the Dolly thing?

The Dolly thing?

You know. The impersonating.

Beanie climbed into the back seat too, then.

Dolly grinned at us. Oh, you know. A few decades.

Wow, said Beanie. And—sorry if this is a stupid question—

Ain't no such thing as a stupid question, doll.

Well—I'm guessing you make a good living off of it? I mean—you look *amazing*—just like Dolly Parton, actually.

I'm sorry, I said to Dolly. That was rude, Beans.

But Dolly smiled again and waved a hand at us. She winked at Beanie. I'd say I do quite well, she said.

The desert was becoming less desert and more populated with little towns, truck stops, gas stations and motels as we approached LA.

Hey, Dolly, Nora said from the front seat, her eyes on the road, What's your favorite Dolly song? Can we have a rendition of it?

Well, I normally charge for a private concert, she said, laughing. And I don't have my guitar. I'll have to scream to get heard over this engine noise.

We can put it on the aux and you can sing along.

She agreed to that, and Beanie found "Coat of Many Colors" on Spotify and played it quietly as the woman sang along. The song was soft and acoustic and very beautiful. Her voice was almost a whisper, perfectly rendered in the real Dolly's cadence.

Your dad would get a kick out of this, I told Beanie after she finished the song and we applauded her.

I can see why you're performing in Vegas, Beanie said. You're the spit of the real Dolly. Your voice is unreal.

I suppressed a smirk.

She's not the real Dolly Parton, Beans, I said, chuckling.

Of course I'm not the real Dolly Parton, Dolly said, her eyes twinkling.

Dolly sang "Jolene" for us then, and we joined in because we knew the words to that one.

Sorry, do you mind if I FaceTime my friend? He's a huge fan of Dolly Parton. He would love to meet you, I said.

Sweetness, you can do whatever you want. You're getting me out of a tough spot here.

Beanie asked Dolly what had been her favorite gig to ever play, while I dialed Gus. Dolly said it was the Rock and Roll Hall of Fame.

I love your commitment to the bit, I said while I waited for Gus to pick up the call, delighted.

Gus answered the phone. He was in bed, the soft green glow illuminating his face on the phone screen, his bare shoulders peeking out from underneath the duvet. He found his glasses and slipped them on, squinting.

It's the middle of the night, babe, he said, half asleep.

I know, I know, I'm sorry, but I wanted you to meet someone.

I handed the phone over to Dolly and grinned as she waved at him and sang a couple of bars of "9 to 5."

Wow. Incredible, I heard Gus say. He sleepily asked her how her Vegas residency had been going. Beanie and I exchanged a look with one another.

Oh, sorry, I said quickly. He thinks you're the real Dolly Parton, I explained.

She laughed. Wouldn't be the first time, doll, she said.

They exchanged some pleasantries and Dolly asked Gus some questions about what he did for work and where he lived and so on. He told her about how much his mother Grace loved Dolly Parton, and would blast her greatest hits in the kitchen on a Sunday afternoon while she did laundry. He would sit at the kitchen table and watch her dancing, totally free, melancholy, wishing she were someone else, and because of that he loved Dolly too.

There was nothing she wanted more in the world, he said. Than to see Dolly Parton live. The music made her cry.

Well, there's no time to waste, darlin'. Come to Vegas.

Gus smiled somberly. She's too ill to make the journey, now, I'm afraid.

I'm sorry to hear that.

Gus sighed and shrugged. It's life, isn't it? It's the way it goes.

They talked some more about his parents. And after a few minutes she said goodbye and passed the phone back to me.

She's brilliant, isn't she? I asked him, grinning down the phone.

I love her, he said. Where did you find her?

On the side of the road.

Where are you at the moment?

We're not far from LA now. Maybe an hour outside.

I've texted you the details of the pharmacy where you can pick up Nora's medication.

Thanks, I replied, moving to the back of the van so Nora couldn't hear us. Beanie and the Dolly Parton impersonator were now playing a travel-sized Connect 4.

How is everything? How's the trip going?

I told Gus about the mess we'd made of scattering Mum's ashes, how we'd lost them and how we'd got them back.

And how's Nora? And Beans?

I felt my shoulders sag.

I don't know, I said. I honestly don't know. I'm constantly terrified that Nora is going to do something—stupid. Beanie is okay, I think. She's dealing with so much. I don't want to put anything more on her.

He smiled sadly. In that moment I decided firmly not to tell him what Nora had told me. I had no idea if he already knew, if she'd already come out to him or he had guessed. Either way, the secret wasn't mine to tell. I wasn't even supposed to know, myself. I glanced at her over the top of the phone as she laughed easily at something Dolly had said.

I wish you were here, I told him. You would know what to do.

He looked at me intensely through the screen, frowning a little, his glasses catching the light. That look. I had only glimpsed flashes of it for years. I felt like it burned directly into the center of my soul. Even through the phone it was powerful. I felt my cheeks go warm. I chastised myself. He probably had no idea what he was doing. In the dark of his bedroom, his head against the pillow, he was pale and serious.

You, he said, are the strongest woman, the strongest person I've ever known. You don't need me. You've got it.

I don't know if that's true, Gus, I said, my voice barely more than a whisper.

He sighed quietly. I wish you could see yourself how everyone else sees you.

Beanie and Nora think I'm on a crusade.

I mean, they're not wrong. I miss you.

I sighed, quiet, small. I miss you, too.

We said goodbye and I hung up the phone, and I suddenly felt that I wanted to cry.

Dolly crawled to where I sat in the back of the van, her stiletto heels digging into the upholstery, and pulled me into a hug.

What's the matter, chicken? she asked gently.

I don't know, I replied. I really don't know.

Beanie was sitting further down the van, closer to the back of Nora's seat. She looked at me with a furrowed brow, as though I were a complicated math problem she couldn't quite put her finger on.

I think I'm still in love with him, I told Dolly in a whisper, my voice barely audible, so that Beanie couldn't hear me.

I knew that it was true, then. Now that I had said it out loud to Dolly Parton, I had breathed life into the idea of it. Every fiber of my body knew the truth of it.

Well, Dolly whispered back. If you're still in love with him, you gotta go get him, right?

I shook the feeling off with a shudder.

Impossible, I replied. It's complicated. We have a daughter together. I nodded at Beanie, who had now climbed back into the passenger seat and was having an animated one-sided conversation with Nora about the *Terminator* movies.

I don't see how that makes things complicated, Dolly said, fairly.

But it'll go wrong, I said. And then we won't be able to co-parent. The most important person is her. If we mess it up, which we *will*, we already messed it up once before, *I* already messed it up. She's going to be the one who gets hurt.

But what if you *don't* mess it up? she asked. What if it's meant to be?

I don't believe in fate, I said flatly.

Well, I do, she replied, and I'm manifesting for you. Okay?

I laughed and shrugged and then Dolly's hair got caught in one of the door handles so we got distracted with untangling her and the conversation ended. We eased into Los Angeles rush-hour traffic, well and truly out of the wilderness now, and overlooking the thick grey haze of the city as we slid through the mountains towards the California coastline.

After Gus had gone to university, I'd taken Nora back to boarding school and checked myself and Beanie into a hostel funded by West Hampstead Women's Centre. Somehow, and without me fully realizing that it had happened until it had, we'd lived there for three years.

I hadn't gone back for Nora.

Gus had stayed true to his word. He'd telephoned every night from his student accommodation in Hull, to say goodnight to Beanie. I'd tried to imagine his life up there: university halls, the union nightclub, the library, the feeling of belonging to a group of people who share a common goal. Sometimes he'd talked about his new law-school friends and I'd dreamed of them, as though they'd been my friends too. Every weekend, Gus had taken the three-and-a-half-hour train journey down to London to spend the weekend with Beanie at his parents', and I had begun to join them on those weekends more and more frequently. I'd found myself in the garden, often, with Grace and Beanie, cultivating rhubarb. We'd grown eighty percent of the Hansons' Christmas dinner in the garden in 2007. The following summer, I'd joined them on their annual summer holiday to the caravan in Colchester for the first time.

I'd felt myself becoming folded into their lives, and for once I hadn't recoiled against it, hadn't instinctively rejected the idea of it.

The difference had been, of course, Gus. What I had told him in the Richmond house in the summer of 2005, before he'd left for university, had seemed to stick.

When he'd looked at me, his eyes had slid over mine, as though he couldn't maintain eye contact with me lest he betray something obscene in the intensity of his gaze.

He wouldn't touch me, at all. Even a brush of the hand at the kitchen sink in his parents' house had made him flinch away.

Over time, it had become easier. We'd settled into a new version of love for one another. Making everything about Beanie had helped. We'd never spoken about how I had ended it. I'd never apologized, even when in the middle of the night I would find myself awake, thinking of him, tears leaking from my eyes with the pain of the deep invisible wound in my chest.

And then, one weekend, in the living room at Grace and Frank's, listening to Dolly Parton on the record player, he'd said to me, quietly, standing in the doorway, I need to tell you something.

Yeah? I said, not looking up from the playdough Beanie was rolling into blobs on the wooden floor.

I met this girl, he said simply.

My eyes shot up at him, my mouth suddenly dry.

Oh, I said. Okay.

Her name's Naomi, he said. She's in my halls. She's studying biomedical science.

Cool, I whispered.

He was watching me with an intensity I hadn't seen for a long time. He was waiting for me to say something, I could tell.

How long? I asked, digging my fingernails into my palms in an attempt to keep my voice from wobbling.

A couple of months, he said. I didn't want to tell you unless—you know . . .

Yeah, no, I get it, I said.

The silence stretched for decades between us. I looked down at the play-dough Beanie had spread all over the floor, and fought the urge to mash it in with my fist.

So, what, you want her to meet Beanie? I asked him.

No! No. God—no—I just wanted to . . .

Wanted to what?

Just let you know. Notify you. As a courtesy?

Okay. Fine. Well, consider me notified.

He sat down on the floor in the doorway and dragged Beanie onto his lap, placing his hand on her little head and blowing a raspberry on her neck, making her giggle hysterically. I loved them both, in my bones. I hadn't thought of having one without the other. The idea of Gus with someone else made me feel nauseous.

You said, he told me quietly as he tipped Beanie upside down and righted her.

I felt as though I couldn't move.

You said that I shouldn't wait, Gus continued.

I know. I frowned at the floor.

Well, then, you can't be angry.

Who says I'm angry? I'm not angry. You're an adult, Gus. You can do whatever you want.

Images of Gus fucking his way around Hull, an entourage of sexy, bespec-tacled biomedical-science girls in lab coats throwing themselves at him at every turn. An image of Naomi, who for some reason had the exact face, shape and build of Pamela Anderson, doing splits naked on Gus's bedroom floor.

I don't care, I told myself. *This is what I wanted.*

I don't think you fully understand how much it fucked me up, he said, later that night, once Beanie was in bed and we were picking playdough out of the gaps in the floorboards.

I felt my face starting to screw up. I said nothing.

We sat in silence on the living-room floor, our hands tacky with play-dough, and after some time he pulled me into his chest. I felt myself go rigid. Gus and I didn't touch anymore. Ever.

But this embrace didn't feel like a test, or a question. It felt like home.

If you want to introduce Naomi to Beanie, I said into his chest through clenched teeth, I think we should talk about that.

God, he said, letting go of me, his eyes sliding away from mine. Yeah. Obviously.

Naomi didn't last that long in the end. But after her there was Gemma, and Danielle, and Charmaine. By the time we got to Lulu it stopped hurt-ing. Gus started looking me in the eye again. Slowly, over time, as we watched our daughter grow, the idea of us became such an impossibility that the pain became more bearable, a low throb in the base of the gut.

How strange that I didn't fully know the father of my baby until our baby was a child. How strange that the love of my life, a love that I had lost, became my best friend. Slowly and in fits and starts, over many years.

Sometimes I let myself feel the pain of what I had done. Sometimes I caught him staring at me as though I were a puzzle he couldn't solve. Beanie started infant school, and Gus finished his degree and got an apprenticeship in a local family law practice.

This was what I would learn to live with.

It was, after all, exactly what I deserved. And Gus deserved so much more than me.

Where do you need dropping off, Dolly? Nora called from the driver's seat.

Are you familiar with Beverly Hills? Dolly asked in reply.

We were in the thick of the city, now. Nora navigated the camper through downtown with the expertise of a local, confident and assured in the face of some of the worst traffic I had ever seen. Los Angeles was—it seemed to me—dirty and unremarkable, architecture on top of architecture on top of advertisement with no discernible pattern or reason. Driving down the Sunset Strip, Beanie and I pressed our noses to the window and then looked at one another, unimpressed.

Nora, on the other hand, seemed to visibly relax the further we got into the city. The pollution and noise seemed to lift her shoulders marginally, as she drove.

I forget that you lived here for three years, I said to Nora, as I watched her navigate the streets, no Google Maps required.

It was four, actually, she said. Remember that?

We were sitting in traffic on Santa Monica Boulevard now, and she was pointing out the window to the south. I recognized the building, the huge complex of towers that it was a part of: Cedars-Sinai.

The hospital? Dolly asked, confused. Of all the buildings in LA, why would she remember that?

When I tried to kill myself, Nora said simply, by way of explanation. The second time.

It wasn't the second time Nora had almost died, though. It was the fifth.

Oh, cool, that's where you ended up? Beanie asked, her voice saturated with fascination. She stared with a morbid curiosity at the hospital buildings as we drove by.

Okay, guys, it's just a hospital, I said, uncomfortable.

I had only been to LA once, and it was to visit Nora after her second suicide attempt. I'd missed most of the city, because my days here had consisted of driving Mum in the rental car from the shitty motel to the hospital and back, and there, and back again; eating pre-made sandwiches out of plastic wrap in the car park; making myself sick from eating too quickly, my stomach turning at the smell of the disinfectant in the corridors. The blueness. Every single hospital was exactly the same.

I was an adult, with a tween kid. It had been over a decade since I'd slept in the same building as Ingrid Olssen. I hadn't spent so much time with Mum since I was a child. She'd slept in the hotel room adjacent to mine as I'd ferried us back and forth to Nora's bedside over the course of a week while the doctors had observed her for any long-term effects on her brain from the oxygen deprivation. Mum had had the cancer diagnosis by then, already, but she hadn't told anyone about it. One night, after visiting Nora to watch her stare at the ceiling, while Mum had talked incessantly about the self-portrait she'd been working on, we'd got back to the hotel and I'd watched as Mum had pulled herself up the staircase using both hands on the handrail, because she hadn't had the strength in her to hold her body up independently.

What's going on with you? I'd asked, my voice harsh. I had no patience for her. She was fifty-three years old but she held herself like she was a septuagenarian. It was almost certainly the eighties cocaine that did it. I had watched a documentary about how they used to cut it with heroin and glass. I didn't offer her an arm to help her up the stairs. In truth, I took some perverse pleasure in watching her struggle. When I was nine or ten, shortly after Nora was born, I had come home from school with a staple embedded in the soft flesh of my ankle. I couldn't remember how it had happened. I didn't really remember the pain. But I remembered how Mum had taken one look at it and said, That's going to make me sick, can't you pull it out yourself?

So I had, with a bag of frozen peas and the pair of pliers Mum used to stretch her canvases.

Nothing's going on with me, she said, breathless, as she finally made it to the top of the stairs. I just don't like being around sickness. It makes me nervous.

That's your daughter in there, I said, trying not to spit the words out, pointing in the rough direction of the hospital. Neither of us could see it from the windowless mezzanine level of the motel four blocks away. But the sentiment was clear.

She muttered something I took as vindictive in Norwegian and wandered away, and I let her go, exasperated and furious.

In the middle of the night, she banged on my bedroom door. I opened it and registered her in her nightdress, her arms bony and sagging. Her hair a wild silver streak down her back.

What's the matter? I asked her.

I hate it here, she said, her teeth clenched. The food is disgusting.

What do you want me to do about it?

Take me home. Take me back to London.

Nora's not well.

Mum swore.

I think she's faking it, she said in Norwegian, her eyes darting from side to side. She always spoke more Norwegian when she was having some sort of episode.

She's putting it on, Mum continued. I can tell from the way she looks at me like she's laughing at me. She's just trying to inconvenience us. She's not getting enough attention, that's what it is. So she drags us all out to this god-forsaken city to fawn over her. Well. I won't have it anymore. I'm not having her dictate how I can live my life. I want to go home. I want you to book me a flight. Now.

I stared at her, feeling all the rage of my thirty years at her hands bubbling over. Her eyes were not focusing on anything in particular. She was staring at the walls, and then the ceiling, and then me, and then the space just behind my left shoulder.

Everyone knows that if you want to die, you just get on with it, Mum said. Anything less and you're doing it for the attention.

I resisted the urge to slam the door in her face then. The tumor in her chest was, at that time and although I didn't know it, roughly the size of a golf ball.

This heat is making me crazy, she said.

The next morning, I called Karoline to confirm that she could be at Heathrow to collect, and drove Mum to the airport. As soon as she had gone through the gate, I walked away, bummed a cigarette off a Polish guy in the smoking area and punched a wall, breaking two of my fingers. I hadn't bothered with health insurance in my eagerness to get over here after we'd received the news that Nora was in the hospital, so I taped my fingers together and necked painkillers for the remaining week I spent in LA. I stayed until Nora was out of the hospital, and drove her to Dad's house before getting on a plane myself and running away. The next time I saw her, or my mother, back in the UK, Mum was almost dead.

I sat alone with Mum one night in the master bedroom, less than a year later, with the tubes coming out of everywhere, the machines making mechanical alien noises.

She cried.

I just want to die, she said. Why won't they let me die?

Everyone knows that if you want to die, you just get on with it, I said, feeling the venom in my mouth as I spat the words out.

She fixed me with a stare that lacked any human emotion, her mouth a grim, thin line.

Get out, she said.

Thank you, I replied, and I ran downstairs and into the back garden and I breathed in the crisp night air. There were no stars, only light pollution and chemtrails. When the staple came out of my ankle at age nine, the skin underneath was pale pink and unspoiled, the loose flap tender and exposed. I enjoyed the spike of pain when I pressed on it, hard, until the tiny cavity left behind by the puncture of the metal flooded over with blood.

Dolly Parton, or rather, the Dolly Parton impersonator, directed Nora out of the main part of the city, away from the dense, packed-in buildings, and up into the hills where the roads were narrow and foliage was lush and vibrant.

I'm just around this next corner, here, she said. Thank you so much for the ride, ladies. I can't tell you how much I appreciate it.

Any time, Nora said, allowing Dolly to squeeze her hand.

Just here's fine, now.

Are you sure?

We were on a narrow road overlooking the city on the left-hand side. The road was steep and I wondered how Nora was going to get the van back down the hill. On the right-hand side, embedded into the rock, was a tall, plush-looking hotel with a broad white canopy stretched across its façade. Nora pulled right up to the front of it and a valet opened the door to the van.

Dolly hopped out and teetered over to the revolving doors, the valet who seemed to know her steadying her with his arm.

Thank you, Carl, sweetie, she said, patting the valet gently on the elbow.

Beanie, Nora and I watched on in total amazement, our faces three "o's of open mouths.

A concierge pulled a side-door open for her, revealing a stunning white marble staircase, presumably leading up to some sort of private suite.

Girls, do you want to stop in for a coffee? Dolly called to us, her hips swinging as she turned to observe us.

None of us answered. We just stared.

Are you the real Dolly Parton? Beanie shouted, her voice pitchy.

Dolly stared at us and laughed.

Oh, honey, she said, through giggles. Please. As if!

We continued to stare.

Well, all right then, bye-bye. Dolly gave us a jaunty wave, the shards of mirror on her catsuit glittering in the golden-hour sunshine. Hope you get your ex back, she yelled at me, still waving. And with that the door was shut and Dolly, or not-quite-but-almost-Dolly, was gone.

The three of us that remained stared at the door, and then at each other.

Excuse me, Beanie called to the concierge who stood now under the canopy at attention, his hat slightly off-center. Was that the real Dolly Parton?

Excuse me, pardon?

That woman who just got out of our campervan. Was it actually, really, Dolly Parton?

I don't know what you're talking about, ma'am, he replied, smiling beatifically.

Get back in the van, Beans, I said. It's not Dolly Parton. And she did.

What did she mean, *hope you get your ex back*? Mum? Was she talking about Dad?

I shrugged and smiled, waving the question away. Somewhere in the distance, a hawk was screeching. The leaves shifted in the breeze.

CHAPTER 25

The more time I spent in Los Angeles, the less it appealed to me.

We dropped the camper van off at the car rental outlet near LAX and got an Uber to our hotel. From here on out, we would be hotel-hopping with a rental car: it seemed unnecessary to camp when we were staying in cities for the rest of the route to San Francisco. We had three nights in LA before we would head up the Pacific Coast Highway to San Francisco. The realization that we were getting closer now made me nervous. I knew that I had some things I needed to fix before we made it to the exhibition. Namely, I needed to get Nora medicated, and I needed—I knew now with absolute certainty—to break up with Richard.

The further we travelled across the western vista of the United States, the surer I was that I needed to do it.

It had to do with a lot of things. It was Beanie. It was the fact he was writing a book about my mum, and was apparently mining the trauma of my family to do it. It was how he spoke about her. Mum. Nora. Like they were exhibits in a museum. It was how he treated our relationship like an idea rather than something that we were experiencing together.

I was beginning to realize how much of an idiot I had been over the past six months.

After I'd unpacked some crumpled clothes from my suitcase into a narrow closet in our triple room, I took a towel and a bottle of water to the outdoor hotel pool, which was on the hot flat roof of the building. Beanie was already suspended in the center of a crystalline blue swimming pool on a pineapple-shaped float, asleep with her heart-shaped sunglasses perched upon her nose, the sun beating down on her. Nora sat under a broad parasol reading a battered copy of *The Idiot*. Far below, the traffic of Western Ave through Koreatown drifted upwards in both the fumes and the incessant noise of engines and horns and roadworks. The sky was a perfect endless blue.

Has Beanie got SPF on? I asked as I sat down on the sun lounger next to Nora's.

Nora licked her thumb and turned a page of her book. I think so, she said.

I stared out at Beanie, her limp legs trailing in the water, and thought I could distinguish streaks of white sunblock on her legs.

I want to talk to you about something, I said to Nora, carefully.

Yeah, I know, she replied.

What do you mean, you know?

You've been acting weird for days. And you have this little look on your face, like you're about to pop me with a pin.

I'm not about to pop you with a pin.

What do you want to talk about?

I exhaled slowly and adjusted the hem of my shorts.

There's a pharmacy in Santa Monica, I said. It's a pharmacy that Gus found. They've got your prescription ready to go, they just need sign-off from your doctor. And we can get all your medication sorted.

Nora went very still.

This again, she said.

Yeah, this, I said.

You know how I feel about it.

I know.

It makes me into a zombie.

I know. But I'm also trying to get you through this trip in one piece.

You weren't there. With Mum. When she started taking tablets. You were already gone by then. By the time she got onto prescription medication.

I felt my stomach twist. The remembrance of how I'd left Nora. How I'd let her down, broken my promise to come back for her.

You know they've got me on alprazolam? That's what Mum was taking, too. She was taking someone else's alprazolam. She was buying it off Pinky. Remember Pinky?

Yeah, I remember Pinky.

Well. Yeah.

I didn't know that.

You wouldn't.

I looked at her, then, ignoring the twist, and took a deep breath, and said the thing I'd been toying with for a while. The last-resort thing.

What if something happens to you, I said, while we're here? What will Beanie and I do? Beanie is going to be traumatized. We would have to take your body back to London. Just imagine that for a second. Imagine what that's going to do to us.

She stared straight ahead, her mouth a thin line, her book forgotten. I felt dirty, manipulative, but I knew it had worked.

I'll talk to my doctor, she said. But you're going to have to do something for me too.

What?

You have to come with me to Dad's.

I gawked at her.

Dad's? What do you want to see Dad for?

Remember when I lived here before? Before I moved back to London, after I—you know—I was living with Dad for a bit. Remember?

I remembered. I remembered picking Nora up from the hospital after she'd been discharged, driving to a house that had a *roundabout* on the driveway, and dropping her and all two of her trash bags of stuff on Dad's doorstep. He lived in a six-bedroomed villa at the foot of Griffith Park, with Marnie and a household staff of three. I'd stayed long enough to see the door open, see her ushered into a cavernous vestibule, and then I'd driven away, got on a plane and got the fuck out of there for good. Until now.

I've got some stuff at Dad's, Nora explained. Things that I need. To finish my thesis.

It wasn't the answer I'd been expecting.

What sorts of things? I asked.

She shrugged. Some notebooks. Some photographs. Tapes.

Tapes? Ever heard of the Cloud?

Shut up. Just some things like that. I need them.

You've been doing fine without them on your PhD for two years.

Well, until you tried to kill yourself for an art project.

The project's changing, she replied, as though she had read my mind.

I narrowed my eyes at her. Changing how?

I don't know yet. But the Control Room isn't dead, is it?

I breathed a sigh. I really, really, want the Control Room to be dead, I said.

She continued, as though she hadn't heard me. The work is still alive. It's breathing. So, I can't kill it. I need to find a new angle.

This is the concrete all over again, isn't it?

It's not the concrete, she said. And—to my surprise—she laughed, if a little maniacally.

Then what is it?

I don't know yet. But it's something I need my notes for.

I leaned back on my sun lounger and let the weight of the air push me further down until I was horizontal and staring directly into the sun.

If I go with you to Dad's, will you take your meds?

Quiet.

I'll think about it, she said.

I reached over and took her hand without looking at her.

I hate Dad, I said, slowly, realizing the truth of the words as they left my mouth.

I know, she replied. I wouldn't ask you unless it was really important.

I know, I said.

That night, Aunt Karoline called me.

Richard says you're coming to the exhibition, she said, her shrill voice disturbing the peace of the bedroom as Beanie brushed her teeth and Nora stared unseeingly at her phone in the dim light of the evening.

Yes, we're coming, I said cagily. Me, Beans and Nora.

Is Nora taking her tablets? Doing her therapy sessions?

I glanced at Nora and she shook her head vigorously at me, her eyes wide.

Nora's fine, I said.

Good, good. I need to dash, darling, the caterer for the launch party is calling.

She promptly hung up.

The next morning, we picked up a new car from a rental company in Hollywood, and Nora drove us up into the hills.

Are you sure about this? I asked for the tenth time that morning. The car was so small compared to the roomy, bulky interior of the camper van. It felt claustrophobic.

Yes, I'm sure, she said. We'll go in, we'll get out, and he won't even know we've been there.

What if he's at home?

Unlikely. It's the middle of the week in early August. He's probably golfing.

What about Marnie?

What about her?

We pulled up to the gated stone house in which Dad lived, at the foot of Griffith Park on a broad street lined with palm trees bending to the east with the force of the Pacific Coastal breeze. I'd never been to Dad's house in Hollywood before, besides the time I'd dropped Nora off on the doorstep and legged it. I had never been invited. Edward Robb had functioned as something of an intermittent presence throughout my life, though as Nora had lived with him for a little while as an adult, I imagined their relationship was slightly warmer, more familial. Nora was much easier to get along with than I was. In the Richmond house, Dad's visits had usually been no more than a weekend in length, during which he'd mostly ignored us unless he'd found it necessary to mete out some sort of parental discipline.

Once, when I was fourteen, I had cut off another girl's ponytail at school.

Her name was Monica Drippings and she'd had a long blonde plait that went all the way to her waist. She'd called Mum a whore in double Biology and before I could think about what I was doing, I had already taken a pair of scissors from the stationery trolley and snipped the pigtail clean off.

It had happened to be one of the rare weekends that Dad had been visiting, in between some bit-part filming commitment at Pinewood. That was him: he would turn up for a few days at a time, between the conveniences of his work schedule, cause a fracas with either Mum, Aunt Karoline, or me, and then he would disappear back to the States for another year, a wad of American dollars pressed into Nora's hands and mine, as though the money—which had been useless to us, anyway—had made up for the lack of his physical presence.

On that Friday, when I'd cut off Monica Drippings's ponytail, I'd got home from school to find him waiting in the conservatory with a stack of pizzas from the takeaway. Nora, four years old, had sat on the floor, chewing through a slice of margherita, her eyes shining as she'd looked up at him.

Mattie, she'd screamed, throwing her arms up as I'd walked into the kitchen holding the detention slip. Pappa's here.

You girls are looking skinny, he said by way of greeting.

I wanted to resist the pizza, but he was right: I couldn't remember the last time I had tasted melted cheese, and I was ravenous. So I sat down with them without acknowledging them, and gobbled my way through three slices so quickly that I felt sick by the end of it.

Where's Mum? I asked him, between mouthfuls.

Gone walkies, he replied. Dad's way of saying that Mum was AWOL.

I've called Karoline, he clarified.

Why? Aren't you staying?

I've got a three A.M. call time, he said, annoyed that I had asked, already moving to stand. I saw Nora freeze as he did. She knew that he was about to leave, and she was calculating what exactly she could do to make him stay.

I slapped my detention slip on the kitchen counter.

You'll probably want to read this, seeing as Mum's not here. You need to sign it.

He picked it up, agitated.

You cut off a girl's ponytail? he asked, his eyes skimming across the note from my biology teacher. He had abnormally pointy eyebrows, and the outer tips seemed to sharpen when he frowned, like the tips of silver knives. He now looked at me with those pointy eyebrows, and in his expression I saw that he didn't recognize me. That somewhere in between his flying visits I had become something that he didn't recognize, something monstrous, a wholly other kind of person.

She called Mum a whore, I said bluntly, holding his gaze.

What's a whore? Nora asked.

You're not allowed to know, I said. It's a nasty word.

Is Mummy a whore?

No, she's not, I said. Dad raised his sharp eyebrows, conspicuously.

He placed the slip back down on the kitchen counter.

I don't know, he said. Why I'm paying for you to go to that school when you're just going to get yourself kicked out.

Don't, then, I said, petulant. I never asked to go to a fancy school. I never wanted you to pay for it.

Your mother said that—

Oh, yeah, and we all know that Ingrid knows best, don't we?

Nora watched us as though she were watching a tennis match. Back and forth and back and forth.

I don't know why you come here, I said, spitting venom, unable to stop myself. It doesn't make you a better person. We don't need your money. We don't want it. Mum doesn't want you here.

You two are my children. I've got every right to have a say—

You literally turn up when it's convenient, and you upset Nora, and then you leave, and pat yourself on the back for doing your fatherly duties for the year. It makes me sick. We're better off without you.

Nora had started crying.

He was a little flabbergasted by the outburst, I could see. But I could feel it boiling up in me and spilling over the edges. All the rage. I could see that he was a little afraid of me. And I leaned into it. I wanted to show him something, something that said *this is what you made me into in the gaps of your attention.*

I was tired of living this life, of being Ingrid Olssen and Edward Robb's eldest daughter. Of feeling surplus. Of having to take care of Nora because neither of them could get their shit together. I wanted to have a normal life with friends who didn't know my mum's name, and a dad who took us to the Natural History Museum, or something, instead of raiding our cupboards for dregs of whisky whenever he visited, and acting surprised that he had living, breathing children, with minds and opinions of their own.

Matilda, Dad said pointedly, firmly, and he took a step towards me.

No, I shouted at him, feeling the rage exploding out of me.

And I slapped him across the face.

There was a moment of silence then. The silence was for all of us, for the space stretching out after the slap, the bit that I couldn't take back.

As soon as I did it, I wished I hadn't.

But I was also secretly delighted with myself. Delighted at the look of shock and fear written across his face.

Stay. Away. From. Us, I told him.

You're a nasty little bitch, aren't you? he said, clutching a cheek that was blooming scarlet.

And then he left.

Mattieeeeeee, Nora wailed after he had slammed the front door, climbed into his convertible Lotus and driven away. Why did you do that? Now Pappa doesn't like us.

I was so furious I barely heard her crying.

He likes *you*, I replied. It's just *me* he's got a problem with.

The next time we saw Dad was about eight months later. He came back for the weekend during another shoot. He brought American candies and a fistful of cash, and he smiled his faltering TV star smile at all of us. He pretended the slap had never happened. But I could tell that he remembered it. Because when he looked at me, his eyebrows became sharper than ever. Razor-tipped. His eyes slid over me, like he wasn't properly seeing me or registering my presence.

We pulled up outside his villa, which was one of the largest I had ever seen. I dared not think about how much it was worth. On the driveway roundabout, there was an elaborate fountain made up of three bronze dolphins squirting water out of their blowholes.

It hadn't changed at all since I had dropped Nora off and run away.

I could still see the look she had given me as I'd watched her in the rearview mirror. Devastation that I had done it, but, also, somewhere deep in her skin, in her bones, she was telling herself, *yeah, I get it, it's what I deserve.*

I'd gritted my teeth and pressed down on the accelerator as she'd been ushered into our father's house.

We're just going to get in and get out and that's it, Nora muttered now as we walked up to the front door and she pressed hard on the mechanical doorbell. The noise of the bell reverberated around us, and moments later a middle-aged woman with close-cropped henna-dyed red hair wearing a mint-green polo shirt and khaki-colored tailored trousers opened the door and squinted at us.

After a moment or two, she said, with recognition in her voice, *Nora?*

Hi, Polly, Nora replied, and she allowed Polly to squeal and pull her into a deep and lingering hug. She seemed to envelop Nora, though she was two inches shorter than her. Nora held on to her.

Don't just stand on the doorstep, Polly said at last. Come in, girls, come in.

She pulled us into the vestibule, which was huge and white with a grand and ornate staircase hugging the far wall, and the floor tiled with chessboard-style marble.

Polly. This is my sister, Matilda, and my niece, Beatrice. Guys, this is Polly, the housekeeper here.

We shook hands awkwardly and Polly stood and beamed at us for a second too long.

Well, she said eventually, still smiling. What can I do for ya?

I'm just here to get some things I left behind, Nora said. Notebooks and stuff. Do you know where Dad might have put them?

Polly led us up the staircase and down the hallway. The walls were lined with photographs of Dad and Marnie at their wedding, which they had had in the Bahamas and forgotten to invite me and Nora to, and various stills of the different shows and movies he had been in. They were everything from the smallest walk-on parts right at the beginning of his career, up to the big retrospective segment he had done the previous year on *McCloy Who's Talking* to celebrate thirty-five years of *Quantum Leap.*

Where are the pictures of you? Beanie asked quietly, her eyes wide as she stared at the walls. I shushed her. We arrived outside a door and Polly stopped us.

Your bedroom, she said to Nora. Nothing's changed since you left, really. You know you're welcome back any time. I'm sure the twins would love to have someone to play with.

The twins? Nora asked, but Polly had already stepped past her and pushed the door open to reveal a huge guest bedroom complete with four-poster bed and floor-to-ceiling French doors leading out onto a balcony with a jaw-dropping view of downtown Los Angeles. Beanie whistled.

Thanks, Polly, Nora said. We won't be long.

Polly waved us off and disappeared while Nora pulled open the closet doors and stepped inside.

They'll be in here, she said, her voice muffled, as she rifled around.

She began to pull out archival boxes.

I filed everything, she said. Before I came back to London.

More boxes. Beanie opened the foldaway French doors and stepped onto the balcony.

Mum, there's a tennis court down there, she called. And a swimming pool.

I took the boxes from Nora and stacked them neatly by the bedroom door. More and more boxes emerged from the closet; we had a pile of four, then seven, then nine.

There's too much here, I said. How are we going to get it all back on a plane?

Nora stood, hands on her hips, a little sweaty from the effort of moving it all. She surveyed the boxes. There was something in her eyes that I liked. The look of someone with a plan. The look of someone excited about their next move, putting together something schemey. These boxes were more than just dusty old notes. They were a sign that Nora was planning for something in the immediate future.

You're right, she said. There's too much here, isn't there.

She sat on the bed and stared at the boxes, at a loss.

What is all this stuff? I asked, lifting a lid and peeking inside one of them.

Don't, she said abruptly and I pushed the lid closed. It's everything from when I lived here. All of the work I put together. The writing and the research and everything else. I've kept records of everything. Of all of the work.

Like Mum, then?

She glared at me, though I hadn't meant it as an insult, for once.

Yeah, like Mum, I guess, she said reluctantly.

I'm sorry, I said. I didn't mean to say that—in that way—

It's fine, she said, sighing. I know you didn't. I just wish that I could have something that isn't part of her, right? That isn't *influenced* by her. That isn't *in conversation* with her.

Her whole body sagged into the immaculately made bed. The corners of the duvet folded back into perfect right angles.

I felt then as though I understood in some minuscule way, for the first time, what it might be like for Nora, as an artist who was at the same time the daughter of Ingrid Olssen. There was something about what she and Mum did that I had always treated with some cynicism. It was because I didn't understand it. The way they dreamed of it. I didn't get the interest, the reams and reams of pages people dedicated to analyzing the work; I didn't believe in it.

I still didn't believe in it, and I didn't think I ever would.

But I saw what it meant to Nora in that moment, and I understood some small aspect of the pain she felt, and the darkness and the cold and the bearing-down-down-down presence of the shadow cast by the brilliant genius of our mum. The shadow in which she lived.

I need these papers, Nora said, staring up at the ceiling. I need them home.

Let's courier them, I said. I don't think we'll even get them all in the back of the car.

Mum, Beanie said. There are kids running around in your dad's back garden.

What? I asked, and walked over to join her on the balcony. Sure enough, down on the freshly trimmed lawn were two blonde-haired toddlers no more than eighteen months old. They were waddling around on the grass with the help of another mint-green-polo-shirted staff member, who was trying to interest them in the flower beds.

Abruptly, my father, Edward Robb, dressed in tennis whites and holding a lowball glass of whisky, joined them on the lawn. He hadn't seen us up here on the balcony.

I watched as he picked each of the toddlers up in turn, blew raspberries on their cheeks and bellies, swung them in the air until they burbled with giggles. The picture of a loving father.

I glanced over at Nora, whose expression of abject horror surely mirrored my own. Her face said that she hadn't known about these tiny humans, either.

They had the jowls of my father, the poor fuckers.

Hey, Dad, I shouted down at him, my voice all accusation and no greeting.

He glanced up at the balcony and squinted at me.

Matilda, is that you? he shouted, his Texan drawl more pronounced than ever.

I walked back into the bedroom, out to the hallway and down the giant staircase, feeling as though I were floating above my own body. He was already in the vestibule when I was halfway down. I stopped and stared at him. He was holding one of the kids. A little girl, blonde and pale, with an abnormally perfect row of baby teeth.

Matilda, he said.

Dad, I replied.

Let me call Marnie.

That's all right.

No. No. I insist.

He looked much older than the last time I'd seen him at the funeral. A middle-aged paunch protruded from his midriff, his skin had a suede-ish quality to it, as though he had spent too much time in the sun and had dried out like a pair of moccasins. On his head, his bald patch was thinly disguised with wisps of silver hair dragged over to the side to cover it.

Light streamed into the vestibule, illuminating him as he pulled out his phone and sent a text, presumably to Marnie.

Daddy, said one of the toddlers in an accent such the perfect imitation of his own it was almost comical. Daddy, ice cream, pleesh.

Daddy, ice cream, please, Dad repeated, delighted. Okay, okay, okay, we'll get you some ice cream. Carly?

As if by alchemy, the polo-shirted woman from the garden stepped out of some side room and ushered the children away, taking the one Dad was holding gently from his arms. By now, Nora and Beanie had joined me on the stairs, both of them very still, as though a sudden movement might spook me like a horse.

Have we entered the fucking *Twilight Zone?* Nora whispered.

You have children, I said to Dad.

Yes, he said. Two of 'em. That one's Liberty Louise and the other one, the one with the pink shoes, that's Denise Diana.

Beanie snorted involuntarily.

Diana's my middle name, Nora said slowly.

Dad blinked at her, as though he had just now registered her presence.

Is it? he said, feigning confusion. Well, Diana's my mother's name, so.

You forgot my middle name, didn't you? Nora said, not unkindly. She seemed faintly amused.

Come have some tea. Polly will make us something, I'm sure.

With hesitant steps and a nudge from behind, I descended the stairs. I looked down at my feet so that I didn't have to look at him. My sneakers were filthy, once white but now coated in the muck and dust of the desert. They seemed even grubbier against the polished white marble of the staircase. Nora was wearing a pair of Crocs that had once been yellow but were now brown. Dad ushered us into an enormous country-house-style kitchen, oblivious to the state of our shoes, and sat us down on barstools while Polly—who looked increasingly uncomfortable—served us iced tea from a pitcher in the fridge.

Polly, you don't have to do that, I said. We can pour our own drinks.

Nonsense, Dad boomed. That's what she's here for, aren't you, Polly?

I glanced at Nora, who grimaced back at me.

What brings you to California, anyhow? he asked. Nora, aren't you meant to be in some sort of secure unit?

We were just trying to get Nora's stuff, Beanie said uselessly. Then we're going to the exhibition. Dad turned his attention to her.

And how's my favorite granddaughter? he asked. How's school going? How's drama class?

It's going okay, Beanie said uncertainly, glancing at me.

She's a straight-A student, I boasted on her behalf, unable to help myself, and she smiled shyly.

Straight-A student, hey? Nice stuff. Nice stuff. I hope you're doing Shakespeare. None of that physical theater shit, you hear me?

When no one responded, he sipped his iced tea thoughtfully and checked his watch.

Marnie'll be here any minute now, he said.

He drummed his fingers against the countertop, not looking at us.

Actually, we're in a bit of a rush, Nora said eventually, her voice a little strained.

Dad, you had a whole two kids and didn't tell us, I said.

They're twins, he replied, as though that was enough of an explanation.

Yeah, and?

His mouth opened and closed and opened again.

Well, you never visit me, he said, his expression darkening. You don't take an interest in my life. I didn't meet Beatrice until she was over a year old. You hate Marnie and you don't even try to hide it.

So? I asked, choosing not to acknowledge the absolute truth of any and all of those statements.

So—why should I have to tell you? You girls. You're not a part of my life anymore.

I felt myself simmering like onions and sugar in a hot pan.

We're not a part of your life, I said, because that's the way you engineered it to be.

I'm not an old man, you know, he continued, ignoring me. I'm not even sixty yet. I deserve to be happy, I deserve to live my life the way I want to live it.

And that's by pretending you have two daughters, not four, I confirmed, seething.

Was Marnie pregnant while I lived here? Nora asked, her brow furrowing as she attempted the mental arithmetic.

Yeah, Beanie said quietly, having already done it for her. She would have been.

Dad, what the actual fuck? I said loudly, standing up.

Well, Nora wasn't well, were you, Nora? We didn't want to send you on a spiral with news that didn't concern you.

News that didn't concern me, Nora repeated, dazed.

I shook my head at him. My expectations were always low for you, I said. But even I didn't think you could stoop to this.

Sit down, please, Matilda, he said, and his voice was heavy and commanding. But I found that I wasn't compelled to obey.

You've always been prone to making a scene, he said. His eyebrows were sharpening at the edges.

Sorry I'm making a scene, I said petulantly. Sorry I'm disrupting your life with my existence.

He slammed his fist on the table, making all three of us jump. What do you want me to do, huh, Mattie? What can I do to make this right?

Nothing, I said, struggling to keep the tremor out of my voice. I watched as one of the twins, having escaped her nanny, poked her head above the windowsill in the kitchen and watched with careful, curious eyes, trained on her father.

I recognized that look. I recognized it in myself, and in Nora, when we were children.

The low ebb of anxiety whenever the phone rang.

The absence of space.

The shadow in the hallway.

I sat down, finally.

When Mum wasn't well and kept ditching us to live alone in that house. I wanted you to come and get us. Why didn't you come and get us, Dad?

Nora sat down next to me and squeezed my hand.

I had asked her about this before, in the hospital, when she was being sectioned, after the third attempt.

It's all about Mum, she said, coming out of a therapy session to sit in the relatives' room with me and spoon orange-flavored Jell-O out of an improbably small translucent plastic cup into her small, dry mouth.

And Dad, she continued. It's all about them. Surprise, surprise. Unresolved childhood trauma. I'm a walking fucking cliché. I am so sick of interrogating my own psyche.

Do you ever wonder what our life would've been like? I asked. If things were different.

If we'd gone to live with Dad in California, you mean?

I nodded.

Yeah, she replied. I wonder every day what it would have been like for us. I wonder whether my brain would be this hell-bent on killing me.

There was no use wondering, of course. The choices our parents had made when we were children had irrevocably molded us into the people we were now. We were too old to change, and too sensible to yearn for an impossible alternative universe.

In every universe, though, I knew that the only constant would be Nora. Nora, an inevitability.

Your mother said the same thing, Dad said sadly.

What do you mean?

In the divorce. She wanted me to take you. So she could go on living the way she was living, without the guilt. But I was the one with stable work. I was the one making something of my life.

He wasn't talking to us anymore. He was trying to convince himself of something.

She wasted it all, he said.

She didn't, Nora said sharply.

Why should I ruin everything I built here so she could ruin herself? he asked the ceiling.

I closed my eyes briefly, feeling my stomach turn to lead.

You're saying Mum tried to make you take us away, I said. That she didn't want us.

He snapped back to me, jaw tense.

Yes, he said. But you knew that, didn't you?

Not in so many words, I replied.

So Mum wanted rid of us, Nora said. And so did you, Dad.

The silence felt like a drowning. I thought of Mum again, building a spindly scaffolding for her dreams so that they wouldn't fall to the ground and suffocate her.

She couldn't just exist, just be. She didn't want to.

And you, Nora said, turning to me. You didn't want us either.

What? I asked.

But before she could answer me, Dad, in his Hollywood-mansion kitchen, took out his wallet.

He said, I want to apologize properly to you girls.

From the wallet—brown leather and embossed with his initials—he pulled a wad of cash and started counting the bills.

Oh, no, Nora said.

I stood up.

I think we should go now, Nora said.

You're a prick, Dad, I said as Nora took me by the arm and attempted to steer me to the front door.

You're a PRICK, I said again, louder, shouting at the back of his head. He put his wallet on the kitchen counter and held his head in his hands. But he didn't turn around.

Denise Diana was standing at the door to the kitchen garden, her eyes big and watchful as Nora wrestled me to the exit.

You know they're not going to stay blonde, I said petulantly. They'll go dark, like we did. It's in the gene pool.

Your mother's gene pool, Dad corrected me swiftly.

Beanie zipped out of the door behind us, still holding a half-drunk glass of peachy-colored iced tea. She stared at it for a second, as if unclear as to how it had got into her hand, and then threw it in a bush.

We didn't even get your stuff, she said to Nora, panicking.

Nora stared at her nonplussed for a moment, and then said, Ahhhh, fuck.

We all three of us looked up at the door, the realization that our exit was about to be reneged upon. Nora hesitated before pressing the mechanical doorbell. The sound reverberated once again all around us, on the inside of our skulls, through the soft tissue of our brains.

As if by some miracle, it was Polly who answered the door again.

Nora, I'm so sorry, I had no idea that you didn't know about—

Nora grasped her hand. This is unfortunately not the shittiest thing our dad has ever done, she explained. Listen, Polly, I need you to courier some stuff for me.

She gave Polly the details of where the boxes ought to be sent while Beanie and I stared out at the bronzed dolphin water feature. The water in the fountain was crystal clear; it looked drinkable.

With one last wave at Polly, who was still standing on the doorstep, her eyes upside-down with sadness, Nora slid into the car, and Beanie and I followed.

I glanced at Dad's house in the rear-view mirror as we pulled away. I felt, rather than saw, Nora deflating beside me.

Never again, Nora said, with some conviction.

Never again, I agreed.

CHAPTER 26

We ended up on the Santa Monica pier.

The afternoon was perfect and crystalline, and the Pacific Ocean below us was overrun with surfers and swimmers. The sky was blue and endless, as it had been since we'd got here.

I feel like we're in a dream, Beanie said as we parked and walked along the seafront, past neatly lined tall palm trees and hot-dog stands and beach calisthenics parks to get to the pier. The END OF ROUTE 66 sign stood poker-straight on the pier. We leaned over the railings and stared down into the water. I could feel the roar of the sea in my bones. I was still vibrating with adrenaline from Dad's house.

I found a food stand and bought three portions of crab sticks and fries. Beanie announced that she was going for a paddle and wandered down to the beach below us. Nora looked at her food, bemused, when I handed it to her.

What's the matter? I asked her.

I'm allergic to shellfish, she replied, her lip curled.

I scoffed. No, you're not.

I am.

Since when?

Since I was fourteen. Aunt Karoline cooked oysters and I had to go to A and E because I had a rash on my chest and I couldn't breathe.

I stared at her.

I have no recollection of this, I said. Whatsoever. Absolutely none.

Nora shrugged. You were already gone by then, she said matter-of-factly.

What's that supposed to mean?

It's just a fact.

I took the crab-and-fries from her hand and threw it in a nearby trashcan.

When are you going to stop punishing me? I asked her, unable to disguise the anguish in my voice.

I'm not, she replied. I stopped caring a long time ago.

I shook my head at her.

You're the only one doing the punishing, she said. You're the one punishing yourself.

I don't believe you, I said.

She grimaced.

I turned out to the ocean, watched the orange blip of Beanie standing in the shallow water fifty feet below us and letting it lap at her bare feet as she ate fries thoughtfully and stared unseeingly at the horizon. It was easier than having to look Nora in the face.

I'm sorry I didn't know about the shellfish, I said quietly.

It's fine, Nora said. I really don't care.

If you say so.

We stood at the railings in a comfortable silence.

When I first moved back to London, Nora said, after some time. Not long after Mum died and I started my PhD. I was trying to work out what I wanted to write about for my thesis, what the work was going to look like. I was having a bit of a crisis, because Mum was dead, right? And I was thinking, what if I can't do it without her, you know? Like, what if I'm actually a shit artist?

You're not a shit artist.

But at the time, I was like, well, what if I could only do it because I was trying to be better than Mum, or different, or antagonistic, or something. And now Mum was gone, and maybe I didn't have it in me anymore. Maybe I'd lost it. There had been this weird thing that happened when she came to LA when I was doing my Master's. She came to see the concrete piece. The response to *My burial*. It was a couple of years before I tried to kill myself. The whole time she was there, in the exhibition space, walking around, watching the film, she had this curious look on her face; it was one I hadn't seen before. Like, a weird *pride*. And then, once she had seen it all, she turned to me and said, Aren't you going to thank me, *kjæreste*?

Thank her for what?

I don't know. For making me the way that I am, maybe.

So, what happened when you moved to London?

Well, I had this terrible allergic reaction. I must have had something with fish in it without realizing. I don't know. Anyway, I had this awful reaction. On my own, in the apartment, and I couldn't find my EpiPen. And I didn't know who to call, and I was on my own.

Nora.

That was the sixth time.

The sixth time, what? I asked her.

The sixth time I almost died.

I counted up the rest on my fingers. The time Mum dropped her as a baby. The bathtub. And then Maurice Hoffmann. The car—I couldn't bear to dwell on that one. And then LA. This one made six. And of course, the Control Room made seven.

Holy shit, I said. You're right.

She grinned at me.

I'm a cheater, she said. I cheat death.

But you shouldn't have to. You should have people there—

She held up a hand to stop me.

I called myself an ambulance, she continued. And I wasn't breathing very well, and I lay down on my bed in this empty apartment, in this part of London that I didn't know very well, and I've never felt so alone in my whole life, which is *really* saying something because I was coming out of the second suicide attempt, right, and I thought to myself, holy shit, this is how I'm going to die.

I'm going to die right here on this mattress, and no one is going to know about it. I'm going to be one of those cases you hear about on the news where they don't find the body for weeks and weeks and by the time someone realizes I'm missing, that I haven't been seen, all of the organic matter of my body will have rotted away and melted through the bedsheets and the mattress and the bedframe and all that'll be left of me is this big, brown, smelly stain. And they'll have to get people in hazmat suits to come and hose me off the bedlinen. And that's all I'll be remembered for. For being the sad fuck who died alone and no one knew.

No one will know, and no one will care.

I realized that I didn't care either. It was almost, like, *peaceful*. The idea of dying. Anything to stop my brain buzzing. Anything for a little bit of quiet.

The idea of my body turning into mulch. Of returning my organic matter to the earth. Of separating myself from the mortal coil. Of becoming part of an expanding universe, like air and stardust and gravity. I realized that it was the only way I could be still.

And that's when I decided to get the cameras, she said.

Nora, I said.

I'm not saying it to get sympathy, she said quickly, cutting me off. I'm not telling you to elicit your pity or whatever. I just wanted to explain that to you.

Yeah, I said quietly, trying to stop myself from crying.

Because I don't think you understand, she said.

No, I replied. I don't understand. And I was crying for real now.

I realized, she said, that no one was coming to save me, ever, ever. No one was responsible for me. So I had to be responsible for myself. Just like when we were kids, right? The only way we were going to survive that house, Mum and Dad, was by saving ourselves. Because no one was going to do it for us. I had to make myself known and knowable and unavoidable. So that's what I did. I saved myself, Matt.

Through an experiment in self-isolation, I said.

Yeah, she replied. Except that the whole world was watching.

She slipped her hand into mine.

It should have been me, I said. I should have been there to save you. I should have been there to shove an EpiPen in your leg. To get you off the bathroom floor.

Maybe, she said.

I was realizing, in that moment, that I hadn't abandoned Nora once. I had done it a thousand times.

I had spent my whole life abandoning Nora.

I should have been there for you, I told her.

You shouldn't have needed to. We can't change it now.

No. We can't. Except I can tell you I'm sorry.

She picked a fry out of my food and popped it in her mouth. Then she immediately spat it out.

That one definitely touched fish, she explained.

I rolled my eyes at her.

We're not responsible for the circumstances of our birth, Nora said thoughtfully. We're not responsible for the Richmond house. For what Mum did, what Dad did. Any of it.

Yeah, I agreed. But we're responsible for everything that came after.

We are.

The sun bore down on us and the sound of the sea got into our bones, and the ground shifted beneath us.

I still thought it in every moment, every in-breath and exhalation. With every blink of the eye or flutter of the pulse I was thinking it. *Please don't die, Nora. Please don't die.*

The world seemed to tip on the axis of it, her alive-ness, her existence within it.

But when we stood up on the pier and watched my kid tap her feet in the water below, and we cried silently into the salt spray, and I saw the way she tipped her face to the sun and squared her shoulders and clenched her fists at the horizon, it felt, just for a single spectacular moment, like she was going to live for ever.

———————

She woke me up in the middle of the night, that night, when she rolled out of bed and crept into the bathroom. I looked over at Beanie, and she was awake too, staring at the ceiling with eyes that shone in the light that filtered through the gap in the curtain. We listened, the pair of us, pretending that we weren't. We listened to her panicked gasping breaths, stifled as though she had both hands over her mouth. As though she were trying not to wake us, as though we ought not to be disturbed. And then, later, she crawled back into bed and I rolled over, feigning sleep, pretending that I hadn't heard her.

Do you think we could go to the Getty today? she asked us the next morning.

The Getty?

Yeah. You know. The museum.

Why do you want to go to the Getty? Beanie asked, sliding her sunglasses onto the bridge of her nose.

Nora hesitated, hugged herself by pulling her elbows closer into her body.

Nora? I asked as she sat down on the bed.

There's a Degas there, she said, pretending that she didn't care.

A Degas?

The artist. Degas.

Yeah. And?

It's one of Mum's favorites. I think we should see it.

Beanie's eyes flashed to mine.

I shrugged exaggeratedly.

Well, my whole day was going to involve sitting on that pool deck and not moving, I said. I'm up for some culture.

It's just the Degas. We don't have to do the whole thing. If I have any more culture, I might die, Nora said. I've got culture coming out my eardrums.

That's the curse of an artist, Beanie said.

The museum was embedded into the side of a hill in the Bel Air area of the city, almost as though it were growing out of the rock face. We parked and queued for a novelty yet stylishly built tram, which would carry us up the sheer face of the cliff to the gloriously, puritanically white set of buildings further up the rock. Everything was unnervingly clean, as though it had just been built last week. Nora shuffled from foot to foot as we waited our turn for the tram, picking at the skin around her fingernails.

It's going to be fine, I told her, though I wasn't sure why I was saying it in that moment, exactly.

As the tram carried us up the cliff, an embarrassingly moving piece of classical music building to a denouement over the tinny speakers, I saw my chance.

After this, will you come and fill your prescription with me? I asked her gently.

She glanced at me, distracted. I can't think about that now, she said.

Just say we can talk about it, I pleaded. Later today. Can we talk about it, please?

Sure, she said. We'll talk about it later today.

The tram shuddered to a stop at the top of the cliff, and opened up onto an immaculate sandstone plaza, with lush greenery and long shadows cast across pale stone steps. It was utopian in its presentation: the air was warm and the museum seemed as though it were an architect's model of itself, clean lines and white walls and water features.

Nora stepped off the tram first, hesitantly. She glanced around, her sunglasses obscuring her expression. She led us through the lobby into the central plaza and we trotted after her towards a building closest to the edge of the mountain, the landscaped gardens below us drawing curious symbols in the ground. The sound of running water was everywhere, water gurgling against pools set in white marble. The sky was a perfect cerulean blue in every direction. Across the freeway, there were mansions set into the hill, surrounded by lush foliage, their swimming pools patchwork crystalline squares of aquamarine against dark coniferous trees that had been taken from their native environments and replanted wholesale along the lines of the roads.

It's in here, Nora said, gesturing for us to follow her across the plaza.

We climbed a grand spiral staircase inside the building to a floor dedicated to nineteenth-century European portraiture. Inside, the walls were dark teals and burgundies, mimicking the style of the galleries in London, I thought, a stark contrast with the blinding whiteness of the rest of the Getty.

Nora led us to the room with the Van Gogh in it. Tourists crowded round it, cameras poised, but we passed it, to the small square self-portrait opposite.

There it is, Nora said.

It was small, compared to the sizes Mum liked to work with. A square of canvas no larger than an outstretched hand. The explainer plaque dated it *about 1857-58.* In the oil itself, the artist, in his twenties, stared out moodily at the viewer, his lower lip jutting out, the light and shadow on his face warping it into something devastating.

Oh, Beanie said. Poor Edgar. He looks sad.

I watched his eyes as they watched me, and felt nothing. But Nora's gaze was fixed upon it.

I tried very hard not to say, I don't get it. And though I was silent, I was sure she heard me. Because she turned around and said, The reason it's special is because it was never meant to be displayed. It was just a study. He was just trying something out. And it came out like this. She gestured at the square of canvas and I nodded, trying to look impressed.

That's why Mum loved it, Nora explained.

Beanie was nodding now.

Yeah, she said. I get it.

Do you? I whispered at her. She furrowed her eyebrows at me.

Human beings, Nora said, are at their very best when they are alone.

And she turned back to the Degas, and I thought she might cry.

Nory? I asked her.

It's fine, she said, not turning to look at us.

Mum, why don't we go and look at the Sudanese vases? Beanie prompted, tugging at my sleeve.

I glanced at Nora again. She seemed not to have heard us. She was still staring at the Degas portrait, oblivious to the gallery around her becoming further and further bloated with tourists clamoring to look at Van Gogh's blue flowers on the wall opposite.

We walked down to the pavilion, leaving Nora behind. We found ourselves out on a pale veranda with tessellating concrete tiles, overlooking the city and the thick brownish haze that emanated from it.

Let's send a picture to Dad, Beanie said, and she snapped a selfie of the two of us above the cityscape on her phone.

That's a nice one, I said absent-mindedly. I was thinking of Nora, standing in front of the portrait, transfixed, as though it had snatched her soul.

I miss Dad, Beanie said.

Yeah, me too, I replied, without thinking, and I saw her grin and immediately regretted my words. God, I hate LA, I said. Look at that. Look at all that pollution.

London is probably just as bad, she pointed out. It's just that you can't see it because you can't get a view of it like this.

I shrugged. I still prefer London to here, I said. Whatever you do, don't go to university here. I won't visit, okay?

Like I didn't visit Nora.

I wouldn't want to be this far away from you and Dad. I don't know how Nora did it.

Well, that's nice to hear.

I leaned against the wall and watched the city, letting out a long breath I didn't realize I'd been holding.

Do you want to know what I think? Beanie said, grinning.

What you think about what?

About you and Dad.

Oh, Beans, why are we still on this?

Because it's important.

I groaned. Okay. Fine. What do you think?

I think that you're still in love with him.

For crying out loud, kid.

Don't deny it. I think you are. You still love Dad. I saw the way you were looking when you were telling Dolly Parton about him in the back of the van.

I stared at her.

Nothing gets past you, does it, big nose?

She shrugged, her grin even wider.

I pulled her into a sideways hug and sighed.

You're not going to drop this, are you? I asked her. I remembered, then, that argument we had had at the restaurant, before everything had started falling apart. How Gus had made Beanie keep his and Lulu's separation a secret from me. At the time I had been furious, sure that I could never forgive Gus for swearing our daughter to secrecy with motivations I couldn't understand. Now, it seemed like a conversation that had happened in another universe.

Nope, she said. I'm never going to drop this.

Okay. Fine. I'll tell you what I think. And then we can never talk about it ever again, okay?

Okay.

I breathed out slowly once more.

I am always going to be in love with your dad, I said to her slowly, and held a finger up at her as she went to react to what I had said. Wait. Let me finish, I said.

I'm always going to be in love with him, I continued. Because we did the most amazing thing together. We made you, and we brought you up, and nothing I ever do for the rest of my life is going to beat that, kid.

But me and Dad. It could never work again between us. Too much has happened. There's too much history there.

But, Mum—

No, Beans. I think you might be too young to understand this, but love isn't the only thing a relationship needs to work. I did some really bad, not good things while I was with your father. I gave up on the relationship. I sent him away, I told him I didn't care, and Gus is the kind of person who doesn't forget something like that. But guess what? Something amazing happened. He moved on. He found someone to love him how he deserved to be loved. And there is no way in hell I would try to sabotage that.

But they broke up—

Let me finish. There is no way I'll ever put myself—or put him—in a position where I could do the same thing again to him. And I wouldn't want to.

I felt my heart tug even as I said it, because I knew the truth of it. The absolute and overwhelming guilt of it.

I'm being honest with you because I think that it's important that you know, I said frankly. And I don't want you to go on thinking that there's some world where me and your dad might get back together. Because there's not, Beans, and I'm sorry to say it. Your dad is going to find the perfect person for him, and they're going to be very happy together. That person isn't me. I ruined it forever. And that's the end of it.

I glanced up at her then, expecting a look of complete devastation on her face, ready to pull her into a hug and apologize but explain that it was important that she understood. But when I looked at her, all I saw was the face of a teenager who was deeply unimpressed by her mother, one eyebrow quirked up, a look that said *I know better.*

What's that look for?

What look?

That look on your face right now.

I haven't got a look on my face.

Yes, you have.

I haven't. I don't know what you're talking about.

I'm literally staring at you, kid. I can see the look.

I think you're mistaken.

Before we could dissolve further into the argument, Nora was strolling towards us out on the veranda. I waved at her as she approached.

Okay? Beanie asked, linking arms with her.

Nora still had her sunglasses on, and I noticed that her lip was quivering.

I'm not feeling very well, she said simply.

I dragged the two of them into my arms.

I'm sorry, I said uselessly.

She turned to look at the view of the city too, then, her sunglasses slipping down her nose, though she pushed them back up. I could see the tears beginning to track down her cheeks and wrapped my arm around her shoulders. Beanie stood on the other side of her and took her hand.

Fuck this fucking city, Nora announced after a moment of silence.

That's exactly what I've been saying this *whole time.*

She cried some more and after a little while she sniffed and wiped her face under her sunglasses with the corner of her sleeve.

Okay, let's go now, she said.

And we strolled back through the ceramics exhibition to the front of the museum, out onto the plaza in its perfect white angularity.

Hey, Mum, Beanie said. Look at that.

She was pointing at a poster that was framed in one of those outdoor advertising Plexiglas coverings, on the side of the building that housed a café and a restaurant.

I looked over at what she was pointing at and almost fell over. There on the wall was a huge, larger-than-life-sized photograph of Ingrid Olssen.

Blahhh, I said, involuntarily.

It's Mum, Nora commented.

Yeah, no shit, I said, feeling my heart palpitating.

We walked over to the poster. Beanie took a selfie with it.

Guys, get in, she said. Come on.

We both did, our faces stony, Nora's nose bright pink.

Overlaying the poster of Mum's face was a contemporary sans serif font, in bold off-white:

INGRID OLSSEN: A LEGACY

SAN FRANCISCO MUSEUM OF MODERN ART

AUGUST 10–OCTOBER 14, 2020

MEMBERS GO FREE

SUPPORTED BY KAROLINE OLSSEN AND ASSOCIATED FUNDING

Oh my God, I said. It's actually happening. It's actually real.

What are we going to do? Beanie asked, staring at the poster, transfixed.

Well, we're going to do what we came here to do, I said uncertainly.

And what's that, exactly? Because a lot has happened and I've kind of lost the thread of—

We're going to stop it, Nora said, her teeth clenched.

She strode over to the poster and yanked it dramatically out from underneath the Plexiglas, and shredded it into tiny pieces with nimble fingers.

We're going to stop the exhibition, she said, her voice heavy with meaning, and then it's finished.

We're going to stop the exhibition, she repeated, talking to herself and not us, the shredded paper fluttering from her fingers in the mountain breeze. And then it's finished.

EXTRACT FROM CHAPTER 23, INGRID OLSSEN:
VISIONARY BY RICHARD TAPER (FORTHCOMING
FROM ORANGE RABBIT PRESS)

Maurice Hoffmann shot Ingrid Olssen's nine-year-old daughter,
Nora Robb, in the summer of 2004 at Olssen's home in Richmond,
UK. Many critics view the shooting as the moment that defined the
final stage of Olssen's career up to her death in 2018, and informed
some of the best work of her lifetime.

There are several explanations for the shooting, and having
spoken to tens of Ingrid Olssen's acquaintances, colleagues,
family members and contemporaries who all claim to have some
information regarding the incident, the waters only become further muddied.

There are no facts that have consensus among all those I
interviewed.

The first fact that is disputed, is that by the time Maurice Hoffmann turned up at Ingrid's Richmond townhouse in the summer
of 2004, the pair had neither seen nor spoken to one another for at
least seven years. Some corroborated accounts place Ingrid's last
meeting with Hoffmann at around August 1997, shortly after her
debut at Grift House Art Festival.

As Olssen's relationship with Hoffmann diminished, her work
took a marked turn away from the clean lines and silkscreens of
the eighties and early nineties. Ingrid's emancipation from Hoffmann coincided with several other significant events in her life. In
quick succession, Olssen undertook a whirlwind romance with
the television actor, Edward Robb, got married and gave birth.
These life events can be traced in the intention of her large oil
works. With *Edward and me on a bed of lies* (1986), the first notable
work in this period of Olssen's life, one can observe the early
tumult of the love affair with Robb, and the way that it was already
turning sour. In Olssen's interbirth period (Matilda born in 1986,
and Nora in 1995), the work is more refined, cleaner and

considered. It is at this time that Olssen briefly returns to silk-screens and repetition, and, in a departure from her portraiture work, creates over a hundred serigraphs of the Richmond house, interposed with southern Norwegian landscapes, in the most comprehensive and varied series of her career. This work is also largely considered by critics her weakest. By the time Olssen is pregnant with her second daughter, Nora, in 1995, she is separated from Edward Robb, and she has painted *My burial*, a piece featuring her younger daughter in utero, and conversely one of her most celebrated giant oil works.

Angelica Hoffmann is the widow of the late Maurice Hoffmann and Director of the Hoffmann Foundation, which offers grants to students from disadvantaged socio-economic backgrounds to pursue an education in the arts. I asked her what she knew about the breakdown of her late husband's relationship with his most famous ingénue.

According to Angelica, the dissolution of the mentor-friendship came down to creative differences.

"There didn't seem to be anything in particular," she told me. "Maurice had always been quite staunch in his beliefs about what constituted good technique, good practice and good manners. In his opinion, Ingrid didn't have any of the three."

After Olssen met Edward Robb, her problems with substance abuse—notably alcohol and stimulants—became a more dominant part of her life. Hoffmann was a teetotaler and spoke vocally throughout his life about his distaste for drug culture in London galleries.

Karoline Olssen calls him a relic. "He was getting left behind. And he didn't like it. So he took it out on Ingrid."

There was no significant moment of climax for Olssen and Hoffmann. By most accounts, their relationship simply faded, and their circles changed, until they were no longer attending the same events, no longer moved in the same crowds, and no longer called upon one another or shared work with one another.

There is another narrative that has emerged since Hoffmann's
death in 2009, and has gathered momentum since Olssen's own
death. Several of Olssen's acquaintances who spent time in her
Richmond home and studio in the nineties, allege that Maurice
Hoffmann was in love with Ingrid Olssen.*

I asked her daughters whether they could confirm the rumor.

According to Matilda Robb, "Mum had a different boyfriend
most weeks, and they were all in love with her. They were all trying
to get something from her. Was Maurice Hoffmann one of them?
I don't know. Probably. They all blurred into one."

Nora Robb says, "When I was five years old, my sister was out
somewhere with her boyfriend and it was just me and Mum in
the house. And an old German-sounding guy with a wide-
brimmed hat and a tweed overcoat came to the house. He and
Mum had a huge argument in the conservatory. She was probably drunk, though I don't remember for certain. Anyway, I
remember watching from behind a floor lamp and I saw him hit
her—hard—in the small of the back. It was a punch rather than
a hit. So hard that she fell to the ground. And then when he left,
she stayed on the floor for a very long time. I'm pretty sure that
man was Maurice Hoffmann. But, you know. I was five. I might
have dreamed it. And stuff like that happened a lot."

Edward Robb also cannot corroborate the rumors, saying that,
"Ingrid barely mentioned Maurice when we were together. It was
almost as though he didn't exist."

But Sadie Nelson, bassist for the band Acid Rain, whose Brit-
pop hit "Virgin Queen" went to number one in 1998, spent several months sleeping on the floor of Olssen's studio in 1995 shortly
after Olssen had given birth to Nora and divorced Edward Robb.
Nelson alleges that she witnessed Hoffmann coming in and out

---

* A statement from The Hoffmann Foundation and Angelica Hoffmann maintains that Maurice Hoffmann was never involved sexually or romantically with Ingrid Olssen when she lived at
his home in Golders Green or otherwise, and that Maurice Hoffmann never at any time engaged
with any sexual relations with any person under the age of consent.

of the house several times a week over the course of those months, and staying for many hours with Olssen in the upstairs rooms of the house. Sadie Nelson was detoxing from heroin at the time and concedes that she may have been hallucinating her dead father.

"There's no way to know for certain," she says.

In addition, recently uncovered financial records from a 2007 court case in which one of Hoffmann's assistants sued the Hoffmann Foundation for unpaid wages after a dispute over copyright, show that Hoffmann was sending Olssen a monthly allowance of nine hundred pounds right up to the shotgun incident. Afterwards, the money stopped. Hoffmann won the case brought against him by his former assistant, though suffered from a cardiac arrest shortly after the trial concluded. He never fully recovered and died in 2009 from complications related to heart disease.

When Hoffmann arrived at the house in Richmond in 2004, with a shotgun that he had taken from a Wiltshire hunting lodge that belonged to his business manager, Olssen had (according to contemporary accounts and notwithstanding unconfirmed sightings such as Nora Robb's) not seen him for several years.

Those present in the house at the time of the shooting were Ingrid Olssen, her sister and manager, Karoline Olssen, and her daughter, Nora Robb. Her elder daughter, Matilda, had already moved away from the family home with her own child, Beatrice, born in November 2002. Nora was nine years old.

"I was nine years old, Richard," she says with some indignation. "There's no point asking me about it."

"Maurice Hoffmann was a man deranged," Karoline Olssen elaborates in a transatlantic accent that seems to invoke her turn as Blanche DuBois in a Woking Theater production of *A Streetcar Named Desire* staged in 1991.

Karoline also corroborates Sadie Nelson's account of Hoffmann's visits to the Richmond house in the 1990s.

On the 2004 shooting, she says that, "He kicked the door down and stomped through the house looking for Ingrid."

"It was more like he wasn't very well," Nora tells me.

Both agree that Hoffmann took aim at Ingrid, and Ingrid ran up the stairs into her daughter's bedroom, where Nora was sleeping. Karoline was on the phone to the police downstairs in the studio when she heard the gunshot.

When asked what she remembers of the incident, Nora recalls that he had "really, really shiny eyes. I've never seen eyes so shiny; it was like they were emitting light. And I remember that my mother was afraid. Terrified. I had never felt fear like that on her."

Ingrid crawled under Nora's bed in an attempt to hide from Hoffmann, who had chased her up the stairs and was searching the rooms for her. When he came into Nora's bedroom, he saw the shape of a body under the sheets, and shot at it without looking. The bullet hit Nora and not Ingrid. She screamed, and Hoffmann, perhaps realizing what he had done, that he had shot the wrong person, a child, fled the house.

Nora was taken to A and E and the wound was treated, with two further operations to remove bullet fragments from her leg needed in the following year. She walked with a leg brace until her thirteenth birthday, though did not sustain any permanent injuries into adulthood. Hoffmann was apprehended in a hired car at an industrial estate in Hampstead some hours later, the shotgun propped up on the passenger seat next to him. Ingrid Olssen refused to press charges against Hoffmann and insisted that the whole thing had been an unfortunate accident. Hoffmann was eventually charged with possession of a firearm without a license and ordered to pay a fine.

It was not until after that evening that the effects of the shooting became fully understood.

"We went through a period in that house where no one was allowed in, and no one was allowed out," Karoline explains. "The only humans allowed inside were myself, Ingrid and Nora. Even Matilda wasn't let in when she knocked on the door."

The guardedness of the Richmond house was symptomatic of a paranoia that permeated Olssen's life and work for several years after the shooting.

"At the time, I was trying to get custody of Nora," Matilda explains. "There had been a few incidents where Nora had been left home alone for days, and she'd been found sleeping in the park because Mum had inadvertently locked her out of the house. I wanted Nora to come and live with me. But I was seventeen, and social services inspected my apartment and said "no". Mum disappeared a lot, but she wouldn't let anyone else in the house to look after Nora while she was gone. Sometimes not even Aunt Karoline. After the night of the shooting, I didn't see Nora for a year, and the following summer I came and stayed with her for a few weeks. I promised her that I would come back for her."

I asked Matilda what she thought of Olssen's work during this period of upheaval, but she didn't seem to understand the question.

It's clear, nevertheless, that Olssen's output at the time was heavily informed by that night and the circumstances of the shooting. Olssen went through a six-month period where her self-portraiture became obsessive, each one more grotesque than the previous, her features distorted beyond recognition. From 2004 to her death in 2018, all Olssen's work was self-portraiture. This late stage of her career is widely considered to be her most prolific, and having produced her finest work.

Karoline Olssen agrees and notes the *Window* series (oil and mixed media on reinforced board, 2006) as a particular standout: six self-portraits conducted at the bay window of the studio at the Richmond house, where Olssen uses the natural light to contort the features of her face into inhuman proportions. Each portrait captures the face at a different time of the day, and each face is more hideous than the last, with protruding cheekbones, sagging eyes and melting jowls. The *Window* series will be placed on public display for the first time ever in 2020 at the *Ingrid Olssen: A Legacy* exhibition at the San Francisco Museum of Modern Art.[*]

Nora Robb remembers the series well, noting that "Mum didn't move from the window for days."

She comments that the series indicates a deep-rooted and pervasive fear in Olssen that had not been present before.

"Something changed in her after the shooting," Nora says. "She had always been kind of chaotic as a person. You know as well as I do. But she had intention in what she did; in her work, in how she lived her life. After Maurice Hoffmann shot me, it was like she'd lost something vital to her continued existence. It was like she had realized her own exposure.

"I think you can see that in her work, and in how she lived her life at the end. She got deep into prescription pills. There was a lot of unpleasant press after the shooting. Lurid false details were printed in the tabloids. We had reporters camped out on our front lawn for days at a time. This is probably the time that Mum stopped engaging with the press altogether. No more getting snapped by the paparazzi, no more interviews, no more gossip rags. By the time she died she wanted nothing to do with any of it.

"But it wasn't just about the newspapers. She had dealt with the tabloids her whole life in the UK. There are pictures of her vagina on the internet from upskirting photos, for God's sake.

"There was something else, I think. Something insidious about being a woman in the public eye. It's that everyone is trying to take something of you for themselves. Everyone was taking something from Ingrid Olssen. Her whole life, whether it was her so-called friends, her sister who she bankrolled, the press, the galleries, her children, her ex-husband, or the other men she was

---

[*] Editor's note: please amend this reference to the exhibition in light of recent events.

involved with, or Maurice Hoffmann turning up at her house to try to take her whole life for himself. Even you, Richard, with this biography. She's dead and there's still someone out there picking at the bones. Everyone wanted a little piece of her, always. And when she was young and optimistic and energetic, that was okay. She was happy to give it all away. But I think that she got to the point where they had all taken so much from her that she had nothing left to give.

"That's what happens to us all. You take, and we give and we give and we give it all away until we have nothing left."

CHAPTER 27

NORA STARED DOWN AT THE PILLBOX ON THE DASHBOARD
AS WE DROVE NORTH TOWARDS MALIBU.

I don't want them, she said.

We had the windows down and the Pacific Ocean on our left. On our right, the rocks and hillocks and sun-baked tundra of the desert and the Santa Monica Mountains sat stark against the glittering teal of the ocean. Nobody was meant to live out here, in this shallow, dry basin of land. Even the asphalt was sun-bleached, pale and dusty.

I'm not taking them, she said again, an edge in her voice, talking about the medication we had collected from the pharmacy in Santa Monica before we'd hit the road for the final leg of our journey.

You can't make me.

I felt my stomach twist, as it did every time we had this conversation.

Are you a doctor? I asked her. Do you know better than your doctors?

In this case, I do, she said, her bottom lip sticking out a little bit. I'm so much better without medication. I feel so much better.

It was true that Nora's hair, under a bright pink baseball cap that belonged to Beanie, and skin, which had caught the sun a little, were looking healthier. She had some color and fullness back to her face. Her eyes didn't seem like they were looking at something that no one else could see. I thought back to when I'd first seen her in the hospital. I'd barely recognized her. She had seemed like all her insides had been drawn out and someone had stuffed her. She'd walked and talked and looked like Nora, but there had been something uncanny in her face that had made her seem like a fake, an imitation, a replica that had all the right parts and features but nothing on the inside. Now, something had come back to her. I hadn't noticed the exact moment it had happened. Somewhere between Phoenix and LA, maybe. But it was there, just a shadow of it.

But.

When you get prescribed something, you take it, I said. It's what you do. You take it because you're sick, and it's going to make you better.

Have you never heard of the opioid crisis? Nora asked me spitefully, and I sighed.

Yeah, she said, victorious, when I didn't reply. I'm not trusting a profession that took money to give people opioids for backache.

I looked at the pillbox again, not bothering to make the argument that it was an NHS doctor, not an American one, who'd written this prescription. It was sitting innocuously on the dashboard. Maybe Nora was right. Maybe her tablets were going to make her worse.

But we won't know until you try, I said aloud.

Matilda, Nora said, exasperated. This is not my first rodeo.

I returned my attention to the road. We were hitting traffic as we drove through Malibu. On the other side of the city, Zuma Beach was awash with surfers running directly into the sea with boards. We queued on the Pacific Coast Highway as cars turned into the township. The lushness of it was bizarre, in contrast with the atmosphere inside the car. The pale beige squares of the beach houses like broken teeth on the rocks. As we moved further away from the pollution haze, the concrete jungle of LA, I felt myself relaxing. Nora picked at her thumbs. Beanie sat in the back and stared out the window. The cliffs, inland, bore down on us.

Look at all those hills, guys, she said, clawing at any handhold that might change the tone of the conversation.

Yeah, Nora said. Look at all those hills your mum can die on.

I slammed on the brakes as the car in front indicated onto the beachfront at the last possible moment.

Idiot, I said under my breath.

You know what? Fuck this, said Nora.

And she opened the passenger-side door of the car and stepped out onto the highway.

NORA? I shouted, but she ignored me, slammed the door, and crossed the four lanes, picking her way through the crawling traffic, and disappearing into the throng of people on the beach.

For fuck's sake, I muttered, and indicated off the highway.

You shouldn't have kept pushing her, Beanie said, quietly, from the back seat, sliding off her headphones. She's not going to take them.

Yes, thanks for your input, I snapped as we parked and locked the car. We walked from the car park to the beach. Despite the warmth of the sun, a strong wind sapped the heat. Our hair whipped around our faces. My skin rose into goosepimples as we stepped onto the beach.

The sand was hot and pale and damp as the tide started the process of dragging itself back out to sea.

After Gus had left for university and I'd made Nora go back to school, I'd gone back to the Richmond house one last time. I had moved into a women's home instead of keeping my promise to Nora, and I'd been pretending that everything would be okay. Our grandfather, Lars, a man neither Nora nor I had ever met, had passed away from liver failure that November, leaving behind a debt-riddled and dilapidated pig farm, and Mum and Karoline had gone to Norway to deal with the probate on his estate. I'd known, then, that Nora would be alone for Christmas. I'd dropped Beanie off at Gus's parents on Christmas Eve, so that she could avoid the canteen-style roast dinner in the group home with a cohort of dispossessed mothers and toddlers, blinking at the fluorescent lights, on Christmas Day. I'd hated that I wouldn't be with Beanie on Christmas, but she would have a better time with Gus, in his spacious and well-heated family home in Chiswick, with his loving and gentle parents and a glittering tree and the scents of cinnamon and ginger-bread and icing sugar in the air. I'd been invited to join them, too, but I couldn't shake the feeling that I was a charity case to Frank and Grace. Gus and I had been navigating the recency of our breakup, and I'd misinterpreted their warmth as pity. Before I'd left that evening for the Richmond house, Frank had pressed an envelope into my hand with a wink and a Merry Christmas. I'd opened it on the bus and found a voucher for ten driving lessons with the West London Driving Academy. The gift—so thoughtful and practical and extravagant and unabashed—had made my throat hurt. I'd hated the way they looked at me. I couldn't handle their expressions of love and welcome. I'd not been ready for it yet. So, I'd left Beanie there to spend her Christmas with Gus and the Hansons, and I'd got the bus to the Richmond house.

I'd knocked and Nora had opened the door. Christmas in this house had tended to be something altogether different from the Hansons'. It had usually involved a flying visit from Karoline, who would bring us a box of Ferrero Rocher from the corner shop and disappear within the hour. By lunchtime, Mum would be three-quarters through a bottle of champagne. Dad would reluctantly call the house phone and force himself through a protracted season's greeting with one or both of us, before promptly claiming connection issues and hanging up. And Nora had been alone in the house with all of that. Her face had changed a lot in the time that she had been at school. The edges of it had been harder, her eyes steelier, her skin paler and her freckles had gone. She was eleven years old, with a bullet wound and a leg brace and abandoned by every member of her family on Christmas Day. Not yet ready to throw herself out of a moving car, but not far off it either. She'd looked older and younger at the same time. She had done her eyes in black kohl pencil, like Mum had often done hers. The effect had been that of a child raiding the face paints.

Hey, Nory, I'd said, unable to stop the sympathetic tone from creeping into my voice. Merry Christmas.

What do you want? she asked, through her teeth. She didn't seem at all surprised to see me, only annoyed.

I just came to find my driver's license. I said, shrinking away from her, feeling the lie roll too easily off my tongue. Gus's parents got me some driving lessons for Christmas.

Good for you, she said sarcastically.

It was true, at least, that somewhere in the house my provisional driver's license lay dormant. When I'd left, I'd only taken the essentials. I stepped into the darkness, under the same pretense. Nora didn't move until I was barging into her. Her whole body a knife. No Christmas lights, no tinsel.

Just bare floorboards and the locked door to Mum's studio. I tried not to look too hard at the peeling wallpaper, the radiator hanging off the wall, the broken banister, and stomped up the stairs.

It's probably in our room, I called down to her, feeling idiotic. Once I've got it shall we go and get a McDonald's or something?

I mentally counted the coins in my pockets as I said it, knowing before I had finished that I certainly didn't have enough to buy a Big Mac and a milkshake.

You can't just barge into my bedroom, Nora shouted after me. She had cut all her hair off and the scraggly ends of it curled around the nape of her neck. She was far too thin. All of the soft edges I knew from the time we had spent together the previous summer were gone. I let myself into the bedroom anyway, which I noticed now also had a lock on the door, same as Mum's studio, and I pulled open the drawers at the vanity. Nora had made the space her own. The walls were overflowing with tacked-up drawings, postcards, posters of bands I'd never heard of.

You don't live here anymore, she said, having followed me up. This is my bedroom.

I love what you've done with it, I said, pausing and looking around. I'd found my license in one of the little drawers on the vanity table, the picture showing a ghost of my sixteen-year-old self, under a bunch of notebooks. I pulled it out and tucked it into my pocket.

I'm serious, Nora continued. You need to get out of my bedroom, Matt.

Can you talk to me properly? I asked her, baffled.

No. I can't. You don't live here, anymore, remember? *You* left. So you can *stay gone* and fuck off, can't you?

I now turned to look at her properly.

What did you say to me? I asked her.

I said, you need to *fuck off.*

She said the words like she'd just learned them, like she was saying them for the first time. They were unfamiliar in her mouth. She would soon have them tattooed on the backs of her ankles, but for now she was stuck in this house, the words sticking in her throat, her eyes huge.

You didn't come back for me, she said.

And she picked up a book from the bed and threw it at my head.

And you *promised* that you would. You said you would come and get me from school. And you didn't. You just ran away and left me.

She threw another book.

Nora! What the hell?

Get out! Her voice rose to a scream. Get out, get out, get out, fuck off, leave me alone, fuck *OFF.*

She picked up another book and lobbed it at me.

Jesus! All right, fine. I'm going.

I sprinted down the stairs and she chased after me, screaming at me and throwing books. Spittle flew from her mouth. As soon as I was out she slammed the old yellow door, hard, so that the glass rattled.

I stared at the door. Directly on the other side of it, I heard her slide down the wood and onto the floor.

Nora? I called tentatively.

You're a *cunt*, Matilda.

I slid down the door on the outside, and I could hear her crying, small broken gasps.

I'm sorry, I said, feeling my throat burn. I wanted to make sure you're okay.

You've been gone for ages, Matt. *Ages.* You said you were going to come back for me.

I know. But things happened—Beanie—

You said you would come back. And now look what's happened.

I wanted to explain to her. How being alone with Beanie, with Gus gone, had turned everything to mush in my mouth. How I felt as though I could no longer live and breathe independently, how I had had to choose one of them: Beanie or Nora. How it felt too hard, how I wasn't good enough to choose both.

Nory, why don't you open the door, and we can go somewhere and get some food?

No. I don't want to see you.

Nora—

I *said*, LEAVE. ME. ALONE.

She yanked open the front door and I fell into the hallway a little bit, the momentum forcing me into the void space. Her eyes blazed with a hatred I had never seen in her before. Hatred that was directed at me.

Nora . . . I said again, but before I could continue, she was out of the house, past me and striding across the green towards the houses on the opposite side. I followed her, tripping over my own feet in my struggle to keep up.

Nora? Where are you going?

She didn't answer, she just walked until she was running, towards the divided highway behind the houses on the other side of the green, through the alleyway into the visitors' car park for the town center, and beyond it to the edge of Twickenham Road.

What are you doing? I shouted at her, over the roar of the traffic, swishing past us at fifty miles an hour, the high keening buzz of car engines in the dark.

What are you doing? I shouted again, and when she turned to look at me, she was smiling.

She stepped out into the oncoming traffic. And I screamed.

I darted forward, as her back foot left the pavement and she stumbled into the road.

This was the first time Nora tried to die, and the fourth time that she almost did.

I scrambled to grab on to her wrist, and I yanked her back as hard as I could.

In the dark, a car squealed on its brakes, its driver slamming on the horn long and hard.

Nora squirmed, trying to get away from me.

No—you don't—I spat the words at her. She roared like an animal.

But I had got my nails into the insides of her wrist and she couldn't get away from me.

I dragged her back onto the sidewalk and threw her on the ground with more force than I'd intended.

On the ground, in the dark, in the right light, she looked just like my daughter.

On the beach in Malibu, my daughter and I wove in and out of strangers with inflatables and body boards and tennis rackets, searching for her.

Can you see her? I asked Beanie, shouting over the roar of the waves.

No, can you?

No.

We marched west along the beach, further away from the city, towards the quieter parts where the waves broke angrily against the dark rocks jutting out from the land.

Maybe she just needs a minute to herself, Mum, Beanie said.

Maybe she needs someone, I countered.

I slid my hand into hers, still scanning the horizon. The water glittered in the late afternoon sunshine; it was almost blinding.

I felt like I was on the other side of that door again, calling to her, listening to her cry but not able to touch her. I felt like I was trying to get to the hospital, Cedars-Sinai in Los Angeles the second time, Homerton the third, or West Middlesex when she was nine with a fresh O-shaped bleeding gunshot wound in her leg.

Every hospital in the world was exactly the same. Looked the same, smelled the same, felt the same, and always and forever blue, blue, blue.

I saw her then, pink baseball cap like a beacon, paddling in a rock pool further up the beach. The water was shallow and warm on the soles of my feet.

Nora, I shouted to her, exasperated. Come on, let's go.

I just need five minutes, she said.

I narrowed my eyes at her then, felt my blood turning warm too.

Okay, I said. That's fine. You take five minutes, Nora. You take all the time you need. I'll just be waiting here.

She gave me a quizzical look.

Waiting here to clean up your mess, I continued, almost shouted, across the beach.

I wanted her to hear me over the waves.

And I wanted her to know.

It's not fair, Nora, I went on, really yelling at her now, not caring whether she wanted to respond or not, feeling the rage bubble, foaming like the surf.

You can't keep doing this to me, I shouted. You can't do this to the people that love you.

She had rolled her shorts up to let the water lap at her knees, and she stood awkwardly in the rock pool, in a strange, angular, unnatural stance.

What do you mean, I can't do this to you? she shouted back. What exactly have I ever done to you, Matilda? What exactly could I have, ever, possibly, done, that hurts you so badly?

I gaped at her, disbelieving.

She went on.

What could I have done that will ever touch the sides of what you did to me?

We were on the side of the divided highway again, then, my sister eleven years old, me twenty, having just dragged her away from jumping in front of a speeding car.

She was on the sidewalk, prone. I had my knee on her chest.

I can't do this, I said, panting, tears streaming down my face. I can't do it.

Well, don't then, Nora shouted up at me, from down on the ground.

Our breath came out in cold, Christmas Eve gusts.

The pain in my chest felt as though it would suffocate me.

Nora lay back on the concrete and stared up at the stars. All the energy gone from her limbs.

It's so loud, Mattie, she said.

What is? I asked her.

She looked up at me, unique devastation writ across her face.

It doesn't matter, she said, quietly, exhausted. I relaxed my knee and she lumbered onto her feet, her legs trembling.

She walked away from me, back towards the green, back towards the Richmond house.

I watched her as she went. She didn't turn around. She wasn't waiting for me.

And I thought of Beanie, and only Beanie, and only myself.

I didn't follow her.

Instead, I turned around and walked away from her.

On the beach in Malibu, she said, What could I have done that will ever touch the sides of what you did to me?

I already felt the tears coming, as though they'd been waiting in the wings. But there it was. She had finally said it.

Despite the tears, despite the way my insides curdled with what I had done, I threw my head back and laughed viciously.

Go on, then, I shouted, a little hysterically. Let me have it.

She picked up a clump of seaweed and lobbed it at me, but it fell short and landed at my feet.

You are a. Selfish.

She lobbed another piece of seaweed.

Self-serving.

Another slimy green plant flung.

Coward.

And another.

Bitch.

The last piece hit me square across the face.

Don't throw stuff at me! I shrieked at her, fully aware of how childish I sounded. I peeled the seaweed off my face and flung it back at her. She yelped angrily as it slapped her on the shoulder.

Mum! Beanie shouted. Nora. Can you *stop*!

There, you've said it now, I shouted at Nora. Happy with yourself, are you? Finally got it off your chest? I'm a terrible person, I know. I left you. I know! I hate myself for it, Nora. I'll never forgive myself. But you need to STOP—

And I kicked some sand at her. She jumped away, lifting her legs comically high.

STOP trying to FUCKING DIE. Okay? I'm SICK OF IT.

And then she charged at me.

I'm not quite sure how it happened. One moment, we were standing on the shoreline, ten yards apart, screaming at each other through the wind.

The next, we were waist-deep in the ocean, and she was chasing me in slow motion through the water.

YOU LEFT ME IN THAT FUCKING HOUSE, she shouted.

Beanie yelled at us on the shore to come back.

I LITERALLY HATE YOU, she screamed at me, over the sound of the waves lapping at her midriff, and I knew by the way she'd made herself hoarse with the force of the screaming, that she meant it with every fibre of her being. YOU'RE AN EVIL HAG.

I LITERALLY HATE YOU, TOO, I screamed back, my eyes burning with angry tears, and in that moment I meant it just as much as she did.

I found a shallow patch and, completely spent, sat down uselessly in the sea, letting the saltwater soak through my clothes.

We rested for a moment, her standing with her hands on her hips squinting up at the sun, her top lip curled up away from her teeth. Me slapping the water with the flats of my hands, sitting on the sand like a toddler with my legs straight out in front of me.

The only sounds were that of the wind, the tide, and our own harried breathing and our hearts in our eardrums.

My whole life has been about people leaving, she shouted over the wind.

I know, I said.

You left me.

I know.

You left me every time that you could.

I know.

Look at what happened to me.

I'm sorry, I shouted at her. I'm sorry. I'll never stop being sorry. For everything. For Mum. For leaving you at school. For leaving you with Dad. For running away and not coming back for you. For not being there.

She stared up at the sun.

I couldn't do it, I shouted. I was afraid. I'm a big fat coward. You're right about that.

I wish things were different, Nora said.

I do, too. I tried to get you out of that house when I left. I promise you I did. Me and Gus, we tried to get custody of you. But they wouldn't let us. Social services, I mean. They thought we were too young to look after you.

You *were* too young.

I guess we were. But I should have tried harder, Nory. I shouldn't have given up so easily. And I'm sorry that I did.

I couldn't tell whether her face was wet from seawater or tears, but I felt my own sliding hot and cathartic down my chin.

But you've got to start doing something, Nora, I said. You've got to start saving yourself. Like you said you would. Okay? Because I can't. I just can't do it. I tried. I really fucking did. But I just made everything worse. I don't think I'm up to it.

I don't think I'm up to it either, she shouted, her voice out of control and desperate.

Well, you've got to be. That's it, Nora. You've just got to. Okay?

Okay. You've got seaweed in your hair.

She waded over to me in the shallows and picked it out.

Thanks, I said, panting.

She held out a hand and I took it. She hauled me onto my feet.

I'm not taking them, Nora said with finality. The tablets. I need to feel everything. Even if it's too loud. Okay?

Okay, I said, and I wondered once again whether I was betraying her.

Several of the surfers further down the beach had stopped and were watching us with some curiosity. I made a futile attempt to brush the sand off my soaking clothes and traipsed back to the shoreline. I had lost a sandal in the chaos, but I now saw that it had washed up on the shore and Beanie was holding it in her hand. She gave it to me as I drew level with her.

It's fine, I said, in response to Beanie's expression, half furious, half quizzical.

It's over, Nora added. It's all going to be over.

We climbed back into the car, still soaking wet. The box of tablets was still sitting innocuously on the dashboard. Nora picked the box up and cradled it gently, as though it were an endangered species. Then she lobbed it out the window.

CHAPTER 28

WE DROVE TO MORRO BAY IN AN UNCOMFORTABLE AND STICKY SILENCE.

Seawater had seeped all the way into the driver's seat of the car, and now the whole lower half of my body was damp and cold. In the passenger seat, Nora stared out the open window as we drove, her teeth chattering a little. In the back seat, Beanie texted.

Who are you chatting to? I asked her.

Dad.

Oh, yeah? What's he saying?

Not much. I just told him about the tantrum you two threw in the sea.

Nora continued watching out the window, pretending she couldn't hear us.

I reached for her across the central console of the car and rubbed her shoulder uselessly. She lifted my hand up to her face, and smiled resignedly at me.

The journey to Morro Bay took three hours, and it was the longest three hours we had spent together since we'd landed in Phoenix. The silence seemed to stretch out on the road before us, endlessly. No one bothered to put on music. The sky, sheet-like, covered us from every direction. The sea to the left of us was choppy.

I pulled into our last stopover before San Francisco. A small turquoise-painted inn on a steep road leading down to the water. The bay itself was calm and flat, fishing boats bobbing gently. A vista of squat single-story cafés and souvenir shops that lined the shores. The sun was setting behind us, casting an eerie shadow across a huge orb-shaped mound out beyond the bay.

Nora and I unloaded our luggage from the boot of the car while Beanie checked us in. The wind was high, and Nora struggled to light a cigarette.

All of this is going to be underwater soon, Nora commented, pausing to look towards the town. It seemed unremarkable: residential and unpretentious and unaccustomed to visitors without surfboards.

Okay, I said.

I still felt it there, but it was less of a stinging and urgent fear, now, and more of a low-frequency ache in the pit of the belly. Nora was going to die. She had almost died seven times already. We were all going to die. And there was nothing any of us could do to stop it.

As we wheeled our suitcases towards the motel reception, the sky turned the color of fire. We turned back to the land and watched the sun inch into the horizon. The majesty of it was impossible to ignore.

Beanie was beside us then, and we watched it together in the parking lot.

That's really something, isn't it? Nora said quietly.

Yeah, I replied. It's really something.

———————

I slept deeply on that last night before San Francisco. I felt no anticipation for what was about to happen. I didn't have any sense of how it was all going to end for us once we got to the exhibition. I was single-minded in my goal, my conviction that we needed to stop it, but besides this absolute I hadn't thought through exactly how I was going to achieve it. I dreamed of being a child in the Richmond house with Nora, very young, when she was just a baby, except I was in the body of my thirty-three-year-old self. The smell of talcum powder and jasmine and milk. The sense that nothing bad would ever happen because we were unspoiled, she was unspoiled, and I could fix things before they got bad. I ran out of the house with her a baby in my arms and when I turned back, the house was on fire, the roof caving in, the windows smashing out. Within moments it was a smoking wreck.

It was early when I woke up. The sun filtered lazily through the slatted blinds, and Nora's body in the bed next to mine rose and fell in a gentle rhythm under the covers. Beanie, the early riser, was already gone from the sofa bed, the sheets screwed up into a ball at the foot of it. I pulled on a jacket and headed out the door and downhill to the sea. The sun was barely up and the pre-dawn sky was the color of pale slate. Out on the water, boats dotted the horizon. Beanie was standing at the foot of the pier. It was high tide and the water lapped at us.

Hello, I said, walking over to her, wrapping my coat tighter around my body to defend against the morning chill.

She smiled weakly at me.

Are you okay? she asked me.

What? Yes. Of course.

Her question surprised me. Of the many times I had asked both her and Nora that question over the last days, it was the first time someone had asked me. I felt then a bone-deep ache of exhaustion come over me.

I just want it to be done, I said to her. I want to finish it and go home.

How are we going to do it?

Do what? Stop the exhibition?

I was thinking we could do an art heist.

I laughed.

Hope you brought a balaclava.

We walked the edge of the bay, heading northwards towards the enormous Morro Rock that jutted out obscenely from the shore, in a comfortable silence.

Let's go and look at the rock, Beanie said, and we hiked the coastal road, out to the mound, all the way to the edge of it and walked around it.

I don't get it, Beanie said. It's just a giant rock.

I think it's volcanic, I commented.

We walked the circumference of it, and on the other side came across a flat, yellow, sandy beach with a gentle ocean overlapping on the sand. It was empty. We took off our shoes and walked its length.

Mum, Beanie said, when we got to the other end of it and the sun was creeping over the inland horizon. I've got something to tell you.

Yeah?

I should have told you it a long time ago.

I glanced over at her and I saw then that she was nervous. Picking at her fingernails like Nora always did. Her hair was still mussed up from sleep. She glanced at me furtively before looking away.

You can tell me, I said to her, turning to her. You know that, right, Beans? You can tell me anything.

Okay. She took one very long and deep breath and exhaled slowly.

Beanie said it with the melodrama and gravitas of the kind that can only be possessed by a sixth-form theater student.

I like girls, she said. I've always known I've liked girls. I'm sorry I didn't tell you before. But I was scared. I don't know what I was scared of, I've always known you'll love me no matter what. But anyway. There it is. I'm gay, I like girls, and if you've got any questions, or whatever, just like. I don't know. Put them on a postcard?

She took a step back from me to survey my reaction, her silver-sparkling Docs dangling from her hands by the laces, catching the light and throwing rainbows across the sand, and she bowed with a Shakespearean flourish.

I studied her and saw that her eyes were shining. Her fingers trembling.

Oh, my girl, I said.

I pulled her into a bone-crushing hug.

Of course I love you no matter what, I told her, tears in my eyes. It's not even a question. I'm so proud of you, kid.

We stood there, in the shadow of the volcanic rock, the rising sun warming our cheeks, for what seemed like an age.

I love you, I said again. So much.

I love you too, Beanie replied. Sorry I didn't tell you sooner.

Sorry I made it so difficult for you to tell me in the first place. I'm such an idiot, Beans, honestly.

We walked slowly back towards the motel, her hand in mine.

How long have you known? I asked her, stupidly.

I don't know. Since before I can remember.

Have you talked to Dad?

Not yet. I will when we get home. I just couldn't not tell you anymore. It was making me feel sick.

As we approached our turquoise-colored building, I saw that Nora was smoking on the balcony in her pajamas, her hair whipping around her face in tendrils. I lifted a hand and waved to her.

NORA, Beanie shouted. I TOLD MUM I'M GAY.

HELL YEAH, BEANS, Nora shouted back, from up on the balcony.

It seemed like the universe was shrinking, now, fast, until it was the size of the interior of the car. At Big Sur, the hairpin bends and sheer drops from the cliff to the sea—though spectacular—made my heart hammer as I maneuvered the car along the single lane highway. The further we climbed, the more saturated the colors became. Nora slept in the back seat with a book over her face. I instructed Beanie to play all our shared favorite music on the aux. Nora loved Fleetwood Mac, but even more so she felt an affinity with Stevie Nicks. We played "Edge of Seventeen" and "Landslide" and "Caroline." Then we played two Foo Fighters albums back to back. Then all the good Janis Joplin ones: "Cry Baby," "Piece of my Heart" and "Me and Bobby McGee," and then Bowie's greatest hits, and then Arctic Monkeys, and then Jefferson Airplane and Kate Bush and Jimi Hendrix. By the time we got to Janis, I knew that Nora was awake by the way she held her body. I could see it through the rear-view mirror. But still she pretended that she was sleeping.

On the descent into San Francisco via Half Moon Bay on Highway 1 morphing into the freeway, the climate changed again: the air moist, the sky overcast and the road lined with thickets of green trees and grass. There was nothing to see here, except endless perfect landscape, the sea, the sky, the mountains behind. It was so picturesque that it exhausted my eyes. The city itself seemed to creep up on us barely noticed. The green became yellow, then brown, then grey, and then once again vibrant as we entered the city proper. San Francisco was expansive, and populous, and urbane. But where Los Angeles was a brown haze of pollution, San Francisco was like a village. The hills were steep and the bay slipped into view like the rising tide. I felt my body relax even as my hands clenched themselves like claws around the steering wheel.

We're here, I said, to no one in particular, to myself. We're here. We made it.

Beanie looked up from her phone. Oh my God, she said. We made it. Nora, wake up.

She reached into the back seat and shook Nora's leg. Nora stretched and peered out the window.

Oh my God, she said, imitating Beanie inadvertently.

I can't believe it, Beanie said, and it genuinely seemed as though she were surprised that we had made it. Are you ready to do an art heist?

Who packed the balaclavas? Nora asked and Beanie grinned at me.

I thought I was going to die in this car, Nora said.

I thought so, too, I replied. She gave me a double thumbs-up in the rear-view mirror.

We dropped our car off at the rental place—the traffic was bad and the public transport good here, so it seemed pointless to keep it—and checked into our Airbnb via a lock-box key. The building was a three-story Edwardian townhouse between the Haight-Ashbury and Castro neighborhoods, with the top floor converted into a B&B-style situation where the owner, Danny, a man in his forties with gentle eyes, lived at the back of a slim corridor. It wasn't dissimilar, actually, to the Richmond house in its composition and style. Only much bigger, and with steep, narrow stairs leading up to the top floor, which left us breathless once we had dragged up our overstuffed suitcases. We had booked three rooms. The whole place had been decked out like a big, fancy, Victorian-era tearoom, complete with dramatic curtains for the bay windows, big brass lamps, twelve-feet-high ceilings to accommodate burning chandeliers that were long gone, original floorboards, and rugs embroidered with fleurs-de-lis. There was a mock drawing room with a large oak mantelpiece and a communal kitchen featuring an industrial coffee maker. It was only lunchtime, but we had left Morro Bay before the sun had been fully up, and had stopped only once for a hasty breakfast of rockfish in Monterey, at a large-windowed diner at the end of the pier overlooking the fat seals sunbathing on the rocks in the harbor. And so, each of us retreated to our rooms, and slept. It was the first time in almost two weeks that I had slept alone, without the soft breathing of my sister and daughter emanating from somewhere else in the room, rhythmic like cicadas on a summer night.

I woke up disoriented, with bright afternoon sunshine streaming through the uncovered window, a full bladder and a horrible taste in my mouth. I showered lengthily, drawing patterns out of the mold in the grouting with my eyes, letting the high-pressure hot water pummel my skin. The bathroom window slid up and opened out onto a view of San Franciscan rooftops and tiny gardens far below. The painted ladies leaned with the tilt of the hills. The lush greenery of the parks to the east leaked into the city, grey and jumbled together, buildings upon buildings, to the west, before sprawling out into the Bay.

After showering, I took out my phone and dialed Richard's number. He answered on the third ring.

Hey! he said cheerily.

Hi, we just got here, I replied.

To San Francisco?

Yes. Where else?

In the background I heard the sounds of spoons against ceramics, clattering plates, muffled conversation; he was in a coffee shop, it seemed.

I've just been doing the final touches on the book before I send it back to my editor, he said. I'll come and meet you somewhere.

Where?

Well. I'm in a café on the harborfront. Fisherman's Wharf. Do you want to come here?

I dressed and texted Nora and Beanie to say I would be gone for a little while, assuming they were sleeping as I had been. Outside, the breeze was cool and soft. My hair was still a little damp from my shower and I could smell the eucalyptus-scented shampoo on it. I navigated to a bus stop and boarded one. It drove in an almost straight line right up to the marina in the corner of the city, where it bridged with Oakland to the east, and the Golden Gate Bridge jutted out of the city to the west. I stepped off the bus and walked along the marina, the sea here choppy and relentless. Out in the bay, the mound of Alcatraz Island rose from the water like a humpbacked whale.

The wind whipped my hair around my face. This was it. We had made it, all the way here.

Now we needed to decide what the hell we were going to do.

I knew exactly what was on the top of my list, but the rest was unclear.

I turned to walk back towards the coffee shop that Richard had sent the details of, steeling myself.

Matilda?

I heard the voice before I saw him. He was standing at the edge of the promenade, right up by where the water met the floodwall. He was wearing a tweed-textured coat and a pair of brown loafers. He was holding two take-away cups.

There you are, I said. Hello, Richard.

I saw you get off the bus from the window of the café, he said, pointing back towards a mahogany-looking 1920s-style coffee shop with huge windows on the corner of the street heading inland. And you walked this way, he continued. I thought you might be lost.

No, I wasn't lost, I said. I just wanted to see the view.

He handed me one of the coffee cups and I took a sip of strong black americano, just how I liked it.

I missed you, he said, smiling weakly.

I missed you, too, I replied, and was surprised to realize that I meant it. But now I knew that it wasn't enough to miss him. Not anymore.

Richard, I need to talk to you about something, I said, my stomach churning.

We sat down on the hard, concrete floodwall.

Are you looking forward to the exhibition launch? he asked, conversationally, touching my arm.

Not really, no, I replied.

You ought to be. This is a special moment for all of us.

I thought you said we shouldn't come.

You won't like it. But it's your prerogative.

Richard, I need to talk to you about—

It's okay, he said. I already know.

What do you already know?

You're leaving me, aren't you?

I looked at him then and I felt my heart swell. He was smiling, but beneath the veneer of his expression there was an acute look of devastation in his eyes.

It's okay, he said, before I could answer him. I understand. I really do.

Will you let me explain? I asked him.

You don't need to. I already know. I get it.

Sorry, what? Are you sure?

He continued, after a deep inhale. I know that you aren't in love with me.

Richard . . . please let me—

I kind of always knew it, to be honest. He turned to look out at the sea with a practiced melancholy about him. I let him speak, and he was speaking more to himself than he was to me.

Right from the very beginning, he said. I knew that you were holding yourself back. Sometimes, when I touched you, you flinched away from me. Did you realize you were doing that? You didn't, did you?

He didn't wait for me to answer.

And I thought, maybe, maybe if I just waited, it would happen for you, too. And then I knew for certain. I knew when I saw the two of you together for the first time, before everything happened, and we ended up here. Because you never looked at me like that, Matt.

I stared at him, my mouth a little bit open.

You never looked at me the way you look at him.

I felt myself sinking into the concrete, the knot in my stomach tightening until it felt like I could no longer breathe.

It's not about Gus, I blurted out, before I could stop myself.

He quirked an eyebrow at me, incredulous.

Really, I said.

If Gus wasn't a part of my life at all, I knew in my bones that I would have felt the same about Richard.

I said to him, my teeth clenched against the wind, There's a feeling that's been creeping up on me, for some time now, that you're a voyeur in my life, Richard. A tourist in all of our lives.

He opened his mouth to protest but I held a hand up to stop him.

And at first, it was good. In the beginning it felt safe, because you were on the inside. It made things easy for us. And you're a good person. And I thought that was enough.

But I've realized something. And it's taken me too long to realize it but here it is. You're not entitled to my life, Richard. You're not entitled to anyone's life. We don't owe you anything. We're not your entertainment, we're not tabloid fodder. We're not topography on which you can map your own hopes and dreams. We don't belong to anyone except ourselves.

Richard chewed at the inside of his cheek, and I realized that my voice had risen an octave.

I don't think you're ever going to understand that, I said.

I'm sorry, he said.

Don't be, I replied. I'm not.

His face fell, and I immediately regretted the harshness of my words, how they might be interpreted. So I took his hand and squeezed.

He smiled sadly at me and squeezed back.

I wish you had just let me believe you were in love with someone else, he said.

Maybe, I replied, ignoring the way my stomach twisted at the truth I was continuing to deny. But you don't deserve that. And nor do I.

We sat and watched the seagulls for a few minutes, before he slipped his hand out of mine.

I'll come and pick up my stuff at some point once we're back in London, he said, matter-of-factly, standing up and brushing imaginary lint from his jacket.

Richard—

Please don't, he said. He held out his hand to me and I thought he was helping me up from the low concrete wall, so I took it, but instead he shook my hand firmly and let go.

It's been a pleasure working with you, Matilda, he said.

And, with his hands in his pockets, he strolled away.

CHAPTER 29

I DECIDED TO WALK BACK THROUGH THE CITY,
MEANDERING THROUGH JAPANTOWN AND
THE THEATER DISTRICT.

I passed jazz bars and pizza places and grocery stores and hotels and sky-
scrapers, the long, straight roads graduating upwards or downwards with
the slopes of the hills. I felt my limbs stretching beneath me as I climbed the
steep inclines. The city was truly beautiful, and thriving and teeming with
life. It reminded me of some parts of London in so many ways: the mish-
mash of the people with the architecture and the neighborhoods. Despite
the density of the buildings, there seemed to be greenness and lushness
everywhere. The air was thin and purifying.

I decided to walk to the Museum of Modern Art, underestimating
how long it would take me and exactly what kind of toll it would take on
my muscles as I power-walked up and down the sloping streets. The
museum was a squat, terracotta colored building that came right up to
the sidewalk, its overbite supported by fat, cylindrical, polished columns.
It competed with the traffic and was bookended by two thick, tall, white
office buildings. Outside, a handful of photographers lined the sidewalk.
I crossed the road to get a better look at it. Hanging from the roof and
draped over the front of the building like a huge flag, was a forty-foot
vinyl banner of my mother, naked, in self-portraiture, and my father,
naked, leaning over her. At the bottom and imposed on the image, the
small text that noted that the painting was a "Detail from *Edward and me*

on a bed of lies (egg tempera on card, 1986), on loan from the permanent collection at the National Gallery, Oslo" was in a rotund sans-serif font. At the top of the billboard, were the words INGRID OLSSEN: A LEGACY.

I stared at the vinyl, flapping in the wind, with my chin up in the air. I stared for so long that I thought it might detach from the building, and flutter all the way down onto the street, onto me, and suffocate me.

But it didn't.

I bought ice cream and beers and bananas from a supermarket and took the Muni back to Page Street, overladen with paper grocery bags.

This is it, I thought, as I let myself into the house and traipsed up the stairs into the Airbnb's communal kitchen. We were the only guests staying at the house, so we had the kitchen space to ourselves. Nora was standing at the counter, brewing coffee in the machine.

This is it, she said, as though she had heard my thoughts when she'd seen me. This is the end.

She reached into the cupboard and took out a second mug. I dumped the groceries on the table and together in a companionable silence we stored them in the fridge-freezer while the coffee brewed.

I feel like we're going to kill Mum, I said to her as I handed her a tub of ice cream.

We can't kill her when she's already dead, Nora replied, but I could see it in her too. The anticipation of what we were about to do. I wasn't sure entirely what it was that we were going to do. All I knew was that it was important, and it was the last bit, and we couldn't afford to get it wrong.

Once everything was put away Nora turned and pulled me, unexpectedly, into a long hug.

What's that for? I asked her.

I'm sorry, she said.

What for?

For throwing seaweed at you and chasing you into the sea. And for everything else.

Don't you ever apologize to me, I told her, and I hugged her back. I'm sorry, too.

This is what she wanted, isn't it?

I thought of Mum, way back in the beginning, before things got too bad. The lemon tree and the smell of her soap and her long, soft hair.

And then of Mum in the final days, the bedroom. The way she held our wrists, one in each of her hands.

Burn it all, she had said. Throw it all away.

Yes, I said. It's what she would have wanted.

She let go of me awkwardly just as Beanie walked into the kitchen, yawning.

What's new? she asked, picking up my coffee and taking a gulp.

Well, I said. I broke up with Richard.

Beanie put the coffee mug down, and clapped once, very loudly, and then picked it back up.

Language, Old Bean, Nora warned. She looked dog-tired, like she hadn't slept at all.

I didn't say anything, Beanie said, grinning. I didn't say a word.

I wanted my apartment, and my own bed, and the familiarity of the sofa and the curtains and the laminate floors that Beanie and I had put in together, haphazardly, when we'd moved in. We'd slid across it in our socks, competing over who could hit the wall harder. We'd given ourselves stitches laughing.

But we weren't there, we were here, and so we got ready for the gallery, trying on our nicest outfits, crumpled as they had been in the bottom of our suitcases, and blow-dried our hair and spritzed perfume and drew on eyeliner. Beanie did her eyes like Mum always used to, rings and rings and rings of black pencil until it looked like the hollows of her eye sockets were showing through the skin.

And then we took a tram to the museum.

We stood outside it, on the opposite side of the street, and I stared up once more at *Edward and me on a bed of lies*. The sun was setting, and a curious quality of light had settled over the building, the street lights not yet lit. Since I had been there earlier in the afternoon, someone had laid out a carpet running into the building, and now behind partitions there were more photographers. I saw Nora shrink. People I didn't recognize stepped out of cars and posed for photographs before walking through the double doors into the lobby. A cluster of fans stood to the side of the building, stopping the attendees for autographs and photographs.

Are you ready? I asked them both as we crossed the street.

Yes, said Beanie.

This is the last thing we need to do, said Nora.

My girls.

We slipped past the photographers, not pausing to pose, and stepped inside the lobby of the building.

Several things happened at once.

The first was that a member of waitstaff thrust flutes of champagne into our hands the moment we touched the gleaming, hyper-polished floor of the inside of the museum. We found ourselves in an expansive entrance area. There was a string quartet in the corner of the room, and many, many people—most of whom I didn't recognize besides a couple of journalists who had interviewed Mum for magazines—milling around in small groups dressed for a cocktail party, talking and laughing.

Someone else came and demanded our jackets, which we shrugged off and handed over. We found that we were chronically underdressed in the midst of a crowd in tuxedos and evening gowns. Glasses tinkling with champagne and laughter and chatter. And then, as though by magic, Aunt Karoline was in front of us, wearing what looked like a pink satin dressing gown, and sucking on an e-cigarette as though it were the only oxygen available in the room.

Girls! she said, loudly, too loudly, almost shrieking, her eyes darting from each of our faces to the next nervously. I didn't think you were coming. Girls. Come and get a drink.

We've already got drinks.

She hovered with us at the doorway, fidgeting.

Have you seen your father? He's here somewhere.

Nora groaned loudly, showing us the whites of her eyes, and no one said anything further for a moment.

You invited Dad to your party? I asked her.

Well, well, she said, muttering more to herself than us. You're here now. You ought to come through and say hello to some people. How was your trip?

She took us to a group of men in suits and introduced each of them by name. I didn't take in a single one.

These gentlemen are from the sponsor, she said. The company that contributed money so we could put on the exhibition.

I know what a sponsor is, I said. Beanie and Nora hung back, exchanging nervous glances with one another. It felt as though all eyes in the room were following us, as though we were a bomb that was about to go off.

And here's Larry Montague, the museum's director. Karoline ushered him forward as though he were a von Trapp child being asked to say goodnight. He nodded courteously at me, but his eyes were on Nora.

Karoline continued round the circle until she had introduced all the different kinds of suits in the group—the herringbones, the dark-navy-blues, and the mottled greys, and then Richard appeared at Karoline's elbow.

Matilda, he said curtly, kissing me on both cheeks.

It's good to see you, I said, feeling my stomach curl.

Yes, he replied.

Karoline was explaining how the evening would go. There would be drinks and chit-chat first, and then we would be taken up to the seventh-floor gallery space to view the exhibition, and then some speeches followed by more drinks and canapés.

I'm glad you're here, girls, she said, seeming to have finally got her bearings and smiling broadly at us, but the smile didn't reach her eyes.

And here's the lady of the hour, she said, taking Nora gently by the hand.

None of this would have been possible without Nora's kind permission to let us display Ingrid's work, Aunt Karoline declared to the room at large.

The men in suits murmured appreciatively. Larry Montague stepped forward and offered her his hand.

Nora Robb, he said, with the look of a fox. I'm a fan of your work.

Nora looked supremely uncomfortable, touched his hand and stared at her shoes. She had forgotten to change into her heels before we left the house, and was still wearing her yellow Crocs, with a black velvet long-sleeved dress that came to her knees. Everyone had noticed the Crocs but no one was pointing them out.

I'm sorry, I said to Karoline loudly, and I felt the old rage beginning to simmer. I tamped it down. Who are these people? I barely recognize anyone here, except you and Richard. No offence, Larry.

Larry pretended he hadn't heard me.

Everyone here is a friend of the exhibition, Karoline said with that same smile that didn't reach her eyes. Everyone here got us to where we are now. In this gorgeous museum surrounded by Ingrid's life's work.

I had no answer for her, so I apologized to Larry Montague and excused the three of us, dragging Nora and Beanie over to the side of the room.

What's the plan? Beanie asked in a conspiratorial whisper, necking the rest of her champagne. It was Moët, the kind that Mum used to drink. The smell of it made me feel a little nauseous. I took Nora's flute from her hand and placed it—and mine—on a passing tray, undrunk.

I don't know what the plan is, I said. I don't know what I was expecting. But it wasn't this. I've never been to an exhibition opening before.

Nora's eyes slid across the room. Don't look now, but Dad's coming over.

Oh, for fuck's sake.

Hello, girls, he said, approaching from behind like a jump-scare. His voice boomed off the polished floor.

Hello, Grandad, Beanie said generously, allowing him to kiss her on the cheek.

It's wonderful to see you all.

We didn't know you were coming, I said pointedly.

Really? I'm sure I told you.

Where's Marnie?

We thought she should stay at home with Denise and Liberty.

Denise Diana and Liberty Louise, Nora intoned.

Yes, Dad replied, his eyes narrowing. Listen, girls, I know we had some unpleasantness in Hollywood. But I was hoping we could get past it. Just for tonight. For your mother's sake.

I glanced at Nora. She stared blankly at the wall.

We don't really have anything further to say to you, Dad, I replied evenly.

His eyes narrowed further, shining. His eyebrows two sharp diagonal lines.

I don't think that's very mature of you, Matilda. You're a grown woman now. It's time to leave the past in the past.

Yeah, sure, I replied. Let's leave the past in the past.

At that moment, the tinkling of a spoon on a champagne flute rang through the room.

Ladies and gentlemen, Karoline called in her high, tight voice, her Scandinavian inflection suddenly extremely pronounced. Please follow me through to the exhibition space.

Well, said Dad. We had better go through, hadn't we?

He marched away, as though desperate to escape us, and caught up with a man wearing a leather jacket ahead of us who looked like he might be Sting, or at least Sting-adjacent.

The attendees—fifty or sixty of them in total—filed into elevators that drew us up to the seventh floor of the building. Once there, we were ushered through a set of double doors. The lights inside were attractively dimmed.

We lagged behind, until we were the last ones in the room, and the double doors were shut firmly behind us.

We saw it immediately.

To be fair, there wasn't really an option to miss it.

It hung, suspended by cords from the ceiling, directly in front of us.

Staring down in all its seven-foot-long glory, was *Girls*.

It was hanging in the center of the room. The pièce de résistance.

And there we were, our likenesses in paint on the canvas. Nora and I, on either side of our mother, little girls, children, rendered in oil in a way that made us appear ghoulish, monstrous, inhuman.

Beside it, a little mounted plaque on a little stand detailed the materials used, the year, and the subjects: *Olssen and her two young daughters, at home in her studio. With thanks to the National Portrait Gallery, London.*

Oh God, I said involuntarily, and I suddenly felt very strongly as though I was going to be sick.

I forgot how massive it is, Beanie said. When was the last time you saw it? In real life?

It was the day I left the Richmond house, I replied. I remembered it clearly. I remembered resisting the urge to drag it away from the living-room wall and put my foot through it, one final parting gift.

I don't remember the last time I saw it, Nora said, standing up very straight. It must have been one of the summers when I was back from school. She loaned it to the National Portrait Gallery in between. And the next time I came back, it was gone.

It was as though it had paralyzed us so that we were rooted to the floor, and we couldn't move. There were other paintings around the room, Mum's work from different periods in her life. The linocuts and the screen-prints. The smaller portraits and series. But none were as big and as imposing as this one. None rendered our faces back at us, distorted beyond recognition, like this one did.

I smelled her then. The smell of her soap—aloe and lavender—on her skin, mixed with linseed oil from the paint, and acetone and stale cigarette smoke and old wood from the brushes. And the Moët, the alcohol on her breath, the smell of rotten meat.

After we sat for this, Nora said quietly.

What?

It was after we sat for this, she repeated. That's when Mum invented Hector. That's when she told us the first Hector story. The story of the day Hector stole the sun.

I stared at her, then, feeling a lump in my throat.

Mum didn't invent Hector, I said quietly, my hands trembling. I did.

She looked at me with sad eyes. No, you didn't. Remember, Matt? The cupboard under the stairs.

And then, suddenly, with vile clarity, I remembered.

One of Mum's parties, one of the loud ones, one of the ones that ran all night with strangers and shouting and smoke coming underneath the studio door. Nora and I had made a nest for ourselves in the cupboard under the stairs.

Sometime in the small hours of the morning, when we'd both been curled up against the exposed bricks, Mum had cracked the cupboard door open and crawled in there with us.

What are you girls doing in here? she'd whispered, her eyes a funny shape.

It's too loud to sleep upstairs, I whispered, half asleep.

Nora stirred and Mum sighed and draped her arms around us, let us snuggle into her, like she used to do before the parties started happening, before the pills and the champagne and sleeping all day in the conservatory.

She hummed to us.

Are you scared? she asked me.

I'm not, I said, defiant. But Nora is.

You don't need to be scared, Nory. Because Hector's in the walls and he's going to look after you.

And she told us the first Hector story.

The story of the day Hector stole the sun.

I felt as though I was going to choke.

Hector who lived in the walls, I said.

You remember, Nora replied.

I remembered. Properly. The whole thing. The first story.

You let me believe that I invented him, I said. Nora nodded and shrugged with one shoulder.

All this time I had been guarding memories from Nora, like fine treasures. Afraid of what the knowing would do to her. What kind of devastation it might bring about in her.

And all this time she had been doing the same for me.

She clenched her fists.

He's still in the walls, she said. He lives in the walls, wherever I go.

I felt my stomach twist.

She wasn't talking about Hector anymore.

We walked through the exhibition, which comprised of four rooms with white walls, pine floorboards and impossibly high ceilings. In each room was more of Mum's work. Some of the pieces I recognized and some I didn't. In the first room there were mostly silkscreens, lithographs and linocut prints that had been made before either Nora or I were born. *Girls* hung oppressively in the middle of the room, suspended from the ceiling. It had been a very deliberate and conscious choice to hang this piece here; most of the room was Mum's early work, which was whimsical and far less expressive in its style, playing with perspective and composition. To me, *Girls* didn't belong in here, chronologically or thematically.

Why do you think they put *Girls* here? I asked Nora, the artist. Maybe she understood something that I had missed.

She stared at it thoughtfully, her tongue sticking out of her mouth a little, like the stalk of a pumpkin.

It's here to shock you, she said. To make you feel small and insignificant and unwanted. This is Ingrid Olssen's world, and you, the viewer, are invited to participate in it for an hour or so. But you need to know that you're not welcome.

We continued into the second room, past a full-length nude of Aunt Karoline on the back wall. It was much clearer in the second room that a thematic choice had been made. Each piece of work hung in here was a self-portrait. The paintings spanned her entire life, almost. Her very first sketches as a teenager, a lithograph, and then several oils, which increased in size and expression through the rest of her life. Text that had been stenciled onto the wall gave some commentary on Olssen's preoccupation with self-portraiture as a means of expressing vulnerability and the most fundamental of human emotions. Her manipulation of the paint ranged from playful to vengeful. The text went on. I wondered who had written it: maybe Karoline, or maybe even Richard.

We continued through the space, and found more. In the third room, there was a small sketch of our grandfather, Lars, who we had never met. I examined it closely. I had never seen it before. It didn't seem particularly good to me; the pencil lines were frantic and there didn't seem to be an effort to capture a likeness. I moved to read the little plaque that was mounted next to the sheet of cartridge paper on the wall. *Ingrid Olssen's only portrait of her father, Lars Olssen, was composed after his death, when she visited him as he lay in state at Stange Church in Hønefoss, Ringerike, Norway.* I looked again at the sketch. Yes, he was absolutely dead, there was no misunderstanding it.

I glanced over at Beanie, who had wandered over to see what I was looking at, and her face was stricken with horror.

Wow, she said.

Yeah, I replied. I didn't even know this existed.

Nora was on the other side of the room and Larry Montague, the museum's director, was trying to talk to her. I sidled over to her and stood at her shoulder.

Just wanted to say how much of a fan I am, he was saying in a Bostonian accent, his hair flipped away from his face. Your concrete piece was just—wow—really something special. Breathtaking.

Thanks, Nora said, her voice toneless.

I've been following the Control Room, he said. I just wanted to come and say hello and check whether you were . . . okay? I saw what happened on the news and I was just—devastated. Karoline told me all about it.

She's fine now, thanks, I interrupted, smiling placidly, my eyes wide. He smiled back at me.

That's good to hear, he said, not getting it. Really good. I was so worried. Anyway, you should go and look at *My burial* if you haven't seen it already. There's a wonderful tribute to you in there, Nora. It was my idea, actually.

My burial is here? I asked him, bristling at the familiar hand he placed on Nora's elbow.

Sure it is, it's through there. He pointed to a little room off to the side of the main exhibition space, its door open and its walls black.

Thanks, Nora said, but she had stopped listening to him. Her eyes were drawn magnetically to the door.

You know—we'd love to have you back here sometime—I would very much like to have a conversation . . .

I followed Nora who, as though in a trance, was now walking towards the door, and Larry Montague dissolved away. It was a small doorway—if you didn't know what you were looking for, you might have missed it.

And inside, on one wall, was *My burial*, complete with a huge rip in the canvas from top to bottom. I knew the story of *My burial* and Grift House: of how Mum put her foot through the painting when Karoline sold it to the bank that would eventually bankrupt her father's farm. Even with the rip, it was obvious how accomplished the work was, even to someone like me. The composition was deeply frightening, a top-down view of a grave with a heavily pregnant woman—Mum being viewed from above, half-buried in dirt, her arms and fingers stretching out towards the viewer, a look of sheer terror on her face.

The light from a projector flickered across Nora's hair, and I then saw what was on the opposite wall.

A projection of Nora's piece, the piece that first got her noticed, also titled *My burial*.

There were two plaques on the perpendicular wall opposite the door. The plaques looked like this next to one another:

My burial (1995)	My burial (2015)
Ingrid Olssen	Nora Robb
Oil on canvas	Digital film and concrete
Associated Funding	Publicly licensed

There was also some stenciled text on the wall, which read:

Olssen's My burial *is a secret double-portrait. At the time of its completion, Olssen was pregnant with her daughter, Nora Robb. Robb, in her own right, is a celebrated performance artist who is known for her provocative work, which often invites its audience to participate in the art. Her response to* My burial *can be seen in her work projected on the wall opposite.*

In Nora's *My burial* (2015), twenty-year-old Nora suspends a camera from the ceiling above a bathtub. We cannot see the camera, as the viewer. We are the camera. Watching her from above. The whole thing is filmed in black and white. Nora is in the bathtub, in only her underwear, like Mum is in the shallow grave in the original *My burial*. Nora lies there for a moment, inert, her eyes knowing something that we (the viewer) don't. Then, from the right-hand side of the screen, a concrete mixer is wheeled into view by an unknown person whose face we don't see. From the spout pours freshly mixed, liquid concrete into the tub. At first, Nora lies stationary and lets it happen to her. And then she begins to struggle. The concrete is in her hair, her armpits, her underwear, her eyelashes. She is struggling not to get it in her mouth. And it is pouring and pouring and pouring until the bathtub is overflowing, and she is almost entirely submerged.

It wasn't concrete, Nora said, over my shoulder, watching the projection. People thought it was so transgressive, she continued. Such a blatant act of self-harm as art. It was perverse, ground-breaking, beautiful, disgusting, all of the above.

I watched her as she took in her own work, her form, drowning in the concrete on the projection, reflected in her dark eyes.

It was custard, she said finally. Just custard. Mixed with baking powder.

It's incredible, Beanie said.

It's shameful, she replied. And I never gave Karoline permission to use it.

She marched out of the room and I could see the anger vibrating through her, just as it did me. We passed a handful more self-portraits on the way through. The *Window* series, of Mum after Maurice Hoffmann had shot Nora. And the last one she'd ever painted, unfinished, the rough lines of the sketch underneath the paint meaning that only half her face, painted with a feeding tube snaking out of her nose and down her cheek, was filled in. We followed Nora at a quick trot back to the first room we had seen, with *Girls* suspended in the center. By the double doors, Karoline was talking to a blond man in a navy suit.

Oh, good! Nora, darling, let me introduce you to—

No, Nora said simply, as she drew level with Karoline.

Karoline blinked at her, baffled momentarily.

You need to take *My burial* off. Now. Take it down, the projection. You had no right.

Darling, it's on YouTube. You gave it a Creative Commons license yourself. It's in the public domain. A thousand versions of it have been replicated over and over again. It's on every art curriculum in the country. You don't own it.

I don't *own* it, Nora said. But I don't want you *touching* it. I don't want you touching it. Take it down.

Before Karoline had a chance to reply, the lights had suddenly come up and the string quartet, who had brought their strings up to the seventh floor, grew quiet.

Just one moment, darling, Karoline said, holding a finger up and swishing her way over to a temporary stage that had been erected at the back of the exhibition space, a microphone stand wobbling in front of her. She daintily tapped her champagne flute into the mic. One of Mum's full-length nudes, with skin that had blue and yellow undertones, hung behind her. The subject of the painting was, once again, Karoline.

Ladies and gentleman. She spoke breathily into the microphone, still affecting a Norwegian accent stronger than the one she truly had. I want to thank you all so much for joining me in the Anselm Kiefer Galleries to launch this wonderful and wide-ranging exhibition in partnership with the Museum of Modern Art here in San Francisco.

What you have before you is the most comprehensive collection of Ingrid Olssen's work that has been displayed publicly, ever.

At this, a wave of applause went around the room. Nora kicked her Croc into the floor, her face the color of poppies.

Avoiding making eye contact with the three of us by the doors, Karoline then spoke in depth for ten minutes about Mum's biography: her start in Hønefoss, her move to London, her mentorship under the German screen-printer, Maurice Hoffmann, before, as an emerging talent, discovering a love and affinity for oils and portraiture in the impasto style of application.

She then, Karoline continued, moved away from the rigidity and repetition of linocuts and serigraphy—a few of which can be seen at the back of this room—and chose to work instead on the manipulation of the materials on the canvas, or board, to communicate the fundamental truth of the emotions of the subject in the application of the paint.

You can see this in her self-portraiture in Room Two, said Karoline. Where we have chosen a selection of her self-portraits and portraits of public figures who were in her life, to demonstrate how her craft evolved throughout her career, and indeed how her personal history was deeply intertwined with her methodology.

In Room Three you will find her famous double and triple portraits. And in Room Four, you will find works that interact explicitly with death as a theme, something which came up many times in Olssen's portfolio.

Karoline stood awkwardly, the echo of the nude version of herself behind her a strange mirage. The nude portrait of Karoline was larger than life-sized, and it hung over her like a bad omen. In it she was younger, in her twenties, the skin taut and pale and rendered to seem lifelike. One arm draped coyly over her head. The blood vessels in her hands just-there, an expression rather than a realistic portrayal. It was a painting that Mum had finished when I was a toddler; I vaguely remembered it from the Richmond house, propped against the back wall in the studio until the next thing came along, Mum hyper-focusing her energy until she had perfected something else, and the new thing had been finished, and the old thing had been hidden behind it.

I could see that Richard and Dad were close to the front of the stage. Richard watched Karoline speak raptly, his eyes shining, and Dad was checking his phone. I looked over at Nora and she seemed to be concentrating very hard, her mouth pressed into a thin line.

I'd now like to invite our primary sponsor for the exhibition up onto the stage, Karoline said, smiling broadly. Please, everyone join me in welcoming Jacques Sallberg to say a few words on behalf of Associated Funding.

There was another polite smattering of applause, which was somewhat obstructed by the fact that everyone was still holding champagne flutes. Jacques, the tall, skinny blond man with brilliant-white teeth that Karoline had been speaking with moments ago, climbed lankily onto the stage, smoothed down his expensive-looking navy suit and approached the microphone.

Associated Funding? I stage-whispered to Nora, bewildered.

She nodded brusquely, her eyes fixed on Jacques, blazing with anger.

I had always vaguely wondered how Karoline had pulled the money together to put on such an extravagant show. I wasn't interested in art or galleries but even I knew that it cost millions of dollars to pull something like this off. Karoline had shipped hundreds of individual pieces of work across the Atlantic Ocean; she had been flying herself and some freelancers back and forth from London for over a year. Conservators, curators, press, marketing. All together it must have cost a fortune, even with most of the artwork coming from Nora, who had, inadvertently it seemed, lent it to the museum for free. Karo herself, despite her airs, I was now almost certain was broke, left with the Richmond house, which was in a state of disrepair, the back end of it subsiding into the soft peat soil, that made it a financial burden rather than an asset. Nora and I had never had an inheritance. Mum had squandered her own money and Dad didn't seem to be aware that we were poor. I had always been too proud to ask him for money, even as a kid, and I knew that if Karo asked him, he would refuse.

But now it became clear. Karoline had put on her show, the vanity exhibition, which was less about Ingrid Olssen's legacy and more about Karoline Olssen's legacy, using money from Associated Funding. The bank that had closed down Olssengården. I knew the story as well as anyone else. I'd seen it in the newspapers, and I'd read it on the internet. And I'd heard it straight from the mouths of my mother and aunt. Associated Funding kept lending and lending and lending, even when they knew that they would never get the money back. And they'd run the Olssen farm into the ground with collateralized debt until our grandfather, Lars Olssen, had been found dead out in the barn one morning by a bailiff who had come to take the pigs, the tips of his fingers and ears frozen solid. They had already repossessed the property before he'd been buried.

I never knew Lars Olssen. I had never thought about him all that deeply, so preoccupied had I been with the behavior, motivations and decisions of his daughters and how they affected my life, my sister's life, and my own daughter's life. To me, Lars Olssen was almost the stuff of mythology. A distant and intangible truth of the existence of the Olssen family and its line. I never knew Mum to speak of him in overly much detail, either.

But I knew what Associated Funding had done to Lars Olssen.

I knew what Mum thought of Associated Funding.

And I knew what she would think of this.

I glanced back to Nora and I sensed an understanding pass between us.

Jacques Sallberg from Associated Funding was talking lyrically about the work the bank did to support cultural endeavors in Europe and the Americas. He then spoke in length about his personal admiration for Olssen portraiture.

Our first encounter with Ingrid Olssen, in fact, he said with a sly grin, has not been in putting together this exhibition.

He surveyed the room, enjoying the audience, his whole body relaxed. He was relishing the moment.

I saw that Nora had clawed her hands into fists.

Jacques Sallberg continued. Indeed, it was at Grift House Art Festival in 1997 that Associated Funding first acquired an original Ingrid Olssen painting, *My burial*, which Olssen promptly destroyed by kicking a hole into the canvas.

The room was filled with muted laughter. Everyone here knew the story, and they knew it well. Ingrid Olssen, the wild card. The loose cannon. The tortured genius. What was she like. Something terrible was happening in front of us. And no one could see that it was happening.

Associated Funding continued with its purchase, nevertheless, Jacques reassured the gathering. And the organization has kindly loaned it to the exhibition. You'll find it on display in an annex off Room Four, complete with the original hole made by the artist's foot.

After Jacques finished his speech, Karoline came back onstage.

I'm delighted to tell you all, she said with aplomb, that Ingrid's daughters, Matilda and Nora Robb, are here with us tonight.

She thrust an elegant, red-clawed hand in our direction, and then—to my absolute horror—every pair of eyes in the room turned to look at us, and Nora in particular.

Girls, Karoline said, still speaking into the microphone. We didn't plan this, but I would love if you could come up and say a few words about your mother.

I glared at Karoline with such ferocity that I thought that she might be

355

incinerated on the spot. And then I looked at Nora, who had turned pale. She shook her head swiftly, with a tiny, marginal movement. I looked at Beanie, who was grimacing.

Everyone in the room was still staring at us, waiting.

Before my brain had caught up with what my body was doing, I found that my legs were moving, and I was walking towards the stage.

CHAPTER 30

A FURTHER POLITE SMATTERING OF APPLAUSE FROM THE ASSEMBLED GUESTS.

And then, as I clambered up onto the black-painted wood, the silence was oppressive.

I moved over to the microphone and Karoline stepped to the back of the stage, all graciousness and humility.

I put my lips to the microphone and heard my own breathing reverberate around the room, from the hidden PA system speakers.

Hi, I said, too loudly, and the microphone squeaked.

I looked back over to Beanie and Nora, at the back of the room, both staring. I felt my pulse in my throat.

I'm Matilda Robb, I said, my voice wobbling. Ingrid was my mum.

I paused, waiting for some kind of response from the crowd, but none was given.

Ingrid Olssen was a complicated person, I said, and she would have hated this exhibition.

There was another rumble of laughter around the room. They thought I was joking.

I'm not joking, I said, louder now into the microphone. She would have hated it.

More laughter.

Jacques Sallberg. I turned to him where he stood at the edge of the room, feeling the anger begin to bubble.

The reason she destroyed *My burial*, I said, wasn't because she was some kook, she wasn't doing performance art, or whatever. She did it because she hated the way big money was dipping its hand into art. She hated that her art was a commercial proposition for people. Like this exhibition, which is, I'm sure, going to make many of you lots of money.

Now no one was laughing.

Associated Funding repossessed my grandfather's farm on the day he died, I said, relishing the way the words sent a hushed silence across the room. I turned to Karoline.

You knew that, Karo, I said. Your own father. You knew what they did to him, and yet you're still letting them put their fingerprints all over Mum's work. What would she say to you, if she were still alive? What would she think?

Karoline had turned an impressive shade of beetroot, at the back of the stage. She was mouthing, with incredible enunciation, *Shut the fuck up*, her eyes wide with meaning. She looked like she was debating whether to rugby-tackle me off the mic.

Speaking of *My burial*, I continued, feeling my heartbeat in my eardrums. Nora Robb never gave permission for her work to be displayed here. And she—and I—insists that it be taken down immediately before it opens to the public.

I looked down and saw Richard, and something like a gleam of triumph in his eyes. He was smiling up at me. Next to him, Dad took a large gulp of champagne and swayed a little on the spot.

Anyway, I said, suddenly exhausted, the anger and the fear dissipating. I looked back out to the crowd and saw nothing but a sea of men in black, navy, herringbone and mottled-grey suits.

I hope you enjoy your little champagnes and your little cocktail party, I said, concluding my outburst. And I hope you enjoy it in the knowledge that Ingrid Olssen, whose legacy you supposedly want to honor, would have hated every single one of you.

I shrugged and Beanie started clapping, alone.

I stepped off the stage and shouldered my way through the stunned crowd, towards the back of the room.

The silence was momentarily oppressive, humming around me as I barged my way through the mob. And then, responding to some hidden cue, the string quartet picked up and the microphone was hastily disconnected and hustled down from the stage by a waiter, presumably so that no one else could give an impromptu speech. I found Beanie and Nora, and we stood and watched. Karoline stood stock-still, frozen in the position at the back of the stage that she had been in when she'd invited me up. She caught my eye and I shrugged at her like, *whattayagonnado?* The crowd was dispersing now, the murmuring of voices growing in volume until suddenly, everyone was back to looking at the art, and not us, and it was as though it had never happened.

Nora took my hand and squeezed it.

Thank you, she said, her face sincere. I smiled at her. The restlessness from before was gone. There was something peaceful about her.

We walked through the rest of the exhibition once more, all four rooms of it, and between us pointed out the things we hadn't noticed the first time round. Like the passport-sized portraits of her, straight on, bouquets of roses in the foreground. The warped perspectives of the composite portraits from her studio. The monstrosity of the final self-portrait, the one done in bed when she was dying.

I don't know what we're going to do, I said to Nora. I don't know how we're going to stop it.

Around us, people everywhere chattered and muttered and observed.

We came back to the first room, and stared up at *Girls*, and stared, and stared, until the whole room was *Girls* and nothing else.

———————

The party was coming to an end and the suits were filtering out of the room. Karoline, now reappeared at the double doors, was air-kissing and laughing and thanking and fawning. I glared at her, and cast about the room for Nora and Beanie. Sometime over the course of the evening we had become separated. The waitstaff were collecting champagne flutes now. The lights were coming up. The suits were less and less and less. And the floors were shiny with polish.

And *Girls* bore down on us.

It bore down, down, down, like the sky in the desert over Boulder City in the RV park, like *Edward and me on the bed of lies* in forty-foot vinyl. Like the museum itself, the weight of it, the Richmond house, crumbling around us, burning down, subsiding into the soft peat of the earth, dissipating until there was nothing but a crater in the library of my dreams. It was the ghosts in the walls, which were here, even now, under the fluorescent light, and it was our heartbeats, heavier now—faster—and *Girls*, us—it was us up there, yes, but it also wasn't, it was the versions of ourselves that we almost became, and then we didn't. It was gravel into a grave over the womb, mineral-rich and tasting of iron-like blood. It was custard poured into a bathtub from a cement mixer in black and white. It was generations of decay, cut out at the source of the rot. It was us, and it wasn't. It was how we got to get away from it all. It was how we got to be free.

I miss her, Nora said, unexpectedly. I hate her, and I miss her.

I thought of the lemon tree.

I hate her and I miss her, too, I said.

She slipped her hand into mine.

It's *Girls*, I said to Nora. It has to be *Girls*. There's nothing else for it.

She nodded solemnly.

We were the last people there, somehow. Me and Nora and Beanie. Even Karoline had disappeared somewhere with Larry Montague and another handful of suits, into the bowels of the museum.

Do we do it now? I asked Nora.

She looked up at *Girls* once more.

Hector was in the walls of the Richmond house.

I could hear him breathing, as a child. I could feel his eyes on the back of my neck.

My heart thrummed with fear when I felt him watching.

Nora could, too. Even as a baby. Her eyes tracing him as he stalked the house, between the plasterboards. His thumbprints behind every surface, pressing through, trying to get out.

We turned him into a story, just as Mum had done that first time, when we'd hidden from her in the cupboard under the stairs, and we made him a hero. We tried to make him save us.

But, truly, the only people who could save us were ourselves. The only person who could have saved Nora was me. And when I couldn't do it, all that was left was Nora.

The robbery turned out to be easier than I could have ever imagined.

We unhooked *Girls* from the steel cords suspending it from the ceiling, and let it drop into our arms. It fell gracefully. It dived into our arms, as though it had been waiting for us to collect it. But then, the weight of it was the problem. It weighed a fortune, and it was cumbersome, and awkward to hold. The wooden frame on the back of the canvas brittle and splintered. The fabric of the painting heavy with paint smeared layer upon layer upon layer.

Her eyes stared at me as she fell, as we fell, directly through me, directly into the center of my being.

Is this what you wanted? I asked her silently, feeling my stomach leap.

We caught it like we were participants in a trust-fall exercise.

As soon as the steel cords disconnected, an alarm sounded. Loudly and obtrusively. I felt my heart sink. How stupid of us. Of course there would be alarms. Of course we couldn't just walk out of an art gallery with a priceless work of art. Of course this was a ridiculous idea.

I thought about running for it anyway, and I could see that Nora and Beans were ready to do the same.

But then, as abruptly as it had started, the foghorn stopped.

We froze, hearts hammering, waiting for someone to come running. One of the security guards posted in the lobby by the doors. Larry Montague with a double-barrel shotgun and unfinished business.

But no one came.

The museum was silent as a grave.

We crept out of the gallery and into the elevator lobby.

At the doors to the elevator, Karoline rounded the corner, alone, and stopped dead. She was still holding a glass of champagne.

We froze—the three of us—mirroring her, as though if we didn't move she might not see us standing there, in the process of stealing one of Ingrid Olssen's most celebrated artworks. It was late, now, past eight o'clock. The sky outside, through tall windows, beginning to turn a dark indigo. The only noise now the buzz of an air-conditioning unit and the strip lights in the galleries. It seemed impossible that we would just be allowed to walk out with it.

Karoline, crystalline blue eyes the color of the desert sky, an e-cigarette hanging from her mouth. She watched us like a cat.

She opened her mouth, I thought maybe to call for someone, to raise the alarm, seeing as the actual alarms had apparently failed to do that job.

Girls now face down, with us at three of its four corners.

We could drop it and let the oils smear against the floor.

We could run.

We could put our feet through the canvas.

We could set it on fire. I had a Clipper in my bra, just in case.

Karoline stared, and looked about to say something. But then a curious expression came across her face.

It wasn't quite the expression of someone who had lost—she wasn't admitting any sort of defeat, no—it was more a look of resignation, and understanding, and admission.

She turned away from us and walked towards the elevator, reached out to press the "down" button with one ruby-hued, sharpened acrylic nail.

She called us an elevator.

And then she walked away.

We left the building, holding *Girls*, as though it were a piece of discarded timber.

And no one stopped us.

There were moments that I caught Nora's eye, as we sat on the bus with it, with Beanie, propped up against the back seats, and we mirrored one another's expressions. Looks of *what the fuck* and *how is this happening* and *we did it* and *I wish we could go back for the rest.*

It had been a moment of shared memory, reiterated. Collective madness. And we weren't achieving what we'd set out to do. The exhibition would go on, no doubt. There was enough of Ingrid Olssen's work left behind that it could. We hadn't, truly, achieved anything. Except perhaps a sense of self-righteousness. A reclamation of ourselves through the eyes of our mother. It was for us just as much as it was for her. But, ultimately, it was for her. It was the last thing we would ever do for her, together.

The bus took us to a car park at the southern foot of the bridge, and we carried the painting off it, each of us heaving it out of the door, maneuvering it around corners and people. It snagged on the door, and the canvas tore, and my heart fell out of me, and then I realized. It didn't matter.

We heaved it up a set of concrete stairs, through the pedestrian access gate and along the sidewalk.

Can a person walk to the center of the Golden Gate Bridge with a seven-foot-long priceless artwork?

In theory, no.

But that's what we did.

The iron railings weren't all that gold, or all that red, after all. Like the rest of it, they were rusty and brown with decades upon decades of peeling coats of paint. The view of the bay was magnificent, better than I ever could have imagined. It was darkening, but we could see water below, the tide thrusting itself towards the beach at Crissy Field, the trail still rattling with joggers and dog walkers taking in the warmth of the sunset.

We dragged it to the center of the bridge, cars roaring past us, impossibly loud, on the freeway. We pressed our bodies against the iron railings to let cyclists past. There was a sign that warned that anyone throwing objects off the bridge would be charged with a misdemeanor. There were several more signs that listed an emergency telephone number for crisis counselling. We dragged it further, towards the point where the suspended metal inverted arc almost touched the railings. The steel cords, thick as limbs, stretched taut on the other side. We rested *Girls* against the railings for a moment and caught our breath. The absolute quiet of our breathing in the dusky air, the wind, at odds with the roar of the water below, the tide ebbed against the city like a piece of complex music.

I panted, my heart hammering from the exertion of carrying *Girls* to its final resting place.

Are you ready? I asked them.

Beanie nodded, her eyes blazing with something new that I hadn't seen in her before, a shadow across her face.

I looked at Nora. She was crumpled up, her hands shaking. Her eyes dark. Her hair whipped around her face and neck like rope. Her jaw set in a hard line, her bottom lip jutting out a little.

Ready, she said.

We picked up the frame of the canvas at the bottom, our fingernails digging into the wood.

And we tipped it over the railings and threw it into the sea.

PARTIAL TRANSCRIPTION OF INTERVIEW NUMBER 3
WITH NORA ROBB [06.05.2020]

R.T.: I think that's a good place to finish, don't you?

[Silence.]

R.T.: Thank you for agreeing to meet with me one last time.
       Talking with me about the Control Room. And in hospi-
       tal, too. I know it's been difficult.

N.R.: You're welcome.

R.T.: Although . . .

N.R.: Although?

R.T.: You told me that you could have died seven times back in
       January when we spoke. But you had six stories. Only this
       most recent incident makes it seven.

N.R.: What's your point?

R.T.: You knew you were going to die, almost, seven times.

N.R.: You're asking me if, back in January, I knew that I was
       going to try to die this summer, in the Control Room.
       You're asking if I was planning it.

R.T.: Well . . . yes, that's exactly what I'm asking.

N.R.: You don't need to look so concerned.

[Silence.]

N.R.: I always knew I was going to die.

R.T.: You—what—

N.R.: Everyone dies. Right? The seventh death was always going
       to happen. And now, I suppose, there will be another.
       One more death. Just one, I hope. That'll make it eight.

R.T.: I'm not sure if I understand.

N.R.: It's the thing about dying, Richard. Everyone's got to do it
       at least once.

CHAPTER 31

We walked back to the city, southwards, over the bridge.

I felt the exhaustion in Nora's body. The blue lights of police vehicles illuminated the visitor center as we headed inland. There was already an SFPD police car waiting for us. I wanted to scream. The exhilaration coursed through me like electricity.

We walked hand in hand and when we got to the pedestrian gate to let ourselves off the bridge, two waiting police officers took me and Nora by the shoulders.

Let's go, ladies, one of them—a blonde woman no taller than Nora—said after she had read us our rights. I signaled for Beanie to get in the back of the car, and then I followed, the police officer's hand still guiding me, while Nora was stuffed in last.

And we were driven away.

I twisted myself round to watch the bridge dissipate into the horizon, the adrenaline still thrilling through my capillaries.

We did it, Beanie said, her voice dazed and trembling.

We did it, I agreed.

I wouldn't be so pleased with yourselves, if I were you, the police officer in the passenger seat said.

It was only then that I started to think about consequences.

There would be press. *Olsen daughters steal priceless painting.*

Criminal charges, probably, for all three of us.

Would I lose my job?

Would Beanie lose her chance at university?

And what about Nora?

It seemed like the weight of imagining that future was going to drown me. It would come, later, eventually, with everything else that followed.

What mattered now was that the only people who were important were here, and we were together, and the universe was expanding.

We bathed in the blue lights. There was euphoria, and terror, and exhilaration, in the faces of my girls.

―――――――

We were fingerprinted and photographed in a dark corridor in a nameless building, and then spent the night, sleepless, in a shared jail cell in the center of downtown San Francisco.

I called Karoline.

No, she said, when I asked her to come and bail us. Absolutely not. Where is it?

She meant *Girls*.

It's in the Bay, I replied, trying to keep the smile out of my voice. Karoline, we need you. Can you help us out?

Have you smoked your socks?

I laughed at that. Fully and a little deliriously.

Okay, but maybe just Beanie? Please?

She hung up on me. And that was my phone call.

I pleaded with the desk sergeant while Beanie and Nora placed theirs.

We're British nationals, I said, trying to keep the growing panic out of my voice. I felt like I was in a dream, like it wasn't happening. What had we been thinking?

Can you at least arrange a lawyer for my daughter?

The public defender doesn't work weekends. He'll be here on Monday, the officer said, her voice not without sympathy.

What are we going to do until then?

She grimaced.

Get comfortable, she said.

We slept lightly throughout the day on Saturday, the sun streaming through the small windows at the highest point of the walls. Outside, the noises of the city went on like nothing had happened.

I had been dreaming of something unpleasant. The smell of smoke in the hallway of the Richmond house. The roof caving in. I was sweating, my clothes twisting around my body, my nostril hairs burning when Nora startled me awake.

What? What is it? I gabbled, flustered. Is Beanie okay?

Yeah, she replied. Everything's fine. She hovered above me, her jaw hard and angular and her eyes dark.

I just wanted to tell you something, Nora said.

What?

I'm finishing the Control Room.

I put my hand up to my face, rubbing the sleep and sweat away.

I want to do something with my work, all the stuff that I'm sending home from Dad's.

Okay, I said.

I want you to help me.

Of course, I said. Of course I'll help.

Mattie, I know that you tried. I didn't always know, when we were kids, and I thought that you were leaving me.

I was, I said, feeling my body sag against the wall. I was always leaving you, Nora. And I should never have run away.

You were doing what you had to do, for you. And for Beanie. It's okay.

She meant it. I could tell. Her whole body was alert with meaning, with the force of what she was trying to tell me.

I want to put on an exhibition, she said. Something that's just mine.

I tensed, feeling the weight of the legacy, once again.

Will you do it for me?

Yeah, I said, after a moment. I'll do it for you.

Thank you. She took my hand and kissed it, a gesture I had never felt from her before.

I felt sleep cloak me once again.

———

Then, in the middle of the afternoon, the heat stifling in the room, cell door was yanked open.

You're free to go, the booking officer told us.

She led us out into the waiting area while we were each given paperwork to fill in, signing our agreement to a court date, and our belongings handed over to us in clear plastic bags. Beanie, as a minor, was given a Notice to Appear—a meeting with a probation officer—while Nora and I were given an arraignment date. The walls were yellow, and the floor was sticky.

Who bailed us? I wondered aloud. Not Karoline, surely? Who did you two call?

Nora shook her head. I called Dad, but I couldn't get through, she said. I couldn't think of anyone else . . . there wasn't anyone . . .

She trailed off and stared at Beanie.

I called Dad, too, Beanie said.

And we walked out into the reception of the building, and saw him, and my heart fell out of me.

The man responsible for our freedom was sitting on one of the plastic seats in a corner, speaking hurriedly into his phone and making notes on a pad balanced atop a coffee cup on his knee.

When Gus spotted us, he hung up and stood, spilling his coffee on the floor. He didn't seem to notice it.

I came here straight from the airport, he said, indicating the duffel bag on the chair next to him, and he dragged Beanie into a hug.

You three, he said, are in big trouble.

He let go of Beanie and turned to me.

And *you*, he said. But he couldn't finish his sentence.

I know, I said. I know, I know.

He smiled at me, at my resignation, and then frowned, as though having an argument with himself.

And the intensity of that look hit me like a freight train once more. So much more powerful in person than it was over a video call. The universe expanding in the dark of his irises.

I realized fully, in my bones and my fingertips and the backs of my kneecaps, exactly how much I had missed him, and how completely I was in love with him, had always been in love with him. It felt as though the floor had vanished from beneath my feet. It felt like the way he looked at me burned directly into the center of my soul.

It hadn't been something in particular, that had made me realize it. More so, it was a knowledge that had crept up on me over the years of a shared life together, but apart. The shared experience of loving our child. The implicit understanding one can have of another human being, of seeing into their soul and seeing the goodness amid the flaws and the rot in between the light, and still loving it anyway.

It's brand-new fresh towels.

It's banana splits and alcoholic coffee and a gentle goodbye.

It's soft soil and the fruits of the lemon tree, big golden orbs, dropping into the garden in the summer, ready to be made into cake.

It's a warm body sliding into bed in the dead of night simply for the feeling of one human being holding another.

It's the experience of making something miraculous together.

And it was—wholeheartedly and with absolute clarity now—the fact that there was no one I wanted to see more in that exact moment than him. It was the fact that he had come, without hesitation, to get us.

It might not be enough. And I wasn't sure that it was. When I looked at him I was in love, but I was also afraid. Terrified that I was about to fuck things up.

How lucky I was, that I had met him so young.

And how moronic I was to have squandered him.

He slipped a hand into mine.

I'm so sorry, Gus, I said.

You're an idiot, he replied darkly.

Why did you come?

My daughter and her mother seem to have got themselves into a bit of legal trouble. What was I going to do, leave you to it? I'm very angry at all of you, by the way.

He looked serious but he couldn't hold the expression, so instead grinned at me—that look again—I couldn't believe, still, that he was here.

He touched his cheek to mine, briefly, and I smelled the shaving cream and toothpaste and the feel of his skin on my cheek. The starch of his collar, crumpled yet clean. His hand on the small of my back.

———

Later that night, I would take him to the waterfront, stare up at the rusted monstrous structure of the bridge, towering above us in the dark, black against the sky, some obscene proclamation of human achievement despite the majesty of the universe, in response to it, the conquering of the land and the elements.

And I would place into his hand the fridge magnet that Beanie and I had picked out for him in Arizona: IT'S SEDIMENTARY, BABY.

I didn't want you to know I'd left Lulu, he would say.

Why?

Because I was afraid of what I would do if you knew. That's why I asked Beans to keep it a secret. I was afraid of how you would react.

What do you mean? I would ask him.

He would look out to the water, his eyes stormy with the argument he had been having with himself.

Then he would look back at me and it would be like the world was fizzing around us. My eyes pricking with tears.

I've been in love with you every day I've known you, Matilda Robb, he would say, matter-of-factly.

Oh, I would reply.

I'm prepared to wait, he would say. I'll wait for ever, if I have to.

You don't need to wait, I would tell him.

You don't need to wait anymore.

And the next day, when we heard the news, he would pull me into him like he had in the bathroom of my apartment, like he'd crawled into bed with me and given me his body. Solid. Human flesh and bone and blood. And in every moment then, and every moment thereafter, I would be falling in love with him.

The thing that Gus taught me is that there is no limit to how much one human being can care for another. That the heart, and the way that it loves, is bottomless and limitless and as infinite as the universe. It will expand forever, to make room for more.

You can feel the universe expanding into itself, only if you let it.

You can feel the heart expanding into itself, only if you let it.

Nora knew that better than anyone.

Tomorrow, and for now, that would be enough.

He would say, how did it take so long?

And I would say, I don't know, but here we are now.

Here we are now.

———

And here we were now. Beanie cleared her throat pointedly and he let go of me.

I've booked you a lawyer registered to practice in the state of California, he said, suddenly all business, squaring his shoulders. I can't defend you over here. I'm not licensed.

We have an arraignment date.

We'll try to move it and get your charges thrown out, he said. But you conspicuously lobbed a very famous work of art off a national landmark, so that's unlikely. It's a misdemeanor so it'll be a fine, and there's sometimes jail time. But you're not citizens so you'll plead no contest and more likely you'll be banned from entering the country for a period of time.

Fine by me, Nora said. I don't want to be here.

He finally turned to Nora and pulled her into a hug, and when he let go she looked as though she was going to cry.

I missed you, he said to her. It's been far too long.

I missed you too, she said, smiling weakly with eyes that shone.

What are we gonna do with you, hey, Nory?

A look of total calm came over her face. The same look she'd had in the exhibition after I'd got down from the stage. The same look that she'd had directly after *Girls* had gone over the railings and unceremoniously hit the water.

You don't have to worry about me anymore, she said. I'm good.

CHAPTER 32

We exited the anonymous office building that was the county jail and came out onto the Mission District, astride the freeway.

The noises of cars and trucks and the city engulfed us. The hum of a place readying itself for a frenzied night. The sun was low and hot in the sky, sinking behind Oakland to the east.

You okay? I asked Beanie as she fished her heart-shaped sunglasses out of her plastic bag and propped them on her nose.

That's the dumbest shit you've ever done, Mum, Beanie said with a grin.

I felt it too. The buzz of exhilaration still thrumming through me. Police sirens wailed along an adjacent road. We walked towards the pier, where yachts bobbed up and down. We looked out to the water and felt the possibility of life stretch out to the horizon, limitless.

As we debated whether we should find something to eat, or go home, or call Karoline, or call our lawyer, I noticed that Nora was walking away from us. I called after her. She turned and as she did, the low-slung sunlight caught her hair and turned it into spun gold. She walked with square shoulders. And her hands loose at her hips.

Nora? You coming? I called to her.

She turned and saw us watching her, and I ran to catch up with her.

We're going to find somewhere to eat, I said.

It's okay, she replied. You go.

I didn't want to leave her.

Are you sure?

She smiled peacefully.

Mattie, she said, her voice heavy with meaning. Remember what I told you. It's all done, now. Everything's done. We can move on.

I don't understand, I said.

She exhaled. You've been running away for a long time.

Nora . . .

You need to stop now, okay? Stop being so scared of chasing what you really want. What you deserve.

I saw every version of her in her face then. A newborn baby, a toddler in the Richmond house trying so hard to get someone to love her. Nora at three, at eight, fifteen, seventeen, a hard set to her jaw, the tattoos on her ankles, the way she pushed me out of the house. The ways she almost died but always saved herself. Nora an artist, in the bathtub, in the Control Room, hovering at the foot of our dying mother's bed. Nora as Beanie saw her. Nora as I saw her and Nora as she saw herself. The freckles scattered across her back. The way she turned her face to the sun, just catching the last embers of it on her skin, and walked away once more.

You go, she called back, lifting one arm into an easy wave. I'll catch up with you later.

Partial transcription of Interview Number 3 with Nora Robb [06.05.2020]

N.R.: Everything I ever was, the good, the bad, the excellent and the imperfect. Everything I ever did was because of her.

CHAPTER 33

IN THE MIDDLE OF THE NIGHT, THAT NIGHT, MY LEGS
WRAPPED AROUND GUS'S, HIS HAIR ON MY CHEEK.

I woke up and I felt an uncontrollable, burning itch across my whole body. It
was so palpable that I thought that my skin might be on fire. I dragged myself
to the bathroom and wrenched off my clothes, stared at my body in the mirror. But there was no rash or sore, despite the burning, scratching sensation
that raked itself across my torso, made my upper arms feel as though they
were on fire, were the skin of a freshly plucked goose. But my body was free
of marks.

I tossed around in bed, unable to get comfortable.

And then, abruptly, at four in the morning or close to it, the itch
subsided.

I drifted off to sleep, momentarily exhausted and relieved that the itch
had gone at last.

By the time I jolted awake moments later, gasping, wailing, remembering
the before, the significance of the burning, it was already too late.

Many things happened in the hours and days after the robbery.

The only thing that mattered was this one:

The coastguard pulled Nora's body, aged twenty-four and eleven-and-a-
half months, out of the water of the San Francisco Bay at six forty-two the
following morning.

CHAPTER 34

I DIDN'T KNOW NORA VERY WELL.

I now understand this fact more tangibly than I ever have before.

But there were certain things that I did know about my sister.

In the days that followed, in the mortuary, the police station, speaking to the TSA agent, my father, Karoline, Gus, our lawyer, all of whom decamped into our rented Airbnb townhouse, I catalogued the things I knew.

Nora liked to sleep in late.

She peeled the crusts off her sandwiches because she didn't like how they felt on her tongue.

She took her tea with milk and two sugars.

Her favorite music was made by people who died too young in the seventies. She liked show tunes played on the piano with a single voice as accompaniment.

She liked to be alone.

No—that's not right—she had learned to be alone as a mechanism for survival.

She sang "Jolene" beautifully.

She didn't believe in God or astrology.

She liked bottled lager and cheeseburgers, and she was allergic to shellfish.

She loved deeply and she didn't know how to show it.

She bit the skin around her fingernails when she was nervous.

She hugged herself by pulling on her elbows when she was upset.

She had two nipple piercings, and one tattoo of a smiley face behind her left ear, and the words *fuck off* across the backs of her ankles. She loved to wear jewelry and enjoyed the sound of bangles jangling on her arms.

She laughed at bad jokes.

She was a meticulously clean person.

She wanted to create something beautiful and meaningful before she was dead.

CHAPTER 35

Karoline and I went to identify her body.

We stood outside in a blue corridor and waited for someone to tell us what to do.

When the time came, I couldn't go inside.

Karoline said, Are you sure? Her eyes looked as tired as I felt, and she touched my hair and curled a coil of it round a finger tenderly.

I shook my head and she went into the viewing room by herself.

I found a bathroom and retched into the toilet.

When Karoline came back, she nodded at me, her skin pale.

They made her look peaceful, she said. At least they made her look peaceful.

I roared.

It didn't seem fair to me that she didn't say goodbye to us, not properly. She just went in the night and left us all behind.

That was the thing I hated her for, in the beginning.

The wreck of it.

It was an inevitability, in many ways.

We told Beanie.

She said, They found her in the water, didn't they.

When I said "yes," she collapsed.

We'd gone to the seaside at Littlehampton for the first time, when I was fourteen and Nora was six, and Mum had been dating Guernsey Steve.

We'd hired pedal boats on the seafront, even though the water had been freezing. Mum and Steve had taken one, and Nora and I the other. She was small for her age. I lifted her into the seat at the water's edge and the attendant kicked us off from the jetty into the choppy, slate-colored waters of the English Channel. The sky was a dark and ominous grey and it was starting to rain. Our pedalo, sunshine-yellow and indenting the water with its bathtub-shaped mass, veered and roiled from side to side with each wave that hit it. We were very quickly afraid. I, fourteen years old, pretended that I wasn't, but I was. Mum had disappeared somewhere along the shoreline. We both knew that she couldn't be relied upon to save us. The water became darker and angrier and more violent the further out we got. Nora stopped pedaling and started to cry. I knew she would never cry in front of Mum, and that she only did now because we were alone. She wasn't crying about the pedalo, or the water, even. She was crying because she was in pain and afraid and she didn't understand why.

I shouted at her to shut up, to help me pedal back to the shore. Because I was fourteen, and I was angry at her for existing, for inconveniencing my escape, and I couldn't do it by myself.

But she couldn't, or wouldn't, pedal. I leaned over the side of the vessel and used my hands as oars, trying to scoop us through the water. It wasn't working, and the sky was dark.

And then, without warning, as though it were the answer to a question that hadn't been asked, Nora was in the water.

It was my turn to scream and cry, then. I screeched for the pedalo vendor on the shore to come and help us. He had put a life preserver on Nora, at least, so she bobbed on the surface of the water. I reached down to her but I couldn't get a good grip on her.

Please don't die, Nora. Please don't die. Whatever you do, don't die.

And the longer she lay in the water, at first thrashing around and screaming and calling for me, the calmer she became. She stopped moving, realizing that if she lay still, she stayed upright. And soon, as though she had commanded them to be so, the waters around her were still and calm, too.

And the sky cleared and she sighed, staring up at the sky, salt staining her red-blooming cheeks, her hair in the water like a dark and many-limbed creature about to pull her small child's body down, her breathing hard and quick.

She was six years old. And she hadn't had her eight deaths yet. She had only almost-died once. Now that she's gone, I think about the water and wonder whether it counts as another. A ninth time to add to her tally.

But it doesn't. Because she decided that she wasn't going to die that day. Because she looked at the sky and said "no."

And when she was done, she pulled herself up onto the boat and we pedaled together back to the shore.

CHAPTER 36

THE UNIVERSE EXPANDED.

And then, rapidly, it shrank.

Something fundamental had been removed from the inside of my body, like my liver or spleen.

Things began to happen around me and I was ushered through them in a daze.

Beanie and I weren't allowed to leave the country until our arraignment, and the gallery agreed not to press charges for theft and destruction of property. The matter was complicated because, technically, Nora owned *Girls*. In return, we donated my half of Mum's portfolio in equal parts to the Museum of Modern Art in San Francisco and the National Portrait Gallery in London, an agreement arranged by Richard, Karoline and Gus.

She would hate this, I told Karoline when she and Gus brought the papers for me to sign.

Who would? she asked me. Nora or Ingrid?

I didn't need to respond. She knew that my answer was "both."

I signed the documents anyway, because, in practical terms, I had no other choice if I wanted to avoid a criminal record for my daughter.

I tasted iron in my mouth.

The exhibition went ahead as planned, though Larry Montague removed Nora's *My burial* (2015) from display. It was unclear whether Nora's demand on the opening night had anything to do with it, or whether it had been deemed tasteless to display it so soon after her death. There was a surge in ticket sales due to the press attention surrounding the theft of *Girls* and Nora's death, and the exhibition's run was extended from October to January. It received mixed to positive reviews from critics.

After we were cleared to leave the States, we took her body back to London.

On the day we arrived back at our apartment, our suitcases still dusty from the desert, I found Chelsea waiting at my front door, sitting on a suitcase of her own.

Oh, Matt, she said, when she saw us. Oh, Old Bean.

We collapsed into her and sobbed like children.

We burned Nora at Mortlake cemetery.

We held a funeral and a wake and I kept waiting for her to turn up. Of course she didn't, because even if she could, she wouldn't. But I kept glancing at the door, as I delivered her eulogy, hopeful, imagining that she would burst through it in a black dress and a pair of yellow Crocs and open the casket to show that it had been filled with custard and baking powder the whole time.

An army of her students from the university arrived with sunflowers, chaperoned into the back rows by the girl with the plait from outside her apartment a lifetime ago.

At the public celebration of Nora's life, which was held in the auditorium at Goldsmiths six weeks after she died, a shy teenaged boy approached me sheepishly. A woman I assumed to be his mother hovered behind him, clasping her hands.

Ms. Robb, he said, his voice shaking. You don't know me, but I wanted to introduce myself. My name's Benny Montgomery.

I took him in and registered the implied significance in his tone.

I know about you, I said, realizing why his name was so familiar. You called the police on Nora when she—the Control Room . . .

Yeah. That was me. I'm very sorry for your loss, Ms. Robb.

I stared at him and felt myself beginning to crumble. I had promised myself that I wouldn't. Not in public, when these strangers and journalists were here, ready to tear us apart again.

Benny was still talking.

I'm sorry I couldn't save her, he said. I'm sorry I couldn't . . .

He trailed off as I took his hand.

You gave me months with my sister I never would have had, I told him. There's nothing more precious to me.

As he walked away, his mother's arms draped across his shoulders, his words rang through me like the chime of a church bell.

I'm sorry I couldn't save her. I'm sorry I couldn't.

———————

I dreamed that she was being buried alive in concrete.

I dreamed that she was under the rubble of the Richmond house and every time I removed a piece of the house to get to her, more rained down from above.

I dreamed—the worst dream of them all—of her body, beached, bloated and blue.

I woke up crying, or screaming, and Gus hushed me out of the cold sweat of the bedsheets, and let me sob into his arms, keening like a wounded animal.

CHAPTER 37

We went back to our lives.

Beanie collected her results at the end of the summer, on a hot, still day in east London, and outside the school gates she slid her thumb under the glue of the envelope as Gus and I watched, quiet.

She glanced over the page, her eyes narrow.

Two As and two Bs, she said, finally.

I clapped my hands and Gus pulled her into a hug, grinning.

You did it, kid, I said, my voice thick with emotion.

She had already done so much more than I ever could, than I had ever wanted. The world was hers.

She looked up at me, her face strained, and I knew she was thinking of Nora. I was too.

That day was a bright spot in a dark few months.

Beanie went back to school, beginning her second year of sixth form, and I back to work, where the problems the children faced mentally, emotionally, became increasingly ghoulish with each passing day. I looked at each child that visited me and thought to myself, *well, I couldn't help her, so how the fuck am I supposed to help you?*

We returned to our apartment at the end of the day and stared at one another blankly, pale-faced and shadowy eyed, and could not think of anything to say to one another, and picked at our food in silence, and went to sleepless nights separately. I had tried to talk to her about what happened. But she wouldn't. She wouldn't leave the house, except for school. We were due to start looking at universities soon. I had gently mentioned to her that it might be a good idea to defer for a year, considering what had happened. She stood up from the sofa and walked out of the apartment, and stayed with Gus for a week.

Gus and I weren't together, but we weren't apart, either. We were feeling it out. The euphoria I had felt in San Francisco when he had kissed me for the first time in fifteen years, had been supplanted by the sickening and deadening sense of loss in the wake of Nora. Now, when I thought of him, I thought of that last night. What I had done wrong. So many things, it seemed. A small part of me wondered whether, if I had gone back to the house with Nora that night, and stayed with her, instead of leaving her and Beanie to go alone to take a walk along the harbourfront with Gus, things might have been different. I played every second of every moment over and over again. Had I missed the signs of something catastrophic? I wondered whether I had catalyzed it with something I'd said or done. Why hadn't I seen that Nora had been wrong, off, close to the edge of something she couldn't come back from? The strange calmness that had come over her in the end. Had she already been planning something then? The mistakes stretched back further. Had I pushed her too hard to take her medication? Had I not pushed hard enough? Should we have ever gone to the exhibition? Should we have ever got on the plane? Now, when I thought of Gus, I thought of those moments, too. And it was unbearable.

I supposed that it was my punishment, finally come at long last.

I couldn't deny that I truly deserved it.

Beanie and I were sitting at the dining table on a Saturday morning, half-heartedly picking at our toast, when my phone rang. It was a US number that I didn't recognize. I showed Beanie the caller ID, frowning, and answered it.

Matilda? came the eerily familiar voice on the other end on the crackling line. It's Polly, I'm Edward Robb's housekeeper—your father's housekeeper—I don't know that you'll remember me.

Her voice was urgent and apologetic.

Hi, I said, remembering the red-haired woman who had helped us at Dad's house in Hollywood in the summer.

I was so sorry not to get over for the funeral, she said. I had to work—

Don't be silly, I said monotonously. Dad and Marnie had both been at Nora's funeral, Marnie impossible to decipher besides being visibly uncomfortable, and Dad stoic before finally, at the wake, breaking down in Karoline's arms and being consoled by an army of well-wishers, none of whom I'd recognized. I'd only spoken to him once through the whole thing. I had found myself standing next to him at the bar, surveying the strangers and wondering which of them Nora knew personally, had intimacy with, if any at all. I hadn't noticed that he'd been next to me. He'd said, unprompted, She called me, you know, the day before.

Yeah, I know.

She called me from jail. She wanted me to come and get her.

Yeah.

I wish I had answered the call.

Well, you didn't, I said.

Maybe I could have said something. Done something to stop her, you know?

I took a gulp of wine from the glass I was holding and stared at him while I considered how to respond. He wouldn't meet my gaze.

There's nothing you could have done, Dad, I said, my voice free of emotion. His shoulders—which had been tensed—relaxed, and he brought a hand to his face.

I know, he said. I know. The mind spirals, though, doesn't it?

It took me a moment to realize that he had taken my words as absolution instead of accusation. I set my glass down on the bar.

After this is done, I told him. I want you to go back to California, and stay there. And you will not contact me, or Beanie, any longer. Do you understand?

A mixture of fear and understanding muddled across his face. And he nodded curtly and turned away. The next time I saw him that day, he and Marnie were climbing into a waiting cab.

Now, on the phone to Polly, it seemed strange that she—who Nora loved—would be required to manage an empty house while he had been here.

Listen, Matilda, I'm calling because I have a small issue here, and I'm so sorry to do this, but I need your help.

What can I do for you?

Well—it's just—I thought they'd come back to us, return to sender, right? But it looks like they've been sitting in some sort of customs facility for months waiting to be checked over. And now there's a courier on his way to the apartment.

What apartment? I asked. What's this all about?

Nora's apartment . . . It's her work, Matilda. Her research. The things she asked me to send home. It's all getting delivered today. This afternoon, between three and five, in fact. I'm so sorry to do this to you, hon—

It's getting delivered to her apartment? I asked.

Yep—it's a south-east London zip code, I believe.

I felt my stomach somersault. I thanked Polly and hung up.

Beanie looked at me quizzically, a piece of toast crust hanging from her mouth.

Want to go get Nora's stuff? I asked her.

I slid the spare key into the lock and braced myself. Truthfully, I had almost completely forgotten about the apartment. The scattering of red-stamped mail on the floor in the entrance hall indicated that Nora was days away from being evicted for unpaid rent. I had already closed down her bank account and was in the process of executing her estate, which consisted of a couple of thousand pounds' worth of savings, a mountain of student debt, and fifty percent of Ingrid Olssen's portfolio, minus one recently destroyed masterpiece. And now, I supposed, there were twenty-plus archival boxes of her own work, due to arrive momentarily, to add to that list.

Beanie and I wandered the apartment, dazed.

I stared at the bathroom door and decided not to go inside.

Instead, Beanie and I took trash bags from the cupboard underneath the sink and set about collecting her belongings.

There weren't many: mainly clothes and books, furniture, and some papers and a desktop computer. We worked in silence, neither of us acknowledging the curious déjà vu of being here, in Nora's apartment, among her things, deciding on what to take and what to leave.

I went through her clothes and they smelled of talc and jasmine, like she did. The scent of her hit me like a punch in the ribs and I sat on the floor in the middle of the bedroom and felt my throat burning with unspent tears.

Of course, the cameras were still there, in the corners of every room.

Beanie was going through the books in the study when the doorbell rang. I answered the intercom and buzzed the delivery through.

They came up on a trolley, three boxes at a time. Beanie and I stood at the door and stared at them. They were unmarked, unremarkable, brown-grey cardboard boxes with lids, just as they had been in Dad's house, except this time they had customs security checking tape wrapped around them. Beanie slid her hand into mine as the FedEx driver brought another three up via the elevator.

Shall we? I asked her.

And, one by one, we carried each box into the living room, which was bare and therefore had a wide empty space in the middle of it for us to stack them.

Once they were all inside, and I had thanked the delivery driver, I closed the front door with a soft click, and joined Beanie to stare at them.

What do you think we should do? she asked me. She might have wanted us to burn them, like Grandma.

True, I replied. But she also might have wanted us to finish the work. She said the Control Room was finished, but she might have had other plans.

One of our last conversations came back to me, then. In the hot, humid jail cell when she'd shaken me from sleep and forgiven me. I had turned it over in my mind countless times since. But I had almost forgotten the other things she had said. The things weighted with meaning.

Tentatively, as though I were committing some sort of sacrilege, I slid the lid off one of the boxes and peeked inside. A stack of notebooks nestled together in there. I picked one up gently, handling it as though it were an artefact. It was soft in my hands, as though it had been worn smooth with use. On the spine, in Nora's block capitals, was handwritten: NORA ROBB, MARCH 2017–MAY 2017.

I put it down, as though it might burn me.

I think they're diaries, I told Beanie. Or maybe notes.

Beanie was staring up at one of the cameras in the corner of the living room.

Hang on a second, she said, and she pulled out her phone.

I frowned at her. What are you doing?

Yeah, I thought so, she said after a moment. She turned her phone so that I would see the screen.

The Control Room is still live, she said. The work is still going.

Sure enough, the Control Room website still had the live feed up and running. Messages of condolence flooded the comments section. The viewer count was ticking up, at the sight of our pixelated figures in the abandoned living space of Nora Robb.

Let's leave it on, I said, and I knew immediately as the words left my mouth that it was the right thing to do. Let's keep it running. Until we have to release the apartment back to the rental agency.

Beanie nodded. I think she would have liked that.

We loaded up a minivan that I had borrowed from a friend from work with the boxes, and the belongings of Nora's that we had decided to keep. Certain items of clothing, an old blanket, a handful of photographs and some books. A beautiful handmade ceramic vase on top of the breadbox. Then we drove to a storage unit in Brentford. The unit I had hired back in 2018 was the size of a shipping container, and climate-controlled; it had to be, because it had half of Ingrid Olssen's portfolio in there, still awaiting its collection, the items inside to be shipped off to SFMOMA and the National Portrait Gallery. Karoline was mediating on which place got which works. I was pretending it wasn't happening.

Beanie and I unloaded the boxes from the car and stacked them neatly in the center of the unit. On all sides, Nora's work was surrounded by huge Olssen canvases.

They'll be gone soon, I said, out loud, and I looked over to Beanie and saw that she was crying.

Oh, Old Bean, I said, pulling her close to me.

I hate it that she's gone, Beanie said, through gasping sobs into my chest. I hate what happened.

I held her while she cried, and I felt my heart breaking all over again. Every day was the turning of the stomach, the unfocused realization all over again, every time we woke up, that she was gone and she would be gone forever.

I understood it completely.

We drove to Richmond Green and watched the birds and talked about Nora.

I don't know what to do, Beanie said. I can't believe this is really happening. It feels like it's not real. I feel like I don't exist anymore, like I'm not a real person.

On the Green in front of us, a border collie chased a pit bull across the grass, kicking up clumps of mud with its hind legs. The mid-afternoon light had a translucent quality to it, the sky an explosion of pink and orange. It was turning into winter fast.

When my mum—Grandma—died, I said, I felt like I wasn't connected to my own body. I felt like my body was doing things without my say-so. It was a very strange feeling. I looked at my hands and felt like they didn't belong to me. I didn't know what it was at the time but I was disassociating. It's a part of grief.

She said, I feel like that too. All the time.

It's going to get easier, Beans, I said. I promise.

She let me pull her into a hug.

I miss her so much, I said. And I let myself silently admit, then, on the Green watching the dog walkers, that I meant both of them.

Me too, Beanie replied.

You exist just fine, I told her. You're a real person just fine.

———————

That night I dreamed of the jail cell, of Nora, and I woke up, startled.

I went in Beanie's room and shook her awake from soft-breathed sleep.

What? she asked urgently. What's the matter?

I know what we're going to do with Nora's work.

Beanie sat up in bed, rubbing sleep out of her eyes, bleary with it.

What are we going to do? she asked.

We're going to put on an exhibition.

CHAPTER 38

By the following January, the only things left in my storage unit belonged to Nora.

Karoline visited me with more papers to sign for the transfer of the Olssen portfolio to the galleries.

Are you coming to the launch, darling? she asked me.

She was talking about Richard's book, which was to be published in the spring, with a newly written afterword on Nora.

I hadn't started thinking about Nora's exhibition yet. It wouldn't happen yet. It would be in months, or years. When we were ready. But it *would* happen. I was determined.

I shook my head "no." Even in death, the specter of legacy haunted me.

I want to talk to you about something else, she said, sucking on a vape in my living room. I've had a surveyor look at the Richmond house, and the subsidence is terminal, I'm afraid. We think that it's unsellable.

I shrugged at her, glancing up from the documents.

Do whatever you want with that house, I said. I don't care.

Well, that's just the thing, she said. I've had an offer from a developer. They have a plan and they want to knock it down.

What are they going to build? I asked.

She shrugged. Some sort of multi-use space, I think. Residential, with a shop and a nursery school on the ground floor. They were talking about mounting a plaque, or something, I think. For your mother. And perhaps we could ask for Nora's name to be added to it.

I looked at her hard in the face, in a way that I hadn't done for years—
maybe ever. I noticed then the resemblance for the first time. The way she
looked like Mum. Only a little bit, around the eyes and in the curve of her
nose. In a way that you could only spot if you knew what you were looking
for. If you already knew that they were sisters. In the same way that Nora
and I had looked alike.

I'm sorry, I said to her.

Darling, she said between vape inhales. Whatever for?

I thought of all the times I had imagined the Richmond house falling to
the ground.

I thought of Hector, stalking through the walls, and the yellow door.

It's yours now, I told her. Burn it to the ground.

————————

Gus and I took the train to Edinburgh with Beanie, with the intention of
touring the university.

Grief comes in waves. Sometimes it is there, in every second of every
waking moment, and it is paralyzing. You cannot think, eat, breathe, or
speak without the presence of them in the intention of every choice you
make. It slides a hand around your esophagus and doesn't let go, until
you can't breathe, until you are choking.

In quieter moments, more bearable moments, the hand is on the small of
your back, guiding your body but never pushing. I liked having that hand
there, even though it was painful, even though sometimes it kept me awake
at night and made me resentful and cruel and unreachable, because it made
Nora's existence more real to me. The fact that she had lived became very
important to me.

The other part of it was the guilt. The raking through of what could have
been done, and how I could have done it better. In the first weeks and
months, it was all I could think of. I drove myself insane running through
every second of every moment in my mind. How could I not have seen it
coming? How was I so selfish, so wrapped up in my own stuff, that I couldn't
have done anything to stop it?

I spent so much time thinking in this way that I almost completely lost sight of the other things that mattered to me, that still existed on this plane, and that I could influence.

My people. My kid, and the love of my life.

In the autumn, Gus asked me to meet him at his house and he drove us back to the school, where we had met almost two decades ago, the bike sheds a little rustier, the brickwork on the walls faded and stained. We walked through the alley across the road to the old people's home on the edge of the park. The spot where we had first met, back when Chelsea and I had been running around setting fires in the woods.

Do you remember this place? he asked me.

Of course, I said, feeling my chest tighten. How could I forget?

He took my hand and led me further along the alleyway, to a nondescript iron-bar gate with a chain and padlock wrapped around it to keep the loitering schoolkids out. He took out a key and unlocked it.

Still holding my hand, he led me through the allotment, along the rows of rhubarb, cabbages, carrots and potatoes, all the way to the end. One unspoiled, untoiled square of perfect brown soil, rich with minerals and water and sunlight.

It's only small, he said. But I thought that it could be a start. Somewhere for you to grow things that isn't your balcony.

He reached into his pocket and handed me a packet of sunflower seeds.

I took them and stared at them, feeling my fingertips fizzing.

We sat down in the dirt and smelled the earth.

The three of us ate cheese-and-pickle sandwiches on the train to Edinburgh, and Beanie said, Will you visit if I go to university in Scotland?

Would you want us to visit? Gus asked her with one raised eyebrow.

Well—*yeah*—obviously. Not all the time. Maybe like, I don't know, once a month? Once a term?

I laughed at her hedging as we got off the train at Edinburgh Waverley and walked through the ornate station and out into the Gothic grandeur of the city. It was drizzling, and the buildings were dark and ominous against a slate-colored sky. Beanie walked ahead of us, gaping up at the architecture, her eyes sparkling and her mouth slack. She gestured for us to follow, her phone out as she navigated us to the hotel.

If she leaves us and moves all the way to Scotland, I said quietly, as Gus slipped his hand into mine, I'm moving here too.

No, you're not, he said, chuckling.

It's so *far*, I moaned. What if something happens? What if we can't get to her? What about train strikes—

She'll be fine, he said smoothly. Look at her.

He pointed ahead at our kid. She had stopped at a roadside coffee truck and was buying takeaway coffees now, chatting easily with the barista and laughing, showing all of her teeth. I hadn't seen her laugh like that for months. Beanie's shoulders were a little higher, and held a little more intention, than they had before the road trip. Mine did too.

She'll be better than fine, Gus amended. She'll be magnificent.

She turned around and waved at us to come and get our coffees.

He let go of my hand to join her.

The rain was subsiding, now. I paused and took in the two of them, arm in arm, silhouetted against a shining, silver pavement that refracted the weak afternoon light.

Beanie turned and looked at me, her face expectant.

Mum? Are you coming?

That morning, before we'd left for the train, on our way out the door, she had handed me a white, unaddressed envelope.

I'd slipped a thumb under the glue, a question in my face.

I just got some of them printed, she'd said quickly, sheepishly. For when I go away to uni. I thought I could do a new photo collage for my new bedroom in halls. Like the one we did together.

Okay . . . I said. So, what's this photo? It's for me?

I drew the single photograph out from the envelope, the back of it facing up, and turned it over.

It was me and Nora.

On the top of the mountain at Bootleg Canyon. Just after we had tipped Mum's ashes into the abyss. Just before we'd slid on metal cables into the abyss ourselves, screaming and happy and alive.

Nora's eyes were bright with something unknowable.

Nora on the left, me on the right. A whisper of a gap between us. The sky big and bright and blue and beautiful.

Underneath, scrawled across the bottom of the photo, in handwriting I recognized as Beanie's, was one word.

Girls.

I think I like this version the best, Beanie said, as I felt the tears slip down my cheeks.

I think I like it the best too, I replied.

Mum? Beanie called once more from up ahead. She and Gus were waiting.

I thought again of the photograph, now mounted with all the others on my own wall back home.

I felt my fingers and my toes and my whole existence, all at once.

I thought of my square patch of dirt, which I would dig and plant and grow in.

The act of living, just being, sometimes felt impossible.

And then—very suddenly and in the moments I least expected it—even in the dying rain, my small world became inexplicably, inconceivably, radically, all I had ever needed it to be.

I sent a silent promise out into the expanding universe.

I waved at them and ran to catch up.

AUTHOR'S NOTE

I am grateful to the people, organizations, and institutions whose friendship, support, service, and work have guided me in shaping this novel, which started out as a story about three women on a road trip in the desert and turned into something completely different and far removed from anything I have ever tried to write before. *Daughters* incorporates a blend of fictionalized people, places, and events inspired by those from the real world, as well as artworks, places, and events that are entirely imaginary. Any inaccuracies in the text, relating to the former, are my own and absolutely, definitely, one hundred percent intentional.

My heartfelt thanks goes to the team at Abrams for their support in publishing this edition of the novel, especially Zack Knoll, Ruby Pucillo, Abby Muller, Eli Mock, Annalea Manalili, Sarah Masterson Hally, Andrew Gibeley, and Taryn Roeder, as well as the sales and marketing teams.

To Charlotte Mursell, there is no one with whom I would rather be on this journey. Thank you for your time, investment, patience, and the downright *alchemy* you unleash on every draft. Your guidance, kindness and generosity continue to build me into a better writer.

To Anwen Hooson, a legend, where would I be without you? Thank you, as always, for "getting it," for giving me confidence to pursue this story, for being my first reader, my first champion, and for your unwavering support.

Thank you to my publishing team at Orion, most especially Sian Baldwin, Juliet Ewers, Helena Fouracre, Snigdha Koirala, and Paul Stark. Thank you to my copy editor, Suzanne Clarke. Thank you to Amber Gadd and

Ryan Laughton for lending your extraordinary voices to the audiobook for *Daughters*.

Thank you to my early readers whose advice and perspective I value above all else: David Anderson, Sara Jafari, Vashti Kincaid, Kenny Murray, Jasmin Nahar, and Ruben Willis-Powell.

Thank you to Emma Jeremy, for being the greatest human being of all time, and for lending me your poem "wet sand" from your collection *Sad Thing Angry* (Out-Spoken Press, 2023) for the epigraph of this book.

I was fortunate to conduct research at some of the locations that feature in the book. Thank you to Jeffrey, Nicholas, Matthew, Deb, Marius, Haris, Jaafar, Riva, Barbara, Vandana, and Blanca for your hospitality and guidance. Thank you most of all to Stefan Knap, who helped plant the first seed of the idea for this story in 2019 in an RV Park in Boulder City, Nevada. Thanks also to Stefan for the castle.

Grift House Art Festival is a loose fictionalization of the Frieze Art Fair in London (they really do have a fleet of Mercedes-Benzes), and much of it was imagined with the help of journalism by Jonathan Jones.

To Eddie, Joel, Sam, Jules, Jamie, Danny, Scott, Matt, Ryan, Charlie, Jordan, Viv, Kirsty, Erica, Becky, Ollie, and everyone else I've inevitably missed. Thank you for your bottomless encouragement. I feel so lucky to know you all.

Thank you to Miles for everything you do to make life good.

Thank you to my family, who, against all odds, continues to put up with my nonsense.

With the publication of *Daughters* I would like to acknowledge the lives of Dain Lewis (1989-2023) and Grant Lewis (1954-2023).

As you might expect, it is not possible, in security terms, to walk out of the SFMOMA with stolen artwork. Nor is it possible to enter the United States with an undeclared Tupperware of human remains. Please don't attempt either.